Dear Reader,

When my editor asked me if I'd do a twisted fairy tale for Harlequin Presents, I knew I had to do "Little Red Riding Hood." Not only is it one of my favorite fairy tales but I already had an image of a big bad billionaire called Jack Wolfe.

Jack was a cynical, scarred, ruthlessly driven alpha guy who could lure any woman into his bed but never wanted to keep them there... Enter Katherine Medford, my Little Red, who's as brave and, frankly, reckless as the fairy-tale chick (seriously, who visits Granny when there's a wolf loose in the woods?). But unlike Little Red, when Katie ends up in Jack's bed, she doesn't need some random lumberjack to rescue her, because she's all about rescuing herself...

One storm-tossed night in Granny's cottage, an accidental pregnancy *and* a marriage of convenience later and my fairy tale was getting a uniquely Harlequin Presents twist as Katie discovers it's incredibly hard to rescue yourself from a wolf, especially if you're starting to fall in love with him!

I loved adding a generous dose of passion, glamour and high-stakes drama to the old tale. I hope you enjoy reading it.

Love,

Heidi x

USA TODAY bestselling author **Heidi Rice** lives in London, England. She is married with two teenage sons—which gives her rather too much of an insight into the male psyche—and also works as a film journalist. She adores her job, which involves getting swept up in a world of high emotions; sensual excitement; funny, feisty women; sexy, tortured men; and glamorous locations where laundry doesn't exist. Once she turns off her computer, she often does chores—usually involving laundry!

Books by Heidi Rice

Harlequin Presents

A Forbidden Night with the Housekeeper
Innocent's Desert Wedding Contract
Banished Prince to Desert Boss

Hot Summer Nights with a Billionaire

One Wild Night with her Enemy

The Christmas Princess Swap

The Royal Pregnancy Test

Secrets of Billionaire Siblings

The Billionaire's Proposition in Paris
The CEO's Impossible Heir

Visit the Author Profile page
at Harlequin.com for more titles.

Heidi Rice

A BABY TO TAME
THE WOLFE

Recycling programs
for this product may
not exist in your area.

ISBN-13: 978-1-335-73846-2

A Baby to Tame the Wolfe

Copyright © 2022 by Heidi Rice

For questions and comments about the quality of this book,
please contact us at CustomerService@Harlequin.com.

Harlequin Enterprises ULC
22 Adelaide St. West, 41st Floor
Toronto, Ontario M5H 4E3, Canada
www.Harlequin.com

Printed in U.S.A.

A BABY TO TAME
THE WOLFE

To my son Luca,

Who will never read this book, but whose childhood obsession with wolves and his gala performance in a Year 6 production of "Little Red Riding Hood" as the wolf led to my love of this particular fairy tale, and thus— eventually—my decision to write this story. I owe you one, my gorgeous boy—which unfortunately does not include a share of the royalties, just in case you were wondering!

PROLOGUE

Katie, I need your help! It's an emergency!

KATHERINE MEDFORD WRAPPED the large black trench coat around her red velvet cape to shield it from the spitting rain as she shot out of the Tube at Leicester Square while reading her sister Beatrice's eighth text in a row.

What was the problem this time? That Katie would have to fix? Because she was already late for her booking. And unlike Bea, who had their father Lord Henry Medford's considerable financial largesse to rely on, Katie could not afford to lose this job or the twenty-pounds-an-hour commission. The phone began to buzz. Katie's thumb hovered over the 'reject call' button as she dodged pedestrians along Charing Cross Road, en route to the children's bookshop where she was supposed to be reading fairy tales to an audience of four- to five-year-olds in ten minutes and counting.

But, as she went to press her thumb down, the image of Bea from years ago aged fourteen, tears streaking down her cheeks, her face a sodden mess of confusion and fear as Katie was marched out of Medford Hall by their father, tugged at Katie's chest. She sighed and clicked the 'accept call' button as she broke into a jog.

'Bea, what's the problem?' she said breathlessly, the corset of her costume holding her ribcage in a vice. 'I'm late. I don't have time for this, unless it really is an emergency- –'

'It's Jack Wolfe,' her sister said, getting straight to the point for once and mentioning the billionaire corporate raider Katie had never met—because why would she, they hardly moved in the same circles. But she knew her sister had got engaged to him a week ago because of the pictures of Bea and her new fiancé all over the Internet.

An irritating ripple streaked down Katie's spine.

Wolfe had been hotness personified in a rough, untamed, wildly charismatic way wearing a perfectly tailored tuxedo. The mysterious scar on his cheek which marred his chiselled features and the tattoo on his neck—just visible above the pristine white dress-shirt—made him look even more darkly compelling next to Bea's bright, willowy blonde beauty. Katie would almost have been jealous of her sister, except she didn't have to meet Jack Wolfe to know he had to be a man like her father.

No, thanks. One overbearing bully is all I need in my life.

'He's invited me for dinner tonight at his penthouse on Hyde Park Corner, just the two of us,' her sister rushed on. 'And I'm scared he's going to want to take our relationship to the next level.'

Katie stopped dead in the street, her heeled boots skidding on the rain-slick pavement. Her fingers tightened on the phone as she registered the panic in Bea's voice.

'What do you mean, you're scared?' Katie gentled her tone to contain her own panic. 'Has Wolfe done something to frighten you, Bea?'

Wolfe was well known for being a rough diamond, with the looks of a fallen angel to go with his stratospheric rise from an East End council estate to the high-flying business circles in which her father moved. But Wolfe was also a big man, tall and strong, with a muscular physique that filled out his tux to perfection.

And that was without even factoring in the scar and the tats. How exactly had he got that scar which the tabloids had been speculating about for years? Was he violent, aggressive, dangerous?

Her own breathing became ragged as she was thrust back to a time long ago when she'd still been a little girl, hazy half-formed memories lurking on the edges of her consciousness. She swallowed down the wave of humiliation that those stupid nightmares still had the power to wake her up on occasion, struggling to escape something she couldn't see but knew was right there, ready to hurt her if she let it. She evened out her breathing... *Don't go there. Focus on Bea.*

'No, Katie, don't be silly. Jack's not like *that*,' Bea replied with more conviction than Katie felt. 'He'd never hurt me.'

'Then why are you scared of being alone with him?'

Bea huffed out a breath. 'Because he'll probably want to have sex and I'm not sure I'm ready. To be honest, I'm pretty sure I won't ever be ready. He's just a bit too much for me. He's ridiculously smart, and he can be very witty, and he's exciting to be with, but underneath all that there's an intensity about him. I have no idea what he's thinking. He's so guarded, it's like a super power. He's way too deep for me. You know how shallow I am.' Bea's manic babbling finally stopped.

There were so many things to unpick in what Bea had confided, Katie didn't even know where to start—not least because she absolutely did not want this much information about Jack Wolfe. But perhaps the most astonishing thing was the two of them hadn't had sex yet. While Bea was pretty flaky, she had dated before. And Jack Wolfe didn't strike her as the kind of guy to remain celibate for months while dating anyone…especially someone he'd asked to marry him. The guy oozed sex appeal. He could probably give a woman an orgasm from thirty paces.

So not the point, Katie.

'You're not shallow, Bea,' Katie said, because she hated it when her sister put herself down. That was their father talking.

'Whatever,' Bea said, sounding exasperated. 'But I still don't think we'd be a good match,' she added. 'At all.' She huffed. 'I'm worried I'll fall in love with him and he would never love me back.'

Say, what now?

'Then why on earth did you agree to marry him?'

Katie asked, walking briskly again as she remembered the children who were sat in a bookstore eagerly waiting for Little Red Riding Hood to put in an appearance. She was glad Bea wasn't in an abusive relationship. But she did not have time to debate her sister's confusing love life right now.

'Because Daddy insisted I say yes,' Bea murmured sheepishly. 'Jack has loaned Daddy some money on generous terms. If Daddy finds out I've broken it off, and if Jack changes the terms, he'll be furious…'

Katie's pace slowed again. She might have guessed their father had engineered this situation. Why couldn't Bea just stand up to him? But she knew why. Bea was scared of their father's temper tantrums, and with good reason… 'Surely you must know you can't marry Jack Wolfe if you don't love him, Bea?' Katie said softly.

'I know I have to break it off, but Katie, it's the pressure. Jack is very hot, but I'm sure he plans to seduce me tonight. And I'm not sure I'll be able to resist him. And once we've slept together it will be that much harder to dump him. I don't want to hurt his feelings.'

Whoa… What the…?

'Bea, you're not serious? Jack Wolfe has built a fortune on being an absolute bastard. His business strategy is to chew up smaller companies and spit them out. You said yourself you don't think he could ever love you. If the guy even has feelings, I'll be astonished.'

'Everyone has feelings, Katie,' Bea countered

gently, making Katie wonder if her sister's airhead act *was* actually an act. 'Even Jack.'

'Do you think he has feelings for you, then?' Katie asked, the stupid ripple turning to a deep pulsing ache in her chest. What was that even about?

'No.' Bea sighed. 'He's very attentive. But he's not at all romantic. He pretty much told me he only asked me to marry him because he thinks I'll make a good trophy wife.'

Oh, for the love of...

'Bea, he sounds worse than Father,' Katie said, exasperated. At least Henry Medford had pretended to love their mother once. 'You shouldn't have let Father bully you into saying yes.'

'I know...' Katie could hear her sister's huff of distress even over the blast of a taxi horn. 'Which brings me to why I rang,' Bea added, her voice taking on a desperate tone that Katie recognised only too well, because it was usually the precursor to Bea asking her to do something outrageous or ridiculous or both. 'Could you go to Jack's place tonight at seven?'

'Why would I do that?' Katie asked. Did her sister need moral support to tell Wolfe the engagement was off?

'He's flying in from New York,' Bea said, bulldozing over Katie's question. 'But I told the doorman, Jeffrey, to expect you so you can wait for him in his penthouse—which is spectacular, by the way,' Bea added, her tone segueing neatly from desperate to wheedling. 'If you're there instead of me when he gets home, you can tell him I'm not going to marry him and I won't have to worry. Then I can tell Daddy *he* broke off the engagement.'

Katie stopped dead again. So shocked she didn't know what to say. Bea had asked her for huge favours before. Favours she'd almost always agreed to because she wanted Bea to be happy, and she knew her sister had a massive problem standing up for herself—thanks to their broken childhood.

Katie had always been there to stand up for Bea when her sister's courage or determination had failed her. But this was…

'You have got to be joking!' Katie cried. 'I can't turn up at his place unannounced to dump him on your behalf. I've never even met the guy.' But even as she said it she felt the little frisson of something… Something electric and contradictory and wholly inappropriate rippling through her tired, over-corseted body. The same something that had rippled through her when she'd studied the photos of her sister and Jack Wolfe together a bit too forensically. 'Plus I won't have time to change out of my Little Red Riding Hood costume,' she added a little desperately. She lived in north North London and she was supposed to be reading fairy tales until six. Assuming, of course, she hadn't already been fired for being late. 'I won't do it, Bea. Absolutely no way…'

But even as she said the words the corset cinched tightly around her thundering heart and Katie could feel her fierce determination not to make an absolute tit of herself slipping out of her grasp.

Bea was her sister and if there was one thing she

would always be prepared to do, it was her sister's dirty work. Because Bea had been there for her when she'd needed her most.

And there was also the matter of the ripple that was still playing havoc with her senses at the thought of a brooding, overbearing billionaire who was the very last guy on earth who should inspire a ripple in a smart, grounded, totally pragmatic, tycoon-despising woman like herself.

Perhaps she needed to meet the man to discover exactly how overbearing, arrogant and annoying he really was, and sort out this ripple once and for all.

CHAPTER ONE

Jack Wolfe glanced at his watch as the chauffeur-driven car pulled up outside the Wolfe Apartments on Grosvenor Place.

Five past three in the morning. Terrific. Only eight hours late.

He rubbed grit-filled eyes as he dragged his stiff body out of the car.

His contact lenses were practically bonded to his eyeballs, and he hadn't slept a wink on the plane. Normally he'd never take a commercial flight but, thanks to an engine problem with the Wolfe jet at JFK, he'd had to fit his six-foot-three-inch frame into a bed built for a skinny ten-year-old.

He checked his phone as he walked into the building and sent a half-hearted nod to the guy on the desk. He'd had no reply from Beatrice, but at least he'd managed to text her from JFK before he'd found another flight and postpone the dinner he'd had scheduled for last night. So she wouldn't be waiting in his apartment.

He stepped into the private lift that would whisk him to his penthouse on the top floor of the building and frowned at the floor indicator. Weird he wasn't more devastated about being forced to postpone tonight's dinner date. Perhaps it was time he addressed why it had taken him so long to fit seducing his fiancée into his schedule.

He liked Beatrice, a lot. And, as soon as he'd begun dating her, he'd marked her out as a perfect candidate for his wife. As tall and beautiful as a supermodel, she had a slightly kooky and admirably non-confrontational temperament which meant they had never had a disagreement. She didn't have a paying job, which meant there would be no conflicts of interest when it came to time management in their marriage—he was, after all, a workaholic.

And best of all, because of her father's position and her aristocratic lineage, she had the class and the social connections he needed to finally break down the last of the barriers still closed to him in the City of London and, more importantly, on Smyth-Brown's board—smoothing the way for the takeover he had been planning for years. So he could finally destroy the man who had destroyed his mother's life.

There was just one problem in his arrangement with Beatrice, though.

Sex. Or, rather, the lack of it.

She'd been hesitant to become intimate at first, especially after she'd accepted his proposal. There was no rush and there was a fragility about her which reminded him rather unfortunately of his mother.

There wasn't much of a spark between them. But

that hadn't bothered him either. He was an experienced guy with a highly charged libido. He'd lost his virginity as a teenager to a woman twice his age—and he'd had a ton of practice since at satisfying women.

The only problem was, after building towards the moment when he would finally make Beatrice his, he really hadn't been anticipating last night's dinner as much as he'd expected—in fact, it had almost begun to seem like a chore. He'd never dated any woman for longer than a few months, so he had been planning to suggest that they conduct discreet affairs once their sexual relationship petered out. But he really hadn't expected to feel quite so jaded before their sex life had even started.

His brow lowered further as the private lift glided to a stop on the fourteenth floor of the building. The bell pinged and the lift doors swished open. Thrusting his fingers through his hair, he stepped into the apartment's palatial lobby area and dumped his luggage next to the hall table.

He was being ridiculous. Seducing his fiancée wouldn't be a chore, it would be a pleasure, a pleasure which was long overdue. He was simply exhausted right now, and frustrated at the prospect of having to delay their first night together for another couple of days at least. He'd never had to be this patient before. Apparently there *was* such a thing as too much anticipation.

The ambient lighting gave the strikingly modern hall furniture a blue gleam, but he resisted the urge to request the main lighting be switched on.

His eyeballs were so damn sore now, they felt like a couple of peeled grapes. No wonder he wasn't in the mood to jump Beatrice or anyone else.

Dragging off his tie and shoving it into his pocket, he headed into the open-plan living area. Floor-to-ceiling windows looked out onto Wellington Arch and the faltering stream of traffic making its way around Hyde Park Corner and up Piccadilly, the dawn creeping up to illuminate Green Park.

Calm settled over him, as it always did when he had a chance to survey how far he'd come from the frightened feral kid he'd once been. He adored this view because it was a million miles away from where he'd started in a squalid, one-bedroom council flat on the other side of London, ducking to avoid his stepfather's fists.

Rubbing his eyes, he walked deftly through the shadows towards his bedroom suite. He entered the bathroom from the hallway and finally managed to claw out his sticky lenses. He was all but blind without them and, after taking a shower in the dull light afforded by the bathroom mirror, he took the door into the bedroom.

Darkness was his friend, always had been, because he had once had to hide in the shadows.

Not any more.

The heady scent hit him as he closed the door to the steamy bathroom. Something spicy and seductive. Had Beatrice come into the bedroom before getting his message his flight had been delayed until tomorrow? When she'd never been in his bedroom before.

But it didn't smell like Beatrice. She had an expensive vanilla scent. This scent was far more arousing. Fresh and earthy—it smelled like ripe apples and wildflowers on a summer day. A wave of heat pounded south and made him smile. Even if he was so shattered he was having scent hallucinations, the instant erection proved he wasn't becoming a eunuch.

His groin continued to throb as he found the huge king-size bed in the darkness and dropped the towel from around his hips.

He climbed between the sheets, his exhaustion still playing tricks with his sense of smell. He closed his eyes, enjoying the deliciously erotic scent and the satisfying warmth in his crotch as his bones melted into the mattress. His mind plummeted into sleep and he found himself in a summer orchard, the ripe red apples heavy on the flowering fruit trees, the scent of earth and sunshine intensifying.

Warmth enveloped him. The sound of a light breeze through the orchard matched his breathing, deep and even, and impossibly sensual. The ache in his crotch throbbed. A sigh—soft, sweet, hot— rustled through the trees and stroked his chest and shoulder as he lay in the sun.

He stretched, turning into the electrifying caress, wanting, needing, more. His searching hands found silky hair, satin skin. He plunged his fingers into the vibrant mass and pressed his palm over velvet-covered curves, the tart apple freshness surrounding him in a cloud of need.

His arousal hardened and the vague thought shimmered through his mind that this would have been the best wet dream he had ever had… But why was his dream woman clothed? And what was she clothed in, he wondered, as his fingers encountered rigid ribbing. At last he found the plump curve of a breast through soft cotton, the nipple pebbling as he plucked it.

The last of the fatigue melted away, his appetite intensifying, energy sparking through his body like an electrical current as he began exploring sweet-scented flesh with his lips, his tongue, his teeth. He nipped and nibbled, kissed and sucked, locating a soft cheek, a tender earlobe, a graceful neck and a stubborn chin… Gasping breaths feathered his face, urging him on.

His mouth finally landed on full lips to capture shuddering moans as voracious and needy as his. Fingertips, firm and seeking, caressed the taught muscles of his abs, sending the electrical sparks deep into his groin. His hands sunk further into the mass of curls and the delicious apple scent became even richer. He held his angel's head to take the kiss deeper, the summer sun warming his naked skin, shining off the plump red fruit and through the vivid green canopy overhead.

A wave of possessive hunger flowed through him as the stiff length of his arousal, so hard now he could probably pound nails with it, brushed more velvet. Was that a thigh? A belly? More damn clothing?

The earthy, erotic apple scent, the heady sobs and those caressing fingers ignited a firestorm that finally centred where he needed it the most.

'Yes.' He groaned. But then suddenly everything changed.

'Wait… Stop…' a groggy voice whispered close to his ear. Then snapped loudly, 'Get off me.'

The panicked cry sliced through the sensual fog like a missile, hurtling him out of the summer orchard and back into the dark apartment. He yanked himself back in the darkness, letting go of the mass of curls, hideously aware the warm, soft, body of his dream woman had gone rigid and become far too real.

'What the…?' He growled, the pain in his groin nothing compared to the sickening, disorienting feeling clutching at his ribs. 'Are you really here?'

'Yes, of course I am!' came the hissed reply. Palms flattened against his chest, probably to push him off, but he was already rolling away, brutally awake now, his head throbbing, the painful erection refusing to subside despite his shattered equilibrium.

A barrage of questions blasted into his muddled brain all at once.

Had he just molested a woman in his sleep? And what the hell was she doing in his bed? In his bedroom? At three in the morning? Because this definitely was not Beatrice.

A dark figure scrambled out of the bed and a switch clicked.

'Argh!' He swore viciously, as the sudden glare turned his eyes to fireballs.

He threw his arm over his face, to stop his retinas from being lasered off, and yanked up the sheet to cover the still-throbbing erection. But not before he caught a blurry glimpse of wild russet hair and bold, abundant curves trussed up in a red and black outfit worthy of a lusty tavern wench in a gothic novel.

Was that a corset? Turning her cleavage into the eighth wonder of the world?

Horror and guilt gave way to shock and outrage as awareness continued to spit and pop over his skin like wildfire. Whatever she was wearing, it wasn't doing a damn thing to calm the inferno still raging in his crotch.

'Dim the lights,' he demanded of the house's smart tech system as his mind finally caught up with his cartwheeling emotions and his torched libido.

Was this some kind of a sick prank, or worse, an attempt at blackmail?

'Who are you?' he demanded as his temper gathered pace.

Whoever she was, it was not his fault he'd touched her. Kissed her. Caressed her... Good God, begged her to stroke him to orgasm... Shame washed over him and the erection finally began to soften.

He cut off the thought of what he'd almost done. He'd been virtually comatose. And he was the one who was naked. And he'd stopped the minute he'd woken up enough to figure out what was going on.

And this was *his* bed, in *his* place.

The lights dipped as requested, the only sound her laboured breathing and his thundering heartbeat as he slowly lowered his arm. He waited for his flaming eyeballs to adjust to the half-light. He couldn't see her properly, his myopia turning her into a series of fuzzy, indistinct shapes. But somehow, even without being able to make out too many details, he could sense her vibrant, vivid beauty— not classy and fragile like Beatrice's but raw and real and way too sensual. The earthy, spicy scent tinged with the ripe aroma of a summer orchard still permeated the room. Not a hallucination, then, but the smell of her.

Other memories flashed back to torment him. The feel of her lush curves—satin and silk against his fingertips—the taste of her still lingering on his tongue—heady and sweet and more addictive than a class A drug.

He thrust clumsy fingers through his hair.

'What the hell are you doing hiding in my bed?' he demanded when she didn't speak, letting every ounce of his outrage and frustration vibrate through the words. 'In the middle of the night...disguised as a Victorian hooker?'

'I'm not dressed as a hooker. This is a Little Red Riding Hood outfit!' The inane reply stumbled out of Katie's mouth, her whole body still vibrating from the shock of Jack Wolfe's touch. Firm, forceful, electrifying. Her mind still reeled from being catapulted out of heaven and into hell in one second flat.

Unfortunately, her body had not got the memo— that she was now in the most compromising, mortifying position she had ever found herself in in her entire life—and that was saying something for someone who had earned a living as a children's entertainer for the past five years.

Her nipples were hard enough to drill through steel and the weight in her sex felt like a hot, heavy brick throbbing in time to her frantic heartbeat.

She'd been fast asleep, dreaming of him… Or so she'd thought. But now her panicked gaze devoured the man himself.

Jack Wolfe, in all his glory.

The snapped photos had not done him justice. Sitting up in his bed with a sheet thrown over the mammoth erection she'd had in her hand only moments before, Jack Wolfe was a smorgasbord of hotness laid out before her on thousand-thread-count sheets.

Her shocked gaze took in every inch of him in the softened lighting. The muscular chest, the broad shoulders, the swirling tattoo of a howling wolf which flared over one shoulder blade and across his left pec—only partially obscured by the sprinkle of chest hair that surrounded his nipples and arrowed down through washboard abs.

She jerked her gaze back up before it could land once again on the tent in his lap.

His eyes narrowed, or rather squinted, and she had the weirdest feeling he couldn't quite see her. His glare didn't alter as she took in the full masculine beauty of his face.

All sharp angles and sensual lines, his bone structure was perfectly symmetrical except for a bump on the bridge of his nose. And the livid scar which sliced through his eyebrow and marred his right cheek. His eyes were a startling, pure almost translucent blue with a dark rim around the edges. And horribly bloodshot.

She noted the other signs of fatigue: the bruised shadows under his eyes, the drawn lines around his mouth. Sympathy and guilt joined the tangle of emotions making her stomach pitch and roll. But at least it went some way to stem the flood of sensation.

'I don't give a damn who you're disguised as,' he finally snarled, the sharp tone cutting through the charged silence with the precision of a scalpel. 'I want to know what you're doing in my bed waiting to jump me in the middle of the night!'

'I… I fell asleep.'

'Well, duh…' The sneer broke through her shock and shame to tap into her own indignation—which had completely malfunctioned in the face of his extreme hotness.

However hot he was, she was not the one who had initiated Kiss-mageddon. Even sound asleep she'd known that was him. His firm touch skimming over her curves, cupping her breasts, tightening her nipples to…

She swallowed.

Focus, Katie, for goodness' sake.

'I didn't jump you…you jumped me,' she managed.

He scraped his fingers through his hair, pushing the short, damp waves into haphazard spikes. 'Fine, we're even there,' he said, the growled concession surprising her a little. Even naked—*especially* naked—he didn't look like the type of guy who backed down often. 'But I still don't know who the hell you are or what you're doing in my penthouse dressed as a porno version of Red Riding Hood!'

Porno…? What the…?

'This costume's not pornographic. It's not even revealing!' she all but yelped, her own outrage finally coming to the fore. *Of all the…* 'I wear this outfit to read fairy tales to four-year-olds and I've never had any complaints.'

His burning, bloodshot gaze skated over her and drowned her outrage in another flood of unwanted sensation. *Drat the man.* 'I expect their fathers enjoy the show even more than they do.'

She sputtered.

But then she glanced down at her costume. Okay, it had become a bit dishevelled during their dream clinch. She hooked the corset at the top, which she'd loosened before taking a quick nap in what she'd thought was a guest bedroom after getting Bea's text telling her she was off the hook and Jack wouldn't be coming home until tomorrow afternoon.

Wrong again, Bea.

There were no personal items in this room, not even any toiletries on the bathroom vanity… Who lived like that? she thought indignantly as she yanked up the cotton chemise under the corset so it more adequately covered her ample cleavage.

It seemed her quick nap had turned into a deep, drugging sleep before he had so rudely awakened her with his hot, firm touch and his voracious…

Seriously, Katie, focus, already.

She struggled to control the burn of humiliation. And arousal. Not a great combination at the best of times. She had to leave ASAP, now she'd finally gathered enough of her shattered wits to think coherently. But she still had a message to deliver.

'I'm here on behalf of your fiancée, Bea Medford,' she said, even though he was still glaring at her as if she'd ruined his night instead of the other way round.

'How do you know Beatrice?' he demanded, the frown on his forehead becoming catastrophic.

She opened her mouth to tell him, then snapped it shut again as her common sense caught up with her panic. The less this man knew about her identity, the better. He might have her sued or arrested. Even if he'd kissed her first, she was the one who had been in his bed, sound asleep at stupid o'clock in the morning. 'Bea wanted me to tell you,' she continued, ignoring his question. 'She's breaking off the engagement.'

The words dropped into silence and a dart of anguish pierced her ribcage. She hated to be the bearer of bad tidings, even to overbearing, staggeringly hot and arrogant billionaires.

But the pang dissipated when she noted his reaction. He looked mildly surprised, supremely irritated but not remotely devastated. And his glare—which was still directed squarely at her, as if *she'd* been the one who had just dumped him by proxy—hadn't dimmed in the slightest.

'I see,' he said. 'And she didn't come and tell me this herself *why* exactly?'

I know, right?

Katie quashed the disloyal thought. She was on her sister's side—*always*.

But it was impossible not to feel at least a little pissed off with Bea when she had to blurt out, 'She doesn't love you, and she didn't want to hurt your feelings.' She left out the bit about Bea's fear of succumbing to Jack Wolfe's all-powerful seduction techniques, because she had no desire to stroke his already over-inflated ego. Again.

Forget thirty paces. The man had almost given her an orgasm in less than thirty seconds while she'd been sound asleep.

Wolfe's glare intensified. 'Duly noted.' He growled without so much as a flicker of emotion.

So Bea had been right—Jack Wolfe certainly did not have feelings for her, at least not feelings that could be hurt. Katie's heartbeat took a giddy leap. She squashed it like a bug. Why should she be pleased by evidence that he was a heartless, manipulative bastard?

This man had proposed marriage to her sister without giving a hoot about her. When Bea was the sweetest, kindest, most beautiful woman on the planet…give or take the odd episode of unnecessary drama and the fact she was too much of a coward to do her own dirty work.

'Although that still does not explain why you were hiding out in my bed in the middle of the night, disguised as Little Red Riding Hooker,' Jack added, snapping Katie out of her revelry.

Little Red Riding…?

She stiffened at the insult, ready to fire something equally insulting back at him, but the scathing retort got caught in her throat when his glowering gaze raked over her outfit again. And what she saw in it triggered a new wave of heat.

'Tough,' she managed, her throat as raw as the rest of her. 'That's all the explanation you're going to get.'

So saying, she turned and grabbed the boots she'd left by the bed.

Time to stop bickering and run.

She heard his shouted demands—something about staying put and giving him a proper answer to his questions—as she sprinted out through the bedroom door.

She wasn't particularly athletic but, now her flight instinct had finally kicked in big time, she raced through the living area faster than a championship sprinter, grabbing her red velvet cape and raincoat en route. The lift doors were open, the lift waiting for her—*thank God*—and she made it inside and stabbed the button before she heard the crash of footfalls. The doors slid closed on the sight of two hundred and twenty pounds of enraged, spectacularly fit male sprinting towards her, wearing nothing more than a pair of hastily donned boxer shorts and an enraged expression.

She tugged on her boots as the lift dropped to the basement, then raced out of the building's garage. It was only once she jumped aboard a passing night bus heading towards North London that the adrenaline high caused by her narrow escape diluted enough for her to breath properly.

She was retiring as a children's entertainer as

of tonight and finally moving out of London. She had enough money saved now, just about, to move the fledging bakery business she'd launched a year ago to the next level.

Her Welsh grandmother had left Katie a cottage in Snowdonia in her will—because she had always been proud of Katie for breaking free of her father's control. Angharad Evans had always despised Henry Medford after the way he had treated her daughter, Carys—Katie and Bea's mother. The mother Katie barcly remembered.

The old cottage in the heart of the forest needed some work after being empty for years, but the beautiful forest glade where the smallholding was situated was like something out of a fairy tale, and satisfyingly remote. And the online business Katie had been building for over a year would be even better there, reducing her overheads once she'd invested in a new kitchen.

It was way past time she started making a life for herself that she loved. Instead of one where she was just squeaking by—and humiliating herself on a regular basis. And, if moving out of London and going into hiding in rural Wales also meant avoiding Jack Wolfe's prodigious temper, his hot body and any fallout from tonight, so be it.

CHAPTER TWO

One month later

'WHAT DO YOU MEAN, I can't drive to Cariad Cottage?' Jack Wolfe stared incredulously at the old farmer, who was staring back at him as if he'd lost his mind.

Maybe he had. Why hadn't he been able to forget the woman who had ruined all his best laid plans four long weeks ago now? So much so he'd finally hired a private detective to find her. And rearranged a ton of meetings first thing this morning to make a six-hour drive to the middle of nowhere just to confront her.

'Not in that, boyo,' the man said in a thick Welsh accent, glancing at the Mercedes Benz EQS convertible Jack had liberated from his garage at five o'clock that morning when he'd finally been given an address and discovered Little Red Riding Hooker was his ex-fiancée's older sister.

'You'd need a tractor, or a quad, maybe,' the farmer added. 'Or you could walk. Take about an hour—maybe two.' He glanced down at Jack's shoes. 'But there's a storm heading in.'

What storm? There had been no mention of a storm on his weather app. The sky above the tree-tops on the edge of the forest was startlingly blue, not a cloud in sight. Perhaps the guy was a friend of Katherine Medford—and was trying to head him off.

Well, you can forget that, mate. He had a score to settle with Miss Red.

He intended to get payback, not just for the broken engagement—which was now threatening to screw up the Smyth-Brown takeover—but for all the sleepless nights in the last month when he'd been woken from dreams of apple orchards and scantily clad wenches to find himself unbearably aroused.

Somehow, he'd become fixated on the woman. And he didn't like being fixated on anyone or anything. It suggested a loss of control he would not tolerate.

She owed him.

'Fine. I'll walk,' he said, tugging up the collar of his jacket and opening the muscle car's boot. He toed off his designer loafers and stamped on brand-new walking boots. He threw the car keys to the farmer, who caught them one-handed.

'There's two hundred in it if you keep an eye on the car for me until I return,' he said.

The man nodded, then asked, 'You want me to send one of the lads with you for an additional price? So you don't get lost.'

'No, thanks,' Jack said. 'I won't get lost.'

He had envisaged this meeting in his mind's eye over four whole weeks and six long hours of driving. He didn't want company.

The farmer didn't look convinced. Jack ignored him and strode off along the rutted track into the shadow of the forest, the earthy scent of lichen and moss lightened by the fresh, heady perfume of wild spring blooms.

The storm hit forty-five minutes later, by which time his feet were already bloody from blisters, his face had been stung to pieces by midges and the phone signal had died, leaving him staggering about in the mud, trying to keep to the track.

The only thing still driving him on in his cold, wet, painful misery was the thought of finally locating Little Miss Riding Hooker again and wringing her neck.

Katie inhaled the lush, buttery aroma of chocolate and salted caramel as she lifted her latest batch of brownies from the oven.

She wiped floury hands on her apron. Only two more batches and she'd be ready to load the quad bike and drive her orders to the post office in Beddgelert. She frowned at the rain hammering against the cottage's slate roof and battering the kitchen windows. That was if the spring thunderstorm which had begun an hour ago ever stopped.

Heavy thuds broke through the sound of hammering rain.

Someone had come to visit? In the middle of a storm? How odd.

Dumping the apron, she headed towards the sound which was coming from the cottage's front door. Probably stranded hikers. It certainly wasn't locals, as they knew to come to the kitchen door.

Poor things, they must be lost and completely soaked. She'd treat them to a cup of hot cocoa and ply them with cookies until the rain stopped—she had to take advantage of every sales opportunity at the moment, given the woeful state of her finances. Who knew installing an industrial-grade kitchen in an off-grid cottage would be so expensive?

The thuds got more demanding as she rushed through the cottage's candlelit interior. The second-hand generator had died an hour ago. Thank goodness for her wood-powered Aga or her whole afternoon would have been a wash-out.

'Open the door.' The gruff, muffled demand sent a frisson of electricity through her. The memory flash—of a taut male body, translucent-blue, blood-shot eyes and a furious frown—was not wanted.

That was four weeks ago—in another life. Stop obsessing about your disastrous encounter with Jack Wolfe.

'Just coming!' she shouted as cheerfully as she could over the hammering.

Impatient, much?

But, when she flung open the heavy oak door with her best 'come buy my cookies' smile, the memory flash flared as if someone had chucked a gallon of petrol on it. And her smile dropped off a cliff.

'Mr Wolfe?' Her numb fingers fell from the door handle as shock reverberated through her system hot on the heels of the five-alarm fire.

Was the man of her wet dreams *actually* dripping a small lake onto her doorstep, his arms clasped around his waist, his broad shoulders hunched against the cold, his dark hair plastered to his head while he wore a designer business suit so drenched it clung to his muscular physique like a second skin?

Or was she having an out-of-body experience?

'*Mr?* Really?' he said, or rather growled, in that gruff tone that had a predictably incendiary effect on her abdomen. 'Let's not stand on ceremony, Red. After all, we've already shared a bed.'

What?

Horrified realisation dawned.

This is not a dream, Katie. Shut the stupid door.

But, before the shock and heat could recede enough for her fingers to get the message, Wolfe had figured out her intention and thrust his foot forward.

The door slammed on his muddy boot. He swore profusely.

'Blast, sorry…' She cringed. She hadn't meant to injure him. *Much.*

He shoved the door open and marched—or rather, limped assertively—past her into her living room, trailing mud, rainwater and his injured dignity with him.

The muscle in his rain-slicked cheek, gilded by

candlelight, twitched like a ticking bomb. But before she had a chance to ask what on earth he was doing in the middle of North Wales, hiking in a thunderstorm—in what looked like an extremely expensive and now totally ruined designer suit—he shivered so hard, his clenched teeth rattled.

And her shocked arousal got bowled over by a wave of sympathy.

While taking pity on him would have been a stretch because—even drenched and freezing, and with several nasty-looking midge bites he still had an aura of ruthless command which would have impressed Attila the Hun—she did not want the surly billionaire catching his death in her cottage or stomping any more mud onto her grandmother's handmade rug.

'There are towels and a shower through there,' she said, pointing towards the downstairs bathroom. 'Take off your suit and drop it outside so I can dry it by the stove. I'll find you something to wear,' she finished with more authority than she felt.

His scarred eyebrow arched and his sensual mouth curved into something halfway between a sarcastic grin and a suggestive sneer. 'You want me naked again so soon, Katherine? I'm flattered.'

He knows my name! Bea, you're a dead woman.

'Oh, shut up,' she managed, flustered now as well as panicked and confused and inappropriately turned on. 'Don't worry. I promise not to even *look* at your dignity this time. Let alone touch it.'

So why are you talking about it, you muppet?

Perhaps because she'd thought about it far too much in the past month.

Heat flared in his now laser-focussed gaze as it raked over her. 'Shame,' he murmured with a rich appreciation she did not have one clue what to do with.

She made a hasty retreat up the stairs to locate something dry for him to wear from the sack of her grandmother's old clothes that she'd recently washed to take to a charity shop in Bangor. Something that would cover his dignity and salvage what was left of her sanity.

Some chance.

She's stunning. Even more stunning than I imagined.

Jack allowed the thought of Katherine Medford's glorious curves in flour-dusted jeans and a worn T-shirt, her shocked emerald eyes, her pale, freckled skin and wild, red hair warm him as he peeled off his sodden clothing, dropped it outside the bathroom door and stepped into the snug shower cubicle.

The water pressure left a lot to be desired, but the heat was welcome as another shivering fit hit him. As he thawed out, his mind began to engage with something other than the visceral shock of Katherine Medford's unusual beauty.

Her cottage—its whitewashed stone and bright-blue gingerbread trim beckoning him out of the storm like a beacon—was cosier and more comfortable than he had expected from the detective's report on her finances. Thunder crashed outside as he dried himself off with one of the fluffy towels neatly folded on the vanity. The smell of apples from her shampoo reminded him forcefully of the erotic orchard he had visited nearly every night for a month in his dreams.

He dragged on his damp boxers, the only item of clothing which had survived the journey. And scowled down at the burgeoning tent in his shorts.

Behave.

She was everything he'd remembered and more—especially now he was wearing his lenses and could see her more clearly. But the resultant effect on his libido and his self-control was not good.

And worse was the way her saucy, sparky attitude affected him. Since when had he found defiance arousing? She'd slammed the door on his foot! And yet, as soon as he'd got inside the house, the thought of chastising her had taken second place to the thought of feasting on her full lips.

He sighed, rubbing his hair dry.

Time to get real. She might look harmless, but he already knew she wasn't. She would not get the better of him. *Again.*

'Here. It was all I could find that looked big enough.' He turned to see a toned arm appear at the door holding a…? He scowled and tilted his head. What was that? It looked like a piece of purple towelling with…were those pink ruffles?

'Great,' he murmured, lifting it from her outstretched fingers. 'Thanks,' he said, not sure he should be all that thankful. The arm immediately disappeared back behind the door.

'Would you like some hot cocoa?' the disembodied voice asked.

'I'd prefer coffee,' he said. Coffee was the least he was going to need to wear the monstrosity she'd handed him. He shrugged on the worn frilly towelling robe. It was tight across his shoulder blades and only just covered his backside. He looked ridiculous in it, but it was warm and dry and smelt of laundry detergent, with a hint of her. He'd worn enough second-hand clothing as a kid to appreciate comfort over sartorial elegance any day.

'I'm sorry, I don't have coffee,' she said, sounding almost apologetic.

'Cocoa it is, then,' he said, then caught another whiff of the delicious aroma which had enveloped him when he'd first stepped into the cottage. 'And a slice of whatever it is you're baking,' he added, his stomach grumbling loudly as he realised he was starving.

'The brownies are not for sale,' she said. 'They're already on order.'

'I'll give you fifty quid per brownie,' he said, not joking.

He heard an astonished huff which made the goose pimples on his arms—and a few other things—stand to attention.

'Okay, sold,' she said, not sounding all that grateful for his generosity. 'But don't think I won't bill you,' she added with a sharp tone that made him smile. He knew the value of something all depended on what someone was prepared to pay for it. And her mercenary zeal was something he could appreciate.

'There's ointment in the cabinet for your midge bites,' she added. 'It'll stop them itching.'

'How much will that cost me?' he asked wryly.

'It's free... For now, but don't tempt me.' The door began to close before she added. 'I've lit a fire in the living room, so you can sit in there once you're decent until the cocoa is ready.'

His smile sharpened as the door snapped shut, his usual confidence when it came to women, and especially this woman, finally returning full-force.

Decent? Is that really what you want? I don't think so, Red. Not from the way your eyes darkened as soon as you spotted me on your doorstep.

Maybe she had a more volatile effect on him than any woman he'd ever dated, but that didn't have to be a bad thing. When was the last time a woman had challenged him? Or made him ache, for that matter, for four solid weeks—enough to have him tracking her all the way to the wilds of North Wales and trashing his favourite suit?

Perhaps his obsession with her was much more straightforward than he had originally assumed. And just as easily remedied.

After tying the belt on the ridiculous robe, he found the ammonia-based ointment in the cabinet and began dabbing it on the bites on his face and neck, surprised when the angry swelling stopped itching.

The grin widened as he touched the robe's *frou-frou* frills. No doubt Katherine had supplied him with this sartorial disaster to threaten his masculinity.

Yeah, good luck with that, Red!

It would take much more than donning a secondhand dressing gown to put a dent in Jack Wolfe's ego. And he intended to make sure Katherine Medford found that out the hard way…

He chuckled. *Pun fully intended.*

CHAPTER THREE

KATIE PERCHED ON the armchair opposite her uninvited guest and watched him devour his third
brownie.

How could Jack Wolfe still look hot wearing her
grandmother's dressing gown? Even the lurid pink
trim hadn't dimmed his forceful masculinity one
bit. Perhaps because too much of his magnificent
chest was now visible in the deep V of the robe's
flounced neckline.

'That's a hundred and fifty pounds you owe me,'
she said, just in case he'd forgotten the agreed price.
Instead of looking outraged, he smiled. Or was it a
smile? It was hard to tell, the sensual curve as cynical as it was amused. She remembered what Bea
had said about him being impossible to read. Her
sister had not been wrong. The man was about as
transparent as a brick.

'And worth every penny,' he murmured, licking
the last of the caramel crumble off his fingertips.

Her heartbeat, which was now beating time with
the torrential rain outside, sunk deeper into her ab-

domen. If he was trying to intimidate her with that sexy glint in his eyes, it was definitely working.

'So, what are you doing in Snowdonia, Mr Wolfe?' she asked, struggling to keep her voice firm—which required every acting skill she'd ever acquired. 'Assuming, of course, it's not an unlucky coincidence you turned up on my doorstep?'

She'd gone over all the possible motives for his appearance—from the bad to the absolutely catastrophic—while waiting for him to emerge from her bathroom and she couldn't think of a single one that might be benign.

Bea had rung her to thank her, the day after the night of the dream clinch, and said Jack had agreed to release her from the obligation without changing the terms of their father's loan.

Lord Medford had still been angry, but at least he hadn't freaked out completely. Knowing what their father was capable of when his plans were thwarted, Katie had been grateful, and also surprised Wolfe had been so amenable. But now she knew why. Obviously, he'd been planning to get payback on the messenger instead: *her*.

'No, it wasn't a coincidence,' he said, his intent gaze causing her goose bumps to get goose bumps. He placed his plate on the table beside the sofa. The pink trim on the robe caressed his pecs. 'I hired a detective to find you.'

She might have been relieved Bea hadn't ratted her out after all if she wasn't shocked at how determined he had been to locate her. Had she really injured his dignity that much? Because, as she re-called, it had been pretty robust.

His gaze skated over her, setting off more bon-fires. 'I never would have guessed you and Bea-trice were sisters.'

She bristled. She couldn't help it. She loved Bea to pieces, but she knew perfectly well that when men met her baby sister—tall, willowy, serene and dazzlingly beautiful Bea—they didn't notice Katie or spot the family resemblance. Unlike Bea, Katie was short, had insane hair and was, well, not exactly slender. She'd learned over the years to embrace her curves—and her chocolate addiction. She'd never be slim or elegant—she'd failed at a ton of yo-yo diets to prove it—but she was happy with who she was now and she was healthy and fit.

'Well, we *are* sisters,' she said. 'As much as I would love not to share any genetic code with my father, he insisted on a paternity test when we were both born to make sure we were his. Because that's the kind of trusting, charming guy he is.'

The muscle in Wolfe's cheek hardened. 'You don't get on with your father?'

'"Don't get on" is a bit of an understatement,' she said, proud her father's scorn no longer had the power to hurt her. 'We don't have a relation-ship. As a teenager, I wanted to be an actress. He had planned for me to marry one of his business associates. So he kicked me out of the house. It was tough for a while, and the actress thing didn't pan out because I didn't have the right "look",' she added, doing air quotes. 'But I've never missed being under his thumb.'

'How old were you when he kicked you out?'

She shrugged. 'Seventeen.' Perhaps he thought she was a fool to have walked away from all that privilege. From what she'd read about Wolfe in the business press, he'd never had any of the advantages she'd been born into. But she didn't care about his opinion. No one got to judge her life choices any more. That was the point.

'That's very young to be on your own,' he said, surprising her when the fierce look on his face became almost sympathetic.

Katie dismissed the giddy blip in her heart rate. She didn't need his pity. 'I wasn't totally alone,' she said. 'My *nain* was still alive then, so she helped me out.'

'Your *nine*? What is that?' he asked, pronouncing the word in English.

'It's Welsh for grandmother.' She glanced around the cottage. 'Cariad was her home. She left it to me five years ago, when she died,' she added, then wondered why she was giving him so much unsolicited information. 'And seventeen's not that young. I was older than you were when you ended up on the street.'

He stiffened, the frown returning.

Touché, Jack. Two can play the interrogation game.

'How did you find out I was once homeless?' he asked, his tone deceptively soft but with steel beneath. She remembered what Bea had said about how guarded he was with personal information. Apparently that hadn't changed.

'I did an Internet search on you after... After that night.'

The frown deepened. 'I didn't know that information was on the Internet.'

'It's not in the UK press, but I found an article written three years ago for a celebrity website in Mexico. They mentioned the rumours about your background while saying how much money you'd donated to a charity for street kids while you were there.' She'd wondered, when she'd read it, if the story had been planted to make him look good. Apparently not, from the way his jaw clenched.

'I see,' he said, then pulled his smart phone from the pocket of the robe and began tapping with lightning-fast thumbs.

She would hazard a guess that when his phone service returned *Estilo* magazine was going to be forced to take down the article.

'So it's true,' she murmured.

His gaze met hers as he pocketed the phone, the guarded look making the blip in her heart rate pulse.

'What is?' he asked evasively.

'That you were homeless as a child,' she continued, refusing to be deflected by the 'back off' vibes.

Shadows crossed his expression and the pulse of sympathy echoed in her chest. Moments ago it would have been impossible to imagine Jack Wolfe had ever been vulnerable and afraid and at the mercy of people more powerful than himself— and even harder to believe she could have anything in common with him. But, as she watched him debate whether to admit the truth or stonewall her, it became less hard.

'I wasn't a child,' he said at last.

'How old were you?' she probed, because the article hadn't been that specific. She'd simply assumed his 'early teens' had to be younger than seventeen.

Again she saw him debating whether to answer her, then he shrugged. 'Thirteen.'

'That makes you a child, Jack,' she said, stunned he could believe otherwise.

'Believe me, I'd seen enough and done enough—*more* than enough—at that age to qualify as a man.' He rubbed the scar on his cheek and the pulse in her chest bounced.

I wonder who gave him that scar?

'And I was certainly never a victim,' he added, dropping his hand. He reached across the space to snag her wrist. 'So you can take that pitying look off your face.'

His touch was electrifying, shocking her into silence when he stood and dragged her to her feet.

He was too close to her, his big body generating warmth, the scent of him enveloping her. Her apple shampoo mixed with a tantalising, musty aroma which threw her back to that night in his bed and into that unbearably erotic dream.

'I don't pity you,' she said, shuddering when he cupped her cheek with his other hand, pushing her wild hair back from her face and hooking it behind her ear. The gesture was disturbingly possessive, but oddly tender too.

'Good,' he remarked, his gaze roaming over her face with a purpose which made her more aware of his addictive scent and the heavy weight sinking into her sex.

'But I do feel sorry for that boy,' she said boldly, ignoring the renewed ache she thought she'd tamed weeks ago.

'Well, don't be. That little bastard is long gone.' His mouth lowered to hers, his eyes dark with arousal now. 'I'm a man now, a man who always gets what he wants.'

She should push him away, tell him to let her go, but she couldn't seem to move, couldn't seem to speak, all her senses focused on his lips and the memory of them skating over her skin, igniting fires which had been burning ever since.

'And what I want now is *you*, Red,' he murmured.

It was an outrageous thing to say. They didn't know each other, they certainly didn't like each other, and it was fairly obvious he was still mad at her for what had happened with Bea...

But, even knowing all that, her heart continued to hammer harder than the rain outside as her body softened into a mass of molten sensation.

What was happening to her? She wasn't a virgin. But she'd never felt anything like this instant, insane chemistry. Her two boyfriends as a teenager had been nothing like Jack Wolfe. They had been friends, not a rich, powerful, ruthlessly driven man who was the complete opposite of sweet or generous or kind.

So why couldn't she tell him to get lost?

He framed her face with both hands. The rough calluses abraded her skin as he tilted her face up to his.

'You want me too.' His hot breath, flavoured with caramel, whispered over her lips. 'Say it.'

She flattened her palms against her *nain*'s robe, wanting to push him away. But then his ridged abs tensed beneath her fingertips.

'Tell me the truth, Katherine.'

'Yes,' she whispered on a soft sob of need.

Yes.

Triumph leapt in Jack's chest, her reluctant acceptance yanking at something deep inside. He slanted his mouth across hers, capturing her startled gasp, and threaded his fingers into her wild hair to hold her steady, releasing the tantalising scent of apples as his body ached.

The firestorm of need that had been propelling him here all along soared as her lips parted, instinctively giving him more access, and he thrust his tongue deep.

She tasted of cocoa and sin —silky, rich, delicious and even more addictive than her brownies. He explored in demanding, hungry strokes, while running his hands down her sides to capture her bottom and press her into his erection. He exploited each sigh, each shudder, scattering kisses across her stubborn jaw, biting into her earlobe, feasting on her neck.

Her kisses, tentative at first, became as fierce and furious as his. He draped her arms around his neck and drew her closer still, stoking the fire until it burned.

Feeling his control slipping, he yanked himself back and held her waist. Her eyelids fluttered open, her expression a picture of stunned arousal and shocking desire.

He let out a gruff chuckle, trying to ease the tension in his gut and calm the driving need to devour her.

'Where's your bedroom?' he asked, surprised he could actually string a coherent sentence together.

She frowned and he could see the wary confusion cross her face.

'What are you scared of, Red?' he coaxed.

Her gaze flared with outrage and a strange pressure pushed at his chest.

She really was glorious when she was mad.

'I'm not scared of *you*, that's for sure.' The fierce denial made her eyes flash with green fire. The desire in his abdomen flared.

Who would have guessed her independence was even hotter than those gorgeous curves or the fiery passion in her eyes?

'Then let's take what we both want,' he said.

It was a dare, pure and simple. A risky strategy for sure—and not something he would normally do. He didn't have to fight for what he wanted—not any more. Everything eventually fell into his lap, women most of all, because he always made sure he held all the cards.

But Katherine was different. Because he wanted her more than he had wanted any woman. She challenged him, excited him, pushed and provoked him. She already knew more about him than any woman he had ever slept with. The compassion in her eyes when she had revealed what she knew about his past had horrified him. And made him want to prove he wasn't that wild, angry kid.

No one looked at him with pity in their eyes. Not any more. He was the master of his own destiny now. And he intended to be the master of hers too.

The thought of how fixated on her he'd become should have made him extremely uneasy. But, as he watched her gaze flare with the same need and the same desperation, and felt her body soften, the fire in his gut became too intense to think about anything but getting her naked and ending this craving to finish what they'd started a month ago.

'Upstairs,' she said. 'First door on the right.'

He swore with relief, then grasped her hand in his and dragged her up the narrow staircase. He had to duck his head under an exposed beam to enter the low-ceilinged room. A flash of lightning illuminated a cosy, unashamedly feminine space. A brass-framed bed had been crammed into the small area and was covered with a home-made quilt and scattered with colourful cushions, the headboard draped with fairy lights. He flicked the light switch but nothing happened.

'The generator's out,' she said over the roar of thunder.

He marched to the window and drew the curtain, gilding the room in a watery light, but it was enough to see her more clearly, and that was all he cared about.

Untying the robe she'd given him, he dropped it on the floor, his skin burning from the sensory overload.

Her gaze darkened as it roamed over him, her breath shuddering out as it snagged on the tattoo he'd had done several lifetimes ago. He'd debated having it removed. The faded artwork had meant something to him once but seemed crude now, and vulgar on the man he had strived to become. But her avid gaze gave him pause.

How could he feel both exposed yet flattered by the desire darkening her eyes? He didn't need her acceptance or her approval.

Returning to her, he lifted the heavy fall of hair off her nape and cradled her head to tug her mouth back to his. Her hands flattened against his abs as he kissed and caressed the stubborn line of her jaw. 'You're wearing way too many clothes. Yet again,' he murmured.

Katie gave a throaty chuckle. 'I know,' she managed.

'Then let's remedy the situation.' Jack grasped the hem of her T-shirt and yanked it over her head.

It was his turn to feel light-headed as he took in the sight of her magnificent breasts cupped in red lace. Dark nipples poked at the sheer fabric, swollen and erect.

He rubbed his thumb across one rigid tip, gratified when she gasped and the nipple drew into a tight peak. He slid the bra straps off her shoulders, then unhooked the lacy contraption to release the abundant weight into his palms.

He lifted them to capture the engorged nipple with his lips. Tracing the puckered areola with his tongue, he choked down a rough chuckle when her fingernails dug into his shoulders. She clung to him as he worked one stiff peak then the other, kissing, nipping, tugging, her body bowing back like a high-tension wire. She panted, her uninhibited response even more exquisite than the feel of her flesh swelling and elongating against his tongue.

Keeping his mouth on her breasts, he released the buttons on her jeans with clumsy fingers and edged the denim off her hips enough to press the heel of his palm into the heat of her panties.

He groaned as his fingers slid under the gusset and found her clitoris, the slick nub already drenched with desire. He felt her contract around his invading fingers as his thumb caressed the bundle of nerves with ruthless efficiency. His own pain and need dimmed in the drive to make her shatter. Just for him.

She clamped down hard on his probing fingers, crying out as the wave hit with stunning force. He held her there, ruthlessly stroking until she slumped against him, limp and exhausted.

The scent of her arousal permeated the room, making his erection buck against his shorts.

I want to be inside her.

The fierce urgency joined the visceral ache. He stripped off the rest of her clothing in record time, then scooped her into his arms and laid her on the bed.

She stared at him, her gaze unfocussed, her breathing ragged, her red hair dark against the light quilt and her skin flushed with afterglow.

She was a banquet he wanted to feast upon for hours. But as he kicked off his boxers, and the painful erection sprang free, he knew the feasting would have to wait, because right now he had to feed the hunger clawing at what was left of his self-control like a ravening wolf.

He slid his arms under her knees to lift her legs high and wide and position the aching erection at her entrance.

'Hold on to me,' he grunted. Katie's hands clasped his shoulders as he thrust deep in one powerful surge.

Her sex massaged his length. So tight. And for one brutal moment he thought he would lose it. But, using every last ounce of his control, he held on enough to establish a rhythm that would drive them both towards oblivion. Together this time.

She opened for him, her body accepting all of his. His grunts matched her soft pants as she met his thrusts. The tide rose, barrelling towards him, and the pleasure and pain combined into a furious storm no less powerful or elemental than the one still raging outside.

Her body clamped down at last, triggering his own vicious orgasm. Shattering in its intensity, the climax gripped him as he soared into the abyss. But, as he crashed to earth, two thoughts slammed into him at once as he collapsed on top of her.

I didn't use a condom.

I want her again already.

CHAPTER FOUR

KATIE'S FINGERS SLID OFF the broad shoulder pressing her into the mattress, Jack Wolfe's erection still solid inside her.

But, as the halo of afterglow faded, the shattering truth settled on her chest. And felt even heavier than Wolfe's muscular body.

What had she done?

She'd never made love before with such urgency, and passion and ferocity—he'd stoked it for sure, but she'd been a willing and eager participant in her own destruction.

He groaned as he rolled off her.

She flinched, aware of the tenderness from their brutal joining and the sticky residue he had left behind.

This man had been engaged to her sister only a month ago. And, even if he and Bea had never slept together, Katie had just crossed a line—an ethical, moral line. She didn't even like the man. And she certainly didn't trust him.

Perhaps she should be grateful they'd got the hunger out of their system that had been building since that night. But her panic only increased when he shifted beside her and laid a possessive hand on her stomach. The heat didn't feel anywhere near as satisfying as it should have, but worse was that sense of connection which couldn't be real.

She shifted, attempting to scoot off the bed, but his hand curled around her hip, holding her in place.

'Where are you going?' he asked.

She was forced to look at him.

His tanned skin glowed in the turbulent light as the storm continued to batter the window. His strong features, marred by that jagged scar, looked saturnine, the unreadable expression doing nothing to contain the storm raging inside her.

'I need to wash up,' she said, horrified at the thought she hadn't asked him to use protection. She'd been blindsided by him, enough to lose not just her control but every one of her scruples and priorities. And that had never happened to her before. Not ever.

And they weren't even dating.

She grasped his wrist to lift his arm off her. He didn't protest as she sat up and scooped her discarded T-shirt off the floor. She tugged it on, feeling brutally exposed.

Bit late for that, Katie.

Thank goodness the T-shirt was long enough to cover her bare bum because her panties had vanished.

As she stood, intending to lock herself in the bathroom until she could figure out how on earth to play this situation, he said softly behind her, 'I'm sorry. I should have used a condom and I didn't. I've never done that before.'

She glanced round, surprised by the apology and by the frown on his face that suggested he was telling the truth. The heat that shot through her already overused body at the sight of him naked and still partially aroused was not at all welcome.

He threw the quilt over his lap, but the lazy movement suggested he was doing it to protect her modesty, not his own.

Not that she had any. Not any more. Not after the way she'd thrown herself at him. And gone completely to pieces at the first touch of his lips, the first intimate caress.

'Are there likely to be consequences we need to address?' he asked, gathering his faculties a lot quicker than she could.

She shook her head. 'Not unless you have any unpleasant diseases,' she managed, so humiliated now she couldn't even look at him. She turned to stare out of the window, the sun finally putting in an appearance and making the raindrops on the forest leaves sparkle.

The cottage was in a small glade with a mountain stream at the back. One of the few memories she had of her mother was from here, smiling when Carys had brought her and Beatrice to Snowdonia to visit their *nain*. Before her mother had died and her father had forbidden them both to visit 'the old crone', as he liked to call Angharad Evans.

When Katie had arrived to clear the place out a month ago, she'd felt instantly as if she belonged here. But she felt lost now, disorientated, as if she'd become someone other than who she had strived to be—smart, independent and accountable to no one but herself. Had she also betrayed Angharad Evans' memory in the process by welcoming a man as ruthless as her father into her grandmother's old bed?

'I'm on the pill to help with my periods,' she murmured, grateful at least that by a stroke of luck an unplanned pregnancy wouldn't be a consequence. But then she wondered why she had explained the information. Jack Wolfe hardly needed to know she wasn't dating.

Perhaps that was why she'd succumbed so easily to the erotic charge which had flared without warning as soon as he'd declared an interest. It had been four years since she'd been intimate with anyone.

But, even as she tried to persuade herself her insane behaviour had been purely physical, she knew it wasn't. After all, it wasn't as if she hadn't had an orgasm in four years. She was perfectly capable of taking care of her own needs in that department. Although not even her vibrator had ever given her an orgasm—two orgasms—so intense she could still feel the dying embers threatening to reignite any minute just at the sight of Jack lounging on her bed like a well-satisfied tiger... Or rather, a well-satisfied wolf.

Wow, pathetic much?

'I'm clean,' he said, interrupting her pity party. 'I have a rigorous medical every year for my company's insurance,' he added, surprising her with his candour. 'And, as I said, I've never had sex before without a condom.'

'Good to know,' she said, trying to find the information reassuring.

'How about you?'

She swung round at the probing question. Outraged, despite the rational part of her brain telling her he had just as much right to ask her about her sexual history. 'I'm clean too,' she snapped. 'As luck would have it, I'm nowhere near as promiscuous as you are.'

He barked out a half-laugh, completely unperturbed by the bitchy response. 'Don't believe everything you read about me,' he said. 'I've become surprisingly discerning in my old age.'

The frank response made her wish she could take back the revealing reply as she recalled he had never slept with her sister. He'd been engaged to Bea for a week and had dated her for over a month. Why hadn't he seduced her sister with the same fierce focus he'd just seduced her with after meeting her exactly twice? And why should it matter when she'd stopped comparing herself to Bea years ago?

His scarred eyebrow arched and a speculative gleam lit his eyes, accentuating the dark rim around his irises. She had the hideous feeling he could see what she was thinking.

'Just out of interest, when *was* the last time you dated?' he asked, the forthright question slicing through her confused thoughts.

Heat scalded her cheeks.

Good grief, she'd never been a blusher, but she'd never met a man who was quite so direct. Or abrupt.

'A while,' she offered, not about to tell him the truth and encourage any more probing questions.

Or, worse, declare herself the loser in the game of
Who's the Most Jaded Person in the Room they
seemed to be playing.

'Exactly how long is a while?' he countered, un-
deterred by her evasive answer.

'That's none of your business, Jack,' she replied,
then realised her mistake instantly when a smile that
had 'gotcha' written all over it appeared.

'So it's Jack now, is it?' He lifted his arms to link
his fingers behind his head as he sat back against the
cushions, revealing the tantalising tuffs of dark hair
under his armpits and the roped muscles on the un-
derside of his biceps that bulged distractingly. 'Progress, at last,' he finished, the smile now full of wolfish
smugness, or smug wolfishness. *Take your pick.*

Was that his real surname, she wondered. Because it suited him almost too perfectly.

'We just made love,' she said. 'Even I can see
the irony in still calling you Mr Wolfe after that,'
she finished, struggling to gain some semblance of
control over the conversation.

'Did we? Make love? Are you sure?' he mocked.
'How quaint.' The smile took on a cynical slant,
which made him look even more jaded—and hot.

'It's a figure of speech,' she said wearily, suddenly tired of the banter and the knowledge she
wasn't as tough and invulnerable as she had always
assumed, or at least not where he was concerned—
which only made this situation more dangerous.
'We had sex, then, if you prefer,' she added, trying
to regain some of her usual fierceness in the face of

extreme provocation. Did he know how shaky she felt right now? She certainly hoped not.

The smile became rueful, which didn't slow her pounding pulse in the least. 'Funny, because it didn't feel like just having sex,' he said. 'I've had a lot of sex in my life and that was… Well, different.'

Had it been? For him too? Despite his vast experience?

She squashed the foolish thought. He was toying with her, seeing if he could unnerve her even more. Why was she letting him?

She dragged her fingers through her hair and tied the wild mass in a ruthless knot as she glanced out of the window. The panic retreated as she noticed the storm had finally passed. The late afternoon sunlight struggled to peek through the trees. 'The storm's over,' she said, far too aware the storm in her gut hadn't abated in the least. 'Your suit should be dry enough to put back on,' she added, the hint so blatant even he couldn't miss it. 'I'll pack you some brownies for the road free of charge,' she finished, knowing she wasn't even going to hold him to the one hundred and fifty pounds he owed her. She needed him gone now, before she lost what was left of her sanity…and her self-respect.

She headed to the door, ready to hole up in the bathroom until he'd left her bed. And she could breathe again.

But as she reached for the doorknob his gruff voice sent unwelcome sensations sprinting down her spine. 'Not so fast, Red.'

She turned. He was still lounging on her bed but

his gaze had become flat and direct, the muscle in his jaw twitching. 'I'm not finished with you yet.'

'Tough, because I'm finished with you,' Katie said with a conviction she was determined to fake until she'd got him out of the house.

She instantly regretted the bold challenge when the brittle light in his eyes sharpened and he let out a rueful chuckle. 'I wasn't talking about sex,' he said, the searing perusal making it very clear he didn't believe her for a second. 'Precisely.'

Her pulse began to punch her collarbone with the force and fury of a heavyweight champion. 'Then what were you talking about?'

'I have a proposition for you,' Jack said, the silky tone underlined with cold hard steel. 'One you won't want to refuse.'

She swallowed down the lump forming in her throat and locked her knees, the arrogance in his tone as disturbing as everything else about him. 'I don't take orders from you, Jack,' she said, determined to believe it. 'Even if we did just sleep together.'

It was a very long time since she'd allowed herself to be bullied by any man. And, whatever his proposition was, she had no intention of accepting it. He unsettled her in ways she had no control over, and that could not be good. But her curiosity got the better of her when she added, 'What's the proposition?'

He lifted his hands from behind his head and placed them on the taut skin of his belly, drawing her attention to the increasingly visible bulge under the quilt. Her gaze shot back to his face as the sensation sunk like a hot brick into her abdomen. But it was already too late, because his lips curved in that sexy smile that told her he had caught her looking.

'Go wash up,' he said. 'I'll meet you downstairs in twenty minutes. We should probably discuss it when we're both fully clothed,' he added. 'I would hate to take unfair advantage of you.'

She glared at him, knowing full well Jack Wolfe would have no qualms about using any advantage, unfair most of all. But she bit her lip, because calling him out on the blatant lie would be tantamount to admitting he *had* an unfair advantage. And being clothed before she challenged him again would be the smart thing to do… Especially after all the stupid things she'd done.

'Fine,' she said, reaching for the doorknob. 'But, just so you know, the answer is going to be no.' She marched out of the room with a flourish, slamming the door on his low chuckle, satisfied she'd managed to get the last word.

As she showered off the evidence of her stupidity, she promised herself that, no matter what his proposition was, however tempting, however tantalising, however hard to refuse, she would send him packing. Because she owed it to the seventeen-year-old kid who had spent a year sofa-surfing through London and doing crummy minimum-wage jobs on nightshifts to gain her independence. She wasn't about to lose it to a wolf.

CHAPTER FIVE

'WHAT DO YOU MEAN, *no*? You haven't heard the deal yet!' Jack stared at Katherine Medford, not sure whether to be frustrated or amused by the stubborn scowl on her expressive face. Although both reactions were preferable to the fierce tug of need she caused simply by breathing—which was starting to annoy him.

'I don't have to listen to the deal. Have you gone completely insane? I don't want to be any man's mistress but, even if I was going to do something as demeaning as that, it definitely would not be with you.'

Jack let out a gruff laugh, releasing the tension in his ribs. Katherine Medford really did look spectacular when she was mad, and she was practically frothing at the mouth now. He needed to get a grip on the effect she had on him. He'd never found argumentative women a turn-on before, but there was something about Katherine's spitfire qualities that fascinated him.

Go figure.

This fascination was purely sexual, though—for both of them—which surely made her even more perfect for the position he was proposing. A lot more perfect than her sister, anyway.

'Why not me?' he asked.

He had expected pushback and had been more than ready to counter it—after all, that was what negotiations were for. And he happened to be good at them. But her vehement rejection of his proposal was a little over the top, even for her.

'Because you're...' she spluttered, her cheeks suffused with that becoming blush which made the freckles across her nose glow. Something he'd noticed earlier when he had been lying in her bed, far too aware of her naked curves silhouetted against the window through her old T-shirt.

'Because you're *you*,' she said, as if that was supposed to mean something. 'Plus you were engaged to my sister about ten minutes ago. And I don't even like you.'

She leant against the kitchen counter where he'd found her after putting on his clothes. The trousers were trashed and the shirt hopelessly wrinkled, but at least both garments were dry.

His lips quirked. 'I'd say we just proved upstairs you like me well enough,' he said.

'I'm not talking about sex. I'm talking about everything else.'

'Such as?' Jack asked. This ought to be good. Was she a hopeless romantic? Under that guise of pragmatism and practicality? He had to admit he was a little disappointed. But he could work with that if he had too.

Perhaps it was pride, or perhaps it was the sexual

obsession that hadn't faded despite their no-holds-barred antics upstairs—but whatever it was, he did not plan to take no for an answer.

She folded her arms, making those generous breasts plump up underneath her T-shirt.

'Such as shared goals, trust, enjoying each other's company,' she spat out, her brows puckering. 'Oh, and how about the biggie? Actually knowing more about you than I could find out in a few hours of searching online or ten minutes spent in bed with you? Such as that, maybe.'

So not a hopeless romantic, then. *Thank God.* Trying to persuade Bea they actually had a future together had always made him feel vaguely uneasy. At least with Katherine he could dispense with any semblance of hearts and flowers. He had decided that marriage wasn't necessary—Smyth-Brown's board could go hang on that one. He'd find another way to appease them long enough to get his hands on the stock he needed for a controlling interest. But having Katherine as his convenient date wouldn't hurt in that regard when he got her to London. She was still the daughter of a lord, albeit an estranged one.

'You spent *hours* searching for information about me online?' Jack asked, starting to enjoy her indignation when her glare intensified. 'I'm flattered,' he mocked, pressing a hand to his heart, even though the truth was he wasn't lying entirely. He'd have preferred her not to have unearthed information he had directed his legal team to have removed but, now she had, perhaps he could use it.

'Don't be,' she said. 'I was curious, that was all. I'm not any more.'

'Are you sure about that, Red?' He snagged her wrist, forcing her to unfold her arms. And felt her satisfying shudder.

She tried to tug free. He held on.

'You really don't want to hear me out?' he coaxed. 'Find out what I'm offering in return for your cooperation? You're in a much better bargaining position than you think.' Especially now he knew how much he enjoyed having her in his bed.

Getting this hunger out of his system, out of *both* their systems, wasn't going to be as easy as he had originally assumed. But, then again, their explosive chemistry would be a good way to enjoy their time together as he finalised the Smyth-Brown takeover and ripped the company Daniel Smyth's family had built over generations to shreds.

While he wouldn't normally have given his opponent a heads-up on how much he wanted to finalise a deal—after all, that was the biggest no-no when it came to deal-making—he could be generous with Katherine to have her where he wanted her.

'I don't care about the details. I don't want to live with you, I don't even want to date you, plus my life and my business are in Wales. It's completely absurd.'

'Is it?' He glanced at the gleaming kitchen equipment he knew she'd gone into considerable debt to finance. One of the biggest mistakes of fledging businesses was to be overexposed to debt in the first year. But her rookie mistake was his gain.

He'd spent twenty minutes upstairs rereading the detective's report on the financial situation of Cariad Cakes Etc and he was more than ready now to go in for the kill.

'How about if I told you in return for your being at my beck and call for—let's say, six months…' that should be more than long enough to get this frustrating, insistent fascination out of his system. '…I would give you a hundred thousand pounds' worth of investment for your business over the next year for a ten percent share of the profits? And a ten-thousand-pound capital injection to cover your current debts.'

Her mouth dropped open, the bright, unguarded hope in her eyes making the slithers of gold in the emerald green glimmer. His chest tightened, surprising him. After all, he never got sentimental about business, and this would be—essentially— a business proposition. But even so he felt oddly deflated when the glimmer dimmed almost instantly.

'Exactly how co-operative are you expecting me to be?' Katie demanded, the brittle, defensive edge making Jack wonder about the young girl who had been forced to leave home to escape her father's influence.

He'd only met Henry Medford a handful of times, and he hadn't liked him—the man was an arrogant blowhard whose conservative investment strategy lacked vision and originality, and he had sensed that Bea was, if not scared of her father, then certainly determined to stay on the right side of him. While he didn't do sentiment, it was Bea's tentative attitude to her father which had persuaded him not to pull the Medford loan after their break-up.

He didn't sense fear from Katherine, but he could see her fierce determination to avoid the influence of any man would have to be overcome. Or at the very least managed.

'As I said, there will be some social requirements. I prefer to date women who elevate my social standing in ways money alone cannot.'

Not entirely true. He didn't give a damn about his social standing normally. But right now dating her would be useful in his quest not to scare off the Smyth-Brown board with what an inside source had told him was their concern about his 'lower-class background'.

'As the daughter of a hereditary peer—even an estranged daughter,' he added. 'You fit the bill.'

She blinked, looking momentarily stunned. 'I'm sorry…what? Did we just time-travel back to the nineteenth century?' Her gaze darkened with pity, making his temper spike. 'We're living in the twenty-first century, Jack. No one cares about titles and lineage any more. Especially not in the City of London. I think you're totally overestimating the importance of social status in your bid for world domination.'

'As you've never come from nothing, I would hazard a guess you know nothing about what it's like to be barred or blocked from your chosen path because of things you cannot change,' Jack said tightly.

'You're right,' Katie replied, the instant capitulation as galling as the sympathy shadowing her eyes. 'Maybe you can't change your past, or where you came from. But surely you're living proof it doesn't have to matter?' The hint of pity in the words loosened the leash on his temper still further. 'For goodness' sake, Jack, you don't even have a cockney accent. Why on earth would you need to date someone like me when you're a gazillionaire?'

He'd worked hard to get rid of his East End accent, he thought resentfully, well aware of the snobbery of his early investors who had been unwilling to put their money into the hands of someone who didn't pronounce their Ts and Hs properly. But he'd be damned if he'd give her more ammunition with which to condescend to him. He'd never been ashamed of his accent, or where he'd come from. He was just aware of how it had stood between him and his goals. And, anyway, having her seen as his date was nowhere near as important as getting her to London so she would be available when he wanted her.

'Frankly, we're getting off the point. I'm not interested in discussing the reasons why I want you on my arm at social events,' he said, resenting the fact she had managed to sidetrack him and touch a nerve he had considered long dead. 'All I'm willing to do is negotiate the terms of your acceptance.'

She huffed out a breath. 'Well, I'm not willing to negotiate it. I don't want to date you for any reason.'

The provocative comment was like a red rag to a bull, triggering every last one of his competitive instincts. Even if he hadn't desired her in his bed for the foreseeable future, her refusal to negotiate was enough to make him determined to change her mind.

'I think you're forgetting I lent your father a large

sum of money on preferential terms,' he said. 'If I call that in, he won't be happy.'

Her eyebrows shot up, the surprise on her face almost comical. 'Really, Jack? Are you trying to blackmail me?' she asked, obviously expecting him to be ashamed of the implication.

He wasn't. In truth, he much preferred using the carrot to the stick when it came to persuading people to do what he wanted, but he hadn't been nicknamed the Big Bad Wolfe in the financial press for no reason. 'I wouldn't call it blackmail, simply a fact.'

Her eyebrows levelled off, her breathing becoming slightly laboured, which only made her more tempting. He clamped down on the inevitable surge of lust, while acknowledging that her inability to hide her response to him was another point in his favour.

'Call in the loan if you want,' she said. 'My father can't bully me any more. And neither can you.'

The bold statement demonstrated a bravery he admired, making it harder than expected to crush her rebellion. 'I'm not sure Beatrice would agree with you.'

She sucked in a breath as the implications of his threat finally dawned on her.

Distress flickered across her features, the obvious fear for her sister making him feel like a bastard, but he ignored the knee-jerk urge to reassure her. He'd given Beatrice his word he would not change the terms of the loan. And, while he could be unscrupulous when necessary, he never broke his word.

But Katherine did not need to know that. Using her concern for her sister against her was simply a negotiating tactic. He didn't need her to think he was a good man—in fact, it was better if she knew he was not.

Even so, he found it more difficult than he would have expected to remain unmoved when she hissed, 'You bastard.'

He shoved his hands into his pockets to resist the urge to touch her again. Crushing her spirit had never been his intention, but he always played to win, and this situation was no different.

You have to say no. This is insane.

Katie stared at Jack Wolfe, the strange feeling of unreality almost as disconcerting as the sensation rioting over her skin.

She loved Beatrice dearly, but it was time her sister stood up for herself. Katie couldn't protect her from their father's temper for ever.

And didn't she have the right to protect herself? Of course, the chance to clear Cariad Cakes' debts was tempting. But if she accepted she would be at Jack Wolfe's mercy.

Oddly, though, it wasn't the thought of the arguments and disagreements yet to come that bothered her. She'd already noticed a big difference between the way Jack Wolfe approached a negotiation and the way her father had bullied her. Jack might be commanding, powerful and ruthless enough to attempt to coerce her over the loan he'd made to her father but, weirdly, she also appreciated the fact he was being so pragmatic about what he wanted. Despite his outrageous suggestion, he hadn't condescended to her, hadn't tried to seduce her and had treated her like an equal. Something her father had never done.

She pursed her lips and crossed her arms over her chest to stop the pulse of connection getting any worse. And making her give in, when she knew it would be foolish even to contemplate becoming Jack Wolfe's trophy mistress.

Jack Wolfe was dangerous—not just to her independence but her sense of self. Because beneath the ruthless businessman was a man who could cut through her defences without even trying.

'Come on, Katherine,' Jack said, obviously tired of waiting. 'Is it really that hard to say yes?' he asked, the seductive tone reverberating in her abdomen as he stepped closer.

The hot spot between her thighs throbbed at the memory of him inside her—hard, forceful, overwhelming.

'It's only six months.' He cupped her cheek, the rough calluses turning the ripples to shudders. 'By which time, we'll have tired of each other. And by then your business and your future will be secure.'

She shifted away from the tantalising caress, her bottom pressing onto the countertop. She must not get carried away again on the tide of passion that had got her into this fix in the first place.

But, instead of crowding her even more, pressing his advantage, Jack remained where he was. He thrust his hands back into his pockets, almost as if he were having to force himself not to touch her.

And something flickered across his face. Something as shocking as it was unexpected.

Yearning.

But it was there one moment and gone the next.

She must have imagined it. Perhaps it was wishful thinking—making them seem like equals when they really weren't. She cleared her throat. Looked away from him. Night had fallen outside, but a full moon cast an eerie glow over the forest glen. Eerie and, compelling. And almost magical.

Snowdonia had given her strength, purpose and a sense of wellbeing ever since she'd arrived here determined to build a new life. But there was still something missing which had nothing to do with her financial instability or the endless stress of not being strong enough to make her dreams come true.

There was a Welsh word for the feeling of something lost, something longed for, connected to their homeland, that couldn't be directly translated into English: *hiraeth*. Her *nain* had explained it to her when Katie had been a homeless teenager but, being English, and never really having had a homeland she cared about, Katherine had never understood it.

But what if the *hiraeth* her mother had felt being away from her homeland, living with a man who had never really loved her, had been something like this deep tug of yearning? A part of her being she couldn't control?

Katie let out a slow breath, her heart galloping into her throat.

She turned back to find Jack still watching, still waiting, any trace of vulnerability in his expression gone.

She unfolded her arms, raised her gaze and ruthlessly controlled the hum of arousal.

'The answer's no, Jack,' she said.

Something leapt into his eyes that looked like regret. But she knew she must have imagined it when his jaw hardened and his gaze became flat and remote.

'Very well,' he said, surprising her with the instant capitulation. But then he stroked her chin with his thumb and the brutal sizzle rasped over sensitive skin.

She stood trapped in his penetrating gaze and regret sunk like a stone into her abdomen.

'But be advised, Katherine,' he said, his tone as harsh as the light in his eyes. 'I never give anyone a second chance.'

It was a warning that should have been easy to reject, but it wasn't, the foolish urge to call him back and say yes to his devil's bargain all but overwhelming when he took her quad keys, promising to have the vehicle returned that evening.

As the front door slammed behind him, her breath guttered out, her body collapsing against the kitchen counter. But the moment of relief did nothing to disguise the hollow weight still expanding in her stomach—which made no sense at all.

CHAPTER SIX

'I'M GLAD TO SAY the nausea is perfectly natural...'
The doctor sent Katie an easy smile in the cubicle
office of the small surgery in Gwynedd.

'How?' Katie asked, confused now, as well as
exhausted. She'd been sick for the last ten days,
every afternoon like clockwork, and it was starting to seriously impact her business. Because baking cookies and cupcakes and brownies when even
the whiff of chocolate or vanilla essence made you
puke was impossible.

It had been over two months since she'd turned
down Jack Wolfe's insane proposition to become
his mistress for six months. But nothing had gone
right since the moment he'd slammed her cottage
door behind him. It was almost as if he'd cursed her.

Sleep had alluded her for the first few weeks—
florid, forceful, disturbing dreams tormented her
every night in which he demanded her complete
compliance and she obeyed without question. She
could still smell him—bergamot and sex—on the
sheets, despite washing them a hundred times.
Could still feel his lips on her breasts, feel the

hard, forceful thrust in her sex whenever she woke from fitful dreams. Then she had become tired and listless, falling asleep at a moment's notice, the thought of him always there, ready to jump her in her dreams.

The phantom sickness had almost been a welcome distraction at first to explain away the general malaise that seemed to have befallen her ever since he had left. This wasn't about Jack Wolfe and his insulting offer. This was about her working herself to the bone.

But in the last week, when it hadn't got any better, she had begun to panic. She couldn't afford to take any more time off work or she would lose her regular customers. She was on the verge of falling behind on her bank loans—and if that happened Cariad Cakes Etc would go under. But, far worse than that, if she lost the business she could end up losing her home, because she'd mortgaged the cottage to pay for the refit. The only upside was she'd saved money on her grocery bill because the last thing she wanted to do was eat.

The gynaecologist sent her a bright if slightly condescending smile. 'You're pregnant.'

'I'm...' The word dropped like a bomb into the silent surgery. For several moments she couldn't even process it. 'But that's not possible. I... I can't be pregnant, I'm on the pill,' she finally blurted out round the wodge of panic in her throat.

The doctor had made a mistake. That was all there was to it.

'I see,' the doctor replied, her brows furrowing.

'Ah yes, I have it here in your notes,' she added, reading off her computer monitor. 'Well, obviously it's extremely rare for this to happen. But no method of contraception is one hundred percent effective, even the contraceptive pill.'

'But…' Katie stared at the older woman, her skin heating under the probing gaze.

'Of course, if you haven't had sex in—'

'I did, but only once. And it was nine weeks ago,' Katie cut in, horrified by the blast of heat that hit her cheeks. 'But… I *can't* be pregnant,' she said again, her voice breaking on the words even as her hand strayed to her belly. Was this actually happening? Had she somehow got pregnant with Jack Wolfe's baby?

Tears prickled behind her eyes as the truth blindsided her.

If their moment of madness had left her pregnant— and somehow, where Jack Wolfe was concerned, it seemed more than possible— she would never be able to forget him for the rest of her life. And she hadn't exactly had much luck with that already.

The doctor's expression went from confident to concerned in a heartbeat. 'Miss Medford, I did a blood test,' she said gently. 'You are definitely pregnant. What happens now, though, is of course your decision.'

Is it?

'At only nine weeks' gestation, you do have options,' the doctor added softly.

Do I?

Why did she feel as if she didn't have a choice,

then? As if it was already too late? The sensible thing to do now would be to have a termination. This pregnancy had been an accident. A mistake. There was no way she could keep her business afloat if the morning sickness and the exhaustion kept up for another week, let alone any longer. And, even if she managed to get through the pregnancy without going bankrupt, how was she going to be able to run a demanding business while looking after a baby? She couldn't afford to pay for child care, or staff—not for a good few years yet, anyway.

But even as the fear and panic overwhelmed her she cradled her stomach and a surge of protectiveness swept through her. That morphed into something powerful and unstoppable.

She breathed out slowly to prevent her frantic heart beating right out of her chest. She'd never planned to be a mother—had never even thought of it. And now was the worst possible time for this to happen—especially with a man as ruthless and powerful as Jack Wolfe.

But what terrified her most of all was the thought of having her life ripped apart once again. The way it had been when she'd been seventeen—and her father had glared at her with hate in his eyes and told her to get out.

She blinked back tears and forced herself to suck in another careful breath… And think.

You've been at rock bottom before but you made a new life for yourself. A better life. By doing whatever you had to do to survive. Why can't you do the same again?

Another breath eased out through her constricted lungs but it felt less painful this time. She caressed her invisible bump.

Okay, kiddo, Mummy's got this. Whatever happens now, we're in this together.

It wasn't until she sat on the local bus back to Beddgelert twenty minutes later, her backpack stuffed full of pamphlets about everything from pregnancy vitamins to the benefits of breast feeding, that the full impact of what she'd have to do next knocked the air out of her lungs a second time.

I'm going to have to see Jack Wolfe again.

Informing the taciturn billionaire that she was pregnant with his child was going to be tough enough. Especially as she was fairly sure he would not be pleased at the prospect. He might not even believe the baby was his.

But what choice did she have? Not only did he have the right to know he was going to become a father, but she would have to ask him for help. She'd already maxed out all her credit cards and the next loan payment was due on Friday. She could ask Beatrice for money, but that would only be a temporary fix, and if her father found out Bea was spending any of her allowance on Katie he would probably cut her sister off too.

The idea of having to travel to London tomorrow, cap in hand, and beg Jack Wolfe for a loan went against every one of her principles. Given the insulting offer she'd turned down two months ago, it would also threaten to destroy every ounce of the independence and self-respect she'd worked so hard to gain since she'd been seventeen. What made it worse was knowing she would be completely at his mercy.

After the endless battles with her father, being at any man's mercy went against the grain. And, having defied Jack once already, she wasn't even sure he'd have any mercy.

Be advised, Katherine... I never give anyone a second chance.

The rocky escarpment of Pen-y-pass disappeared behind them as the bus travelled into the lush green valley of Nant Gwynant.

Jack might be forceful and overwhelming. But what scared her most was how vulnerable she felt at the moment. If he knew she was pregnant, would he use it against her? What if he had found someone else to be his mistress? Would that be a good thing or bad thing? What if he demanded she get an abortion? He couldn't *make* her do anything, but somehow giving him the power to try scared her even more.

Of course, she wouldn't be able to hold off telling Jack about the pregnancy for very long. But why did she have to tell him everything straight away? Surely she'd be in a better bargaining position if he didn't know? Asking him to reconsider the offer of financial help for her business would be hard. Especially as she wasn't even sure any more whether or not she wanted to be his mistress.

After all, however adamant she'd been two months ago, she still hadn't forgotten the effect he had on her—not even close. But telling him about the pregnancy and throwing herself on his mercy—or lack of it—felt so much more risky.

This was just another negotiation, she told herself staunchly, but it was one she had to make work for her and her baby and her business. The last thing she should do, given what a skilful negotiator Jack was, was give him an even stronger bargaining position.

'Mr Wolfe, there's a Miss Medford downstairs in reception. She doesn't have an appointment, but she insists she knows you, and the front desk asked me to check with you first before they send her away.'

Jack's head lifted at his PA Gorinda's comment. The bump of exhilaration annoyed him. 'Do you know *which* Miss Medford?'

'No, Mr Wolfe, but apparently she's been very persistent.'

'Uh-huh,' he murmured as the bump went nuts.

It had to be Katherine. He hadn't spoken to Beatrice since she'd broken off their engagement, and she didn't have the guts to come to his office without an appointment. Katherine, on the other hand…

'I did tell them there was no way you would—'

'It's okay, Gorinda.' He cut her off. 'Have them send her up.'

Gorinda disguised her astonishment with a quick nod, like the first-class professional she was.

As Jack waited for Katherine to arrive, he got up and paced across the office. He should have told her to go to hell. She'd rejected his offer two months ago now. He'd intended to forget her as soon as he strolled out of her cottage. To find someone else. But it hadn't quite worked out that way. Not only had he not been able to forget her, no other woman had come close to exciting him the way she did.

None of them had Katherine's vibrant hair, her lush curves, her quick wit or her sharp, intelligent emerald eyes. And not one of them made him ache.

He'd come to the conclusion that, if he couldn't have her, he didn't want anyone else. Which was infuriating.

How had she captivated him so comprehensively? When her rejection still stung, reminding him of the feral kid he'd once been…? On the outside, not wanted and never to be invited in.

He returned to his desk, determined not to let her see his agitation—or his excitement at the thought of seeing her again.

Several eternities later, Gorinda stepped into the office with Katherine. After announcing his uninvited guest, his PA left and shut the door.

He took his time staring at the woman who still occupied far too much of his head space.

In a tailored pencil skirt, a silk blouse and low heels, her wild hair pinned on top of her head in a ruthless up-do, she looked more sophisticated than he'd ever seen her. But the power suit and heels couldn't disguise her lush curves or dewy skin. Or the way the buttons of her blouse strained against her cleavage. Was he imagining it, or did her breasts look even more spectacular than he remembered?

'Hello, Katherine,' he said, his tone huskier than he would have liked. He remained seated, keeping his expression flat and direct, even as the bump in his heart rate accelerated. 'To what do I owe the unexpected pleasure?' he added, doing nothing to hide the slice of sarcasm in his tone.

Her cheeks turned a delectable shade of pink. The inconvenient arousal flowed south.

Damn, I still want her—too much.

He shifted in his seat, the sudden recollection of wrapping his lips around those hard, swollen peaks aggravating his temper, not to mention the ache in his pants.

The sour taste in his mouth wasn't far behind, though. She had to be here to renegotiate his offer. Why he should be surprised, he had no idea. But what surprised him more was his disappointment. She'd rejected him when he'd offered her a generous deal two months ago. He'd told her then she wouldn't get a second chance and he still meant it. However much he might still want her.

'Hello, Jack,' she said. 'Can I sit down?'

He swept his hand towards the leather armchair on the other side of the desk. 'Go ahead. You've got five minutes to say whatever you came to say,' he said, gratified by the flash of annoyance before she managed to mask it.

Damned if he didn't still find her rebelliousness a major turn-on.

But as she crossed the room and sat down he frowned. Had she lost weight? Because he could still recall every luscious inch of her in far too much detail and, apart from her breasts, her curves didn't look as much of a handful as he remembered. Not only that, but she moved stiffly, without the confident energy of two months ago.

As her face caught the sun streaming through the office windows, he noticed the tight line of her lips and the bruised shadows under her eyes that she'd tried to mask with make-up.

He stifled the concern pushing against his chest and forced it into a box marked 'not your problem'.

She'd probably been working herself to the bone to make a go of her failing business. But why should he care? He'd offered her a way out. And she'd thrown it back in his face.

He glanced at his watch. 'You've got four minutes now,' he said.

'I wanted to ask about the financing you mentioned two months ago.' She leaned forward, offering him an even better view of her cleavage—which had to be deliberate. 'It's been…' She sighed, the gushing breath weary. 'More of a challenge than I thought to keep up payments on my loans. If you're still interested in investing, I could offer you twenty-five percent instead of ten.'

His disappointment at the evidence that she could be bought after all was tempered by the surge of triumph. He had her where he wanted her now. But he'd be damned if he'd give her an easy ride. 'And the deal I discussed?'

'I'd be willing to do that too, of course,' she said without a moment's hesitation. 'With the six-month time limit you mentioned, obviously.'

'And what exactly would you be prepared to do for this investment?' he asked, keeping his gaze fixed firmly on the blush which was now spreading across her neck.

'Whatever you want me to do,' she said softly.

His chest tightened with anger. 'Uh-huh,' he ground out, holding on to his fury with an effort. 'And what do you envisage that entailing?'

He'd intended to pay to relocate her to London for six months, because their affair would have to be at his convenience, not hers. But if they had decided to sleep together—to get this damn chemistry out of their system—he had never intended to buy her cooperation in that regard. But she'd never given him the chance to explain any of that two months ago. She'd simply jumped to the conclusion he would be paying her for sex—and had rejected him out of hand.

He steepled his fingers to stop them shaking as the fury started to consume him. 'And if I said I didn't just want to date you socially? That I wanted you in my bed for the duration? What then?' he asked, finally pushing the point.

Her eyes widened, the flash of anxiety going some way to satisfy his sense of outrage.

That's right, Red, let's see how far you're willing to go!

Her face fell, the blush blazing now as the last of the eager hope he had glimpsed died. He'd shocked her. And insulted her. Just as he'd intended.

But just as he was sure she would finally realise how insulting that proposition was, to both of them, she said, 'Okay, if that's what you want.'

The anger flared, but right behind it was astonishment. And that heady shot of arousal still throbbing in his groin.

How could he still want her when she was only offering herself in exchange for payment? Had her outrage at the cottage all been an act?

Of course it had, he thought viciously, surprised to realise he actually felt disillusioned when he'd figured he had lost all his illusions years ago.

He was a deeply cynical guy because he'd had to be. He'd come from the very bottom and made it to the top. And he'd had to fight like hell to scale every rung of that ladder. He couldn't afford sentimentality or loyalty unless it benefitted his bottom line.

But although he'd been angry when he'd walked away from her—because she'd denied him something he wanted—in the weeks since he'd been captivated by the notion that Katherine Medford might actually be the real deal. Someone prepared to put their dignity and self-respect before money. And status. And benefitting their own bottom line.

The sour taste in his mouth made his lips twist in a cruel smile. 'I see,' he said, letting his gaze roam over her, the perusal deliberately insulting as he got up from his desk. He walked towards her, suddenly determined to punish her for destroying the image he'd had of her... And get some much-needed payback for the snub that had bruised his ego more than it should have.

What a fool he'd been, wasting months getting hung up on a woman who didn't even exist.

He beckoned her out of the seat. She stood, wary

eyes searching his face, her magnificent breasts rising up and down with her staggered breathing.

She chewed on her lip while her deep-green eyes dilated to black. Satisfaction flowed through him.

'What…what do you want?' She wrapped her arms around her waist, holding in her shudder of response, but he could see the peaks of her breasts standing to attention beneath her blouse.

Red, we both know you want me as much as I want you.

He let the cruel smile spread, damned if he was going to leave her with any pride. People had thought they were better than him his whole life. And he'd taken great pleasure in proving them wrong. She was no different from all the rest.

He leaned closer, close enough to take in a lungful of her tantalising scent—apples and earth and pure, unadulterated sin. The burgeoning erection hardened enough to brush against her belly and he heard her sharp intake of breath, felt the judder of reaction course through her body.

He shoved his fists into his pockets, determined not to touch, not to take. This time she was going to come to him.

'I want you to show me what you've got,' he whispered against her neck. 'That's worth a hundred grand of my money, Red.'

He straightened away from her.

Her expressive features tightened and resentment sparkled in her eyes, highlighting the shards of gold in the emerald green.

There she is.

His breath clogged his lungs and desire flared, crackling in the air between them like an electric force field. But, before he had a chance to register the jolt of excitement, she lifted her arms and grasped his shoulders.

Her fingernails trailed across his nape, sending arrows of sensation shooting through his spine, straight down to his groin. And then she lifted her face to his, offering herself with a boldness, a determination, that robbed him of breath before she rose up on tiptoes and pressed her lips to his in a defiant kiss.

Elemental need exploded like a firework display in his gut, and all thoughts of payback, of punishment, were obliterated by the furious juggernaut of desire too long denied.

Her lips opened on a staggered breath and he thrust his tongue deep, capturing each startled sob of her surrender. He yanked his clenched fists out of his pockets and grasped her hips to pull her vibrating body against the brutal ridge in his trousers. He ground the erection against her, each stroke of his tongue, each brush of his shaft, driving him closer to the edge.

His hands skimmed up her side and cradled her breasts. She bowed back and he dragged his mouth down to suckle the frantic beat in her neck. He fumbled with her blouse, giving a staggered groan as the buttons popped. Lifting the fragrant flesh free of its lacy prison, he traced the engorged peak with his lips but, as he trapped the swollen flesh against the roof of his mouth and suckled hard, she bucked in his arms and cried out—the shocked gasp one of pain, not pleasure.

What the…?

'Ow!'

Her distress doused the fire and he released her so abruptly, she staggered backwards. He caught her elbow before she could fall over the armchair.

'How…?' he managed, his pulse thundering so hard in his ears he was struggling to hear, let alone think.

What had just happened? One minute they had been devouring each other, and then…

She tugged her arm free, her movements jerky, frantic, her eyes downcast, her body shaking with the same tremors wracking his own. He watched her gather the remnants of her blouse. The blouse he'd torn off her.

'Did I hurt you?' he asked, his voice raw.

How the hell had everything got out of control so quickly? He'd been ready to take her right here in his office. The point he'd been trying to make—which seemed petulant and pointless now—was instantly forgotten in the maelstrom of needs triggered by her glorious defiance and the touch of her lips on his.

She shook her head, but her chin remained tucked into her chest and he couldn't see her face. She was still shaking, her knuckles whitening on the torn silk.

Guilt washed through him. He tucked his thumb under her chin and drew her face up to his. 'Katherine, did I hurt you?' he asked again.

Her eyes—that deep, vibrant emerald—were mossy with distress, but devoid of the accusation he had been expecting. 'No,' she murmured, the apologetic tone only confusing him more. 'It's just, I'm a lot more sensitive there.'

His gaze dipped to her full breasts now plumped up under her tightly folded arms. 'Okay,' he said, still trying to figure out where that cry of pain had come from.

'Oh, God,' she whispered, clasping her hand over her mouth. 'Where's the nearest toilet?'

Her features drew tight, a sheen of sweat popping out on her brow, her face turning grey beneath the impressive beard burn starting to appear on her cheeks.

'What?' he asked, the concern he'd tried to contain earlier expanding like a beach ball in his gut.

'Your nearest toilet, Jack!' Her voice rose in distress. 'Where is it?' she cried. 'I'm going to throw up!'

He pointed to the office's large *en suite* bathroom, shocked and confused now, as well as extremely turned on.

She shot out of the room so fast, an apple-scented breeze feathered across his face. Two seconds later, the sounds of violent retching echoed around the silent office.

What the hell is going on?

He walked across the carpeted floor, propped his shoulder against the door jamb, the beach ball expanding as he watched her bent over the toilet bowl, puking her guts up.

He supposed he ought to be offended, embarrassed even, that his lovemaking had made her violently ill. But he was still reeling from the sudden shift from incendiary lust to total disaster—and the feeling he'd just been kicked into another dimension without warning.

The erection finally deflated—mercifully.

Perhaps he shouldn't be surprised, given Katherine had a habit of bringing enough drama into his life to put a TV soap opera to shame. But, as he rinsed a face cloth out in the sink, confusion gave way to curiosity and concern. And a ton of unanswered questions bombarded him all at once.

Why had she come here? And, more importantly, why *now*? Because her motives didn't seem nearly as straightforward as he'd assumed. If she was really an opportunist, an unscrupulous femme fatale prepared to sell her body to rescue her business, why hadn't she agreed to become his mistress two months ago?

The gruesome retching finally subsided and she collapsed onto her bottom. Sitting cross-legged on the floor, she didn't just look tired, she looked shattered and fragile. In a way she never had before. Fragile, defensive and…guilty.

What did she have to feel guilty about?

He handed her the cool cloth, ignoring the residual buzz as their fingers brushed.

'Thank you,' she said, wiping her mouth before folding the cloth with infinite care and pressing it to her burning cheeks. 'It's okay, that's the worst of it over,' she murmured, as if this had happened before.

He crouched beside her, unable to resist the urge to swipe his finger across her clammy forehead and tuck a stray strand of hair behind her ear. She trembled, but didn't draw away from his touch. Her gaze met his at last. The guilty flush highlighted her pale cheeks.

His what-the-hell-ometer shot into the red zone and the wodge of confusion and concern threatened to gag him.

'Why did you come to me?' he demanded, his guts tying into tight, greasy knots. Was she seriously ill?

'I told you, I need money to save my business,' she said, but she ducked her head again.

'Don't give me that crap,' he said, annoyed with her now, as well as himself. Why had he believed so readily that the bold, beautiful, belligerent and stunningly defiant woman he had left behind in Wales had become some conniving little gold-digger in the space of a few months?

He grasped her chin, losing his patience as the sense of detachment, cynicism and ruthlessness which he had relied on for so long became dull and discordant. He shouldn't care why she was here, why she needed his money so badly, but he did.

'Tell me the truth. Are you seriously ill?' he asked.

She puffed out a breath. 'No.'

The relief he wanted to feel didn't come. 'Then why did you just lose your lunch in my toilet?'

The guilty flush became so vivid it would probably be visible from Mars. 'Because I'm pregnant,' she replied. 'With your child.'

CHAPTER SEVEN

'You... What?' Jack murmured, his voice rough with shock, and Katie watched his gaze drop to her belly.

Katie's still tender stomach flipped over as his knees dropped to the bathroom tiles, his balance shot, as well as his usual cast-iron control.

'It was an accident,' she said. 'I can take a DNA test once it's born, if you don't believe it's yours,' she added, expecting to see suspicion, even accusation, on his face.

When his gaze rose, though, he still looked dazed. But then two creases appeared between his brows.

She braced, ready for anger, but all he said was, 'How long have you known?'

'Since yesterday,' she replied. 'I'd been sick on and off for two weeks and it was affecting my work.' She knew she was babbling, but she couldn't seem to stop, wanting to fend off the accusations that were bound to come soon. He'd treated her with contempt as soon as she'd arrived. Which only made her more determined to hold her ground, to get what she needed before he found out how much she needed it.

But his expression remained oddly unreadable.

'It's not easy baking when even the scent of food makes you nauseous,' she finished.

'No doubt,' he said, his gaze drifting back to her belly. 'I thought you were on the pill.'

Oddly, the question lacked the cynicism she'd expected, but even so she went on the offensive.

'I *was* on the pill. But it was low-dosage and I'd only been on it for a week. Even so, the doctor said it's extremely rare.' Feeling stronger, she added an edge to her voice. 'It seems you have extremely fertile sperm.'

'Who knew?' His lips quirked, the hint of wry amusement surprising her even more. Did he think this was funny? But as he continued to study her in that unnerving way he had, as if he could see past every one of her defences, his brow furrowed again. 'Why didn't you tell me about the pregnancy as soon as you arrived?'

She cursed her pale skin as the tell-tale heat crawled up her neck.

'Because I didn't want to get the third degree about how it had happened. Or have you try to talk me into an abortion,' she said, knowing she had been right not to blurt out the truth and give him even more power to hurt her.

Anger spread up her chest to disguise the hurt as she recalled the insulting way he'd treated her. Had he even really still wanted her? Or had he simply intended to humiliate her, get her to show him how much she still wanted him, before he slapped her down?

She'd put everything into that kiss, had lost herself in it seconds after he'd responded, but had he? She wasn't even sure about that any more. Had it all been a game to him to make her go insane with lust just so he could humiliate her more when he rejected her?

'What the hell makes you think I'd try to force you to have an abortion?' he asked, surprising her again. Because he didn't look superior or in control any more. He looked furious.

'Because...' She sputtered to a stop. He actually looked really offended. 'Well, aren't you?' she managed, her righteousness faltering a little.

'Do you want to have the child?' he asked.

Emotion closed her throat. The baby felt so real to her now, even though, according to all the research she'd done in the last twenty-four hours, it was no bigger than a grain of rice.

'Yes, I do want it, very much,' she said without hesitation around the thickness in her throat.

'Then I will support your choice,' Jack answered without an ounce of sarcasm. Or even any apparent resentment.

Katie's jaw went slack. To say she was surprised by the statement would be a massive understatement. She wasn't just surprised—she was stunned speechless.

'Really?' she whispered at last. 'You're not angry?' she asked, not sure she could believe him as she struggled to contain the painful hope pressing against her chest wall.

Was this just another trick? Surely it had to be? She would have expected a man as cynical as him to feel trapped, or at the very least suspicious. She certainly had not expected him to so readily believe not only that the baby was his, but that her pregnancy had genuinely been an accident.

'I pay for my mistakes,' Jack said. 'And this is my fault, not yours. I should have worn protection and I didn't.'

Our baby is not a mistake.

It was what she wanted to say. But as she opened her mouth to protest Jack stood up and, taking her elbow, pulled her to her feet.

'I do have some conditions, though.'

'What conditions?' She stared at him, trying to decipher what was coming so she could ward it off… But as usual his expression gave nothing away.

How could he be so controlled when her emotions felt as if they were being squished through a meat grinder?

'We need to be married—until after the baby's born. No child of mine will grow up without my name.'

'You don't have to be married to me to give the baby your name,' Katie began. 'You can just put your name on the birth…' He pressed his finger to her lips, silencing her.

'You were happy to sleep with me for a hundred-thousand-pound investment in your company about

ten minutes ago, Katherine. So why should marriage be a problem?'

'I know, but…'

'But nothing. We can separate in…' He paused.
'When is it due?'

'I won't know for sure until I've had the first
scan,' she countered, beginning to feel totally overwhelmed again, and not liking it.

'Ball park,' he said.

'January.' She huffed.

'We can separate in February, then. I'll have it
written into the contract.'

'What contract?' she asked, her voice rising. He
was trying to railroad her. *Again.*

'The contract you're going to sign before the
wedding in four weeks' time.'

'What?' She actually squeaked. He wanted to
get married in a month? 'I haven't even agreed to
marry you yet.'

'But you will. You know as well as I do, you're
all out of options, or you wouldn't have come to me
begging to prostitute yourself.'

'I didn't beg!' she gasped, outraged. 'You insisted.'

'And you agreed—then you kissed me as if your
life depended on it. And we both went off like a
couple of rockets on Bonfire Night, coming within
one sensitive nipple of doing each other on my desk
in broad daylight when any one of my employees
could have walked in on us. So let's stop arguing
about semantics.'

She glared at him but couldn't help but feel her panic ease a little.

At least he hadn't been faking his response any more than she had. She wasn't sure if their uncontrollable chemistry was necessarily a bonus in an already overwhelming situation. But it felt important that in at least one part of their relationship they were equally compromised.

'I need time to think about all this,' Katie murmured, suddenly unbearably weary, the emotional rollercoaster of the last twenty-four hours taking its toll as he led her back into his office.

She sat heavily in the armchair, the feeling of her life spinning out of control again doing nothing to ease her surprise when he squatted in front of her and placed warm palms on her knees.

'What is there to think about, really?' Jack murmured. 'This is a business deal which will give me what I need—a chance to elevate my social status and ensure the child is not born a bastard—and give you what you need—a chance to save your company and allow it to grow.'

He glanced at her stomach again. The muscle in his jaw tensed. Perhaps he wasn't as nonchalant about the pregnancy as he seemed. 'And give the child my financial support for the rest of its life.'

The child.

The impersonal description reverberated in Katie's skull—pragmatic and painfully dispassionate.

Her heart shrunk in her chest.

The baby really was nothing more to him than a

mistake he had to rectify. Had she really believed he would feel any differently? And why would he?

She cleared her throat, trying to dislodge her sadness at the realisation her child wouldn't have a father in anything other than a financial capacity.

So what?

She didn't *want* Jack to be a father to this baby. She knew what it was like to grow up with a father who thought of you as a commodity, or a burden. Why would she wish that on her own child? She needed to deal with the practicalities now. Nothing else.

'What exactly would the marriage entail?' she managed to ask. 'Would I have to leave Wales?'

He stood up and walked to the desk. Leaning against it, he folded his arms over his broad chest as he studied her. The beard burn on her cheeks from their earlier kiss began to sting as his eyes heated with something which looked like more than just practicalities.

'Yes. You would live with me wherever I happened to be, travel with me and attend public and private events as my wife when required.' He paused, his gaze skimming her belly again. 'And your condition allows.'

'But my home and my business are in Wales.'

'You'll need to base yourself and your business in London. This is a marriage of convenience,' he said, his gaze darting to her stomach again. 'But it's not going to do the business interests we talked about much good unless it appears real. I'm afraid that's non-negotiable. I'm sure we can figure out a manageable schedule for your social responsibilities as my wife.' He frowned. 'How long has the vomiting been going on?'

She blinked, the question feeling way too personal in what—for him, anyway —appeared to be a business negotiation.

Get real, Katie, that's exactly what it is. And what you want it to be.

'Two weeks now,' she said. 'But it wasn't as bad today as it has been. I think it might finally be getting a bit better.'

His brows climbed up his forehead. '*Seriously?* It's been *worse* than the exorcism routine I just witnessed?'

She let out a half-laugh, the tension in her gut easing at his horrified expression. For a split second it almost felt as if they were a real couple. But she sobered quickly, setting aside the fanciful notion. One thing she mustn't do was mistake his concern for his business priorities with any real concern for her. Or their baby. Of course he didn't want his trophy wife projectile-vomiting at inopportune moments.

'The good news is I've never been sick in the evenings,' she said. 'So social engagements shouldn't be a problem.' Of course, she usually felt exhausted by the end of the day, but he didn't need to know that yet. Hopefully the fatigue would fade too, and not having the stress of figuring out how she was going to keep her business afloat would surely help. Of course, she wasn't familiar with the kind of high-society events he was probably referring to. She would have to wing it, but she'd be damned if she'd let him know she wasn't up to the job he was offering her.

And it *was* a job. A job she was being handsomely paid for—something she would do well to remember.

He nodded. 'Good, although I doubt I'll have to make too many demands on your time. I'm not a social animal at the best of times. I'm sure we can make the marriage convincing with a few well-timed engagements...' His gaze intensified and awareness rippled over her skin. 'Especially given our extraordinary chemistry.'

Her heart bobbed into her throat and the familiar ripple shot down her spine. 'Right, about that...' Her gaze dropped away from his. 'What if I didn't want to sleep with you?'

The silence seemed to stretch out for several endless moments.

It was a lie, and she was sure he knew it. After all, she'd kissed him senseless less than ten minutes ago.

But she wasn't sure she *could* sleep with him especially while carrying his child, and not risk getting much more invested in their fake marriage than she should. Her emotions were screwy enough already.

Gee thanks, pregnancy hormones.

Sleeping with him had already had major consequences—throwing her life into complete turmoil while he seemed mostly unmoved. She didn't want to put herself at any more of a disadvantage.

He was watching her with a typically inscrutable expression but the muscle in his jaw was twitching again.

He didn't like the suggestion. But then, to her surprise, he shrugged. 'Suit yourself.'

'Really?'

'Of course,' he replied. 'Whatever we do together in private will be by mutual consent. That was always going to be the case. It was you who made that assumption two months ago that I would be paying you for sex.'

'Okay,' she said, feeling both chastised and embarrassed. As well as uncertain. She hadn't exactly received the concession she'd been asking for—a marriage in name only. And, given that his seduction techniques so far had turned out to be extremely effective...

Oh, for goodness' sake, Katie. Stop creating problems where there aren't any. Yet. So what if Jack Wolfe could seduce a stone? You can cross that bridge when you come to it. Time to quit while you're ahead.

Jack Wolfe was right about one thing: she was all out of options.

'So what's your answer, Katherine?' he asked, the negotiations clearly over.

She concentrated on the twitch in his jaw and controlled the familiar shot of adrenaline that was always there whenever he looked at her with that laser-sharp focus.

Take the risk. You need this—for your business and your baby. And, remember, he can't hurt you unless you let him.

'Okay,' she said. 'I guess we're getting married, Mr Wolfe.'

CHAPTER EIGHT

'I NOW PRONOUNCE YOU man and wife.'

The vicar's voice echoed in Katie's chest like the heavy clang of bells that had greeted her when she'd arrived at the historic chapel nestled in the heart of Bloomsbury ten minutes ago. She stared at her hand, weighed down by the gold band studded with diamonds Jack had eased onto her ring finger a few moments before.

Breathe, Katie, breathe.

She blinked and tried to release the air trapped in her lungs—which was starting to make her ribs ache under the bustier the stylist had insisted needed to be worn with the lavish cream silk designer wedding gown she had seen for the first time that morning.

You agreed to this, now you have to make it work. For the baby's sake.

Not easy, when she hadn't had a chance to draw a full breath since the moment she'd agreed to Jack Wolfe's devil's bargain just four weeks before.

The minute she'd said those fateful words, Jack had taken charge. At first she'd been too shocked at the speed he'd set things into motion to really object.

He'd been unhappy at her insistence she had to return to Wales that day. Despite her exhaustion, she'd managed to stand her ground, and had felt as if she'd achieved a major concession after she'd agreed to travel home in a chauffeur-driven SUV and return to London as soon as was feasibly possible.

After a sleepless night at Cariad—spent considering and reconsidering what she'd committed to—she'd discovered the next morning that the big concession in his office had been an entirely Pyrrhic victory. A battalion of people began to arrive at the cottage in a steady stream of all-terrain vehicles.

First had come world-renowned London obstetrician Dr Patel and her team who had explained that, with Katie's permission, her pre- and antenatal care was being transferred to the consultant's exclusive clinic in Harley Street. After a thorough check-up, and a long chat with the highly professional and wonderfully reassuring doctor—together with an assurance that Jack Wolfe would be footing the clinic's astronomical bill—Katie had swallowed her pride and agreed to switch to her care. Perhaps Jack's high-handed decision to hire the obstetrician without Katie's input didn't have to be all bad. This was his baby too, after all. Maybe this was a small sign he was beginning to take that on board.

After Dr Patel had left, a PA called Jane Arkwright had arrived, hired to help Katie relocate her business over the next two weeks. Again, Katie had forced herself not to overreact. This was what she'd agreed to. She just hadn't thought it would happen quite this quickly. Luckily Jane was efficient and personable, and had helped to prevent Katie's anxiety hitting critical mass when she'd introduced her to a team of solicitors and accountants with a batch of documents for her to sign—including a pre-nup, a framework for what appeared to be extremely generous child support payments once the baby was born and a host of other legal and financial agreements about Wolfe Inc's investment in Cariad Cakes Etc.

Eventually, though, even Jane's capable presence couldn't stop Katie from freaking out. Why did everything have to be done in such a rush? Couldn't they postpone the wedding for a few more weeks at least?

Eventually, Katie had insisted on contacting Jack. But this time she had been unable to budge him an even an inch—as his calm, measured voice had explained, everything was exactly as they had agreed. And the wedding was already booked for as soon as legally possible. Again, as they had agreed.

Yup, his decision to let her return to Cariad had been nothing more than a clever negotiating tactic to lure her into a false sense of security before the full force of his will bowled her over like a tsunami.

And so it was two weeks later, as the afternoon light fell on the forest glade, she had locked up Cariad for the next seven months and had been directed by Jane to the all-terrain chauffeur-driven SUV for the six-hour drive to London, with the moving vans following behind.

When she'd arrived in Mayfair at midnight, though, she hadn't been driven to Jack's penthouse but to a newly purchased and luxuriously furnished six-bedroomed townhouse on Grosvenor Square with a full staff—including a personal chef, a stylist and a housekeeper—ready to cater to her every whim over the following two weeks while she 'settled into' her short-lived life as Jack Wolfe's fiancée.

Jack, though, was nowhere to be seen. Katie's relief had quickly morphed into consternation, however. After all the panic on the drive down about whether or not she would be moving into Jack's penthouse, she'd been deflated to discover her new fiancé had been *en route* to New York for a month-long trip when she'd called him two weeks ago— and that he would not be returning to London until the day of their wedding.

The days that followed had seemed to accelerate at speed through a packed schedule of visits, meetings, appointments and events all expertly curated by Jane. They'd involved everything from interviews to hire her new bakery team, to endless fittings at a designer couturier in Covent Garden to supply her with a lavish new wardrobe for the role she was about to play. She'd been too preoccupied and frankly numb to spend time dwelling on Jack's absence. And too tired each evening to do anything but fall into a dreamless sleep.

In truth, the only thing she'd still felt she had any real control over when the day of the wedding had dawned was her pregnancy. Thanks to lots of help-ful advice from Dr Patel, and her insistence Katie listen to her body clock and delegate where appro-priate so she got all the sleep she needed, the nausea and fatigue had begun to subside. But everything else—her new home, her new business premises in Hammersmith and the team she had begun to build—had started to feel like a strange dream she might wake up from at any time.

Somehow, her life had been so comprehensively overpowered by Jack Wolfe's organised assault on it over the past month, she'd even forgotten to stress about the prospect of her wedding until a few mo-ments ago when she'd stepped into the chapel—to see him standing at the end of the aisle with his back to her.

As if the first sight of him again since she'd been ushered out of his office four weeks before—looking tall and indomitable in an expertly tailored wedding suit—hadn't been shocking enough, the panic she'd kept so carefully at bay during the last few days began to cinch around her ribs along with the bustier as she made her way down the aisle on the arm of his COO, Terry Maxwell.

She'd been offered the chance to invite guests but, once she'd discovered Jack was only inviting a few of his key staff, she'd declined, simply invit-ing Jane, who Katie had discovered was a sturdy port in the storm of her new reality.

This wasn't a real wedding. And it would have been beyond awkward to invite any of her friends, and especially Bea. After all, she could still hear her sister's gasp down the other end of the phone line when she'd told her of the marriage and the pregnancy. Bea had been her usual sweet self after the shock had worn off, and had tried to sound positive and encouraging on Katie's behalf, while Katie had been able to hear the barely disguised disbelief in her voice, wondering what had happened to her sensible sister.

Katie had channelled every acting skill she'd ever acquired to sound like a woman in love and hold back the desire to confide in her sister. Jack's legal team had insisted she sign a non-disclosure agreement preventing her from revealing the truth about the arrangement to anyone but they need not have bothered. She'd made a promise. A promise she refused to renege on.

As the vicar's words declaring the marriage complete floated up to the chapel's elegantly carved vaulted ceiling, Katie forced herself to raise her gaze from the ring.

Fierce purpose flared in Jack's eyes.

Maybe the marriage was fake, but it didn't *feel* fake as his piercing gaze proceeded to roam over her face with a possessive hunger that stole her breath.

'You may kiss the bride, Mr Wolfe,' the vicar announced with an avuncular chuckle.

Katie clutched the bespoke bouquet of Welsh woodland wild flowers—ivy, daisies and enchanted nightshade. It had been handed to her by the florist what felt like several lifetimes ago. Her gaze darted to the smiling clergyman and then back to Jack.

The sensual smile touching his lips, full of

knowledge and purpose, and sent the twin tides of panic and arousal rippling through her already overwrought body.

Public displays of affection had been part of their written agreement. But, when she'd agreed to that aspect of their deception, she hadn't factored in a proper wedding with a dress, a ring and a thoughtfully designed bouquet, not to mention a ceremony in one of London's most exclusive chapels, which he'd somehow managed to pull off in less than a month.

Katie had simply assumed Jack would probably want to do something basic and understated. But, when Jane had outlined the plans for the 'big day', Katie had resigned herself to going through with it, understanding that the elaborate dog-and-pony show Jack had insisted on had to be part of the push to make the marriage seem real. So why hadn't she been better prepared for this kiss?

Her lips pursed to stop the hum of sensation getting any more pronounced as Jack's gaze lowered pointedly to her mouth. Katie's eyes fixed on his face as she tried to convey her feelings to him telepathically.

Could we please get this over with ASAP?

But Jack, being Jack, seemed in no hurry whatsoever to rush the kiss that would seal their devil's bargain.

The knowing smile spread across his features, making her sure he knew exactly how the molten weight in her belly had lodged between her thighs.

She struggled to remain calm as her breathing

sawed out through congested lungs and Jack took his own sweet time lifting the jewelled veil over her head. He then spent another infinitesimal age arranging the tulle with careful precision over the hairdo a team of stylists had spent hours taming into an artful chignon threaded through with more woodland flowers.

His gaze met hers at last and his thumb skimmed down her burning cheek—possessive and electric. The contact startled her, making the fire flare at her core.

She stiffened, desperate to temper her reaction, not wanting to give him the satisfaction of knowing how easily he could turn her into a mass of pulsating sensations. But she realised she had already given him all the ammunition he needed when he leant down, his thumb sliding under her chin and sending the darts of heat shimmering south, to whisper into her ear, 'Relax, Red, I won't bite. Unless you want me to.'

Before she could think of a pithy response, his lips found hers and the last of her composure shot straight up to the vaulted ceiling.

His tongue licked across the seam. Her mouth opened, surrendering to him instinctively, just as it had done four weeks ago. The lava swelled and pulsed as he explored in expert strokes. His all-consuming kiss dragged her into a netherworld of passion and provocation as her tongue tangled with his.

And every last coherent thought flew right out of her head—bar one.

More.

Treat Yourself with 2 Free Books!

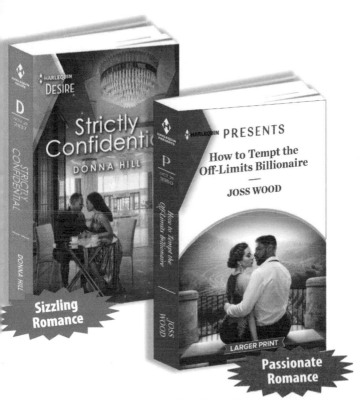

Sizzling Romance

Passionate Romance

Get ready to relax and indulge with your FREE BOOKS and more!

Claim up to FOUR NEW BOOKS & TWO MYSTERY GIFTS – absolutely FREE!

Dear Reader,

We both know life can be difficult at times. That's why it's important to treat yourself so you can relax and recharge once in a while.

And I'd like to help you do this by sending you this amazing offer of up to FOUR brand new full length FREE BOOKS that WE pay for.

This is everything I have ready to send to you right now:

Try **Harlequin® Desire** books featuring the worlds of the American elite with juicy plot twists, delicious sensuality and intriguing scandal.

Try **Harlequin Presents® Larger-Print** books featuring the glamorous lives of royals and billionaires in a world of exotic locations, where passion knows no bounds.

Or **TRY BOTH!**

All we ask in return is that you answer 4 simple questions on the attached Treat Yourself survey. You'll get **Two Free Books** and **Two Mystery Gifts** from each series you try, *altogether worth over $20!* Who could pass up a deal like that?

Sincerely,

Pam Powers

Harlequin Reader Service

Treat Yourself to Free Books and Free Gifts.

Answer 4 fun questions and get rewarded.

◄ **DETACH AND MAIL CARD TODAY!** ►

	YES	NO
1. I LOVE reading a good book.	◯	◯
2. I indulge and "treat" myself often.	◯	◯
3. I love getting FREE things.	◯	◯
4. Reading is one of my favorite activities.	◯	◯

TREAT YOURSELF • Pick your 2 Free Books...

Yes! Please send me my Free Books from each series I select and Free Mystery Gifts. I understand that I am under no obligation to buy anything, as explained on the back of this card.

Which do you prefer?

❏ **Harlequin Desire®** 225/326 HDL GRAN
❏ **Harlequin Presents® Larger-Print** 176/376 HDL GRAN
❏ **Try Both** 225/326 & 176/376 HDL GRAY

FIRST NAME   LAST NAME

ADDRESS

APT.#   CITY

STATE/PROV.   ZIP/POSTAL CODE

EMAIL ❏ Please check this box if you would like to receive newsletters and promotional emails from Harlequin Enterprises ULC and its affiliates. You can unsubscribe anytime.

* * *

Jack drove his tongue into the warm recesses of Katherine's mouth, devouring the taste he had become addicted to. A taste he'd spent the last four weeks away from his new bride to control.

The fire roared in his gut, turning his flesh to iron as the kiss went from controlled to desperate in a heartbeat. He grasped her cheeks to angle her head and take the kiss deeper, to devour more of that glorious taste and her elemental response.

She kissed him back, her tongue duelling with his as they consumed each other in fast, greedy bites.

He heard the sound of the bouquet dropping onto stone tiles, then her hands slipped under his waistcoat, grasping fistfuls of starched linen. Her whole body shook as she clung to him, as if she were caught in a storm and he were the only thing anchoring her to earth.

His muscles tensed, the desire to scoop her into his arms and carry her to some dark, secret corner of the chapel all but unbearable.

'Mr Wolfe, perhaps you and your bride would like to sign the register?' The vicar's voice seemed to drift into his consciousness from a million miles away, through a heady fog of heat and yearning, then registered in his brain like a bombshell.

He tore his mouth from Katherine's. She was staring at him, her eyes glazed, her full lips red and swollen from the ferocity of the kiss. Her expertly arranged hair hung down on one side, tugged from its moorings by his marauding fingers.

She let go of his shirt.

How can she still drive me insane so easily?

He cleared his throat to dislodge the rock pressed against his larynx and sucked in an unsteady breath, far too aware of the heavy erection pressing against his boxers.

It was a good thing the tailor had insisted the wedding trousers be fitted loosely or he would be giving the whole of the congregation a clear demonstration of how much he wanted his wife.

His wife.

The thought struck him for the first time that maybe this arrangement, this deal, wasn't going to be as manageable as he needed it to be. And that was without even factoring in the problem of her pregnancy.

He'd travelled all the way to New York to get a grip on his reaction to her. The fact he couldn't stop thinking about her, had even dreamed about her, had only made him more convinced distance was his best strategy, for the time being at least.

It had nearly killed him a month ago to keep his reaction to the news of her pregnancy in check. He had never planned to father a child for the simple reason he had no clue *how* to be a father, and he knew he didn't have the tools necessary to learn.

But, as he had crouched beside her in his office bathroom, the shocking discovery of her condition had been swiftly followed by another, even more disturbing, revelation.

While he didn't want to care for this child in anything other than a financial capacity, he did care for

Katherine Medford. Enough to want to protect her and her business. Enough to want to mitigate the ravages of what he'd done to her body. Enough to ensure this child had his name. In the weeks since, he'd persuaded himself that the visceral reaction had to come from a need to be a better man than the man who had sired him.

Katherine had simply triggered that knee-jerk reaction with her suggestion he might try to bully her into a termination. At first he'd been furious at the whispered comment, but he'd come to accept that had to be why he had been so determined to get her to agree to this marriage. And why he had been so focussed on getting the deed done as soon as possible.

When she'd told him in his office she didn't want to sleep with him, he'd of course had an equally visceral and enraged reaction. It had taken him every single day since to get a grip on that. And realise that giving in to their sexual chemistry would be a bad move—until he was in complete control of everything else about this arrangement.

But his hard-earned control had started to slip the moment she had appeared at the back of the chapel in a swathe of seductive silk, her wild, red hair tamed beneath the wispy veil.

His breath had backed up in his lungs and he'd been... Mesmerised. Enchanted. Bewitched. And angry—with himself most of all. Because the deep yearning squeezing his ribs had reminded him of that feral kid huddled in a doorway in the West End, watching the theatregoers stroll past him on their way to the Tube—rich, clean, well-dressed, beautiful people who'd had everything, while he'd had nothing.

Katie's wedding dress should have looked classy and demure—it was what he'd requested—but the shimmering fabric had hugged Katherine's curves like a second skin, sliding sensuously over her generous hips and those high, full breasts—made even more glorious by her condition.

The evidence of her pregnancy had horrified him that day in his office, but some aspects of it now only turned him on more—which made no sense whatsoever.

She'd walked towards him—her stride bold and determined—but then he'd seen the flicker of anxiety as she reached him. It had required a titanic effort to remain aloof and in command of his senses during the endless ceremony until the vicar had finally declared them man and wife.

But, when he'd heard the invitation to kiss his bride, he'd seen the note of panic and defiance in her expression. The answering tug of possessiveness—still tempered by the memory of that kid yearning for things he couldn't have—had made him determined to stake a claim. To prove to everyone—and Katherine most of all—she belonged to him.

And before he'd had a chance to think better of the impulse, he'd leaned in, inhaled a lungful of her provocative scent, seen the shocked arousal making the gold shards in her eyes gleam... And all hell had broken loose.

He'd stayed away from her precisely to avoid this

uncontrolled reaction. Given their chemistry, he had no intention of having a platonic marriage, but he also had no intention of letting the hunger blindside him again, the way it had in Wales—and all those days ago in his office—until he figured out how to compartmentalise his reaction to her condition.

Distance hadn't worked, though, because his hunger for her had only become more insatiable, his desire more volatile.

Terrific.

He had a four-hour reception booked at an exclusive private members' club that he owned in Soho—entirely for the benefit of the press and his business associates.

Even better.

How the heck was he going to get through that, not to mention their first night together in the new house, without giving into this insane chemistry again?

Passion rippled through his body as he nodded to the vicar, who was watching them both with thinly disguised astonishment, his cheeks mottled with embarrassment.

'Cool, lead the way,' he said. He clasped Katherine's hand. The ring dug into his palm as he felt the tremor she couldn't disguise. He led her into the vestry to get the last of the ceremony over with. A ceremony that didn't feel nearly as pragmatic as it had when he'd originally planned it.

Katherine followed behind him, for once willing to be led without an argument. Probably because she was still as shell-shocked by that damn kiss as he was.

This hunger wouldn't last. It couldn't. But he planned to treat it with extreme caution nonetheless, because he'd never experienced a need this intense or this unstable.

Controlling it completely obviously wasn't going to happen, but no way was he unleashing this fire again until he was absolutely sure he would not get burned—any more than he had been already.

Katie struggled to hold on to the ripple of reaction as Jack's warm palm settled on her back and he leaned close to be heard over the conversations buzzing around them in the sumptuous Soho club.

'We should head back to the house,' Jack said.

It had been her first assignment as Jack Wolfe's trophy wife and she felt as if she'd done her best. She'd made pointless small talk with a host of celebrities and VIPs, got besieged by photographers shouting her name as they'd entered the venue and had managed to appear calm and collected as Jack had introduced her and they'd received a ton of champagne toasts, good wishes and inquisitive comments laced with innuendo.

The decision had been made—according to Wolfe Inc's press secretary—not to announce the pregnancy until she was showing. Katie had been pathetically grateful for that, because answering all the probing enquiries from Jack's friends and acquaintances about their whirlwind courtship had been tough enough.

She supposed she had to thank Jack for that, too. He'd more than kept up his side of the bargain, playing the solicitous bridegroom with a predatory determination which had deflected anyone who got too close. As she'd struggled to adjust to all the attention, Jack's presence by her side had made her feel strangely protected, until she'd remembered it was all an act. And, as the evening had worn on, fending off unwanted enquiries about their love affair hadn't been anywhere near as tough as stopping herself from dissolving into a puddle of need every time she'd got a whiff of his scent. Or felt the firm touch of his palm caressing her back.

Like now.

The effect he had on her had only got more intense and overwhelming as he'd remained diligently by her side through the champagne reception in the club's lavish atrium, a five-course meal of cordon bleu cuisine devised by the club's Michelin-starred chef—which she'd barely touched—and the never-ending parade of witty and heartfelt speeches.

She stiffened as his calloused fingers stroked her spine where the gown dipped, brutally aware of how addicted she had become to his clean, spicy scent. Surely that had to be the pregnancy hormones?

'Are you sure?' she whispered back, but had to stifle a yawn, the stress of the event and her struggle to keep her traitorous emotions in check—plus the fact she hadn't been able to have her usual nap this afternoon—finally taking their toll.

His lips quirked, but as his gaze raked over her the riot of sensations only intensified. How could he seem so detached? When she was burning up inside, both exhausted and on edge? Why wasn't he still struggling with the after-effects of that wedding kiss the way she was? Was her constant awareness of him *really* just the pregnancy hormones? Because the thought of going back to the house, of being alone with him again for the first time in weeks, was not helping to keep those hormones in check—especially after five solid hours of being the sole focus of his attention. Would he expect them to have a wedding night? And how was she going to resist him if he did?

He glided his thumb under her eye. 'Yes, I'm sure. You look shattered.' He glanced at her plate. 'You hardly ate a bite. Is it the nausea?'

She shook her head. 'No, it's mostly gone. I'm only sick occassionally now.'

Something she would have been a lot more grateful for if it hadn't made her even more aware of him. The morning—or rather, afternoon—sickness had once been a great way to dull this incessant attraction... Now, not a chance.

'Good,' he said, then lifted his hand to waylay one of the eager young assistants who had been hovering around them all day. 'Jenny, have the car brought round discreetly. Mrs Wolfe and I are leaving—with the minimum of fuss, if possible.'

'Yes, sir, Mr Wolfe.' The young woman, who had to be about the same age as Katie, bounced to attention so sharply Katie almost expected her to salute.

During the last few hours, she had noticed the deference with which all Jack's employees treated him, but also the fact he seemed to know all their names. She dismissed the sentimental thought, though—just because he was a good employer wasn't going to make *her* job any easier.

Despite Jack's request, it took a long twenty minutes for them to extricate themselves from the reception and the amused and ebullient well wishes of everyone from Jack's best man—an ex-rapper called Alphonse Parry who had been one of Jack's earliest business partners—to the hat-check girl, which only made Katie feel like more of a fraud.

A sleek black car was waiting at the back of the club. Jack dropped Katie's *faux* fur wrap over her shoulders while the driver opened the door.

'If you want to stay and chat, I don't mind heading back on my own,' she managed, trying to disguise the shiver which had nothing whatsoever to do with the evening breeze pebbling her skin.

He let out a wry laugh, his scarred eyebrow arching. 'Don't you think our guests might get suspicious if I let my bride go home alone on our wedding night?'

Damn. Busted.

'Oh, right—yes, of course,' she murmured, feeling like a clueless idiot.

How could she forget this was all an elaborate charade to give her child a name, keep her business afloat and allow him to…? Well, she wasn't even really sure *what* he was getting out of this, given that she definitely didn't buy the excuse he'd given her in Wales three months ago. The wedding reception had been full of some of the most important people in the global business community, every one of them falling over themselves to be nice to Jack, and her by proxy.

How could dating, or indeed marrying, a lord's daughter make him any more of a big cheese in the City of London? The fact he hadn't bothered to invite her father—thank God—surely only confirmed that?

As they settled into the car's warm interior together, the smell of new leather went some way to covering the scent of him. She had to be grateful he made no move to close the distance between them once the car pulled into traffic.

She stared out of the window, the Ritz hotel's sign reflecting off the glass as the car turned into Piccadilly. Perhaps now would be a good time to press him more on his motivations. But did she really want to know the real reason he had been so set on this marriage? Wouldn't it only complicate things further?

'You don't have to be concerned, Katherine,' he said, breaking the uncomfortable silence.

Her head whipped round as the husky timbre of his voice had the familiar ripple shooting up her spine.

He was watching her with the same intensity he had been watching her with for most of the day, ever since she'd stepped into the chapel.

She had begun to wonder during the evening if he was keeping an eye on her—ready to correct her if she said or did something to give away the real circumstances of their marriage. But there was no judgement in his gaze, only an unsettlingly direct concentration.

'We'll sleep apart tonight. Consummation of this marriage is not part of the arrangement,' he murmured.

Why not?

The thought popped out of nowhere, making the ripple sink into her sex and start to glow.

'Good to know,' she murmured, trying to sound as nonchalant as he did. And to remember she didn't want to sleep with him, because this whole situation was already disturbing enough.

His lips twisted in that disconcerting smile, but his gaze only sharpened. And she had the awful feeling he could see right through her show of indifference.

'Although on the evidence of this afternoon's kiss and the one in my office a month ago,' he continued, the relaxed tone comprehensively contradicted by that focussed gaze, which was making sensation rush over her skin like wildfire, 'I doubt we'll be able to keep our hands off each other for very long.'

'I know,' she said.

He chuckled, but the sound was as raw as she felt.

'Good to know you know that,' he said, echoing her earlier statement.

She let out an unsteady breath, the bustier so tight around her ribs she was surprised she didn't pass out. Clearly, pretending she could resist the insistent pull between them hadn't been such a smart move, because it felt as if he held all the power now that she'd been forced to admit the truth.

'So why aren't we having a wedding night?' she challenged, trying to grab some of that power back.

His eyes widened at the direct question and she felt the instant rush of adrenaline at the realisation she'd disconcerted him. For once. Instead of the other way round.

'Is it because of the baby?' she added, when he didn't reply.

He stared, then turned away. 'No,' he said.

On the one hand, she believed him. After all, he wouldn't have kissed her with such hunger if the pregnancy had been a turn-off. But she had touched a nerve without intending to. And the questions that had been burning in the back of her mind, the ones she'd been determined not even to think about, pushed to the front.

'Do you want to talk about it?' she asked.

'Talk about what?' he asked, turning back, but the confident smile had flatlined.

No, he definitely did *not* want to talk about the pregnancy. But somehow his stubborn refusal only made her more determined to press him on it, despite her own misgivings.

They'd both been knocked off-kilter by the pregnancy. She got that. But why hadn't she questioned the hasty arrangements that he had insisted upon, and which had unnerved her so much? The speed of her relocation to London, the lavishness of today's event, the opulence of the house he'd bought for her to live in, the attentiveness with which he had

treated her during the ceremony and the reception
and even the mysteriously opaque motives for insisting on this marriage in the first place. Because
every one of those things had disturbed her in the
last month. Had he rushed her into this commitment as an elaborate way to avoid having this conversation? Maybe even to avoid thinking about it?

And, if he had, why had she fallen for it so easily? She'd told him she'd decided to have the baby,
and he'd accepted it without question. But she had
no idea how *he* felt about it because she hadn't
asked.

'Do you want to talk about becoming a father?'
she asked patiently, aware she was tiptoeing through
a minefield but not able to deny her curiosity any
longer. No, this wasn't just curiosity about him and
the kind of father he would make. It was much more
fundamental than that. She needed to know if he
would ever be able to think of their child as anything other than a mistake to be rectified, a debt to
be paid. And, if not, why not?

'Do I *want* to talk about it?' he mused. 'No, not
particularly.'

'Why not?' she pressed, refusing to be put off
again.

His gaze locked on hers, the scar on his cheek
flexing. 'Because I do not intend to be a part of
its life.'

The dismissive answer and the brutal, brittle tone
in which he delivered it had her heart contracting
in her chest. It felt like a crushing blow. Which was

ridiculous, really. After all, his response only confirmed what she had already suspected.

He was being honest with her. She didn't know him well, but what she did know—that he was ruthless, driven, and uncompromising enough to buy her cooperation to further his own business ends—probably meant it was a good thing he did not want to be involved in her child's life. After all, her own father had been physically present but emotionally absent throughout her childhood, and that had somehow been worse. Surely it was better not to have a relationship with your father than to have one that was so dysfunctional it made you feel unworthy, unwanted?

But, when his gaze flicked away again, she got the sense he wasn't telling her the whole truth.

The car glided to a stop outside the Mayfair townhouse, and he remained seated while the chauffeur got out and opened her door. As she slipped out of the vehicle, she couldn't help asking, 'Are you coming inside?'

'Do you wish to consummate the marriage tonight?' he countered, the ruthless demand in his voice shaking her to the core. And putting the power firmly back in his hands, as she was sure he had intended.

'Yes… I mean, no.' She scrambled to regain the ground she'd lost. 'Oh, I have no idea.'

His harsh laugh only made her feel more confused. And more powerless. A part of her *wanted* to lose herself in the sex, to take the physical pleasure he offered so she could forget about all the things this marriage would never offer her—security, companionship, maybe even love with a man who might one day come to care for her as well as her child.

But, with her emotions so raw, she knew giving in to that urge tonight would be a very bad idea. Because she wasn't sure she could avoid the intimacy with anything like the efficiency he clearly could.

'Which is it, Mrs Wolfe?' he asked.

'No,' she said with all the conviction she could muster.

'Then I think it's best if I return to the penthouse,' he said, but he reached forward and ran his thumb down her cheek with a possessiveness that stopped her breath. 'You know where to find me, when you're ready to stop running,' he added.

She drew her head back.

He signalled the driver. After she had stepped out of the car, she watched it pull away, the traitorous desire still pulsing in her core.

As she lay in bed half an hour later, her hand curled around her stomach. She felt weary to her bones, the odd feeling of dissatisfaction joined by the terrifying thought her life had just taken an even bigger leap into the unknown.

CHAPTER NINE

'WHAT THE HELL do you mean, the Smyth-Brown board still won't let us bid on the final share allocation?' Jack shouted. He'd had yet another sleepless night alone in his penthouse. The truth was he'd been tying himself in knots ever since tying the damn knot with Katherine three days ago.

He wanted his new wife to come to him. Wanted her to admit how much she needed him so he could forget about the devastated look in her eyes when he'd been straight with her about what he planned to offer this child.

He hadn't lied about that, but the sheen of sadness in her expression still managed to get to him. It made him feel guilty about something he had never promised and could not change. Which made no damn sense whatsoever.

And now this! The main reason he'd decided to go for this marriage—well, one of the main reasons anyway—was to finally get the old fossils on the Smyth-Brown board to agree to Wolfe Inc's bid for the controlling interest of the company. The original plan—way back when he'd first proposed to Beatrice—had been to use the marriage as leverage, to make them stop looking at him as a marauding corporate raider from the wrong side of the tracks and begin to see him as a settled family man they could trust.

His motives had become considerably more confused since then, thanks to his obsession with Beatrice's sister and the idiotic decision not to use a condom. But, if he couldn't even get this much out of the marriage, he was going to go completely insane.

'Jack, chill out,' Terry Maxwell murmured, completely unperturbed by his meltdown.

Terry was his right-hand man, his fixer, his *consigliere* and his chief financial strategist all rolled into one. Terry didn't do deference because he'd been in Jack's employ since Wolfe Inc had made its first million.

It had never bothered Jack before, but his temper surged when Terry added, 'Someone leaked the fact you're not living with your new bride. Daniel Smyth is not the only one beginning to question the authenticity of the marriage.'

'What?' Jack ground out the word, so furious and frustrated, he would not be surprised if steam began to pour out of his ears. 'Who leaked it? I want them fired immediately.'

How dared that son of a bitch question *his* integrity, especially with women, after what the guy had done to his mother?

But, before Jack could begin to work himself up into even more of a temper, Terry said, 'Jack, it could be anyone—you've been photographed coming and going from your penthouse. Perhaps the more cogent question is *why* aren't you living in Grosvenor Square with your beautiful wife?'

'That's none of your damn business,' Jack shot back, but he could hear the defensiveness in his voice as he strode to the windows of his thirty-fourth-floor office and glared at the view of the Shard on the opposite bank.

It wasn't Terry's fault he'd got into this fix with Katherine, allowing his libido and his pride to dictate his actions.

'Fair point,' Terry said, still not bothered in the least by Jack's temper tantrum. 'But, whatever your reasons, there might be a way to quash the rumours, thus fixing the problem with the Smyth-Brown takeover, while also giving the grand opening of Wolfe Maldives next month a huge publicity boost.'

Jack broke off his contemplation of the City skyline. 'Which is?' he asked, not particularly liking the sympathetic smile on his advisor's weathered face.

Terry didn't know about the true nature of his marriage, or Katherine's pregnancy, because Jack had kept all those details on a strictly need-to-know basis to stop any unwanted questions and ensure the smooth passage of the Smyth-Brown buyout. Or so he'd thought.

'The resort is already fully operational. All the staff have been hired and Wolfe Resorts' marketing division have been inviting journalists, travel bloggers and vloggers to try out the six-star experience over the last couple of weeks…' Terry began in a measured tone. 'But we can get rid of the media for a much better publicity coup.'

Jack turned round completely, to skewer his right-hand man. 'Get to the point, Terry.'

'Jack, the place is a prime honeymoon destination…' Terry stared right back at him.

'So?' Jack said, but he could already see where this suggestion was leading, because the familiar pulsing in his groin that had plagued him ever since he'd confronted Katherine on the limo ride back to the house in Mayfair on their so-called wedding night had gone into overdrive.

He had every intention of seducing his wife, and soon. He certainly didn't plan to wait much longer to settle that aspect of their relationship to his satisfaction. Especially as he knew full well her reluctance to welcome him into her bed had nothing whatsoever to do with a lack of desire. But spending any quality time with her was out. The last thing he wanted was to be subjected to another conversation like the one they'd had in the limo.

He hadn't married her to have an actual relationship with her. That had been the whole point of contracting her to *pose* as his wife—which she seemed to have conveniently missed. Of course, the pregnancy complicated that somewhat. But he didn't talk about his past, or his motives or feelings, with anyone. And certainly not with women he was sleeping with… Or intended to sleep with. Especially when they had the unique ability to blindside him with lust—the way Katherine did—and were also carrying his child.

'Jack, don't be deliberately obtuse,' Terry said, looking pained now. 'You've just got married. Wolfe Maldives isn't due to open for another month. A two-week honeymoon there with your blushing bride would garner the kind of organic global media reach your PR department would have wet dreams about for years.'

No way in hell.

That was what his head shouted but, even as he opened his mouth to tell Terry to forget it, the image of Katherine in a skimpy bikini, strolling out of the lagoon's glittering blue waters, those generous breasts bouncing enticingly as she moved, blasted out of his subconscious and sunk deep into his abdomen.

Damn.

He closed his mouth. And frowned.

As much as he hated to admit it, Terry had a point. The truth was, he didn't give a damn about the golden PR opportunity. But the chance to have Katherine all to himself—where he could seduce her in private—held some obvious advantages. Surely he'd already done enough to disabuse her of any sentimental notions she might have had about this marriage?

'Two weeks is too long,' he said, his voice dropping several octaves as more images of Katherine— wet and willing in a luxury beach setting—began to galvanise his resolve. 'I can't afford to spend that much time away from the business.' Which wasn't a lie.

Having Katherine all to himself in paradise— and making every one of the prurient fantasies he'd had about her since their first merry meeting come true—was appealing to all his baser instincts. But he wasn't about to push his luck.

'Really?' Terry looked sceptical. 'You haven't taken a proper holiday in the ten years I've known you.'

'I'm a workaholic, Terry. I like working. I can't spend a fortnight twiddling my thumbs just for a good photo op.' Not that he planned to be twiddling *his* thumbs, exactly.

Terry sent him a garrulous look. 'How about ten days, then?'

'A week,' Jack countered. 'We'll leave tomorrow night,' he added, the adrenaline rush surging at the thought he would only have to endure one more night—two at the most—without Katherine in his bed. 'In the Wolfe jet.'

He sat behind his desk, feeling more settled than he had in days. Hell, weeks. Make that four months ago. Ever since the first time he'd set eyes on his future trophy wife in her Little Red Riding Hooker outfit. He smiled. Maybe he could get her to bring it so he could peel it off her, the way he'd dreamed of doing ever since that night.

'That's great, Jack.' Terry rubbed his hands together with undisguised glee. 'I'll talk to Sully in the marketing division and the resort management team. And I'll let Gorinda know so she can rearrange your schedule. Do you want her to inform Mrs Wolfe of your plans?'

He looked up from his desk. 'Nah, I'll speak to her myself,' he said as the surge of adrenaline took on a fiercely possessive edge. 'Tell Gorinda I'll be eating in Grosvenor Square tonight.'

It was way past time he started laying down the law in this marriage—which was supposed to be for *his* convenience, not hers. He'd paid handsomely for the damn privilege after all. He'd been considerate—mindful of her delicate condition and the huge changes he was imposing on her life and her business. But she'd said herself at the reception that the sickness wasn't a big problem any more. He knew from his business manager's report that Cariad Cakes was now firmly established in its new premises in Hammersmith, and he had seen the way she'd looked at him on their wedding night. She was as hungry for him as he was for her. And he'd given her three long days and nights to come to terms with the way things were, which was more than long enough.

CHAPTER TEN

'JACK, YOU'RE HERE!' Katie stopped dead at the entrance to the dining room, a mix of shock and panic and exhilaration duelling in her chest at the sight of her husband sitting at the table where she'd eaten alone for the last three nights.

His white business shirt was open at the neck to reveal a hint of the tattoo across his chest, the sleeves rolled up tanned, muscular forearms, his hair mussed and his jaw darkened with a day's beard. The scene should have felt at least a little bit domestic. But it didn't. The possessive glint in his eyes echoed in her abdomen.

Yeah, right. Jack Wolfe is about as domesticated as his namesake.

'And you're late,' he said as his penetrating gaze glided over her flour-stained clothing and the weary set of her shoulders. 'You're working too hard.'

'Well, there's a lot to do,' Katie said a little defensively, disconcerted by the note of concern and the fact it made her feel cherished when she knew it wasn't real. 'I would have left earlier, though, if I'd known you were joining me for dinner...' she said, trying at least to *sound* like a dutiful wife. After all, it was what they'd agreed on. Although, she hadn't felt like a wife in the three days since their wedding. He hadn't even contacted her.

At first, she had fretted she'd somehow offended him by being honest with him and not inviting him into her bed. His comment about the baby had upset her, making her feel uniquely vulnerable, but not seeing or hearing from him for three days had only made the unsettled feeling worse...not that it was exactly calm at the moment.

How did he manage to throw her for a loop simply by breathing?

'I didn't expect to see you tonight,' she added rather inanely as he picked up one of the freshly baked bread rolls laid out on the table by the kitchen staff.

'Last time I looked, this was my house,' he said as he buttered the roll, watching her intently as she walked to the place setting at the other end of the table.

'Are you planning to move in, then?' she asked, not entirely sure how she felt about the prospect. The twin tides of panic and exhilaration now danced a jig in her chest, and a few other places besides.

She couldn't avoid him for ever, and she really didn't want to. Surely getting to know him better had to be a good thing? Especially as she'd come to the conclusion—after three days of overthinking what he'd said about fatherhood—that perhaps she just needed to be patient with him.

He'd said he didn't intend to play a part in the

baby's life. But maybe that would change. The pregnancy had to have been a major shock for him too—however good he was at hiding it. And he didn't have the same physical connection with their grain-o'-rice as she did. Of course, the baby would seem like a totally abstract concept to him at this point.

'Not tonight,' he said as a waiter arrived with the first course.

The exhilaration dimmed a bit as a beautifully prepared salad made up of crisp romaine lettuce, finely sliced radishes, carrots, apple and endives, and drizzled with a creamy dressing, was placed in front of her.

'Oh… Okay,' she said, trying to hide her disappointment. She tucked into the salad. Her appetite had returned full force in the last few weeks, despite all the tension over her situation with Jack but, as she wracked her brains to figure out what he was doing here, she couldn't swallow a bite.

'We're heading to the Maldives tomorrow night for a week,' he said. 'So you'll need to brief your team at the bakery and have the housekeeper arrange your packing.'

Katie dropped her fork onto the plate, so shocked by her new husband's bland pronouncement, she barely noticed the splatter of salad dressing hitting the table cloth. *'What?'*

He let out a gruff laugh, but his gaze remained locked on hers, more provocative than humorous. 'I believe it's the usual protocol after a wedding to have a honeymoon.'

'Except this isn't a usual wedding, is it?' she said. 'I haven't even heard from you in three days.'

He placed his knife and fork on the plate, before trapping her again in that blazing blue gaze. 'Have you missed me, Mrs Wolfe?'

Yes, you stupid...

She quashed the unhelpful thought before it could burst out of her mouth and give him even more power.

'I'm just saying, this isn't a normal marriage.'

He picked up his cutlery again, speaking in a conversational tone as he sliced through an endive leaf. 'Perhaps not, but I thought you understood the marriage has to appear to be real.'

'But... There was nothing about a honeymoon in the contract,' she floundered. She didn't want to go on some romantic getaway with him—for a whole week—even if it was only for the sake of appearances. She was having enough trouble sitting across the dining room from him without getting fixated on the way his shoulders strained the seams of his shirt, or recalling the rigid, resistant look on his face when she had asked him about his thoughts on fatherhood.

Getting to know him slowly, and carefully, with a full staff in attendance was one thing. Surviving a week of his focussed attention while battling her own insecurities was quite another. How would she be able to deny the insistent need with him right there? Sleeping with him would fundamentally change the parameters of their agreement in a way that could be dangerous if she wasn't emotionally prepared for the change.

'If you read the small print, it stated you would be required to travel with me,' he continued in that forceful, pragmatic tone that got on her nerves. 'This honeymoon is part of that commitment. You signed it, Red. Are you trying to renege on the deal already?'

'No, but…' She gathered her ragged breathing, forcing herself to remain calm. She'd known he would be dominant, demanding. She'd expected that. She must not lose her temper, because that would just give him the upper hand, especially as she was beginning to think he enjoyed provoking her.

'You said we could negotiate our work schedules. I can't very well leave my business for a week with less than a day's notice.'

He glanced at his watch. 'Our flight isn't leaving until eight tomorrow night, so you've got most of the day to brief your team.'

'Fine, but it's still too soon to relinquish—'

'There's an excellent Internet connection where we're going.' He cut her off, the prickle of impatience sending an answering prickle of irritation through her. 'You'll be able to check in with your team if necessary.'

Standing, he dropped his napkin on the table.

'But this isn't fair,' she said, annoyed when she heard the whiney tone of her own voice. 'I don't *want* to go to the Maldives.'

With you. Alone. On a fake honeymoon. Which will mean nothing to you and might mean something to me.

He strode towards her and tucked a knuckle under her chin to brush his thumb over her bottom lip.

She jerked her head back, but it was already too late. He had to have seen the awareness flare at the brief touch.

He planted his hands in his pockets, the smile as smug as it was predatory. 'I understand very well, Red. You think by avoiding each other this incessant heat will just go away. It won't.'

'But what if I'm not ready?'

His scarred eyebrow lifted, his cast-iron confidence completely undimmed by her declaration.

Damn him.

'I told you anything we do in private would be your choice. That hasn't changed.'

'Then why are you insisting on going to—?'

'However…' He interrupted her. *Again!* 'I did not agree to pretend the heat between us doesn't exist. Personally, I believe enjoying it for as long as your condition allows will make this marriage a lot more pleasurable for both of us. And trying to avoid it will only increase the problem. So I guess the battle lines are drawn.'

The tell-tale weight sunk into her sex as he returned to his seat and finished his salad. She sucked in a breath, too furious to speak.

Of all the arrogant, high-handed, conceited, overbearing...

She picked up her knife and fork again, ignoring the tremble in her fingers. Fine, she'd go on his stupid honeymoon and show him he couldn't bend her to his will. But she'd refuse to be bulldozed back into his bed… By his hungry kisses, his addictive scent or that seductive promise in his cool blue eyes…even if it killed her.

Although it very well might.

After a frantic day spent running through recipes, answering countless emails, checking orders and getting her new business manager up to speed on all the commitments she was being forced to cancel for the next week, Katie was holding on to her indignation by a thread when her car arrived at Heathrow the following evening.

Instead of being dropped off in Departures, though, they were met by a passport official before being whisked through the airport, the lights of incoming planes shining in the night sky overhead. The car drove past the airport buildings to arrive at a huge private hangar behind one of the runways. A sleek silver jet took up all the available space as the car parked beside the metal steps.

She swallowed heavily as the driver opened her door then began unloading the luggage the staff must have packed earlier that day—*three* suitcases worth of luggage containing clothes she had never seen.

She frowned. Up until now, she'd really been far too preoccupied with the pregnancy, the wedding, the huge changes to her business and her constant panic about how to navigate the deal she'd made with Jack without losing her mind to think too much about the world of luxury she had entered. A world she'd been excluded from ever since she was a teenager. A world she'd left without a backwards glance.

But, as she climbed the steps into the jet, it occurred to her Jack Wolfe's lavish luxurious world was way, *way* more exclusive than her father's. She'd come from money and, although she'd never enjoyed the strings attached when she'd lived under her father's control, she knew how this world worked. Or at least, she had thought she did. But, even as the daughter of a British lord, she'd never travelled on a private plane—or had a passport official give her a personal service. Or had three huge suitcases full of clothes she'd never worn packed for her by someone else for a week-long holiday.

Except it's not a holiday, it's a honeymoon.

She puffed out her cheeks, the frustration that had been building ever since Jack's high-handed demand yesterday at dinner giving way to something a lot less fortifying and more disturbing.

She'd barely had time to think in the past month. Perhaps that was why it hadn't really occurred to her until this moment that *everything* about her new life with Jack Wolfe was way outside her comfort zone.

As she stepped into the plane's interior, she was greeted by a hostess uniformed in the red and black colours of the Wolfe Inc logo. The middle-aged woman smiled and took her coat, before directing her to the plane's interior.

'Mr Wolfe is seated in the lounge area, waiting for you, Mrs Wolfe,' she said.

Mrs Wolfe.

She'd been addressed by her married name several times since the wedding. But it had all seemed like an elaborate act until now. A knot formed in her stomach to go with the one in her throat.

She nodded, suddenly feeling woefully under-dressed in the worn jeans and plaid shirt combo she had been wearing all day to direct traffic in Cariad Cakes' industrial kitchen.

Jack sat in one of the large cream leather arm-chairs in the plane's lounge, typing something on his phone. The cabin was darker than she had ex-pected, the lighting no doubt subdued for take-off. A single spotlight turned his short dark hair to a gleaming ebony and cast his handsome features into stark relief. He hadn't shaved all day, and the be-ginnings of the beard shadowing his jaw, together with the scarred eyebrow, made him look even more rugged and untamed than usual, despite the sharply tailored suit trousers and ubiquitous white shirt per-fectly fitted to his muscular torso.

'Mrs Wolfe has arrived, sir,' the hostess an-nounced behind her.

Jack's blue gaze locked on her face as he clicked off the phone. 'Good evening, Mrs Wolfe,' he said, the polite greeting loaded with a meaning that felt anything but polite thanks to the feral gleam in his eyes and the husky timbre of his voice.

She'd expected him to have his army of assis-tants with him on the flight but, as the hostess ex-cused herself to prepare for take-off, Katie realised they were alone.

'Hi,' she said, but the word came out on a high-pitched squeak. Mortified, she cleared her throat of the rubble gathered there, and tried again. 'Hello, Jack.'

'Glad to see you made it in time for take-off,' he said, the slight edge suggesting he hadn't appreciated being kept waiting.

She hadn't arrived with only minutes to spare deliberately—she'd been extremely busy all day—but his tone still rankled.

'Did I have a choice?' she snapped.

A sensual smile—part arrogance, part amusement and yet full of approval—had her heartbeat leaping in her chest. She *knew* he enjoyed provoking her. But why hadn't she realised until now how much more he enjoyed it when she rose to the bait?

He chuckled. 'I can't very well go on a honeymoon on my own, now, can I?' he said, the mocking twinkle in his eyes making him look even more attractive.

The bastard.

Oddly—given her anxiety about what exactly they were going to be doing in the Maldives, and her indignation at the high-handed way he'd sprung this trip—she found her own lips twitching.

'I suppose not,' she conceded as she took the seat opposite him. She sunk into the soft, buttery leather, suddenly aware of how exhausted she was. The extreme fatigue of her early pregnancy had been replaced by a more manageable tiredness in the last few weeks, but she'd been on her feet most of the day—and coping with the inevitable sexual tension of being in Jack Wolfe's orbit didn't help.

'Although you may wish you had after a week

stuck with me spinning my wheels,' she offered. 'I don't think I'm the "lying on the beach" type.'

It wasn't a lie. She couldn't remember the last time she'd taken a break, let alone been able to afford a holiday. She'd been working two or three jobs at a time ever since she'd left home—and even before leaving home she'd had a secret Saturday job because she'd wanted to be as financially independent as possible from her father.

'Neither am I,' Jack murmured. The approval in his gaze became hot and fluid, causing awareness to sizzle over her skin. 'I guess we'll have to find a way to keep each other occupied.'

The sizzle flared across her collarbone and rose into her cheeks.

His gaze narrowed on her burning face and the knowing smile widened.

If only she could conjure up a smart, pithy comeback, but it would have been next to impossible to fake indifference, even if she hadn't been dead on feet.

The pilot's voice rang out over the intercom to inform them they had just been given a departure slot and would be taking off in ten minutes.

Katie fastened her seat belt as instructed and glanced out of the window, realising the plane was already moving and had left the bright interior of the hangar. The lights of the terminal building as they passed it illuminated the congested lines of passengers waiting impatiently at their departure gates.

She sighed and rolled her head back, only to get trapped once again in Jack's watchful gaze. But the sizzle dropped to a distant hum as fatigue settled over her like a warm blanket.

Her mouth cracked open in a huge yawn. 'Good to know there's at least one advantage to having a gazillionaire for my fake husband.'

His right eyebrow rose, drawing her attention to the scar, which had begun to mesmerise her. Curiosity and sympathy joined the potent hum of arousal.

Who *had* given him that scar? It must have hurt so much.

'Which is…?' he asked, the smile gone.

'No boarding queues,' she murmured, then shifted round in her seat away from that disturbing all-seeing gaze. Yawning again, she slipped off her shoes, snuggled her head into the soft leather and tucked her aching feet under her bottom.

She blinked at the red lights on the plane's wing tip flashing as they swung towards the runway. The jet engine's powerful rumble seemed to amplify the insistent hum in her abdomen but, as the plane accelerated down the runway, she couldn't seem to keep her eyes open. Eventually the flashing light dragged her into the darkness and she let herself fall under its spell.

Jack stared at his wife as the jet lifted into the night sky, not sure whether to be bemused or beguiled by the sight of her curled on the seat opposite, fast asleep.

Her russet hair haloed around her head, tendrils escaping from the practical ponytail to curl down her neck. Chocolate stains covered her well-worn jeans and the green and brown plaid shirt.

She looked like a lush tomboy, the light flush on her freckle-dusted skin only adding to the spike in his groin. A few buttons had come undone on her shirt, giving him a tantalising glimpse of her cleavage as she slumbered, her body contorted into what looked like a very uncomfortable position.

She had been exhausted when she arrived. He had seen it in the smudges under her eyes and the lipstick that had been chewed off her lips hours ago. The stab of guilt joined the ache in his groin.

He shifted in his seat, visions of her soft, satiny flesh, that rich spicy scent of salted caramel, ripe apples and wild flowers permeating the cabin.

His gaze dipped and he imagined easing open the other buttons on her shirt, nuzzling the soft fragrant skin of her cleavage as it was revealed inch by tantalising inch, kissing the pulse in her collarbone, unhooking her bra, lifting her breasts free and sucking the plump pink nipples until they hardened against his…

He swore softly and swung his head away from her slumbering form to glare out of the aircraft's window. He gripped the arm rests as the inevitable wave of heat swelled. He sucked in a tortured breath. When had he ever been tormented to this extent by any woman? It was becoming ridiculous. Not to mention distracting.

Christ, if she knew the hold she had on him she would surely exploit it.

The carpet of city lights below them disappeared as the jet headed into cloud cover and began to level off at its cruising altitude.

The hostess appeared. 'Mr Wolfe, the bed chamber is ready for you and your wife,' she said, sending him a rather too amused smile.

'Right, thanks,' he murmured. 'If you could leave us, please.'

The woman immediately got the message and left.

He reached for his laptop, planning to work until Katherine awoke. But, as the minutes ticked past, he found it impossible to concentrate on the bids being put in place for the Smyth-Brown shares, something which should have had all his attention.

He sighed and closed the laptop. Hell, he'd have to check the contracts another day. It would be several months yet before the takeover was finalised and he could finally get his revenge on the man who had discarded his mother.

He had time.

His fervour for the fight would come back as soon as his new wife had become less of a distraction. Sun, sea, sand and lots of mind-blowing sex would cure this strange *ennui*.

His gaze landed back on Katherine, who had contorted herself into another uncomfortable-looking shape. He could smell her. The tantalising earthy aroma sent another unwelcome surge of arousal through his system.

She huffed and shifted, drawing her knees up and her chin down to snuggle tighter into the seat's headrest, almost as if trying to protect herself from something. Her eyelids flickered with dreams, her brows furrowed and her lips pursed into a tight line, her breathing becoming rapid suggesting, whatever the dreams were, they weren't happy or benign.

The shaft of guilt hit more forcefully. He dismissed it. She looked healthier than she had when she'd come to his office and told him of the pregnancy. A week in paradise would be good for her.

He tilted his head to one side to study her, while ignoring the tightness in his chest at the thought of what might be causing her unpleasant dreams.

Surely her nightmares had to be due to the uncomfortable position she was trying to sleep in? Nothing more disturbing than that. Even though it would be torture for him, she was clearly too tired for them to satisfy this hunger tonight.

He undid his seatbelt and approached her. Clasping her shoulder, he rocked her gently. 'Katherine, wake up and I'll show you to the bedroom.'

When she didn't stir, he tried again.

She shook her head, moaned and turned away from him.

'Damn,' he whispered. She really was shattered.

Unclipping her seatbelt, which had become tangled around her hips, he hooked one arm under her bent knees, the other across her back and scooped her up against his chest.

Her cheek nestled against his collarbone, her body soft and pliant and satisfyingly substantial in his arms, her warm breath tickling the skin under his chin. Heat gathered and throbbed in eddying waves in his groin, adding to the torture as he carried her through the darkened cabin and opened the narrow door to the master bedroom.

The hostess had turned down the bed, and a night light embedded in the headboard had been switched on, casting an eerie glow. But, as Jack deposited his cargo in the middle of the smooth satin comforter, Katherine's eyelids fluttered open. Trapped in her emerald gaze, her pupils dark and unfocussed, his breath squeezed his lungs. And his heart hammered against his ribs in hard, heavy thuds.

Thoughts of taking advantage of her drowsy, semi-conscious state bombarded his tortured body. He imagined joining her on the bed, stripping off her clothing, undoing his trousers to free the strident erection and thrusting heavily into the tight, wet heat.

But then her hand reached up to cradle the taut muscle in his cheek, the gentle touch soothing the rampant thoughts—as if he were a wild beast and she a fairy-tale maiden come to rescue him from his own depravity. Before he had a chance to make sense of the ludicrous notion, her fingertip stroked the jagged scar.

His heartbeat slowed, every part of his being focussed on that consoling, feather-light caress, and for one terrifying moment he almost believed it would cure the pain of his past.

'Does it still hurt?' she asked, her voice thick with sleep, her faced softened by the dream-like quality of someone who was not fully aware of what they were saying or doing.

He shook his head, but the relentless, insistent desire shifted, swept along by something a great deal more disturbing… Longing.

'Who did it?' she asked, still caressing the torn, ugly flesh, the symbol of how defenceless he'd once been.

'The man I thought was my father,' Jack said as the truth released from his chest in a guttural whisper.

Anguish shadowed her eyes, the glint of moisture reflecting in the half-light and making him aware of the gold flecks in the emerald-green. But then she blinked and a single tear dripped from the corner of her eye to roll down the side of her face. 'I hate him,' she said.

Shock washed through him like acid as his heart clamoured and roared, the desire returning in a heady rush but driven this time by the brutal yearning.

He grasped her consoling fingers and dragged them away from the ruined flesh. He levered himself off the bed. Her gaze remained riveted to his, conveying emotions he didn't want to see, didn't even want to acknowledge, but could feel turning the weight in his chest into a ten-ton slab of reinforced concrete. 'Go back to sleep, Katherine. I'll see you in the morning.'

He left the room, closed the door behind him and headed into the other bedroom. Not caring any more about the torturous desire still throbbing in his groin.

Because he had a much bigger problem to deal with now. How the hell was he going to lift this concrete slab off his chest while spending a week in paradise with the woman who had dumped it there in the first place?

CHAPTER ELEVEN

KATIE SHIELDED HER EYES against the early-morning sunlight glittering on the turquoise blue of the lagoon. A lagoon which stretched for miles towards the horizon in every direction—literally a vision of paradise.

A salt-scented breeze moved through the palm trees that fringed the beach, adding a hushed rustle to the tranquil day. The translucent sea lapped against the shoreline in desultory waves. Standing on the bedroom terrace of the stunning steel-and-glass structure that was Jack's house on the island, she wondered where her so-called husband was.

Is he avoiding me?

She'd awoken yesterday, after eleven hours virtually comatose, when the private jet had touched down in Malé at midday. She and Jack had been driven by limousine from the airport through the colonial town to the port, where a motor launch had waited to whisk them across the water towards the Ari Atoll and Wolfe Maldives' private island.

One thing she remembered clearly was waking up in the plane's bedroom, alone, strange dreams still intruding on her consciousness—of Jack, his face tense, cautious and wary, shock and brutal sadness clouding his eyes. Even now, twenty-four hours later, she could still feel the texture of his scar against her fingertips, the warm skin ridged and torn. She gripped the balcony railing. Had she touched him in her sleep? Had he carried her into the plane's bedroom?

The man I thought was my father.

His gruff whisper murmured through her memory, as it had so many times on their strangely stilted journey from the airport to the island, and during the afternoon and evening she'd spent alone in the house after he had disappeared with some excuse about having to work.

Had he *actually* confided in her? The words had been full of bitterness but tinged with vulnerability— as if his answer had been wrenched from his very soul. Or had she imagined the dream-like encounter on the flight?

She had considered asking him about it during the limousine transfer to the port in Malé and the breathtaking journey on the motor launch across the vast blue sea. But he had been preoccupied ever since they'd left the airport, either talking on his phone, reading contracts or tapping out messages on his laptop. In fact, she'd barely exchanged two words with him since she'd walked into the jet's lounge area, feeling well-rested but still confused and on edge, to find him waiting for her, his watchful gaze holding so many secrets.

He'd been tense, brooding, the withdrawn quality

telling her louder than words to keep her distance. And, even though she had decided any intimacy between them would be dangerous, she had missed the mocking, dominating—and impossibly hot—man who had invited her on this trip in the first place.

When they'd arrived at Wolfe Maldives—which had appeared like a tropical oasis in the midst of the never-ending blue, the main building a white wood-framed colonial palace which blended into the palm trees—Jack had disappeared with a team of his assistants and the resort's managerial staff.

So this was going to be a working honeymoon, then? Funny he hadn't mentioned that when she'd been freaking out about it at dinner three nights ago.

After he'd left her, she had ignored the pang of regret and concentrated on the tour she was given of the stunning facilities: two swimming pools, a fully equipped gym and several different dining areas, including one on a floating platform in the lagoon, draped in white linen that billowed in the breeze. There were tennis courts, a spa and a seasports area equipped with everything from jet-skis to paddle boards and snorkelling equipment, plus a dive hut where a diving instructor had offered to introduce her to the wonders of the reef that surrounded the island during her stay.

Then she'd been driven in a golf buggy to the Owner's Cottage on the other side of the island. Whoever had named it a cottage had clearly been delusional. Cariad was a cottage. The two-storey stone and glass structure perched on the edge of a white sand cove was nothing short of a palace.

After exploring the five-bedroom house and its grounds while the staff unpacked their luggage, she had been served a three-course meal on the veranda by the charmingly discreet staff…while Jack had been conspicuous by his absence.

After watching the sinking sun create a sensational light show of pinks and oranges and flaming reds from the jetty, she'd headed to bed, feeling anxious but also lonely.

Where was he?

Did Jack plan to join her in the master bedroom tonight? How would she feel if he woke her? Should she have stayed up to greet him when he finished his work commitments? What was her role here? Because she had no idea.

But, when she'd woken this morning, the bed beside her had been empty. And, after she'd checked the property to find another one of the bedrooms slept in but still no sign of Jack, the bewilderment and loneliness turned to agitation.

She frowned, the stunning, sun-drenched scenery doing nothing to dispel the knots in her belly that had been forming since yesterday.

Now she knew a little of how Mrs Rochester must have felt—the unwanted bride hidden away and going insane in the attic. Albeit this was a luxury paradise attic where every possible amenity waited to distract her from the fact her new husband wanted to have nothing to do with her…

Not that they were a *real* husband and wife, she

told herself staunchly, but still it felt as if she'd been brought to the Maldives under false pretences. What had become of the man who'd teased and tormented her, who had insisted the heat between them needed to be dealt with? And what exactly was she supposed to do about the fact she was starting to want it dealt with too?

She breathed in the clean, salty air, the sun warming her skin. Was it possible that what had happened in the plane's bedroom hadn't been a dream? Was it behind his disappearing act? Was Jack running scared now?

And, if he was, what did she want to do about it?

Find him. Because avoidance clearly isn't working. It's just making me more insane.

They had six more days together in paradise and six months until the baby was born. She was tired of running—not just from the insistent desire, but the strange connection they seemed to share. She needed to discover if what he'd told her about the scar was true. Because that furious jolt of compassion for him, and the brutalised boy he'd been, was still there throbbing under her breast bone like an open wound.

Maybe the sensible thing would be to forget about what she thought he'd said to her. It would be horribly embarrassing if she'd conjured the whole scenario up from some desperate desire buried deep in her psyche. Always a possibility.

But she'd never been sensible when it came to relationships. She'd always been reckless, impulsive and passionate. It was how she'd survived on her own for years, especially after her grandmother's death. Why she'd been in Jack Wolfe's penthouse that night at her sister's request. And probably one of the reasons why she had agreed to this marriage in the first place.

Her decision to sign on Jack's dotted line had never been as simple or straightforward as she'd wanted to believe—it hadn't just been about the unplanned pregnancy or her desperation to get out from a mountain of debt and turn her business into a going concern. It had also been about that fierce, intense desire in Jack's eyes whenever he looked at her and the strange sense that he saw her in a way no other man ever had.

Maybe that intense yearning was simply about sex for him, but it was about more than that for her. And it was time she acknowledged it and found a way forward.

Striding back into the bedroom, she donned one of the designer swimsuits that had been brought for her. The one-piece had a fifties vibe, cut high on the leg with a criss-cross design across her chest that lifted her breasts, while the vibrant letter-box-red matched the russet tones of her hair. Although the costume didn't show as much flesh as the bikinis, it flattered her hour-glass shape and gave her a confidence she needed.

She tied up the unruly locks of her hair in a casual knot, slathered all the places she could reach in sun lotion then added a pair of denim cut-offs, some beach sandals and a lose-fitting white linen shirt to her ensemble. She wasn't about to throw herself at the man if he didn't want her. But she refused to allow him to dictate all the terms of their marriage. He'd dictated enough already.

After downing a cup of mint tea and a bowl of the home-baked granola and fresh fruit laid out by the invisible staff on the stunning black quartz breakfast bar, she headed out onto the stone pool-terrace.

She squinted into the sunshine. It had to be getting close to ten o'clock. She'd been up for over an hour and Jack was still nowhere in sight.

He's definitely avoiding me.

Her heartbeat ticked into her throat, her breathing the only sound as silence greeted her.

A pair of sandy deck shoes had been left beside one of the loungers. *Bingo.*

The oval pool sparkled in the sunlight, fringed by large planters of exotic tropical flowers and shrubs. On one side of the beach beyond was the wooden jetty from where she had watched the sunset the night before, a gleaming motor launch and a couple of jet-skis docked at the end. As she scanned the cove, her gaze caught on a glimmer of movement about a mile out, coming around the point on the other side of the bay.

She shielded her eyes. Was that a dolphin?

But as the sleek shape drew closer she recognised it as a man swimming, or rather powering, across the lagoon in fast, efficient strokes, his dark hair and tanned skin contrasting sharply with the bright, translucent turquoise of the sea.

Jack! My invisible husband.

The knots in her stomach grew, and her thigh

muscles quivered as he strode out of the water and onto the beach below the terrace. Dragging off a pair of goggles, he picked up a towel left on the sand and scrubbed himself dry in brusque strokes.

She stepped back into the shade of one of the flowering scrubs, the knots in her stomach tightening.

His muscular arms and wide shoulders glistened in the sunshine, the wet swimming shorts clinging to his thighs and hanging from his lean waist, displaying the ridge of his hip flexors. After rubbing the towel through the short strands of hair, he dragged off the shorts.

The last of her confusion and irritation dried in her throat, turning to something that felt uncomfortably like shock… And awe. It was the first time she'd seen him naked since he had disrobed in the grey, shadowy light of Cariad's storm-tossed bedroom.

Even though he stood a good twenty feet away, the bright sunshine made the view a lot clearer. The tickle of panic in the back of her throat—at the spectacular sight of Jack Wolfe stark-naked—was nothing compared to the flood of sensation working its way up her torso as she took her time devouring every detail—the tan demarcation line on his hip, the bush of black hair framing the long column of his sex before he hooked the towel around his waist.

Apparently Jack worked out… A lot. Something she hadn't registered the last time she'd seen him naked in the furore of need. During her lonely granola breakfast, Katie had rehearsed a script of all the things she wanted to say to Jack when she finally located him. But as he groped around on the sand, then picked up a pair of spectacles, every last word of those imagined opening gambits were whipped away on the breeze along with the last of her temper. And all that was left was the knot in her throat, the sultry insistent ache in her abdomen and the clatter of her heart beating against her ribs.

Jack wore glasses. How had she not known that?

As he headed towards the house with his head down, running his fingers through the cropped hair, she had a sudden vivid memory of the night they'd met and his unfocussed gaze as he'd glared at her. How myopic was he? Because it had seemed for a minute as if he'd had to use touch to locate his spectacles.

As he drew close, she stepped out from behind the plant.

Show time.

His head rose and he stopped dead. Tension rippled through his body, but even behind the lenses of his glasses—which had darkened in the sun— she could see something fierce yet guarded flash across his face. Surprise and desire, certainly, but also a wary alertness.

And suddenly the last of her doubts disappeared. He *had* said those words to her about the scar in the jet two nights ago. It hadn't been a dream. Was that why he had been avoiding her?

Compassion blindsided her.

'Katherine,' he murmured, managing to temper his reaction sooner than she could. 'You're awake?'

He sounded surprised as his possessive gaze took in everything, from her scarlet toenails in the open sandals to the damp tendrils sticking to her neck.

'I've been up for an hour,' she said, determined not to get sidetracked by the hum in her abdomen or the electrifying awareness that pulsed around them.

'Why didn't you come back last night?' she asked.

'I did,' he said, deliberately misinterpreting her question. 'You were asleep.'

'Don't lie.' She crossed her arms over her chest. 'You've been avoiding me, Jack. Why?'

'Because I've been busy.' Jack ground out the words, struggling to keep his voice firm and even when everything inside him was clamouring to touch her, to taste her, to scoop her into his arms, tear off the shorts that barely covered her butt, tug down the swimsuit peeking out from beneath her shirt and fill his mouth with the taste of salt and apples on her breasts.

Hell, how could he still want her so much after swimming for miles and burying himself in work yesterday to keep the hell away from her? Shouldn't this hunger have faded by now, or at least become a lot more manageable? Especially as she knew things about him now he didn't want anyone to know.

When they had arrived yesterday, he'd only planned to stay away from her for an hour or two, but the yearning had only become more insistent as the afternoon had worn on.

He needed to be able to control it, or he might blurt out something else. And he already hated that she'd caught him without his lenses in. The heavy glasses always made him feel weak, reminding him of the child he'd been, trying to dodge fists he couldn't see.

'Doing what?' she asked.

'Surely you can't be bored already?' he countered, damned if he was going to answer any more of her questions.

'We're supposed to be here on our honeymoon, Jack,' she countered right back. 'Don't you think the staff will find it odd if all you do while we're here is work…?' Her gaze dipped. 'And swim.'

Of course they did. He'd seen the confusion on the resort manager's face when he'd insisted on spending all afternoon and evening going over the specs for the press launch in a month's time.

'They're well paid not to question what I do,' he muttered, making the implication clear that she had also been well paid not to question him and not to confront him.

He was damned if he'd be found wanting by someone he'd paid to be his wife…

'Are you avoiding me because of what you told me about your scar?'

The gentle enquiry—and the astuteness behind it—shocked him so much, he couldn't hide his reaction.

Her gaze darkened, piercing the protective layer he'd always kept around his emotions.

'So you remember that?' he growled.

The sick nausea in his stomach was nothing to the surge of fury making his chest hurt. This was why he had never confided in anyone. Why the hell had he confided in her? Giving her ammunition against him? It made no sense, and the compassion in her gaze shook him to his core.

She nodded, the emerald eyes sparking with a sympathy he despised.

He didn't need or want her pity. He'd made a staggering success of his life, despite his squalid and violent beginnings—maybe even because of them.

'I hope he paid for what he did,' she said, her voice breaking slightly, as if she were holding back tears.

'He had his reasons.' He had no desire to talk about the man who he had feared and loved in equal measure until he had realised Harry Wolfe had never wanted him any more than Daniel Smyth had.

Her eyes widened, the shocked distress calling to something deep inside him that he had no intention of acknowledging.

'What possible reason could he have for mutilating a child?' she whispered.

'He discovered I wasn't his son,' Jack said, his thumb stroking the ragged flesh—until he became aware of what he was doing and dropped his hand.

Instead of ending the conversation as he'd hoped, Katie simply stepped towards him, invading the personal space he so desperately needed.

'That's not a reason, Jack,' she said softly. 'To hurt someone who loved him.'

'I didn't love him.' The denial scraped over the jagged boulder which had formed in his throat. 'He

was a violent, abusive bastard to me and my mother
for as long as I can remember. I was glad I wasn't
his. It gave me an excuse to leave that place and
never look back.'

Except he *had* looked back, many times, the brutal shame still lurking in some dark, unbidden corner
of his heart. The picture he'd tried so hard to sup-
press flickered into his memory of his mother's face
the last time he'd seen her. The once soft, beautiful
skin had been strained and tear-streaked, puffy with
exhaustion, desperation and the drugs she'd used to
forget as the paramedics had arrived.

*Don't tell them who did this, honey. Please don't,
or he'll be even angrier.*

Who had really been the monster? The man who
had destroyed his mother, or the boy who had forced
her into his arms then left to save himself?

Stepping closer still, Katherine placed her warm
palm on his scarred cheek. 'I'm glad you got out.'

He jerked back, jolted out of the miserable rem-
iniscence. Grasping her wrist, he pulled her hand
from his face. 'Don't…' he said.

She stared at him, her eyes bold and unashamed.

Vicious sensation prickled across his sun-
warmed shoulders and sank deep into his abdomen,
the need as swift and visceral as it had ever been.

To hell with it. There was no containing it. And
he'd be damned if he'd even try any longer.

'Don't touch me,' he said, his thumb pressing
against the inside of her wrist, feeling the rampant
pulse, her instinctive response only making the

swift, visceral need all the more brutal. 'Not unless you've changed your mind about sleeping with me.'

He expected her to retreat, to fall back on the lie she'd told him before they'd arrived on the island, but instead her expression remained open and unguarded, the hunger clear and unashamed. He dragged her into his embrace, until her soft curves pressed against the hard line of his body.

She didn't flinch, didn't fight him, her breath coming in ragged pants. Then she licked her lips and the fierce arousal turned to pain, his yearning flesh hardening against her belly. He breathed in a lungful of her smell, the rich, earthy scent beneath the aroma of sun cream and sweat sending his senses into overdrive.

'Admit you want me, Katherine,' he demanded. 'And I'll stop avoiding you.'

Shocked arousal dilated the vivid green of her irises to black. 'I want you.'

His raw groan echoed across the pool terrace as he lifted her into his arms. 'Wrap your legs around my waist.'

She grasped his shoulders and obeyed him as he captured her mouth, devouring her in greedy bites—the way he'd dreamed of doing for days. He thrust his tongue deep to capture her startled sobs and marched across the pool terrace and into the house.

All that mattered now was sinking into her again, driving them both to oblivion and claiming what was his so he could forget the things she'd wrenched out of him.

She didn't know him—not really. And he didn't want her to know him.

This was all he wanted from her, the only connection that mattered to him.

This is dangerous, and you know it.

Katie's brain tried to engage, but the rush of adrenaline and the swell of tenderness was unstoppable as Jack strode into the house and took the stairs to the mezzanine.

Her heart pumped hard, sensation spreading through her body like wildfire. He held her easily, as if she weighed nothing at all, while his kisses devoured her neck, her collarbone.

At last, he dumped her onto the huge, canopied bed where she'd slept alone the night before.

A glass wall looked out onto the bay, the diamond-white sand giving way to the iridescent turquoise sea. She lay dazed and disorientated as he dragged off the towel. His arousal jutted out from his belly, thick and long and aggressive, somehow. Her gaze lifted to the tortured expression on his face that matched the giddy, relentless desperation in her heart.

Why had she insisted on provoking him, even knowing the danger? But she couldn't look away from the tight, barely leashed need on his face and the thick jut of his erection as he joined her on the bed. Pushing her legs apart with one insistent thigh, he dragged her shorts off. Then he groaned, thumbing her turgid nipples through her swimsuit.

'A one-piece?' he murmured. 'Just kill me now.'

A chuckle rose up her torso at his look of consternation, but then strangled in her throat as he lifted the swollen flesh over the top of the suit and traced his tongue around one yearning peak.

'Tell me if it hurts...' He growled as he gathered the hardening peak between his lips.

'It doesn't!' she gasped as he suckled with unbearable tenderness.

She rose off the bed as the drawing sensation arrowed into the molten spot between her thighs, the ache intensifying.

She squirmed and writhed, the pleasure too much and yet not enough as he feasted on one nipple then the other.

She grasped his head to drag him closer and dislodged the glasses.

He swore softly and levered himself off the bed. 'Wait there. And take that damn one-piece off. I need to get my lenses in,' he said. 'I'll be damned if I do this blind.'

She lay on the bed, trying to gather her wits, or what was left of them. But her panting breaths only made her feel more light-headed, more disorientated.

She should call a halt to this—forget the harsh sadness in his eyes when he had told her about his past. But something stopped her, and she knew it was a great deal more than just the promise of having the desperate hunger finally fed.

She still lay there, the emotions churning in her gut, her heart pummelling her ribs when he returned. The glasses were gone—the intimidating erection wasn't.

She drew herself into a sitting position. 'Perhaps we shouldn't…'

'I think we both know it's too late for that,' he cut her off, then grasped her wrist and dragged her off the bed until they stood toe to toe. She'd lost her sandals on the way into the house, her bare toes sinking into the deep carpet, but his urgent erection was nowhere near as overwhelming as the turmoil in his eyes.

He cupped her cheek with a shocking gentleness that weakened her knees. He threaded his fingers into her hair and the loose knot tumbled down.

'We need this,' he said.

She opened her mouth, wanting to deny it, but then he placed his mouth on the pummelling pulse by her collarbone. The protest lodged in her throat as he dragged off her shirt… And the words that would release her from the silken web imprisoning her refused to come.

He peeled the suit from her body in one forceful glide.

In the half-light of her granny's cottage at nightfall, her body had been sheltered, obscured, but here the glaring sunlight spotlighted every flaw, every imperfection. But he didn't seem to notice, his urgent hands stroking her to fever pitch.

At last he found her sex and began to torture and torment with insistent fingers.

He sank to his knees and cupped her hips before prising her legs apart. But a position that should have made him less dominant only made him more so as his gaze locked with hers and his tongue trailed up the inside of her thigh.

She shivered, sinking her fingers into his damp hair. She shuddered as he lapped and lathed, finally parting the curls hiding her sex to lick at her clitoris at last. The swell built, staggering in its intensity, shattering the last of her resistance and charging through her body on a tidal wave of stunned pleasure.

As the brutal orgasm subsided, she stood, shaking, exhausted. He rose to his feet to tower over her. 'It's too late to escape me, Red. You're mine now, in the only way that matters.'

She should reject the brutal cynicism, the claim of ownership. She would never belong to any man— but she no longer had the strength to resist it.

Pressing her back on the bed, he climbed over her. Scooping up her legs, he lifted her knees, spreading her wide open for the brutal invasion. He anchored the huge erection deep in one slow, mind-altering thrust, impaling her to the hilt.

Her body contracted, struggling to adjust to the thick invasion, while dragging him deeper still as she clung to his broad shoulders. He began to move in a harsh, relentless rhythm, his breathing as ragged as her own.

The pleasure rose again with brutal speed, furious, overwhelming, rushing towards her on another wave. Her fingers dug into broad, sweat-slicked muscles, trying to concentrate on the physical. But the turmoil in her chest refused to subside as the tsunami bowled over her again, and she heard him shout out as he collapsed on top of her.

* * *

Katie lay dazed for what felt like an eternity, Jack's shoulder digging into her collarbone.

She drew in a shuddering breath and let it out again, waiting as the serene wave of afterglow faded into something hollow and deeply unsettling.

Groaning, Jack pulled out of her at last. She felt the loss of connection instantly. After gathering the last remnants of her sanity around her, the flight instinct that had deserted her so comprehensively minutes ago returned in a rush. She edged to the side of the bed.

He'd torn the swimming costume when he'd dragged it off her, so she scooped up the shorts. Embarrassment heated her cheeks as she tugged them on, forced to wear them without underwear.

'Hey, where are you going?'

The gruff voice behind her had her glancing over her shoulder.

He reclined in the bed, the white sheet lying low on his hips, one arm slung behind his head, the other flat against his stomach, a watchful, questioning light in those crystal-blue eyes.

Her thighs twitched and her sex pulsed, making her aware of the soreness where he had plundered her so convincingly.

'For a walk,' she said, desperate to get away from him and the brutal feeling of connection.

He wasn't the boy who had been scarred by a violent stepfather. He was a forceful, dynamic and scarily controlled man who was going to become a father himself but had no intention of becoming part of his child's life. Perhaps his past explained why he didn't *want* to be a father, but it also meant he was less likely to change his mind.

As she went to stand, he lurched across the bed and grasped her wrist.

She lifted her hand, trying to wrestle it free of his grasp. 'Jack, I have to…'

'Don't go,' he said, the request cutting her protest off at the knees. Her hand dropped to the bed, still manacled in his. 'Stay.'

'I don't think that's a good idea,' she said, but she could hear the foolish hesitation in her own voice. What was wrong with her? What was she hoping was going to happen?

And how could the yearning still be there? Now they'd fed the hunger?

Except it didn't feel fed…not even close. Her gaze lingered on the smooth contours of his chest, the bunch of muscle and sinew, the faded ink.

'Why not?' he asked, but then his lips twitched, as if he were holding back a grin. 'We're on our honeymoon.'

'Yes, but it's not a real honeymoon,' she countered, still trying to cling to what was left of her common sense. Even as a niggling voice at the back of her head kept saying… *Why not stay and find out if there could be more?*

Hadn't they both been running for too long? Didn't she owe it to their child, his child, at least to try?

He fascinated her—his facets, his mood swings and all the carefully guarded secrets that lurked behind his eyes. She was attracted like a moth to a flame, the danger only making him more intriguing.

He had given her something this afternoon, a small glimpse of himself. How could that be bad?

'Right now, it feels real enough,' he murmured, his voice a rough burr of sound that seemed to scrape across her skin like sandpaper.

Sitting up, he turned her body until they sat together on the side of the bed, his thighs bracketing her hips, one large hand resting on the barely-there curve of her belly, his chest hot against her back. He hooked her hair behind her ear to expose her neck and nuzzled the sensitive skin over the galloping pulse.

'Come on, Katherine. We might as well make the most of this chemistry while it lasts,' he murmured. 'What have we got to lose?'

'But what if it never ends?' she asked, then realised how gauche that sounded when he chuckled.

'You don't have a lot of sexual experience, do you, Red?'

She shifted round, trying to see his face. 'I have enough,' she said indignantly.

He skimmed his finger down her nose, the gesture gentle and mocking, but also strangely approving.

'This won't last,' he said, his eyes flaring with fierce need. 'Nothing this good ever does.' The echo of regret made her heart pulse hard.

'But this wasn't supposed to be real,' she finally managed to blurt out as the heat gathered and twisted while his lips roamed over her skin, making her tender sex ache all over again. 'That was the deal.'

Did he know what he was asking of her? What he was risking?

His soft chuckle echoed across her nape before he bit softly into her earlobe.

'Deals can be renegotiated,' he said. 'If both parties are amenable.'

His hand drifted beneath the open fly of her shorts, his fingers delving, exploring.

She jolted as he found her clitoris, still wet, swollen and far too sensitive.

She gripped his wrist, trying to stop the devious, devastating caresses that were turning her into a mass of desperation all over again. How did he do that? So easily? How did he make her forget all her priorities, make her stop thinking and only feel?

His hand stilled, but his voice still held the hint of amusement and the purr of command as it whispered across her neck. 'Shh, Katherine. Let me prove to you how good this is.'

Her grip loosened, her head dropping against his shoulder as the last of her objections drifted away on the tide of pleasure, the pulse of emotion. He circled the slick flesh—tantalising, tormenting. Tortured sobs issued from her lips as a cloud covered the sun and she saw their reflection in the window glass.

His big body surrounded hers, his tanned hand working against the open fly of her shorts with ruthless efficiency. His mouth suckled and nipped at the pulse in her neck, but the sensation concentrated in her sex. His other hand covered one naked breast, moulding the round weight then rolling and plucking the engorged nipple, sending more darts to her core. She quivered and moaned as her back arched, pushing herself instinctively into the devastating caresses—wanting, needing, more.

'Please... I...' she whispered, begging him to take the ache away.

'That's it, Red. Come for me again,' he demanded, just as his fingers found the epicentre at her core. The ache exploded, the earthquake of pleasure too pure, too strong.

She flew again, bowing back, crying out, the climax overwhelming her. And knew, whatever came next, she couldn't run from him any more.

Later, much later—after a shared shower, an exhilarating ride out into the bay on the motor launch, a meal on the terrace delivered on mopeds by two waiters who disappeared as soon as they had served it and another tumultuous and exhausting lovemaking session—Katie lay in Jack's arms again and listened to the slow murmur of his breathing.

Somehow she'd agreed to make this a real honeymoon... Or rather, real enough.

The sun dropped towards the sea, the kaleidoscope of red and orange reflected off the dark water, but felt nowhere near as dramatic as the conflagration in her chest.

Had she done the right thing, giving in to her fascination with Jack? How could she not...? When she was so tired of fighting it? Tired of pretending the need didn't exist? And tired of denying the compassion she felt for the boy who lurked inside the man?

'Consider the terms of our contract renegotiated, Katherine,' he murmured against her nape, his hand absently caressing her stomach where their baby grew.

Her heart bumped into her throat.

But when he relaxed behind her, his breathing becoming deep and even against her back, it took her for ever to fall asleep too. Because she knew she'd just taken a step into unguarded, unknowable territory. A step into no man's land, despite all her best intentions. Just as she had done when she had left her father's house all those years ago.

On one level it terrified her. The only question now was, could she be strong enough, smart enough, patient enough, resilient enough to find out if Jack might one day take that step with her... or would it be another step she would have to take alone?

CHAPTER TWELVE

One month later

'WHERE IS MRS WOLFE?' Jack demanded of Katherine's housekeeper, Mrs Goulding, as he marched into her office in the basement. He'd searched the Mayfair house and couldn't find his wife.

'She had an appointment in Harley Street this afternoon,' Mrs Goulding replied.

The anticipation—which had been expanding under his breastbone and making it virtually impossible for him to concentrate on the endless conference calls he'd had that day to finalise the last of the Smyth-Brown takeover—popped like an overblown balloon.

'Is everything okay?' he asked, his impatience—because she hadn't been here when he had arrived, as she normally would be—turning into something else.

He'd left her in the early hours of the morning to return to his penthouse after spending most of the night ravishing her. She'd been deeply asleep, which wasn't like her at all. She'd been working hard recently on her new business after taking the decision to open a small shop in Knightsbridge to make her online bakery brand more visible.

It had been three weeks since they'd returned from their so-called honeymoon in the Maldives and the need hadn't abated one bit. If anything it had got considerably worse. But what was perhaps a great deal more concerning was the unsettled, agitated feeling that had begun to assail him whenever Katherine was out of his sight.

He had become obsessed with his trophy wife.

The rest of the week in the Maldives—after she had agreed to sleep with him—had been nothing short of idyllic. But not for the reasons he would have assumed.

She had been as eager as he to indulge their sexual connection. In fact, she had thrown herself into it with as much enthusiasm as he had. They'd made love on the beach, by the pool and on the power launch while anchored off one of the deserted islands on the atoll, after a morning spent snorkelling on the reef. And every night, every morning and many of the hours in between, when he'd woken dreaming of her, to find her body curved into his, wet and eager as he woke her.

She hadn't denied him once, had even initiated the contact on more than one occasion, her tentative, adorably artless attitude to sex becoming almost as demanding and adventurous as his by the time the trip had ended.

He'd remained living in the penthouse—to get the distance he needed—and she hadn't objected.

He'd almost been disappointed when she had failed even to comment on his decision. While he still had his clothes in the penthouse, and despite his best intentions to ensure he continued to live his own life, he spent every night with her in Grosvenor Square before returning home, often in the early hours of the morning, to wash and change before heading to his office.

Keeping his belongings in the penthouse had become inconvenient, so he'd been forced to move some items into the house here. Again, she hadn't commented, hadn't pushed. She probed occasionally about his past, his childhood, but had allowed him to deflect those questions easily. And, when she had made offhand comments about the baby, the pregnancy, she hadn't pressed when he had failed to engage.

He should have felt fine. Their life was just as he wanted it, just as he had envisaged it when proposing this marriage.

So why wasn't he content?

Perhaps because it wasn't just the sex that had captivated him since they had returned. He also enjoyed the conversations in the evenings when he arrived from the office to find her in her study, video calling her team or strategising with her marketing manager, or in the kitchen, rustling up something delicious after giving the chef a night off.

During those conversations he had discovered exactly how smart, erudite and witty Katherine was, her intelligence and single-mindedness a match for his own. They'd argued about politics, culture and sport, and had talked at length about her business plans and her long-term goals. She'd come to him with queries, questions, hiring problems and strategy suggestions, and he'd been happy to help.

And she'd quizzed him about his own business. Because he had deflected any personal questions about his childhood, he had refrained from asking about hers, even though he was hopelessly curious now about *her* past. He wanted to know how she had survived after being kicked out of her home at seventeen. And how she had managed to retain such an optimistic and surprisingly naive attitude towards the generosity of the human spirit when he most certainly had not.

And why couldn't he stop thinking about her even now?

It would be pathetic, if it weren't so disturbing.

'I don't believe anything is wrong, sir,' the housekeeper said. 'It may be a scheduled appointment.'

It may be? What if it wasn't? Surely she would have told him if it was routine? She'd mentioned her antenatal appointments in the past. And he'd made a point of not engaging with the information. He didn't want to give her false hopes where his involvement with the child was concerned. But, even so, he knew she would have said something if she was going to be late home. They had a ball to attend tonight, which was why he had arrived home early... That and the fact he seemed less and less able to stay at the office when he knew she awaited him at the house.

Katherine had been tired last night, after returning from a concert they'd attended at the O2. He'd sourced the box seats because he'd caught her dancing to one of the famous band's songs a few weeks ago, and had watched her unobserved, charmed by the sight. He should have left her alone last night and returned to the penthouse after dropping her off, but he hadn't been able to stop himself, the excuse of ensuring she was okay having morphed into something urgent and unstoppable once they'd got to her bedroom.

The guilt that had been sitting at the back of his mind all day tightened its claws around his neck now like a malevolent beast.

Her subdued mood last night had left him holding her a little tighter as he waited for her to drift to sleep in the early hours of the morning. And it had been harder than ever to pull himself out of the bed and leave her to return to his own place.

Deepening their relationship was not part of the deal. And not something he wanted. Because it would only complicate things when he had to let her go. But perhaps he should have stayed with her last night.

'How was she this morning?' he barked, not quite able to keep the frantic urgency out of his voice.

Damn. If he'd woken up with her he would know the answer to this question. Why hadn't he stayed?

'She seemed tired, Mr Wolfe,' the housekeeper said. 'But then she had an early morning meeting, so she had to leave an hour ahead of her usual schedule.'

'She... What time did she get up?' he rasped, the malevolent beast beating on his ribs now.

'Six o'clock.'

He swore under his breath, the guilt and panic turning to anger. She hadn't fallen asleep until two a.m. Why hadn't she told him she had to be up so early? He wouldn't have kept her up half the night if she had.

'Is there a problem, Mr Wolfe?' the housekeeper asked.

Yes, there's a damn problem. My wife may be seriously unwell and it's my fault. And her fault, for not telling me to leave her alone.

His mind reeled, the unguarded feelings starting to overwhelm him.

'No,' he snapped. He headed back through the house towards the entrance hall, tugging his phone out of his pocket en route and speed-dialling Katherine's number. But as he charged down the hallway, intending to drive straight to Harley Street, an echo of his phone's ring tone sounded.

He stopped in the entrance hall to see his wife standing by the front door.

'Katherine!' He charged towards her and grasped her shoulders as the panic surged. 'Are you okay? What were you doing at the doctor's?'

'Jack?' Her eyebrows launched up her forehead, but he could see the fatigue still shadowing her eyes. 'What are you doing here so early?' she said, apropos to absolutely nothing.

'I asked first,' he said. 'What's wrong?' He forced himself to stare at the slight mound of her stomach, which he had noticed more and more in the last few weeks whenever they made love. 'Is it the pregnancy?'

'Nothing's wrong,' she said, but he could hear the weary note in her voice as she tried to shrug off his hold. His grip tightened.

'Jack, you need to let me go,' she said with strained patience, as if he were holding her for the fun of it. As if his head wasn't starting to explode. Why the hell couldn't she give him a straight answer? Was something seriously wrong and she didn't want to tell him?

'My phone's ringing and I need to answer it,' she added, cutting through the flash flood of disaster scenarios in his head.

He cursed, letting go of her with one hand, to fish his own phone out of his pocket and turn it off.

The confusion in her eyes darkened. 'Why were you calling me?'

'Why the hell do you think?' he shouted, frustration and fury pushing up his throat to party with the guilt and panic. 'You're always at home when I get here in the evening. You weren't here, and then Mrs Goulding told me you were at the doctor's and I—'

'It was a routine scan,' she interrupted.

The panic babbling stopped so abruptly, his fingers loosened.

She shrugged out of his hold.

His temper ignited. 'Well, that's just great!' he said, pushing the guilt back down his throat with an effort. 'Why didn't you tell me you had an appointment?' Had she planned to freak him out deliberately?

Was this some kind of dumb test? To push him into admitting she meant something to him? Something more than they'd originally agreed on?

Because of course she did. Maybe this arrangement had no future, but he'd been sleeping with her every night for over a month—hell, he'd even started to neglect his business so he could spend more time with her.

The endless meetings and problems he had to attend to, being available twenty-four-seven to his managers and advisors, had become a chore over the last three weeks. He had turned down a ton of business trips—had even chosen not to travel to the product launch in Tokyo of a new tech company he'd acquired last year when it had clashed with the opening of Katherine's shop. Because he hadn't been able to bear to spend forty-eight hours away from her.

Of course, he could have insisted as per their original contract, that she travel with him. But he simply hadn't had the heart to tear her away from her business when she was clearly so excited about developing it.

And then there were their weekends, when he'd started to make excuses to be with her. He'd always worked at weekends in the past. But gradually, after they'd returned from the Maldives, he'd begun concocting reasons to contact her, spend quality time with her. And not just to coax her into bed. They had taken drives in the countryside, long walks in the park, watched movies in the house's basement cinema, or frolicked in the lap pool he'd had installed in the two-hundred-foot garden.

Yet another sign of how dependent on her company he had become.

He'd tried to convince himself it was still all about the sex—the quality time just an intriguing prelude to jumping each other. But this incessant need that never seemed to end—no matter how many times he took her, how many times they took each other—had forced him to realise that wasn't the whole truth. She meant something to him. Much more than she should. But instead of looking guilty or even contrite, she stared back at him now as if he'd lost the plot.

'Why would I tell you about the scan, Jack?' she asked with a weary resignation that made his ribs contract around his thundering heart. 'When you're not interested.'

She went to pass him, but he grabbed her arm. 'Wait a minute. What is that supposed to mean?'

'Why don't you figure it out?' she said, the sudden snap in her tone surprising him. He shook off the residual hum of guilt. *He* wasn't the one in the wrong here. She should have told him she had a doctor's appointment. So he hadn't had to find out from the housekeeper. End of.

'You think I don't care about your welfare?' he demanded, the turmoil of emotions making his anger surge. 'Of course I care. I care about you. A lot. *There*. Are you happy?'

But, instead of looking smug, her chin tucked into her chest as she sighed.

When her gaze lifted back to his, he could see the shocking sheen of tears. The sight punctured the self-righteous fury with the precision of a high velocity bullet, leaving shock in its wake.

'No, Jack,' she said, so quietly he almost couldn't hear her. 'I'm not happy.'

A single tear slipped from the corner of her eye before she could wipe it away with an impatient fist. And the shock reverberated in his chest like an earthquake.

She dug her teeth into her bottom lip to stop it trembling, her gaze bold and determined, but also somehow broken. The emerald-green, sparkling with all the tears she refused to shed, only crucified him more.

This was what he'd been determined to guard against—why he'd snuck out of her bed each night even though the desire to hold her, to keep her safe, had been all but overwhelming. Why he'd forced himself not to ask all the questions he wanted answers to about her father, her past, about the strong, clever teenager he wished he'd known back when they'd both been still too young to protect themselves.

And, because of that, he heard himself ask a question he knew he shouldn't want the answer to… but did.

'Why aren't you happy?'

Katie stared at her husband, her limbs saturated with exhaustion. The sight of him—strong and indomitable and hopelessly wary—was making sensation flutter and glow in her belly even now.

He'd taken off his jacket and tie, his short hair stuck up in spikes as if he'd run his fingers through it several times. His gaze roamed over her, his eyes searching and a little wild, as he pressed a warm hand to her shoulder then stroked his thumb down her arm.

The prickle of sensation which was always there when he touched her rolled through her. But with it came the fierce pulse of emotion she no longer had any control over.

She'd thrown herself into this relationship in the weeks since they had returned from the Maldives, forced the emotion down and let the heat take over so she could give them both time. To get to know each other, to feel comfortable. But as they'd begun to settle into a routine, the more Jack had let her see of that runaway boy who needed love the way she had, the harder it had been not to push, not to probe, not to beg for more.

Every time he made love to her with such fervour then left her sleeping alone. Every time they had a discussion about business, marketing or her latest cupcake recipe but he'd deflected any questions he deemed too personal. Every time she sent him an email with her latest schedule of antenatal appointments and scans but she got no response.

She blinked, the prickle of sensation turning to something deep, fluid and even more disturbing.

She didn't *want* to feel this way. Didn't want him to show her this side of himself. A caring, tender, nurturing side she was sure he didn't even realise he possessed. Because the more she saw of it, the more real their relationship seemed.

Like the time he'd caught her dancing in the kitchen and she'd seen the spontaneous, boyish smile curving his lips. Or the times he had suggested, more and more of late, that they do something together at the weekend, that he didn't need to work. Like the tension in his jaw she'd begun to notice whenever she yawned and he asked if she were okay. Or the leap of hunger and something more—something rich with relief and even joy— that turned his blue eyes to a rich cobalt when he came here each evening and found her.

And the moment last night, when she'd discovered he had paid a small fortune for tickets to a sold-out concert because he believed she liked the band that was playing. She hadn't even realised it was the same band who had done the song she had been dancing to several weeks before until he'd mentioned it oh, so casually. A part of her had been overjoyed. But another part of her had been devastated. How could he be so observant, so thoughtful, and yet not know how much it meant to her?

And how was she supposed to stop herself from falling hopelessly in love with that man?

But this afternoon had been the wake-up call she needed. The signal she had to start demanding more of him, or she would be lost. She'd seen her baby's three-dimensional image on the ultrasound equipment. She'd devoured the incredible sight of its tiny nose and mouth, the closed eyelids, its long limbs—just like its father's. She'd laughed at Dr Patel pointing out it was sucking its thumb, and shed a few stunned tears when she'd made the decision to find out the baby's sex after the doctor had told her she had a clear image of its sexual organs.

All those emotions had bombarded her—excitement, awe, wonder... And yet at the same time her heart had felt as if it were being ripped away from her chest wall. Because she'd experienced all those incredible, life-altering moments alone. Because Jack had chosen not to be there with her.

It hurt even more to see the stunned compassion on his face now, the wary confusion at her tears. And the defensiveness in his eyes. Because a part of her knew the words he had just flung at her like missiles, words which had stunned her, were true. He *did* care about her. Probably much more than he wanted to. But how could that be enough? For her or their baby?

'Why aren't you happy?' he'd asked her, as if he really didn't know.

Maybe he didn't.

She sucked in an unsteady breath, determined not to let another tear fall. She hated tears. They didn't solve anything. And she refused to be that woman who broke down rather than ask for what she wanted.

She'd been trying to have this conversation for weeks, and it had been like thumping her head against a brick wall, but he had given her an opening this time, and she would be a fool not to take it.

'You know, I saw our baby properly for the first

time today on the ultrasound,' she said as conversationally as she could manage.

Something flickered in his eyes, something wary, tense and instantly guarded. But when he didn't say anything, didn't stop her or try to deflect the conversation as he always had before, the fragile bubble of hope expanded in her chest.

'Dr Patel told me what she thinks the sex is. Would you like to know?'

He stared at her, his expression unreadable.

'Of course, it's not one hundred percent, but Dr Patel was pretty sure. She said about eighty-five percent sure.' She was babbling now, but when his gaze shifted to her stomach, as she had seen it do so many times in the last few weeks as her bump had become more pronounced, the bubble grew. 'Aren't you even a little bit curious?' she asked.

His gaze lifted back to her face. He wanted to say no. She could see it in his eyes. So she blurted it out before he could stop her... 'It's a boy.'

His brows rose, the slash of colour on his cheeks hard to interpret. Was he pleased, surprised, indifferent? Why couldn't she tell even now? How did he manage to keep so much of himself back? Not just from her, but from their child? Would it always be like this?

Was this still all about that young boy he wouldn't talk about? The lost, brutalised child he'd given her a glimpse of in the Maldives and then refused to acknowledge ever since?

He looked away from her and she could see he

was struggling from the tell-tale muscle twitching in his jaw. But what was he struggling with?

'I was thinking of the name Daniel,' she ventured.

His head swung back round. 'No. I don't like that name.'

'Oh, okay,' she managed, but her heart soared. It was the most he had ever given her. The first sign he cared enough about this baby to have a preference. Maybe this didn't have to be a lost cause. Had she given up far too soon? Allowed her own feelings for him to colour the progress they'd made? Feelings that perhaps weren't as unrequited as she'd assumed. Perhaps this wasn't so much about him but about her, and her own desire to protect herself. She was letting everything get mixed up in her head because she was scared too. Scared he would reject her the way her father had. But he'd already given her so much more, without even realising it.

'If you've got any suggestions, I'm all ears,' she managed, her throat thickening with emotion again. Did he know how significant this moment was?

The discomfort in his face was clear. Obviously, he did. But then he murmured, 'I'll think about it.' He glanced at his watch. 'We're supposed to be going to the Collington Charity Ball tonight.' His penetrating gaze searched her face, the wariness returning full force. 'You're tired. If you'd rather avoid it, I can make your excuses.'

Not on your life.

Her heart galloped into her throat, the stupid bubble of hope expanding so fast it was almost choking her. He'd said he cared about her. He'd clearly freaked out when he'd thought she was ill. And he had offered an opinion about the baby's name. And okay, it *had* been reluctantly, but after weeks of what had felt like no progress she was not about to let this shining, shimmering gift horse out of her sight.

'Give me an hour to dress,' she said, and left him standing in the hallway, the weary resignation lifting off her shoulders as she all but skipped up the stairs.

It wasn't enough, but it was enough for now. This didn't have to be about his past or hers. This could be about their future. A future she suddenly felt sure was so much brighter now than it had been an hour ago in the ultrasound suite.

Jack Wolfe *could* be a father. All she had to do was let go of her own insecurities long enough to show him.

A boy?

The information reverberated in Jack's skull, doing nothing to deaden the fear that had been tormenting him for close to an hour as he paused in the doorway of his wife's suite.

She stood in the next room, checking out the fit of her dress for tonight's ball in the mirror, unaware of his presence.

His breath got trapped in his lungs.

The rich, red satin hugged her bold curves, lifting her full breasts, accentuating her lush bottom. The pale skin revealed by the gown's plunging back and the sprinkle of freckles across her bare shoulder blades were given a pearly glow by the room's diffused lighting. He wanted to put his lips at the base of her spine, trail kisses up the delicious line of her backbone to her nape.

He knew exactly how she tasted there, in the hollow beneath her earlobe. And how she would respond—first with surprise, then with excitement, exhilaration and a hunger which matched his own—holding nothing back.

He shoved his hands into his pockets and forced himself not to walk into the room and begin unravelling her outfit. Because in the last hour the flicker of joy, of belonging, of protectiveness which always assailed him when he returned to the house in Mayfair, seemed somehow threatening in a way it never had before.

She moved, revealing the compact curve of her belly, and the fear dropped into his belly like an unexploded bomb. The jumble of emotions which had been festering for an hour collided as he recalled the hope in her eyes. The last thing he wanted to do right now was escort her to the VIP charity event, to parade her in front of a load of other men like a trophy, an acquisition, even though that was exactly what she was supposed to be.

This arrangement had always had a sell-by date. How had he lost sight of that in the last month? After tonight he would have to re-establish the emotional distance he'd lost, or how else would he be able to control the deep pulse of regret, of longing, of loneliness which was already building when he was forced to let her go?

He cleared his throat and she swung round. The

brief flicker of joy in her emerald eyes that he'd seen so many times in the past few weeks wrapped around his heart, scaring him even more.

'Jack?' she whispered, the sound raw. 'Is it time to go?'

He made himself walk into the room, aware of her appreciative gaze gliding over his figure in the tailored tuxedo. 'Yes, we should probably make a move,' he said, trying to keep his tone impersonal, to cover the emotions churning inside him and stop himself from blurting out what he wanted to say to her.

This isn't a marriage of convenience any more.

But even the thought of saying those words made him feel weak and pathetic and needy.

He placed a hand on her bare shoulder, felt her shudder of response. But, instead of placing his lips on the fluttering pulse in her collarbone, he slid his palm down her arm then lifted her fingers to his lips.

'You look beautiful,' he said as he kissed her knuckles and watched the leap of joy flicker again in her eyes at the inadequate complement.

He straightened and let her hand drop, the fear gripping his throat again.

'Jack, is something wrong?' she asked, pressing her palms against the smooth satin of the dress, her gaze far too astute.

'We need to go or we'll be late,' he said.

Her throat contracted as she swallowed. 'Okay.'

He didn't want to hurt her, but he knew he would, because he could never be the man she needed.

CHAPTER THIRTEEN

'How about Sebastian? Or Luca? I've always liked Luca,' Katie offered, excited as the chauffeur-driven car stopped in front of the ornate redbrick façade of the Drapers' Hall where the charity ball they were attending was being held.

Jack sent her a quelling look. 'We're here.'

She grinned back at him, refusing to be put off by his usual reserve when it came to talking about the baby. Talking about their son. The giddy hope had her beaming smiles and even waving at the barrage of press photographers as Jack escorted her into the hall. The smile didn't even dim as Jack led her into an imposing marble-columned ballroom, the gold leaf glimmering in the light of the chandeliers.

For once she didn't feel like a complete fraud as Jack introduced her to the array of VIP guests and business people who always gravitated towards her husband when they arrived at these sorts of events.

My husband.

Funny that tonight she actually felt like Jack's wife. And the mother of his child. Obviously this was still an arrangement, a bargain, a marriage with a sell-by date stamped on it. But they'd taken a huge step forward tonight. Not just when Jack had told her he cared about her, but when he had kissed her hand with such tenderness, such reverence, in her dressing room. She felt closer to him now than she ever had before.

She cupped her belly absently, excited about the pregnancy in a way she had never been before. What if they could do this together? What if she didn't have to do this alone?

She felt as if she were floating— with only Jack's stalwart presence by her side to anchor her to earth—as the evening sped past. She chatted enthusiastically about everything from how to bake the perfect brownie, with the French ambassador, to the wonder of Wolfe Maldives with an award-winning actress who was heading to the resort next month after her current film finished shooting. For once the small talk wasn't a chore and she didn't feel as if she was lying when she talked about her honeymoon or her husband.

But, after two hours on her feet, Katie began to flag.

'You look tired. Would you like to return home?' Jack asked but, just as she placed her fingers on his forearm for some much-needed support, about to give him a resounding yes, his muscles became rigid. His face hardened as his gaze locked on something over her shoulder.

She turned to see a tall, elegant, older man walking through the crowd straight towards them.

'Who's that?' she asked, concerned at the cold light that had entered Jack's eyes.

'No one,' he said, the bite in his tone chilling.

But, before she could say more, the man reached them. 'Mr Wolfe, I presume,' he said, the quirk of his lips doing nothing to dispel the hostile tone.

The man had a patrician handsomeness, the few lines on his tanned face making it hard to tell how old he was—probably in his mid-sixties, with his carefully styled hair more salt than pepper. There was something, though—about the line of his jaw, the powerful way he moved, the brilliant blue of his eyes—which looked familiar.

Who was he? Katie was sure she had never met him, but she instinctively didn't like him, any more than her husband seemed to.

'I understand you are now our majority share-holder...' The man paused dramatically, the cold gleam in his eyes becoming laser-sharp, then murmured, 'Son.'

Jack jolted as if he'd been shot.

'I see you thought I didn't know,' the man continued, when Jack remained silent, the enmity thick in the air. Katie's skin chilled and her stomach jumped as realisation dawned—the physical similarities between them glaringly obvious now.

Was this man Jack's biological father?

The thought stunned her on one level, but horrified her on another, because there was no joy in the meeting—on either side.

The man gave a grim chuckle, both superior and condescending. 'My dear boy, did you really believe

I would allow an upstart like you to own Smyth-Brown if I didn't want you to?'

Katie hated him, whoever he was, for treating Jack with such obvious contempt. She could feel the muscles in Jack's forearm flexing beneath her fingertips as he struggled to control his reaction.

'It won't make a difference,' Jack said, the words ground out on a husk of breath. 'I intend to destroy your legacy,' he added. 'For what you did to my mother.'

Katie's heart broke at the pain she could hear in Jack's voice, and the bone-deep regret she could see etched in the rigid line of his jaw.

But, instead of being cowed by the threat, the man—Jack's father—simply smiled, the tight line of his lips devoid of humour. 'Hmm, I see. Interesting you would blame me for her idiotic decision to marry that oaf,' he said as if he were having a conversation about the weather rather than an event that had robbed Jack of his childhood. 'Although it is a pity the brute maimed you.'

'You son of a…' Jack launched forward, his anger exploding as he grabbed the older man by his lapels.

Katie grasped his arm. 'Jack, don't. He's not worth it,' she pleaded, suddenly desperate to get him away from here. To protect him from the prying eyes of the growing crowd, riveted to the developing altercation.

She knew how much Jack valued his emotional control and his standing in the business community. Something he'd worked his whole life to gain.

And she suspected a public fight was just what this bastard wanted—to expose Jack as a brute, an oaf, like the man who had scarred him.

What gave him the right to do that? When he had no part in Jack's life—or the phenomenal success he had made of it?

Jack's gaze met hers and she saw the flicker of confusion beneath the fury before the anger was downgraded enough for him to release his captive so abruptly, the man stumbled backwards.

'We should leave,' Katie said gently, touching his cheek, forcing him to look at her. Her heart yearned to tell him the words she realised she should have told him weeks ago. But she couldn't say them here, so she tried to convey them telepathically.

I love you. You matter to me. Whatever he did to you doesn't. Not any more.

He nodded, but as he gripped her hand, intending to lead them both out of the ballroom, the bastard stepped into her path.

'So this is the delightful Mrs Wolfe,' the man said, offering her his hand as if he hadn't just tried to emotionally destroy her husband. Katie ignored it.

'Daniel Smyth at your service, my dear,' he added.

Daniel.

Before she had a chance to register the name and what it might mean, his cold gaze skimmed over her belly then lifted back to her face, the satisfied smile even more chilling. 'Did you know, my dear, I required my son marry as part of the deal for him to acquire Smyth-Brown. I needed an heir, but I really didn't think he would be quite so accommodating as to provide me with two heirs for the price of one so soon.'

What?

'Get out of our way,' Jack snarled, shoving Smyth back as he strode past him and led her out of the ballroom, the click of camera phones and the man's cruel laughter following in their wake.

'Do you really believe you can destroy my legacy, boy?' he shouted after them, sounding vaguely mad. 'When you *are* my legacy?'

Katie felt stunned, shaky, disorientated, her mind a mass of confusing emotions as Jack led her to the waiting car and helped her inside.

'Jack… Why—?' she began as the car pulled away from the kerb, suddenly desperate to contain the fear contracting around her ribs and making it hard to breathe.

'I don't want to talk about it,' he cut her off, the tone rigid with barely leashed fury as the car drove down Piccadilly towards home.

Except it isn't his home.

Her body trembled as her hands strayed to her belly.

It's my home and our baby's home. Not his. Because he doesn't want it to be. Any more than he will ever want us.

Her mind struggled to engage with the thoughts careering around in her head. The emotions battered her as the hope she'd nurtured so diligently and so pointlessly for so long finally began to die.

He sat beside her saying nothing, offering no explanation, no solace, no comfort.

The hideous things that had happened to him as a child didn't give her a connection with him, she realised. They didn't have a shared pain after both having been rejected by their fathers. This was *his* pain. A pain he guarded so jealously, so relentlessly, he had married her just to destroy the man who had caused it.

The silence stretched, creating a chasm between them, until the distance felt like millions of miles instead of only a few feet.

The car pulled into the driveway of the Grosvenor Square house. Jack got out, dismissed the chauffeur and walked round the car to open her door.

She stepped out into the night, still dazed. His warm palm settled on her back to direct her into the house, the traitorous ripple only damning her more as he closed the front door and helped her off with her wrap.

'Thank God that's over with,' he said, his hands cupping her stomach as he dragged her back against his body, his lips finding the rampant pulse in her neck.

She jolted as ripples flooded her core at the feel of his already burgeoning erection pressing into her back.

His mouth devoured the spot under her earlobe he knew was supremely sensitive.

'Let's go to bed,' he suggested, but the raw, seductive command—one she had succumbed to so many times before—finally tore away the last of the fog until all that was left was the pain.

And the stark, gruelling light of truth.

'No,' she said, lurching out of his arms, wrenching herself away from the traitorous need.

'Damn it. I need you tonight, Katherine,' he said, his voice raw, his expression more transparent than she had ever seen it before.

She could see the hurt, the anger, the bitter confusion and the desperation the encounter with his father had caused. But she could also see in the rigid line of his jaw, in the anger sparking in his eyes, that this wasn't about her, about them, and it never had been.

She was nothing more than a temporary port in a storm, their marriage nothing more than a convenient means for him to get his revenge for everything he'd suffered in childhood. Her heart broke for that brutalised child…but there was another child now, one who needed her love and support more.

She steeled herself against the desire to soothe, to console, to take the pain away the only way he would let her. And forced herself to say what she had to say.

'I can't do this any more, Jack. You need to leave.'

'What…? Why?' Jack yelled, the stubborn refusal on Katherine's face—and the pulse of desperation swelling in his groin—all but crucifying him.

'Because it's not me you need, Jack,' she said, her voice breaking on the words and only crucifying him more. 'It's your revenge.'

The fury surged. The fury that had been building ever since Daniel Smyth had strolled towards him with that smug, entitled smile on his face and

Jack had been forced to face the sickening realisation that the son of a bitch had played him all along.

He knew who I was. Right from the start.

Daniel Smyth had got the board to insist Jack marry above his station so he could make the kid from a run-down council estate whom he had discarded before he'd even been born somehow worthy to become his heir. And Jack had eventually fallen right into the trap.

But that horrifying revelation, the cruel trick he'd allowed himself to fall for, wasn't nearly as gutting as the closed expression on Katherine's face now.

If only he could just lose himself in her. Forget about tonight, about his past, about the whole sick, stupid mess. He knew none of it would matter any more. After all, he hadn't really married her to get the shares. He'd married her for a host of other reasons. But as he lifted his hand to touch her cheek, to draw her back in, she stepped back.

'When you said you didn't like the name Daniel, I thought we were having a discussion about our son.'

He let his hand drop. So they were back to that. 'Katherine, I told you I can't—'

'But tonight I found out,' she cut him off, the quiver of regret in her hushed tone crushing him, 'I found out it had nothing to do with him. It was just another part of your past you won't allow me to see.'

'I told you on our wedding night what I can offer the child,' he said, even though it felt like a lie now. 'And what I can't.'

She simply stared at him, the gleam of tears almost more than he could bear. 'I know,' she said, so softly he almost didn't hear her. 'And I believed you then. But that was before I fell in love with you.'

'You…' The flood of need hit him square in the chest. But right behind it was the fear. 'No, you don't…' he said, locking away all the emotions he couldn't afford to feel.

One side of her mouth quirked in a sad half-smile, but the sense of hopelessness hovered like a dark cloud in the hallway. 'I spent the whole of my childhood trying to make my father love me. I can't do that with you, Jack. I won't.' Her hand covered her stomach where their child grew. 'I have to protect myself and my child. I don't want you here any more.'

She turned and walked away from him.

He stood, rigid with shock and anger for several seconds, desperate to chase after her, to make her want him, the way he had so many times before.

But the scar burned on his cheek, the agony real again, and so raw.

He'd begged Harry Wolfe to want him, to care about him, because he'd felt so scared. So desperate. And all it had done was left him more alone. He'd be damned if he'd make that mistake a second time.

She would come back to him. On his terms. And, until she did, he would survive without her.

But as he marched out of the house, and slammed the door behind him, it felt as if part of his heart was being wrenched from his body.

The bitter irony was, it was the part of his heart he thought he had killed a long time ago.

CHAPTER FOURTEEN

'GORINDA, I NEED you to speak to Dr Patel's office again. I'm paying the damn bills for my wife's care. I expect to be given regular updates on her condition and I've heard nothing in two weeks,' Jack announced as he marched past his PA into his office.

Two damned weeks Katherine had been sulking. And he was through playing nice, with her or the obstetrician who was charging a fortune for her care. He needed to know she was okay, that was all. Was it too much to ask he be kept informed?

'Mr Wolfe, I've spoken to Dr Patel's administrator several times already.' Jack glanced up from his desk to see his PA's harassed expression. 'I'm afraid she says they can't give you updates on Mrs Wolfe's care without your wife's permission. It's a matter of patient confidentiality.'

'She specifically asked I not be informed?' Jack demanded, the shock combining with the frustration and fury...

The last two weeks had seemed like two years. He'd waited for her to contact him, to call him, to ask him to return to the house in Mayfair.

But she hadn't.

He wasn't sleeping, was barely eating, the yearning to hold her, to make love to her, even to see the changes the pregnancy had made to her body, so intense he could barely function.

For two weeks he'd waited for the yearning to stop so he could return to who he had been before he had met her.

A man alone. A man apart.

But, as he stared at his PA's flushed face, the brutal stab of rejection made him realise that Katherine had destroyed that man—somehow—so comprehensively, he didn't feel like a success any more. He didn't even feel happy in his own skin.

The unfulfilled desire, the physical longing that woke him from fitful dreams—leaving him hard, ready, aching and groping for her in his bed, only to find it empty—was bad enough. But the emotions he couldn't control, the nightmares he couldn't contain, were so much worse. The thought of a lifetime without her smile, her quick wit, her passion, or her companionship, was destroying him from within. And he didn't know how to overcome it. Hell, he even missed her smart mouth and her absolute refusal to do as she was told.

'Apparently she did, Mr Wolfe,' Gorinda replied, sounding almost as weary as he felt.

So Katherine had cut him loose. She'd told him she loved him. But she'd lied.

Devastation hit him.

He thrust his fingers through his hair, only to become aware his hands were shaking. How had she come to mean so much to him when she was never meant to? And how did he make this pain stop now?

He got up from his desk to stare out at the City's skyline—the gothic splendour of Tower Bridge, the gleaming mirrored sheen of The Shard on the opposite bank. It was a view that had once had the power to excite and motivate him, to make him proud of how far he'd come, but today, like every day for the last fortnight, the view seemed dull and listless, ostentatious and unimpressive.

'Dr Patel's receptionist did mention Mrs Wolfe is going to be at the clinic this morning,' Gorinda added. 'Perhaps you could join her there? To find out how she is?'

He swung round at the tentative suggestion to find Gorinda watching him with sympathy in her warm brown eyes.

But I don't want to be a part of the baby's life...

The automatic thought echoed in his head. But even thinking it felt like a lie now. It wasn't that he didn't want to be a part of this baby's life, it was that he was scared to be. Sure he'd fail at fatherhood... The way he'd failed at so much else.

'Okay,' he heard himself say.

And suddenly it all seemed so simple.

He *had* to fix this. To hell with his pride, his fear of fatherhood, his fear of asking her—no, *begging* her—to take him back, his fear of letting her see the frightened boy instead of the man he had become... None of it meant anything any more without her.

Why had it taken him so long to realise she had always been what was missing in his life?

'Rearrange my schedule and text me the address,' he said as he charged back out of the office. Of course, he had absolutely no idea *how* he was going to fix it. Or even if he could fix it. He'd just have to wing it, he thought, with a great deal more confidence than he felt.

'Yes, sir,' Gorinda replied.

If Katherine didn't want to see him, he'd just have to deal with that when he got to the clinic. But he couldn't stay away from her… Or the baby… Not a moment longer…

'I'm sorry, Mr Wolfe, your wife is having a private consultation.'

'I don't care.'

Katie shifted on the bed at the shouted comments coming from outside the ultrasound suite.

'What on earth…?' Dr Patel murmured as she put down the tube of gel she had been about to put on Katie's stomach and clicked off the machine.

But before either she or Katie could do anything more the door burst open and Jack strode in.

'Mr Wolfe! I'm sorry, you'll have to leave…' The doctor began, but Jack marched right past her, sat down in the chair beside the bed and lifted Katie's hand.

'Let me stay, Katherine. I want to meet our son,' he said, his voice thick with desperation, his eyes wild with urgency and something else…something so naked and unguarded, she wondered for a moment if she was dreaming. If she had conjured up this moment from weeks of crying herself to sleep each night.

'Jack…' she finally rasped.

'Please,' he said, and the gentle buzz of his kiss jolted her out of her trance.

'Could you leave us for a minute?' she said to Dr Patel, somehow managing to remain calm while she struggled to sit up and place a sheet over her belly.

Dr Patel nodded and left the room.

'Jack, what are you doing here?' she managed around the painful lump in her throat.

He looked distraught, she realised. But beneath the wild intensity in his expression she could also see determination. And need.

He placed his palm on her belly and rubbed the sheet so gently, she felt tears sting her eyes. 'I want to meet him too,' he said. 'Please, let me.'

She placed her hand over his, but as the joy throbbed heavily in her chest right behind it was the brutal weight of sadness, the hollow ache she had struggled to come to terms with for so long.

'Okay,' she said.

She wanted Jack to be part of his baby's life. And whatever had made him change his mind, she would always be grateful for it. But she knew there was so much else she wanted from him that she could never have. And she couldn't let the hope back in again, or it would destroy her.

'Thank you,' he said, his head dropping down until his forehead rested on her belly. He caressed the bump, his shoulders shuddering with the release of emotion. 'I'm so sorry for being such a coward.'

'Jack, it's okay.' She touched a shaky hand to his

head and let her fingers stroke the short silky strands, her heart shattering in her chest. 'I would never stop you from being a part of the baby's life. You can come with me to the scans from now on. And once the baby's born you can have all the visitation rights you want.'

He lifted his head suddenly, dislodging her hand. 'But I don't want visitation rights,' he said.

'Why not?' she asked, her throat so clogged with emotion now, she could barely talk.

He whisked away the tear that had fallen from her lid. 'Because I want us to be a family. I want to move in with you, have a real marriage, stop running and start building something that will last.'

'Really?' she said but, even as the balloon of hope expanded so much that it began to hurt, the insecurities she thought she'd jettisoned so long ago flooded back.

'Of course, Katherine,' he said, as if the answer she had failed to grasp was obvious. His face softened. 'I've been an idiot. Too much of a coward, to tell you the truth. That I was terrified of becoming a father. Because I didn't know how...'

'Having met your biological father,' Katherine said, the anger that still lingered after their encounter with Daniel Smyth sharpening her words, 'I understand why you might be wary. But you're not like him, Jack. You never could be.'

'I know,' he said. 'Which is why I told my broker to sell the damn shares on the way here. I don't want any part of his company. Not even to tear it to pieces.'

'You...you don't? But why?'

'Because you were right,' he said, his eyes shining. 'I don't need my revenge if I can have you instead.' His hand caressed the mound of her belly. 'And this fella too.'

His eyes met hers and she could see every single thing he was thinking for the first time ever... She saw sincerity, desire, fierce determination, even fear, but most of all desperate, unguarded hope.

'I need you, Katherine,' he said. He thrust his fingers through his hair, looking momentarily dumbfounded. 'Hell, I think I started to fall for you that first night when you were wearing that ridiculous outfit and I couldn't even see you properly. But I could sense your bravery and your boldness and I knew I wanted you, more than anything in the world.' He groaned.

'You...you do?' she croaked, so shocked by the heartfelt declaration, she could barely breathe, let alone think. But the insecurities were still there, asking... How could she trust him? How could she be enough, when she never had been for anyone before now?

'Yeah,' he said. His hand, trembling with emotion, gripped hers so tightly, it was as if he was holding her heart. 'I do.'

She shook her head but, despite the love that flooded through her, she tugged her fingers out of his. 'How can you be sure?'

'What? What do you mean?' he asked, his voice raw.

'How do you know I'm enough now, when I wasn't before?'

'Stop it, Katherine,' he said, looking desperate again. 'I'm telling you I love you. Why won't you believe me? Is this something to do with that bastard Medford? You think I'm like him?'

'No,' she said. 'But…' She stared at him, her heart breaking. But she couldn't back down again, couldn't just accept this at face value. 'Maybe it is. I always thought I'd got over his rejection. That it didn't matter to me. But maybe I never stopped being that girl in some ways. Because I want to believe you, but I can't.'

He took her hand again and held it, his gaze steady, direct, unbreakable. 'Tell me what I need to do to make it right.'

She eased herself onto her elbows until she was sitting up. 'Can you…can you tell me what Daniel Smyth did to make you hate him so?'

'I don't hate him. I don't even care about him any more. I told you that,' he said, but she could hear the defensiveness. And knew she needed to know all of it if she was ever going to put her doubts to rest. She needed to know he trusted her enough to let her in. All the way in. It was a big ask. She got that. And maybe this was about her insecurities as much as his. But she deserved to know or she would never be able to let go of the thought that she was still just a port in a storm, someone he might decide to discard again.

'I know.' She touched his scarred cheek, her heart breaking as she felt him lean into the caress instinctively. 'And I believe you. But I still want to meet that boy. To know him. To understand him.'

So I can love all of him, if he'll let me.

'You don't want to know him. Believe me,' he said, the bitterness thick in his tone. 'He was a little—'

'No, he wasn't,' she interrupted him. 'He was scared and alone, the way I was. What did he do to you, Jack?'

'Daniel Smyth tried to force my mother to have an abortion.' The words guttered out, making the anguish tighten in her belly. *Oh, no.*

'She didn't, obviously, or I wouldn't be here. But that's how she ended up with my stepfather. She wasn't self-sufficient like you are,' he said, his voice so quiet, it barely registered. But still she felt the jolt of pride at the approval in his tone, her doubts starting to drift away. He had always seen her for who she really was, had always admired the things about her her father had despised. How could she have forgotten that?

'Is that why you insisted on marrying me?' she asked, touched beyond belief. He had been showing her all along, who that boy was, and she hadn't even realised. 'Because he'd refused to help her?'

He stared at her, his gaze guarded again. 'Well, it's not the only reason.' He ran his palm over her belly again, caressing, sending the urgent desire through her body and making her smile. 'I wanted you. And… I needed you. But I didn't want to admit it. Not even to myself. Because it scared the hell out of me.'

'Oh, Jack.' She threw her arms around his neck, the happy tears flooding out—with no help whatsoever from the pregnancy hormones, for once. 'Yes. I love you. Let's be a family.'

'Wait a minute!' He drew back and held her at arm's length, his gaze confused. 'That's it? That's all you needed to hear?'

She nodded and grinned, despite the tears clogging her throat and rolling down her cheeks. 'I've been an idiot too. You showed me that boy. I just didn't see him. We're equals. That's all I needed know.'

'Thank God,' he said, then pulled her into his embrace and buried his face in her neck as she told him how much she loved him amidst watery kisses.

And when they finally got to look at their baby together for the first time, ten minutes later—and Jack bombarded poor Dr Patel with a ton of questions it would never even have occurred to Katie to ask—Katie knew for sure that neither of them would ever be alone again.

Because they had each other. Always.

EPILOGUE

Five months later

'WHAT BIG LUNGS you have, Master Wolfe.' Jack grinned down at the angry little face of the baby held securely in his arms as the tiny infant screwed up his eyes and launched into another angry, ear-splitting wail.

'All the better to drive us both mad with!' His wife grinned tiredly from the bed across the room.

'Shh, shh, little fella. It's okay. Daddy's here,' Jack said as he rocked the baby while crossing the room—to absolutely no avail. Young Master Wolfe was not happy. 'Sorry, Red,' he added, aware of how tired Katherine looked. 'I was hoping we wouldn't wake you.'

It was midnight. They'd only brought their son home this morning after Katherine had endured a twenty-two-hour labour. Jack adored his son to pieces, his awe and gratitude knowing no bounds when the baby had been handed to him after he'd cut the umbilical cord at the midwife's suggestion.

But no way in hell were they ever having another

child. The labour had nearly killed him, and watching Katherine battle bravely through so much pain still had anxiety gripping his throat. He intended to wear condoms now for the rest of eternity.

If she ever wanted to sleep with him again, which was debatable. Because he wouldn't blame her in the slightest if she refused to allow him within ten feet of her naked body after what she'd been through less that twenty-four hours ago.

'It's okay,' Katherine murmured sleepily and sat up in bed—looking ludicrously serene and happy for a woman who had just survived what he considered to have been a major war.

Lifting her breast out of the feeding bra, exposing the plump nipple, she reached tired arms towards Jack. 'Give him to me,' she said, stifling a yawn. 'He probably just wants to feed.'

'Damn, seriously! He's done nothing but eat since we got home,' he murmured as he resolutely ignored the shot of arousal at the sight of his wife's glorious breast and handed her their precious little bundle of absolute fury.

The baby found the nipple, latched on immediately and began sucking furiously as if he'd been starved for hours, while his little fist finally stopped moving and settled against his wife's cleavage.

Another shot of arousal rippled through Jack's system…

What was wrong with him? Was he some kind of animal that he could get turned on by the perfectly natural sight of Katherine feeding their son?

'He's definitely a boob man, that's for sure,'

Katherine said, her lips quirking in a cheeky smile that had his heart thumping his chest in hard, heady thuds. 'Not unlike his father.'

He chuckled, releasing the tension in his chest and letting go of the guilt.

God, but he loved this woman so much. How could she be so relaxed, so competent, taking this scary new experience called parenthood in her stride, when he was so useless? But he knew why. Because she was brave and smart and beautiful inside and out. And she had a wicked sense of humour that matched his own.

'Yeah, well, I hope he realises I'm gonna want those boobs back eventually,' Jack said wryly, joy bursting in his heart when she chuckled back.

'That may take a while, given how sore his mum is all over.'

'No worries,' Jack said, knowing if sexy banter was all he was going to get for a while it was more than enough. 'I can wait.'

She sent him a tender, welcoming smile as he climbed onto the bed beside her. He slung an arm around her shoulders and pulled her against his side, impossibly grateful for the companionship, the feeling of home she had created for him over the last five months...

He watched his son's cheeks gradually stop moving and the plump red nipple drop out of his mouth as he drifted back to sleep, as if by magic. Jack pressed a gentle kiss to his wife's temple while the wonder, the love—that was never far away when he watched his wife and child, his family—swelled in his chest, making it a little hard for him to breathe.

'Thank you, Mrs Wolfe,' he said softly.

'You're welcome, Mr Wolfe,' she whispered back. She lifted her head to smile at him. 'We really ought to give Master Wolfe a name, don't you think?' she said.

'How about Greedy?' he said.

She gave him a nudge in the ribs. 'I'm serious.'

'Okay, what do you want to call him?' Jack said, aware of a tickle of apprehension in his throat at the thought of this conversation. After all, the last time they'd discussed naming their son, he'd nearly torpedoed their whole relationship. 'I'm happy with anything you like,' he said, determined to make amends.

She gave him a patient, probing look. 'Okay, I like Aloysius.'

What the actual...?

'Okay,' he said, appalled and trying not to look it. 'Really?' he asked, when he spotted the mischievous twinkle in her eyes.

'No, not really... For goodness' sake, Jack. This is supposed to be a joint enterprise. I don't want to decide something so important on my own.'

'Okay,' he said carefully. But the apprehension still gripped his ribs. 'I just don't want to mess it up, like I did the last time.'

Katie stared at her husband and wanted to laugh and cry at the same time.

He'd been a wonderful father already. And an incredible partner over the last few months as they had navigated this stunning, life-altering and extremely scary experience together—of learning how to love each other, and how to prepare to become parents.

Not that there was really much you could do to prepare for something so momentous. She knew he was terrified of making a mistake, just like she was. She had seen how freaked out he'd been during the labour.

How much he already loved their son, though, and what an incredible father he was going to be, was plain to see. The mix of astonishment and tenderness on his face every time he held the baby with such care, talked to him in that deep, comforting and impossibly patient voice or even changed a nappy with a ridiculous amount of proficiency for a novice was both heart-meltingly sweet and stupidly sexy.

But he still had insecurities. She knew that. They both did. Insecurities which might take a lifetime to overcome. After all, neither of them had much of a blueprint for what a happy, contented, functional family life even looked like, let alone how to create it. She felt sure, though, that they would figure it out... But only if they figured it out together.

She sighed. 'You're not going to muck it up, Jack. Unless you let me call the baby Aloysius without an argument.'

He laughed and squeezed her shoulders. 'Point taken.'

His gaze drifted from her face and back to their son, who was now sound asleep in her arms.

He touched a finger to the baby's downy cheek, cleared his throat and murmured. 'You said you liked Luca… Did you mean it?'

Her heart bounced against her ribs. 'You remembered that?' Why was she surprised, when he had always been stupidly observant, even when she didn't want him to be?

'Of course,' he said.

'Yes, I meant it. I love the name Luca,' she said.

He nodded. 'Good, because so do I.'

Kissing her tenderly on the lips—as her heart felt as if it were about to burst out of her chest with love—he held her securely in his embrace then murmured to their son. 'Hello, Luca Wolfe. Welcome to the family.'

* * * * *

Caught up in the magic of
A Baby to Tame the Wolfe*?*
Then don't miss these other Heidi Rice stories!

Innocent's Desert Wedding Contract
One Wild Night with Her Enemy
The Billionaire's Proposition in Paris
The CEO's Impossible Heir
Banished Prince to Desert Doss

Available now!

#4025 THE BILLIONAIRE'S BABY NEGOTIATION
by Millie Adams
Innocent Olive Monroe has hated Icelandic billionaire
Gunnar Magnusson for years...and then she discovers the
consequences of their electric night together. Now she's facing
the highest-stakes negotiation of all—Gunnar wants their baby,
her company and Olive!

#4026 MAID FOR THE GREEK'S RING
by Louise Fuller
Achileas Kane sees himself as living proof that wedding vows are
meaningless. But this illegitimate son can only gain his inheritance
if he weds. His proposal to hotel chambermaid Effie Price is simply
a contract—until they seal their contract with a single sizzling kiss...

#4027 THE NIGHT THE KING CLAIMED HER
by Natalie Anderson
King Felipe knows far too much about the scandalous secrets in
Elsie Wynter's past. But with her stranded in his palace for one
night only, and their mutual desire flaring, he can think of nothing
but finally claiming her...

#4028 BOUND BY A NINE-MONTH CONFESSION
by Cathy Williams
Celia is unprepared for the passion she finds with billionaire
Leandro, let alone finding herself holding a positive pregnancy
test weeks later! Now they have nine months to decide if their
connection can make them a family.

#4029 CROWNING HIS KIDNAPPED PRINCESS
Scandalous Royal Weddings
by Michelle Smart

When daring Prince Marcelo Berruti rescues Clara Sinclair from a forced wedding, he makes international headlines. Now he's facing a diplomatic crisis...unless he claims the beautiful bride-to-be himself!

#4030 DESTITUTE UNTIL THE ITALIAN'S DIAMOND
by Julia James

Lana can't believe the crushing debts her ex left her with are forcing her to make a convenient marriage with ruthless Italian Salvatore. But while her head agrees to take his name, her body craves his forbidden touch!

#4031 INNOCENT IN HER ENEMY'S BED
by Dani Collins

Ilona is aware that Leander will do anything for revenge against her stepfamily. She just never pictured herself becoming his ally. Or that the sensual back-and-forth between them would lead to their marriage bed...

#4032 HIS DESERT BRIDE BY DEMAND
by Lela May Wight

Desert prince Akeem wants to show first love Charlotte what she gave up by turning her back on him. Then their secret tryst threatens to become a scandal, and duty-bound Akeem must make an outrageous demand: she'll be his queen!

*Desert prince Akeem wants to show first love Charlotte
what she gave up by turning her back on him. Then their
secret tryst threatens to become a scandal, and
duty-bound Akeem must make an outrageous demand:
she'll be his queen!*

*Read on for a sneak preview of
Lela May Wight's next story for Harlequin Presents
His Desert Bride by Demand*

"Can you explain what happened?" Akeem asked. "The intensity?"

Could she? Nine years had passed between them—a lifetime—and still… No, she couldn't.

"My father had a lifetime of being reckless for his own amusement—"

"And you wanted a taste of it?"

"No," he denied, his voice a harsh rasp.

"Then what did you want?" Charlotte pushed.

"A night—"

"You risked your reputation for a night?" She cut him off, her insides twisting. "And so far, it's been a disaster, and we haven't even got to bed." She blew out a puff of agitated air.

"Make no mistake," he warned, "things have changed."

"Changed?"

"My bed is off-limits."

She laughed, a throaty gurgle. "How dare you pull me from my life, fly me who knows how many miles into a kingdom I've never heard of and turn my words back on me!" She fixed him with an exasperated glare. "How dare you try to turn the tables on me!"

"If the tables have turned on anyone," he corrected, "it is me because you will be my wife."

Don't miss
His Desert Bride by Demand,
available August 2022 wherever
Harlequin Presents books and ebooks are sold.

Harlequin.com

Natalie Anderson

PRINCESS'S PREGNANCY SECRET

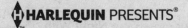

HARLEQUIN PRESENTS®

Recycling programs
for this product may
not exist in your area.

ISBN-13: 978-1-335-41939-2

Princess's Pregnancy Secret

First North American publication 2018

Copyright © 2018 by Natalie Anderson

Printed in U.S.A.

www.Harlequin.com

Natalie Anderson adores happy endings, so you can be sure you've got happy endings to enjoy when you buy her books, she promises nothing less. She loves peppermint-filled dark chocolate, pineapple juice & extremely long showers, plus teasing her imaginary friends with dating dilemmas! She lives in New Zealand with her gorgeous husband & four fabulous children. If you love happy endings too, come find her on Facebook.com/authornataliea, Twitter @authornataliea, or natalie-anderson.com

Books by Natalie Anderson

Harlequin Presents

Claiming His Convenient Fiancée
The Forgotten Gallo Bride
Pleasured by the Secret Billionaire
Mistress Under Contract
Bought: One Night, One Marriage
His Mistress by Arrangement

The Throne of San Felipe

The Secret That Shocked De Santis
The Mistress That Tamed De Santis

The Royal House of Karedes

Ruthless Boss, Royal Mistress

Harlequin KISS

Whose Bed Is It Anyway?
The Right Mr. Wrong

Visit the Author Profile page
at Harlequin.com for more titles.

To my family, for your patience, belief,
bad-but-good puns and supreme fun...
We are such an awesome team, and
I am so very lucky.

CHAPTER ONE

DAMON GALE STALKED the perimeter of the crowded ballroom, dodging another cluster of smiling women whose feathered masks neither softened nor hid their hunger as they stared at him.

He shouldn't have discarded his mask so soon.

Turning his back on another wordless invitation, he sipped his champagne, wishing it contained a stronger liquor. Women wanted more from him than he ever wanted from them. Always. While they agreed to a fling—fully informed of his limits—when it ended, recriminations and resentment came.

You're heartless.

He smiled cynically as the echo rang in his head. His last ex had thrown that old chestnut at him a few months ago. And, yes, he was. Heartless and happy with it.

And what did it matter? For tonight business, not pleasure, beckoned. Tonight he was drawing a line beneath a decades-old disaster and tomorrow he'd walk away from this gilded paradise without a backwards glance. Just coming back had made old wounds hurt like fresh hits.

But for now he'd endured the outrageously opulent entrance, navigated his way up the marble staircase and walked through not one but five antechambers. Each room was larger and more ornate than the last, until finally he'd reached this gleaming monstrosity of a ballroom. The internal balcony overlooking the vast room already brimmed with celebrities and socialites eager to display themselves and spy on others.

Palisades palace was designed to reflect the glory of the royal family and make the average commoner feel as inconsequential as possible. It was supposed to invoke awe and envy. Frankly all the paintings, tapestries and gilded carvings exhausted Damon's eyes. He itched to ditch his dinner jacket and hit one of the trail runs along the pristine coastline that he far preferred to this sumptuous palace, but he needed to stay and play nice for just a little while longer.

Gritting his teeth, he turned away from the lens of an official photographer. He had no desire to feature in anyone's social media feed or society blog. He'd been forced to attend too many of these sorts of occasions in years past, as the proof of the supposed strength of his parents' union and thus to maximise any political inroads they could make from their connections.

The bitterness of their falsity soured the champagne.

Fortunately *his* career wasn't dependent upon the interest and approval of the wealthy and powerful. Thanks to his augmented reality software company, he was as wealthy as any of the patrons in attendance at this palace tonight. But even so, he was here to make the old-school grace and favour system work for him just this once. Grimly he glanced over to where he'd left his half-sister only ten minutes ago. The investors he'd introduced her to were actively listening to her earnest, intelligent conversation, asking questions, clearly interested in what she was saying.

That introduction was all she'd agreed to accept from him. She'd refused his offer to fund her research himself and, while it irritated him, he didn't blame her. After all, they barely knew each other and neither of them wanted to dwell on the cancerous and numerous scars of their parents' infidelities. She had her pride and he respected her for it. But he'd been determined to try to help heal two decades of hurt and heartache caused by lies and deception, even in some small way, given his father's total lack of remorse. From the intensity of that discussion, it seemed his job was done.

Now Damon turned away from the crowds, seeking solace in solitude for a moment before he could escape completely.

Symmetrical marble columns lined the length of the room. On one side they bracketed doors to the internal courtyard currently lit by lights strung in the trees. But on the other side the columns stood like sentries guarding shadowy alcoves.

A wisp of blue caught his eye as he approached the nearest column and he veered nearer. A woman stood veiled in the recess, her attention tightly focused on a group of revellers a few feet away. Her hair was ten shades of blue, hung to her waist and was most definitely a wig. A feathery mask covered half her face like an intimate web of black lace. Her shoulders, cheekbones and lips sparkled in a swirling combination of blue and silver powder.

Damon paused, unable to ignore the way her long dress emphasised every millimetre of her lithe body, clinging to her luscious curves and long legs. Despite that sparkling powder, he could see the tan of her skin and it suggested she was more mermaid than waif. She definitely spent time in the sun and that toned body didn't come from sitting on a spread towel doing nothing.

She was fit—in all interpretations of the word—but it was her undeniable femininity that stole his breath. Her pointed chin and high cheekbones and perfectly pouted lips were pure prettiness and delicacy, while her bountiful breasts were barely contained in the too-tight bodice of her midnight-blue dress.

She hadn't noticed him as she stood still and alone, watching the crowd. So he watched her. Her mask didn't hide her emotions—while her intentions were not obvious, her anxiety was. Something about her stark isolation softened that hard knot tied fast in his chest and set a challenge at the same time.

He was seized by the desire to make her smile.

He was also seized by the urge to span his hands around her narrow waist and pull her close so he could feel the graceful combination of softness and strength that her figure promised.

He smiled ruefully as raw warmth coursed through his veins. Its unexpected ferocity was vastly better than the cold ash clogging his lungs when he'd first arrived. Perhaps there could be a moment of pleasure here after all, now his business was concluded and that personal debt paid.

He quietly strolled nearer. Her attention was still fixed on the people gathering in the glittering ballroom, but he focused on her. She hovered on the edge of the room, still in the shadow. Still almost invisible to everyone else.

Her breasts swelled as she inhaled deeply. He hesitated, waiting for her to move forward. But contrary to his expectation, she suddenly stepped back, her expression falling as she turned away.

Damon narrowed his gaze. He had his own reasons for avoiding occasions like this, but why would a beautiful young woman like her want to hide? She should have company.

His company.

He lifted a second glass from the tray of a passing waiter and stepped past the column into the alcove. She'd paused in her retreat to look over that vast room of bejewelled, beautiful people. The expression in her eyes was obvious, despite the mask and the make-up. Part longing, part loneliness, her isolation stirred him. He spoke before thinking better of it.

'Can't quite do it?'

She whirled to face him, her eyes widening. Damon paused, needing a moment to appreciate the layers of sequins and powder on her pretty features. She was so very blue. She registered the two glasses he was holding and darted a glance behind him. As she realised he was alone, her eyes widened more. He smiled at her obvious wariness.

'It's your first time?' he asked.

Her mouth opened in a small wordless gasp.

'At the palace,' he clarified, wryly amused while keenly aware of the fullness of her glittered lips. 'It can be overwhelming the first time.'

Fascinatingly a telltale colour ran up her neck and face, visible despite the artful swirls of powder dusting almost every inch of her exposed skin. She was *blushing* at the most innocuous of statements.

Well, almost innocuous.

His smile deepened as he imagined her response if he were to utter something a great deal more inappropriate. Her body captured his attention, and he couldn't resist stealing a glance lower.

Heat speared again, tightening his muscles. He dragged his gaze up and realised she'd caught his slip. Unabashed he smiled again, letting her know in that time-worn way of his interest. She met his open gaze, not stepping back. But still she said nothing.

Alone. Definitely unattached. And almost certainly on the inexperienced side.

Damon hadn't chased a woman in a long while. Offers from more than willing bedmates meant he was more hunted than hunter. He avoided their attempts to snare him for longer, bored with justifying his refusal to commit to a relationship. He had too much of what women wanted—money and power. And yes, physical stamina and experience. Women enjoyed those things too.

But the possibilities here were tempting—when she reacted so tantalisingly with so little provocation? Those too-blue eyes and that too-sombre pout were beguiling.

He'd barely expected to stay ten minutes, let alone find someone who'd rouse his playful side. But now his obligation to Kassie had been met, he had the urge to amuse himself.

'What's your name?' he asked.

Her pupils dilated as if she was surprised but, again, she said nothing.

'I think I'll call you "Blue",' he said leisurely.

Her chin lifted fractionally. 'Because of my hair?'

He had to stop his jaw from dropping at the sound

of her husky tones. That sultriness was at complete odds with her innocent demeanour. She was as raspy as a kitten's tongue. The prospect of making her purr tightened his interest.

'Because of the longing in your eyes.' And because of the pout of her pretty mouth.

'What do you think I'm longing for?'

Now there was a question. One he chose not to answer, knowing his silence would speak for itself. He just looked at her—feeling the awareness between them snap.

'What should I call you?' she asked after a beat.

He lifted his eyebrows. 'You don't know who I am?'

Her lips parted as she shook her head. 'Should I?'

He studied her for a moment—there had been no flash of recognition in her eyes when he'd first spoken to her, and there was none now. How...*refreshing.* 'No,' he said. 'I'm no one of importance. No prince, that's for sure.'

Something flickered in her eyes then, but it was gone before he could pick it up.

'I'm visiting Palisades for a few days,' he drawled. 'And I'm single.'

Her lips parted. 'Why do I need to know that?'

That sultry voice pulled, setting off a small ache deep in his bones. He didn't much like aches. He preferred action.

'No reason.' He shrugged carelessly, but smiled.

Her lips twitched, then almost curved. Satisfaction seeped into his gut, followed hard by something far hotter. Pleasure. It pressed him closer.

'Why are you all alone in here?' He offered her the second glass of champagne.

She accepted it but took such a small sip he wasn't sure that the liquid even hit her lips. A careful woman. Intriguing.

'Are you hiding?' he queried.

She licked her lips and glanced down at her dress before tugging at the strap that was straining to hold her curves.

Definitely nervous.

'You look beautiful,' he added. 'You don't need to worry about that.'

That wave of colour swept her cheeks again but she lifted her head. There was an assuredness in her gaze now that surprised him. 'I'm not worried about that.'

Oh? So she held a touch more confidence than had first appeared. Another shot of satisfaction rushed. His fingers itched with the urge to tug the wig from her head and find out what colour her hair really was. While this façade was beautiful, it was a fantasy he wanted to pierce so he could see the real treasure beneath.

'Then why aren't you out there?' he asked.

'Why aren't you?' Alert, she watched for his response.

'Sometimes attendance at these things is *necessary* rather than desired.'

'These "things"?' she mocked his tone.

'It depends who's here.'

'No doubt you desire these "things" more when there are plenty of pretty women.' She was breathless beneath that rasp.

But he knew she was enjoying this slight spar and parry. He'd play along.

'Naturally.' Damon coolly watched her over the rim of his glass as he sipped his drink, deliberately hiding his delight. 'I am merely a man, after all.' He shrugged helplessly.

Her gaze narrowed on him, twin sparks shooting from that impossible blue. 'You mean you're a boy who likes playing with toys. A doll here, a doll there…'

'Of course,' he followed her smoothly. 'Toying with dolls can be quite an amusing pastime. As can collecting them.'

'I'll bet.'

He leaned forward, deliberately intruding into intimate space to whisper conspiratorially, 'I never break my toys though,' he promised. 'I take very good care when I'm playing.'

'Oh?' Her gaze lanced straight through his veneer, striking at a weak spot he didn't know he had. 'If you say it, it must be true.'

Appreciating her little flash of spirit, he was instantly determined to take very great care…to torture her delightfully.

'And you?' he asked, though he already suspected the answer. 'Do you often attend nights like this?' Did she play with toys of her own?

She shrugged her shoulders in an echo of his.

He leaned closer again, rewarded as he heard the hitch in her breathing. 'Do you work at the hospital?'

Tonight's ball was the annual fundraiser and, while he knew huge amounts were raised, it was also the chance for hospital staff to be celebrated.

'I…do some stuff there.' Her lashes lowered.

Wasn't she just Ms Mysterious? 'So why aren't you with your friends?'

'I don't know them all that well.'

Perhaps she was a new recruit who'd won an invitation for this ball in the ballot they held for the hospital staff. Perhaps that was why she didn't have any friends with her. It wouldn't take long for her to find a few. Some surgeon would snap her up if he had any sense. Then it wouldn't be long before she lost that arousing ability to blush.

A spear of possessiveness shafted through him at the thought of some other guy pulling her close. Surprising him into taking another step nearer to her. Too near.

'Do you want to dance?' He gave up on subtlety altogether.

She glanced beyond him. 'No one is dancing yet.'

'We could start the trend.'

She quickly shook her head, leaning back into the shadows so his body hid her from those in the ballroom. Damon guessed she didn't want to stand out. Too late, to him she already did.

'Don't be intimidated by any of that lot.' He jerked his head towards the crowds. 'They might have the wealth but they don't always have the manners. Or the kindness.'

'You're saying you don't fit in either?' The scepticism in her gaze as she looked him over was unmissable.

He resisted the urge to preen in front of her like some damn peacock. Instead he offered a platitude. 'Does anyone truly fit in?'

Her gaze flashed up to his and held it a long moment. Her irises were such a vibrant blue he knew they had to be covered with contacts. The pretence of polite small talk fell away. The desire to reach for her—to strip her—almost overwhelmed him. Now *that* was inappropriate. He tensed, pushing back the base instinct. Damn, he wanted to touch her. Wanted her to touch him. That look in her eyes? Pure invitation. Except he had the feeling she was too inexperienced to even be aware of it.

But he couldn't stop the question spilling roughly from his lips. 'Are you going to do it?'

Eleni Nicolaides didn't know what or how to answer him. This man wasn't like anyone she'd met before.

Direct. Devastating. *Dangerous.*

'Are you going to do it, Blue?'

'Do what?' she whispered vaguely, distracted by the play of dark and light in his watchful expression. He was appallingly handsome in that tall, dark, sex-on-a-stick sort of way. The kind of obviously experienced playboy who'd never been allowed near her.

But at the same time there was more than that to him—something that struck a chord within her. A new—seductive—note that wasn't purely because of the physical magnetism of the man.

He captivated every one of her senses and all her interest. A lick of something new burned—yearning. She wanted him closer. She wanted to reach out and touch him. Her pulse throbbed, heating need about her body—to her dry, sensitive lips, to her tight, full breasts, to other parts too secret to speak of...

His jaw tightened. Eleni blinked at the fierce intensity that flashed in his eyes. Had he read her mind? Did he know just *what* she wanted to do right now?

'Join in,' he answered between gritted teeth.

She swallowed. Now her pulse thundered as she realised how close she'd come to making an almighty fool of herself. 'I shouldn't...'

'Why not?'

So many reasons flooded her head in a cacophony of panic.

Her disguise, her deceit, her *duty*.

'Blue?' he prompted. His smile was gentle enough but the expression in his eyes was too hot.

Men had looked at her with lust before, but those times the lust hadn't been for her but for her wealth, her title, her virtue. She'd never been on a date. She was totally untouched. And everyone knew. She'd read the crude conjecture and the jokes in the lowest of the on-line guttersnipes: *THE VIRGIN PRINCESS!!!*

All caps. Multiple exclamation marks.

That her 'purity' was so interesting and so important angered her. It wasn't as if it had been deliberate. It wasn't as if she'd saved herself for whichever prince would be chosen for her to marry. She'd simply been so sequestered there'd been zero chance to find even a friend, let alone a boyfriend.

And now it transpired that her Prince was to be Xander of the small European state of Santa Chiara. He certainly hadn't saved himself for her and she knew his fidelity after their marriage was not to be expected. Discretion was, but not that sort of intimate loyalty. Or love.

'Do you ever stop asking questions?' she asked, trying for cool and sophisticated for these last few moments of escape.

Wishing she could be as accepting as so many others who didn't doubt their arranged marriages. Because this was it. Tomorrow her engagement would be formally announced. A man she'd barely met and most certainly didn't like would become her fiancé. She felt frigid at the thought. But those archaic royal rules remained unchallenged and offered certainty. The Princess of Palisades could never marry a commoner. This disguise tonight was a lame leap for five minutes of total freedom. The only five minutes she'd have.

'Not if I'm curious about something.'

'And you're curious about—'

'You. Unbearably. Yes.'

Heat slammed into every cell. She couldn't hold his gaze but she couldn't look away either. His eyes were truly blue—not enhanced by contacts the way hers were—and hot. He seemed to see right through her mask, her carefully applied powder, her whole disguise. He saw the need she'd tried to hide from everyone.

She was out of place and yet this was her home— where she'd been born and raised and where her future was destined, dictated by duty.

'You have the chance to experience this…' he waved at the ballroom full of beautiful people '…yet you're hanging back in the shadows.'

He voiced her fantasy—reminding her of her stupid, crazy plan. She'd arranged for a large selection of costumes to be delivered to the nurses' quarters at the hospital for tonight's masquerade. No one would know that one dress, one wig, and one mask were missing from that order. All done so she, cloistered, protected, precious Princess Eleni, could steal one night as an anonymous girl able to talk to people not as a princess, but as a nobody.

She could be no one.

And yet, when it had come to it, she'd swiftly realised her error. She'd watched those guests arrive. Clustered together, laughing squads of *friends*—the kind she'd never had. How could she walk into that room and start talking to any of them *without* her title as her armour? What had she to offer? How could she blend in when she hadn't any clue what to discuss other than superficial niceties? She'd ached with isolation, inwardly mocking her own self-piteous hurt, as she'd uselessly stared at all those other carefree, relaxed people having fun.

Privileged Princess Eleni had burned with jealousy.

Now she burned with something else, something just as shameful.

'I'm biding my time,' she prevaricated with a chuckle, drawing on years of practising polite conversation to cover her shaken, unruly emotions.

'You're wasting it.'

His bluntness shocked that smile from her lips. She met his narrowed gaze and knew he saw too much.

'You want a night out, you need to get out there and start circulating,' he advised.

Her customary serene demeanour snapped at his tone. 'Maybe that's not what I want.'

The atmosphere pulsed between them like an electrical charge faulting.

Heat suffused every inch of her skin. Now she truly was unable to hold his gaze. But as she looked down he reached out. The merest touch of fingers to her chin, nudging so she looked him in the eye again. She fought to quell the uncontrollable shiver that the simple touch generated.

'No?' Somehow he was even closer as he quietly pressed her. 'Then what do you want?'

That she couldn't answer. Not to herself. Not now. But he could see it anyway.

'Walk with me through the ballroom,' he said in a low voice. 'I dare you.'

His challenge roused a rare surge of rebellion within her. She who always did as she was bid—loyal, dutiful, serene. Princess Eleni never caused trouble. But *he* stirred trouble. Her spirit lifted; she was determined to show strength before him.

'I don't need you to dare me,' she breathed.

'Don't you?' He called her bluff.

Silent, she registered the gauntlet in his hard gaze. The glow of those blue eyes ignited her to mutinous action. She turned and strode to the edge of the alcove. Nerves thrummed, chilling her. What if she was recognised?

But this man hadn't recognised her and she knew her brother would be busy in the farthest corner of the room meeting select guests at this early stage in the evening. Everyone was preoccupied with their own friends and acquaintances. She *might* just get away with this after all.

'Coming?' She looked back and asked him, refusing—yet failing—to flush.

He took her hand and placed it in the crook of his elbow, saying nothing, but everything, with a sardonic look. The rock-hard heat of his biceps seeped through the fine material of his tailored suit and her fingers curled around it instinctively. He pressed his arm close to his side, trapping her hand.

He walked slowly, deliberately, the length of the colonnades. To her intense relief, he didn't stop to speak to anyone, instead he kept his attention on her, his gaze melting that cold block of nervousness lodged in her diaphragm.

It turned out she'd been wrong to worry about recognition. Because while people *were* looking, it was not at her.

'All these women are watching you,' she murmured as they drew near the final column. 'And they look surprised.'

A smile curled his sensual lips. 'I haven't been seen dating recently.'

'They think I'm your date?' she asked. 'Am I supposed to feel flattered?'

His laughter was low and appreciative. 'Don't deny it, you do.'

She pressed her lips together, refusing to smile. But the sound of his laugh wasn't just infectious, it seemed to reach right inside her and chase all that cold away with its warmth.

'There.' He drew her into the last alcove, a mirror of the first, and she was appallingly relieved to discover it too was empty at this early hour.

'Was that so awful?' he asked, not relinquishing her hand but walking with her to the very depths of the respite room and turning to face her.

Inwardly she was claiming it as a bittersweet victory. A date at last.

'Who are you?' She felt foolish that she didn't know when it was clear many others did. 'Why do they look at you?'

He cocked his head, his amusement gleaming. 'Why do *you* look at me?'

Eleni refused to answer. She was *not* going to pander to his already outsize ego.

His lazy smile widened. 'What do you see?'

That one she could answer. She smiled, relishing her release from 'polite princess response'.

'I see arrogance,' she answered boldly. 'A man who defies convention and doesn't give a damn what anyone thinks.'

'Because?'

She angled her head, mirroring his inquiring look. 'You don't wear a mask. You don't make the effort that's expected of everyone else.'

'And I don't do that—because why?' His attention narrowed laser-like in its focus on her.

'Because you don't need to,' she guessed, seeing the appreciation flicker in his eyes. 'You don't want their approval. You're determined to show you don't need *anything* from them.'

His expression shuttered, but he didn't deny her assessment of him. Her heart quickened as he stepped closer.

'Do you know what I see?' Almost angrily he pointed to the mask covering most of her face. 'I see someone hiding more than just her features. I see a woman who wants more than what she thinks she should have.'

She stilled, bereft—of speech, of spirit. Because she did want more and yet she knew she was so spoilt and selfish to do so. She had *everything*, didn't she?

'So what happens at midnight?' That tantalising smile quirked his lips, drawing her attention to the sensuality that was such a potent force within him.

She struggled to remind herself she was no Cinderella. She was already the Princess, after all. 'Exactly what you think it will.'

'You'll leave and I'll never see you again.'

His words struck deep inside her—sinking like stones of regret.

'Precisely,' she replied with her perfectly practised princess politeness.

She shouldn't feel the slightest disappointment. This was merely a fleeting conversation in the shadows. Five minutes of dalliance that she could reminisce over a whole lot later. Like for the rest of her life.

'I don't believe in fairy tales,' he said roughly, his smile lost.

'Nor do I,' she whispered. She believed in duty. In family. In doing what was right. Which was why she was going to marry a man she didn't love and who didn't love her. Romance was for fairy tales and other people.

'You sure about that?' He edged closer still, solemn and intense. 'Then flip it. Don't do the expected. Don't disappear at midnight.' He dared her with that compelling whisper. 'Stay and do what you want. You have the mask to protect you. *Take* what you want.'

She stared up at him. He was roguishly handsome and he was only playing with her, wasn't he? But that was…okay. Intense temptation and a totally foreign sensation rippled through her. The trickle soon turned into a tsunami. From the deepest core of her soul, slipping along her veins to ignite every inch of her body.

Want.

Pure and undeniable.

Couldn't she have just a very little moment for herself? Couldn't she have just a very little of *him*?

He couldn't hide his deepening tension. It was in his eyes, in the single twitch of the muscle in his jaw as the curve of his smile flatlined. That infinitesimal *edge* sharpened. But he remained as motionless as the marble column behind him, hiding the ballroom from her view. Waiting, watching.

Take what you want.

That dare echoed in her mind, fuelling her desire.

She gazed into his eyes, losing herself in the molten steel. She parted her lips the merest fraction to draw in a desperate breath. But he moved the moment she did. Full predator—fast, powerful, inescapable—he pressed his mouth to meet hers.

Instinctively she closed her eyes, unable to focus on anything but the sensation of his warm lips teasing hers. Her breath caught as he stepped closer, his hands spanning her waist to draw her against him. She quivered on impact as she felt his hard strength, finally appreciating the sheer size of the man. Tall, strong, he radiated pure masculinity.

He took complete control, his tongue sliding along her lips, slipping past to stroke her. Never had she been kissed like this. Never had *she* kissed like this, but his commanding passion eviscerated any insecurity—and all thought. Lost to the sensation she simply leaned closer, letting him support her, pressing her into his iron heat.

Heavy, addictive power flowed from him to her as he kissed the very soul of her. His arms were like bars, drawing her against the solid expanse of his chest. A moan rose in the back of her throat and he tightened his hold more. She quivered at his defined strength—not just physical. It took mental strength to build a body like his, she knew that too.

Her legs weakened even as a curious energy surged through her. She needed him closer still. But his hand lifted to cup her jaw and he teased—pressing maddeningly light kisses on her lips instead of that explosive, carnal kiss of before. She moaned, in delight, in frustration.

At that raw, unbidden response, he gave her what she wanted. Uncontrolled passion. She clutched at him wildly as her knees gave out—swept away on a torrent of need that had somehow been unleashed. She didn't know how to assuage it, how to combat it. All she could do was cling—wordlessly, mindlessly begging for more. The intensity of his desire mirrored her own—she felt him brace, felt the burning of his skin beneath her fingertips as she touched his jaw, copying his delightful touch.

But now his hand stroked lower, pressing against her thigh. Breathless she slipped deeper, blindly seeking more. But she felt his hesitation. She gasped as he broke the kiss to look at her. Unthinking she arched closer, seeking to regain contact. But in the distance she heard a roaring. A clinking of—

Glasses. *Guests.*

Good grief, what was she *doing*?

Far too late those years of training, duty and responsibility kicked in. How could she have forgotten who and where she was? She could not throw everything away for one moment of *lust*.

But this lust was all-consuming. All she wanted was for him to touch her again—decisively, intimately, now.

Brutal shame burned from her bones to her skin. She had to get alone and under control. But as she twisted from his hold a long tearing sound shredded the unnatural silence between them. Time slowed as realisation seeped into her fried brain.

That too tight, too thin strap over her shoulder had

ripped clear from the fabric it had been straining to support. And the result?

She didn't need to look to know; she could feel the exposure—the cooler air on her skin. Aghast, she sent him a panicked glance. Had he noticed?

Of course he'd noticed.

She froze, transfixed, as his gaze rested for a second longer on her bared breast before flicking back to her face. The fiery hunger in his eyes consumed her. She was alight with colour and heat, but it wasn't embarrassment.

Oh, heavens, no.

She tugged up the front of her dress and turned, blindly seeking escape.

But he drew her close again, bracketing her into the protective stance of his body. He walked, pressing her forward away from the crowd she'd foolishly forgotten was present. And she was so confused she just let him. Through a discreet archway, down a wide corridor to space and silence. He walked with her, until a door closed behind them.

The turn of the lock echoed loudly. Startled, she turned to see him jerkily stripping out of his dinner jacket with barely leashed violence. His white dress shirt strained across his broad shoulders. Somehow he seemed bigger, more aggressive, more sexual.

Appallingly desire flooded again, rooting her to the spot where she clutched her torn dress to her chest. She desperately tried to catch her breath but her body couldn't cope. Her lips felt full and sensitive and throbbed for the press of his. Her breasts felt tight and heavy and, buried deep within, she was molten hot and aching.

All she could do was stare as he stalked towards her.

All she could think was to surrender.

CHAPTER TWO

'SLIP THIS AROUND your shoulders and we can leave immediately.' He held the jacket out to her. 'No one will...' He trailed off as she stared at him uncomprehendingly.

He'd only been stripping in order to *clothe* her? To protect her from prying eyes rather than continue with... with...

Suddenly she was mortified. She'd thought that he'd been going to—

'No.' She finally got her voice box to work. 'No. That's impossible.'

Nervously she licked her lips. What was impossible was her own reaction. Her own *willingness*. Horrified, she stepped away from the temptation personified in front of her, backing up until she was almost against the wall on the far side of the room.

He stood still, his jacket gently swinging from his outstretched hand, and watched her move away from him. A slight frown furrowed his forehead. Then he shifted, easing his stance. He casually tossed the jacket onto the antique sofa that now stood between them.

His lips twisted with a smile as rueful as it was seductive. 'I'm not going to do anything.'

'I know,' she said quickly, trying and failing to offer a smile in return.

She wasn't afraid of him. She was afraid of herself. Her cheeks flamed and she knew a fierce blush had every inch of her skin aglow. Shamed, she clutched the material closer to her chest.

This had been such a mistake. More dangerous than she ever could have imagined. Her breathing quickened again. She was so mortified but so *sensitive*. She glanced at him again only to have him snare her gaze in his. He was watching her too intently. She realised that his breathing was quickened, like hers, and a faint sheen highlighted his sun-kissed skin.

'Are you okay?' he asked softly. 'I'm sorry.'

But he didn't look sorry. If anything that smile deepened.

But she also saw the intensity of the heat banked in his expression and something unfurled within her. Something that didn't help her resistance.

'It wasn't your fault,' she muttered. 'It's a cheap dress and it doesn't really fit that well.'

'Let me help you fix it,' he offered huskily. 'So you can get out of here.'

'I can make do.' She glanced at the locked door behind him. 'I'd better go.'

She knew there was another exit from the room, but it was locked by the security system. She couldn't use it without showing him she was intimate with the palace layout. He could never know that. Maybe she could drape the blue and purple hair of her wig over her shoulder to hide that tear.

'Trust me,' he invited gruffly. 'I'll fix your dress. Won't do anything else.'

That was the problem. She wanted him to do something. Do *everything* or *anything* he wanted. And that was just crazy because she couldn't set a lifetime of responsibility ablaze now. What made it worse was that he knew—why she'd moved to put not just space, but furniture between them.

'You can't get past them all with that strap the way it is now,' he muttered.

He was right. She couldn't get away from him either. Not yet.

So she stepped nearer, turning to present her shoulder with the torn strap. 'Thank you.'

Holding her breath, heart pounding, she fought to remain still as he came within touching distance. The tips of his deft fingers brushed against her burning skin as he tried to tie the loose strap to the torn bodice. She felt it tighten, but then heard his sharp mutter of frustration as the strap loosened again.

She inhaled a jagged breath. 'Don't worry—'

'I'll get it this time,' he interrupted. 'Almost there.'

She waited, paralysed, as he bent to the task again, trying desperately to quell her responsive shiver to the heat of his breath on her skin but he noticed it anyway. His hands stilled for that minuscule moment before working again.

'There,' he promised in a lethal whisper. 'All fixed.'

But he was still there—too close, too tall, too everything. She stood with her eyes tight shut, totally aware of him.

'You're good to go.'

Good. She didn't feel like being good. And she didn't want to go.

She opened her eyes and saw what she'd already felt with every other sense. He was close enough to kiss.

She shook her head very slightly, not wanting to break this spell. 'It was a dumb idea. I shouldn't have come.'

She hadn't meant to tell him anything more but the secret simply fell from her lips.

'But you've gone to such trouble.' He traced one of the swirls of glitter she'd painted on her shoulder. His finger roved north, painting another that rose up her neck, near her frantically beating pulse, and rested there.

'You shouldn't miss out.' He didn't break eye contact as he neared, but he didn't close the half-inch between their mouths.

She had to miss out. That was her destiny—the rules set before she was even born. Yet his gaze mesmerised, making her want all kinds of impossible things. Beneath those thick lashes the intensity of his truly blue eyes burned through to her core.

'You'd better get back out there, Blue.' He suddenly broke the taut silence and dropped his hand. His voice roughened, almost as if he were angry.

'Why?' Why should she? When what she wanted was right here? Just one more kiss? Just once? Hot fury speared—the fierce emotion striking all sense from her. 'Maybe I can…' she muttered, gazing into his eyes.

'Can what?' he challenged, arching an eyebrow. 'What can you do…?'

She tilted her chin and reached up on tiptoe to brush her lips over his. Sensation shivered through her. This was right. This was *it*.

He stiffened, then took complete control. He gripped

her waist and hauled her close, slamming her body into his. She felt the give of her stupid dress again. She didn't mind the half-laugh that heated her.

'You can do that,' he muttered, a heated tease as he kissed her with those torturous light kisses until she moaned in frustration. 'You can do that all you like.'

She did like. She liked it a *lot*.

Kisses. Nothing wrong with kisses. Her bodice fluttered down again, exposing her to him. Thank goodness. His hands took advantage, then his mouth. The drive for more overwhelmed her. Never had she felt so alive. Or so good.

She gasped when he lifted her, but she didn't resist, didn't complain. He strode a couple of paces to sit on the sofa, crushing her close then settling her astride his lap.

She shivered in delight as he kissed her again. She could die in these kisses. She met every one, mimicking, learning, becoming braver. Becoming unbearably aroused. Breathless, she lost all sense of time—could only succumb to the sensation as his hand swept down her body, down her legs. Slowly he drew up the hem of her dress. His fingertips stroked up her hot skin until he neared that most private part of her. She shivered and he lifted his head, looking deep into her eyes. She knew he was seeking permission. She wriggled ever so slightly to let him have greater access because this felt too good to stop. Still watching her, he slid his hand higher.

'Kiss me again,' she whispered.

Something flared in his eyes. And kiss her he did, but not on her mouth. He bent lower, drawing her nipple into the hot cavern of his mouth while at the same time his fingertips erotically teased over the crotch of her panties.

Eleni gasped and writhed—seeking both respite from the torment, and more of it. No one had touched her so intimately. And, heaven have mercy, she liked it.

She caught a glimpse of the reflection in the mirror hanging on the opposite wall. She didn't recognise the woman with that man bending to her bared breasts. This was one stranger doing deliciously naughty things with another stranger—kissing and rubbing and touching and sliding. Beneath her, his hard length pressed against his suit pants. It fascinated her. The devilish ache to explore him more overtook her. She rocked against his hand, shivering with forbidden delight. She was so close to something, but she was cautious. He pulled back for a second and studied her expression. She clenched her jaw. She didn't want him to stop.

'Take what you want,' he urged softly. 'Whatever you want.'

'I…'

'Anything,' he muttered. 'As much or as little as you like.'

Because he wanted this too. She felt the tremble in his fingers and it gave her confidence. Somehow she knew he was as taken aback as she by this conflagration. She might not have the experience, but she had the intuition to understand this was physical passion at its strongest.

Her legs quivered but she let him slide the satin skirt of her dress higher. It glided all the way up to her waist, exposing her almost completely. Her legs were bared, her chest, only her middle was covered in a swathe of blue. She sighed helplessly as that hard ridge of him pressed where she was aching most.

She struggled to unfasten his shirt buttons; she

wanted to see his skin. To feel it. He helped her, pulling the halves of his shirt apart. For a moment she just stared. She'd known he was strong, she'd felt that. But the definition of his tense muscles—the pecs, the abs—still took her by surprise. The light scattering of hair added to the perfection. He was the ultimate specimen of masculinity. She raised her gaze, meeting the fire in his, and understood the strength he was holding in check.

'Touch all you like,' he muttered, a guttural command.

She liked it *all*. Suddenly stupidly nervous, she pressed her palm over his chest—feeling the hardness and heat of him. But she could feel the thump of his heart too and somehow that grounded her. She read the desire in his eyes, intuitively understanding how leashed his passion was. That he, like she, wanted it *all*.

'Touch me,' she choked. Her command—and his reply—dislodged the last brick in the wall that had been damming her desire inside. She did not want him to hold back with her.

He caressed her breasts with his hands, teasing her as she rocked on him, rubbing in the way the basic instinct of her body dictated—back and forth and around.

'So good,' she muttered, savouring the pressure of his mouth, the sweep of his hands, the hardness of him under her. 'So good.'

It was so foreign. So delicious. Feverish with desire, she arched. Pleasure beyond imagination engulfed her as faster they moved together. Kisses became ravenous. Hands swept hard over skin. Heat consumed her. She moaned, her head falling back as he touched her in places she'd never been touched. As he brought her sensuality to life.

She heard a tearing sound and realised it had been the crotch of her panties. They'd not survived the strength of his grip. She glanced and saw he'd tossed the remnants of white silk and lace onto the wide seat. Now she could feel his hand touching her again so much more intimately.

'Oh.'

She dragged in a searing breath and gazed into his eyes.

'That's it, Blue,' he enticed her in that devilish whisper. 'Come on.'

She couldn't answer—not as his fingers circled, and slipped along the slick cleft of her sex, not as they teased that sensitive nub over and over and over. She bit her lip as that searing tension deep in her belly tightened. She rocked, her rhythm matching the pace of his fingers as they strummed over and around her. He kissed her, his tongue soothing the indent of her teeth on her lip, then stroking inside her mouth in an intimate exploration of her private space. Just as his finger probed within her too.

She tore her mouth from his and threw her head back, arching in agony as she gasped for breath. He fixed his mouth on her breast, drawing her nipple in deep. Pleasure shot from one sensitive point to another, rolling in violent waves across her body. She shuddered in exquisite agony, crying out as she was completely lost to this raw, writhing bliss.

When she opened her eyes she saw he was watching her, his hand gently stroking her thigh.

She breathed out, summoning calm and failing.

Giddy, she gazed at him, stunned by the realisation that she'd just had an orgasm. She'd let him touch her and kiss her and he'd made the most amazing feelings flood through her. But the hunger had returned already and brought that special kind of anger with it.

That emptiness blossomed, bigger than before. There was more to this electricity between them. More that she'd missed. More that she wanted.

A chasm stretched before her. A choice. A line that, once crossed, could never be reclaimed. But it was *her* choice. And suddenly she knew exactly how she wanted this one thing in her life to be. Within her control.

For this first time—for only this time—she wanted physical intimacy with a man who truly wanted her back. A man who wanted not her title, not her purity or connections. Just her—naked and no one special. This man knew nothing of who or what she was, but he wanted her. This was not love, no. But pure, basic, brilliant lust.

Just this once, she would be *wanted* for nothing but herself.

Almost angrily she shifted on him, pressing close again, kissing him. He kissed her back, as hard, as passionate. She moaned in his mouth. *Willing* him to take over. But he drew back, pressing his hand over hers, stopping her from sliding her palm down his chiselled chest to his belt.

'We're going to be in trouble in a second,' he groaned. 'Stop.'

She stared dazedly into his face as he eased her back along his thighs, almost crying at his rejection.

'I need to keep you safe,' he muttered as his hands

worked quickly to release his zipper. 'One second. To be safe.'

She couldn't compute his comment because at that moment his erection sprang free. Never had she seen a man naked. Never had she *touched*. He reached into his trouser pocket and pulled out a small packet that he tore open with his teeth. Her mouth dried as she stared avidly.

Of course he was prepared. He was an incredibly handsome, virile man who knew exactly how to turn her on because *he* was experienced. He was used to this kind of anonymous tryst and he definitely knew how to make a woman feel good. And that was…*okay*.

As she tore her gaze away from the magnificence of him she caught sight of their reflections in that gleaming mirror again. The image of those two strangers— half naked and entwined—was the most erotic thing she'd ever seen in her life. Their pasts didn't matter. Nor did their futures. There was only this. Only them. Only now. She turned back to look at the overwhelming man she was sitting astride with such vulnerability— and with such desire.

Princess Eleni always did the right thing.

But she wasn't Princess Eleni tonight. She was no one and this was nothing.

'Easy, Blue.' He gently stroked her arm.

She realised her breathing was completely audible— rushed and short.

'Just whatever you want,' he muttered softly.

He wasn't just inviting her. He was giving her the choice, *all* the control. Yet his voice and his body both commanded and compelled her own and there was no choice.

This once. This *one* time. She wanted everything—all of him. She shimmied closer. The sight of his huge straining erection made her quiver and melt. She didn't know how to do this. She looked into his eyes and was lost in that intensity. And suddenly she understood.

She kissed him. Kissed him long and deep and softened in the delight. In the *rightness* of the sensation. She could feel him there beneath her. She rocked her hips, as she'd done before, feeling him slide through her feminine folds. His hands gripped her hips, holding her, helping her. She pressed down, right on that angle, every sense on high alert and anticipation. But her body resisted, unyielding.

She *wanted* this.

So she pushed down hard. Unexpectedly sharp pain pierced the heated fog of desire.

'Blue?' A burning statue beneath her; his breathing was ragged as he swore. 'I've—'

'I'm fine,' she pleaded, willing her body to welcome his.

'You're tight,' he said between gritted teeth.

'You're big.'

He filled her completely—beneath her, about her, within her. The force and fire of his personality scalded her. Her breath shuddered as she was locked in his embrace, and in the intense heat of his gaze.

'Have I hurt you?' His question came clipped.

'No.' It wasn't regret that burned within her, but recognition. This was what she wanted. 'Kiss me.'

And he did. He kissed her into that pure state of bliss once more. Into heat and light and sparkling rainbows and all kinds of magic that were miraculous and new. Touching him ignited her and she moved restlessly, eager to feel him touching her again too. That fullness between her legs eased. Honeyed heat bloomed and she slid closer still to him. She sighed, unable to remain still any more. His arms tightened around her, clasping her to him as he kissed her back—exactly how she needed. *Yes.* This was so good, it had to be right. He shifted her, sliding her back, and then down hard on the thick column of his manhood.

He suddenly stood, taking her weight with no apparent difficulty. Startled, she instinctively wrapped her legs around his waist. He kissed her in approval and took those few paces to where that narrow table stretched along the wall. He stood at the short end and carefully placed her right on the edge of it, then slowly he eased her so she lay on her back on the cool wood. Her legs were wound around his waist, her hips tilted upwards as he braced over her, his shaft still driven to the hilt inside her. That mirror was right beside her now but she didn't turn her head to look again at those strangers; she couldn't. Her wicked rake claimed every ounce of her focus.

'This is madness,' he muttered. 'But I don't care.'

Nor did she. This moment was too perfect. Too precious. Too much to be denied.

His large hands cupped her, holding her as he pressed into her deeply, and then pulled back a fraction, only to push forward again. Again, then again, then again. Every time he seemed to drive deeper, claiming more and more of her. And she gave it to him. She would give him everything, he made her feel so good. He gazed into her eyes and in his she saw the echo of her own emotions—wonder, pleasure, *need*.

She'd never been as close to another person in all her

life. Not so passionately, nakedly close. Nor so vulnerable, or so safe. Never so free.

She kissed him in arousal, in madness, in gratitude. Trusting him implicitly. He'd already proven his desire to please her.

'Come again,' he coaxed in a passionate whisper. 'I want to feel you come.'

She wanted that too. She wanted exactly that.

He touched her just above the point where they were joined, teasing even as he filled her. She gasped as she felt the sensations inside gather once more in that unstoppable storm.

'You…please…' she begged incoherently as she feverishly clutched him, digging her fingernails into his flesh. She wanted him to feel the same ecstasy surging through her. She needed him on this ride *with* her. As she frantically arched to meet him she heard his groan. His hands gripped tighter, his expression tensed. She smiled in that final second. She wanted to laugh. She wanted to revel in it and she never, ever wanted it to end.

His face flushed as sensation swept the final vestige of control from his grasp. Pleasure stormed through her again, surging to the farthest reaches of her body. She sobbed in the onslaught of goodness and delight and his roar of satisfaction was the coda to her completeness.

Her eyes were closed. She could hear only the beating of her heart and his as they recovered. She was pinned by his weight and it was the best feeling on earth.

But then laughter rang out. Not hers. Nor his.

'What's in this room?'

Eleni snapped her head to stare at the door as someone on the other side tried the handle.

'Hello?'

More laughter reverberated through the wood.

Reality returned in a violent slam, evaporating the mist of delight. Suddenly she saw herself as she'd look to anyone who burst through that door—Princess Eleni of Palisades, ninety per cent naked, sprawled on a table with her legs around the waist of some stranger and his body ploughed deep into hers.

Sordid headlines smashed into her head: *shameless wanton...a one-night stand...the eve of her engagement...* There would be no mercy, no privacy—only scorn and shame. She had to get out of here. Aghast, she stared up at the handsome stranger she'd just ravished. What had she done?

Damon watched his masked lover's eyes widen in shock. Beneath the blue sparkled powder, her skin paled and her kiss-crushed lips parted in a silent gasp. This was more than embarrassment. This was fear. He was so stunned by her devastated expression he stepped back. She slipped down from the table and tugged at her crumpled clothing. Before he could speak someone knocked on the door again. More voices sounded out in the corridor.

Her pallor worsened.

'I'll get rid of them,' he assured her, hauling up his trousers so he could get to the door and deny anyone entrance to the room. He was determined to wipe that terror from her face.

He pressed a hand on the door. Even though he'd locked it, he couldn't be sure someone wouldn't be able to unlock it from the other side. He listened intently, hoping the revellers would pass and go exploring elsewhere. After a few moments the voices faded.

He turned back to see how she was doing, but she'd vanished. Shocked, he stared around the empty room, then stalked back to where she'd been standing seconds ago. Only now did he register the other door tucked to the side of that large mirror. There were two entrances to this room and he'd been so caught up in her he'd not even noticed.

He tried the handle but it was locked. So how had she got through it? Keenly he searched and spotted a discreet security screen. Had she known the code to get out? She must have. Because in the space of two seconds, she'd fled.

Just who was she? Why so afraid of someone finding her? Foreboding filled him. He didn't trust women. He didn't trust anyone.

If only he'd peeled off that mask and seen her face properly. How could he have made such a reckless, risky decision?

Anger simmered, but voices sounded outside the other door again, forcing him to move. He glanced in the mirror at his passion-swept reflection. Frowning, he swiftly buttoned his shirt and fixed his trousers properly. Thank heavens he'd retained enough sense to use protection. But as he sorted himself out he realised something he'd missed in his haste to ensure that door was secure. The damn condom was torn. And more than that? It was marked with a trace of something that shouldn't have been there. He remembered when she'd first pushed down on him. When she'd inhaled sharply and tears had sprung to her eyes.

Uncertainty. *Pain.*

Grimly he fastened his belt. He'd been too lost to lust to absorb the implications of her reaction. Now his gut tensed as he struggled to believe the evidence. Had she given him her virginity? Had she truly never had another lover and yet let him, a total stranger, have her in a ten-minute tryst in a private powder room?

Impossible. But the stain of her purity was on his skin. His pulse thundered in his ears. *Why* would she have done something so wild? What was her motivation?

Hell, what had *he* been thinking? To have had sex with a woman he'd barely met as fast and as furiously as possible? Almost in public?

But her expressive response had swept all sensible thought from his head. She'd *wanted* him and heaven knew he'd wanted her. He was appalled by his recklessness; his anger roared. But a twist of Machiavellian satisfaction brewed beneath, because he was going to have to find her. He was going to have to warn her about the condom. The instinct to hunt her pressed like the blade of a knife. She owed him answers.

Find her. Find her. Find her.

His pulse banged like a pagan's drum, marching him back to the busy ballroom. He even took to the balcony to scan the braying crowd, determined to find that blue hair and swan-like neck. But he knew it was futile. The midnight hour had struck and that sizzling Cinderella had run away, never wanting to be seen again.

Least of all by him.

CHAPTER THREE

'YOU LOOK PEAKY.'

Eleni forced a reassuring smile and faced her brother across the aisle in his jet.

'I have a bit of a headache but it's getting better,' she lied.

She felt rotten. Sleeplessness and guilt made her queasy.

'The next few weeks will be frantic. You'll need to stay in top form. They want the pretty Princess, not the pale one,' King Giorgos turned back to the tablet he'd been staring at for the duration of the flight.

'Yes.'

She glanced out of the small window. Crowds had gathered with flags and celebratory signs. She quickly dug into her bag to do a touch-up on her blush, thankful that the jet had landed them back on Palisades.

Giorgos had escorted her on a three-day celebration visit of Santa Chiara to meet again with Prince Xander and his family. Not so long ago she'd have inwardly grimaced at her brother's smothering protectiveness, but she'd been glad of his presence. It had meant she'd not been left alone with Prince Xander.

The Shy Princess captures the Playboy Prince...

Their engagement had captured the imaginations of both nations. Her schedule and the resulting media interest had been beyond intense these last few weeks. At least all the appearances had kept her too busy to think. But late at night when she was alone in her private suite?

That was when she processed everything, reassuring herself she was safe. She would never tell anyone and that man from the ball would never tell anyone. He didn't even know who she was. She didn't know his name either. Only his face. Only his body.

She shivered but forced another smile when her brother glanced at her again. 'I'm going to go to my hospital visit this morning,' she said brightly.

Giorgos frowned. 'You don't wish to rest?'

Always protective. And also, always frowning.

She shook her head.

It had been nothing more than a sordid physical transaction. A ten-minute encounter between strangers. And surely, *please*, *please*, *please*, she would soon forget it. Because right now the memories were too real. She relived every moment, every word, every touch. And the worst thing? She wanted it again, wanted more, wanted it so much she burned with it. And then she burned with shame. Tears stung at the enormity of her betrayal. She was now engaged to another man yet all she could think of was *him*, that arrogant, intense stranger at the ball.

Thankfully displays of physical affection weren't 'done' between royals so the few 'kisses for the camera' on her tour with Prince Xander had been brief— her coolness read by the media as shyness. In private her fiancé had seemed happy to give her the time and space to adjust.

It was Giorgos who had asked if she was going to be happy with Xander and who'd reassured her that her fiancé's 'playboy' status was more media speculation than solid truth. For a moment she was tempted to confess her dreadful affair, but then she saw the tiredness in the back of her brother's eyes. He worked so hard for his people.

And she couldn't bear to see his crushing disappointment. She remembered how Giorgos had teased her with big-brother ruthlessness and laughter. But how he'd aged a decade overnight when their father died. Under the burden of all that responsibility he'd become serious, distant and more ruthless, without that humour. She understood he was wretchedly busy, but he'd tried his best for her—sending people to educate her, protect her, guide her. He just hadn't had the time himself. And she could not let him down.

He believed Xander to be the right fit for her—from a limited pool of options—and perhaps he was. So she'd make the best of it.

For Giorgos.

But the thought of her wedding night repulsed her. As crazy as it was, that brief conversation with that stranger at the ball had engendered far more trust in her than any of the discussions she'd had with polite, well-educated, aiming-to-please but ultimately careless Prince Xander. She simply didn't want him like that. She shivered again as that cold, sick feeling swept over her.

'I don't want to miss a visit,' she finally answered as she rose to disembark the jet.

She needed to do something slightly worthwhile because the guilt was eating her up. Her brother nodded and said nothing more. If anyone understood duty before all else, it was he.

An hour later, as she walked the corridor towards her favourite ward, that cold queasiness returned.

'Princess Eleni?' Kassie, the physiotherapist escorting her to the ward, stopped.

From a distance Eleni registered the woman was frowning and her voice sounded distanced too.

'Are you feeling okay?'

Damon Gale was barely existing in a state of perpetual anger. He hadn't left Palisades without trying to find and warn his mystery lover there might be consequences from their time together. He'd described her to his half-sister Kassie, but she'd not been able to identify the woman either. No one could. None of his subtle queries had given any answers. Where had she disappeared to so quickly? Heaven knew, when he found her he was giving her a piece of his mind. But at night she came to him in dream after dream. He woke, hard, hungry and irritable as hell. There was so much more they should have done. But now she was hiding. Not least the truth about who she was. Why?

He loathed nothing more than lies.

So this morning, weeks since that damn ball, he'd once again flown back to Palisades. Now he waited for Kassie at the hospital in her tiny office, looking at the clever pen and ink drawings of the child patients pinned to the noticeboard.

He heard a footstep and a low, hurried whisper just outside the door.

'Ma'am, are you sure you're feeling all right?'

That was Kassie. Damon's muscles tensed.

'I'm just a bit…dizzy. Oh.' The woman groaned.

He froze, shocked at the second voice. He *knew* those raspy tones. She spoke in his dreams. Every. Damn. Night.

'Do you need a container?' Kassie asked delicately.

'I had a bug a few days ago but I thought I was over it or I'd never have visited today,' the woman muttered apologetically. 'I'm so sorry. I'd never want to put any of your patients at risk.'

'They're a hardy lot.' Now Kassie's smile was audible. 'I'm more concerned about you. Are you sure I can't get a doctor to check you over?'

'No, please. No fuss. I'll quickly go back to the palace. My driver is waiting.'

Palace? Damon was unable to move. Unable to speak. His woman had known the security code to get through that second door in the palace. Did she work there? But she'd said she worked at the hospital. That was why he was back here again.

'Maybe you should rest a moment,' Kassie urged softly.

'No. I need to go. I shouldn't have come.'

Damon stood. Those words exactly echoed ones he'd heard that night at the masked ball. Those exact tones in that exact, raspy voice. It was *her*.

He strode across the room and out into the corridor. But his half-sister had her back to him and she was standing alone. Damon looked past her and saw no one—the corridor ended abruptly with a corner.

'Who was that?' he demanded harshly.

Kassie spun, startled. 'Damon?' She blinked at him. 'I didn't know you were coming back again so soon.'

'I have another meeting,' he clipped. 'Who were you talking to?'

'I'm not supposed to say because her visits are strictly private,' Kassie answered quietly. 'But she wasn't feeling well today and left early.'

'Whose visits?' What did she mean by 'private'?

'The Princess.'

Damon stared dumbfounded at his half-sister.

Princess Eleni of Palisades?

Wasn't she the younger sister of King Giorgos, a man known for his protectiveness and control over everything—his island nation, his emotions, his small *family*. Hadn't he been the guardian of the supposedly shy Princess for ever?

Now the covers of the newspapers at the airport flashed in his mind. He'd walked past them this morning but paid little attention because they'd all carried the same photo and same headline—

A Royal Engagement! The Perfect Prince for Our Princess!

But the Princess was not perfect. She'd fooled around with a total stranger only a few weeks ago. And now she was engaged. Had she been rebelling like some wilful teen? Or was there something more devious behind her shocking behaviour? And, heaven have mercy, how *old* was she?

'What do you think was wrong with her?' he asked Kassie uneasily. He needed to get alone and research more because an extremely bad feeling was building inside him.

'I'm not sure. She was pale and nau—'

'Where did she go?' he interrupted.

Kassie was staring at him. 'Back to the palace. She visits my ward every Friday. She never misses, no matter what.' Kassie ventured a small smile. 'She doesn't seem your type.'

He forced himself to answer idly, as if this didn't matter a jot. 'Do I have a type?'

Kassie's laugh held a nervous edge as she shook her head. 'Princess Eleni is very sweet and innocent.'

But that was where Kassie was wrong. Princess Eleni wasn't sweet or innocent at all. She was a liar and a cheat and he was going to tear her to shreds.

Thank God he finally knew where and how he could get to her. He just had to withstand waiting one more week.

CHAPTER FOUR

IN HER BATHROOM Eleni stared at her reflection. Her skin was leached of colour and she felt sick and tired all the time. Wretched nausea roiled in her stomach yet again, violent and irrepressible. She'd been avoiding mirrors since the ball. She couldn't see herself without seeing those two strangers entwined...

It had been over a month since that night. Now she gazed at her breasts and held in her agonised gasp. Was it her imagination or were they fuller than usual? That would be because her period was due, right? But finally she made herself face the fact she'd been trying desperately to forget. Her period was more than due. It was late.

Two weeks late.

She'd been busy. She'd been travelling. Her cycle could be screwed up by nerves, couldn't it?

Frigid fear slithered down her spine as bitter acid flooded her mouth again. Because a lone, truly terrifying reason for her recurring sickness gripped her.

Surely it was impossible. She'd seen him put on that condom. She couldn't possibly be pregnant. That foul acid burned its way up into her mouth. She closed her eyes as tears stung and then streamed down her face. She needed help and she needed it now.

But there was no help to be had. She had no true friends to trust. Her childhood companions had been carefully selected for their families' loyalty to the crown and swiftly excised from her life if they'd slightly transgressed. There were acquaintances but no real confidantes and now most were in continental Europe getting on with their careers.

Eleni had studied at home. It was 'safer'; it endorsed their own, prestigious university; it was what Giorgos had wanted. She'd not argued, not wanting to cause him trouble.

She was terrified of troubling him now.

But she was going to have to. Shaking, she showered then dressed. She quickly typed an email to Giorgos's secretary requesting a meeting for this evening. Her brother was busy, but Prince Xander was arriving from Santa Chiara tonight for a week's holiday with her. They'd be travelling to the outer islands to spend more time together. She was dreading it. She had to speak to Giorgos first. She had to tell him the truth.

Still incredibly cold, she grabbed a jacket and stuffed a cap in the pocket while her maid, Bettina, phoned for her car.

It was far later than when she usually went to the hospital, but she was desperate to get away from her suite where her maid was lining up sample wedding dresses from the world's top designers. The only thing she could do while waiting to meet Giorgos was maintain some kind of schedule. Given she'd left her visit so abruptly last week, she couldn't miss this week as well. She'd control the nausea and control her life.

Once she got to the hospital she asked Tony, her security detail, to wait for her outside. But she didn't go into the ward, and instead walked along the corridor to the other side of the building. She tugged on the cap and headed out to the private hospital garden. She needed to steel herself for the polite questions from the patients she'd come to help entertain. But she'd been lying all day, every day for the last few weeks and it was taking its toll. Telling people over and over again how excited she was at the prospect of marrying Prince Xander was exhausting. And horrible. But the bigger the lie, the more believable it apparently was.

She leaned over the wrought-iron railing, looking down at the river. She was going to have to go back and front up to Giorgos. Her gut churned, but it wasn't the pregnancy hormones making her nauseous now. How did she admit this all to him?

I'm sorry. I'm so sorry.

Sorry wasn't going to be good enough. She dreaded sinking so low in his eyes. Never had she regretted anything as much as her recklessness that night at the ball.

A prickle of awareness pressed on her spine—intuition whispered she was no longer alone. Warily she turned away from the water.

'You okay?' The man stood only a couple of paces away. 'Or are you feeling a little blue?'

The bitterness in that soft-spoken query devastated her. It was *him*. Her blood rushed and the edges of her vision blackened as she shrank back. Something grasped her elbow tightly, the pain pulling her from the brink of darkness.

'It's okay, I'm not going to let you fall.'

He was there and he was too close, with his words in her ear and his strength in her grip and his heat magnetic. *Oh, no. No.*

'I'm sorry.' Eleni ignored the sweat suddenly slithering down her spine and snapped herself together.

He released her the second she tugged her arm back, but he didn't step away. So he was close. Too close.

'I don't know what came over me.' She leaned against the railing, unable to stop the trembling of her legs or the jerkiness of her breathing.

'Yeah, you do.' He leaned against the wrought iron too, resting his hand on the rail between them. Not relaxed. *Ready to strike.*

Tall, dark and dangerous, he looked like some streetwise power player in his black trousers, black jersey, aviator sunglasses and unreadable expression.

'There's no point trying to hide any more, Eleni,' he said. 'I know who you are and I know exactly what your problem is.'

She froze. 'I don't have a problem.'

'Yeah, you do. You and I created it together. Now we're going to resolve it. Together.'

All strength vanished from her legs. They'd *created* it? The full horror hit as she realised he *knew.*

'I'm sorry,' she repeated mechanically. 'I don't know who you are and I don't know what you're talking about.' She willed her strength back. 'If you'll forgive me, I need to go.'

'No.' He removed his sunglasses. 'I won't forgive you.'

Her heart stuttered at the emotion reflected in his intense blue eyes. Accusation. Betrayal. Anger...and something else.

Something she dared not try to define.

She clenched her fists and plunged them into the pockets of her jacket, fighting the paralysis. 'I have to leave.'

'Not this time. You're coming with me, Eleni. You know we need to talk.'

'I can't do that.' Why had she thought it wise not to tell her security detail where she was going?

'Yes, you can. Because if you don't...'

'What?' She drew in a sharp breath as a sense of fatality struck. 'What will you do?'

Of course it would come to an ultimatum. The determination had been on his face from the second she'd seen him. He was livid.

'You come with me now and we take the time to sort this out, or I tell the world you're pregnant from screwing a stranger at the palace ball.'

His tawdry description of what they'd done stabbed. It hadn't been a 'screw'. It had meant more than she could ever admit to anyone.

'No one would believe you,' she muttered.

'You're *that* good at lying?' He was beyond livid. 'You want this scandal dragged through the press? That you're going to marry a man without telling him that you're pregnant, most probably by another?'

She flinched at his cruelly blunt words but she latched onto the realisation that he wasn't *sure* the baby was his.

'You want the whole world to know that you're not the perfect Princess after all?' he goaded her relentlessly. 'But a liar and a cheater?'

'I've never been the perfect Princess,' she snapped back, defensive and hurt and unable to stay calm a second longer.

'Come on.' The softness of his swift reply stunned her.

Her heart thundered. He'd echoed the forbidden words from weeks ago. Heat flared. So wrong.

'I can't,' she reminded him—and herself—through gritted teeth. 'My fiancé is arriving in Palisades tonight.'

'Really?' He glared at her. 'That cheating life is what you really want?' His frustration seeped through. 'That's why you're standing by the river looking like you're about to throw yourself in? You're lost, Eleni.'

'You don't know what I am.'

He knew nothing about her and she knew as little about him—not even his damn name.

Except that wasn't quite true. She knew more important things—his determination, his strength, his consideration.

And *her* guilt.

'The one thing I do know is that you're pregnant and the baby very well might be mine. You owe me a conversation at least.'

He wasn't going anywhere and he was perfectly capable of acting on his threat, she knew that about him too. She tried to regain her customary calm, and decided to bluff. 'So talk.'

'Somewhere private.' He glanced up at the multi-storeyed hospital building behind her. 'Where we can't be seen or overheard.'

That made sense but it was impossible. She shook her head.

'My car is just around the corner,' he said, unconcerned at her latest refusal.

Her heart thudded. She shouldn't go anywhere alone with any man and certainly not this one.

'I'll go straight to the media,' he promised coolly. 'And I have proof. I still have your underwear.'

She was aghast; her jaw dropped.

'You *wouldn't*,' she choked.

'I'm prepared to do whatever is necessary to get this sorted out,' he replied blandly, putting his sunglasses back on. 'I suggest you walk with me now.'

What choice did she have?

She hardly saw where she was going as she moved back through the hospital, then to the right instead of the left. Away from her guard. Hopefully Tony wouldn't notice for a few minutes yet—in all her life she'd never caused trouble for him.

She slid into the passenger seat of his car.

'Five minutes,' she said just as he closed the door for her.

He was still laughing, bitterly, as he got in, locked the doors and started the engine. 'You might want to put on your seat belt, because it's going to take a little longer than that this time, sweetheart.' He pulled out into the road. 'We have a lifetime to work out.'

'Where are you taking me?' She broke into a cold sweat.

'As I said, somewhere private. Somewhere where we won't be disturbed.'

'You can't take me away from here.' Frantically she twisted in her seat, terrified to see the hospital getting smaller as they moved away from it.

'I know how quickly you can move, Eleni. I'm not taking the risk of you running from me this time.'

Surprised, she turned to face him.

'Relax.' He sent her an ironic glance. 'I'm not going to hurt you, Princess. We just need to talk.'

Sure, she knew he wouldn't hurt her physically. But in other ways? She tried to clear her head. 'You have the better of me. I don't even know your name.'

'So you're finally curious enough to ask?' His hands

tightened on the steering wheel. 'My name is Damon Gale. I'm the CEO of a tech company that specialises in augmented reality. I have another company that's working on robotics. Most women think I'm something of a catch.'

Damon. Crisp and masculine. It suited him.

'I'm not like most women.' She prickled at his arrogance. 'And a lot of men think I'm a catch.'

'You definitely took some catching,' he murmured, pulling into a car park and killing the engine. 'Yet here we are.'

Eleni looked out of the car window and saw he meant literally. He'd brought her to the marina. 'Why are we here?'

'I need the certainty that you won't do one of your disappearing acts, but we can't have this argument in the front seat of a car and...' He hesitated as he stared at her. 'We need space.'

Space? Eleni's heart thundered as she gazed into his eyes. Beneath her shock and fear something else stirred—awareness, recognition.

This is the one I had. This is the one I want.

Suddenly that forbidden passion pulsed through every fibre of her being.

Unbidden. Unwanted. Undeniable.

CHAPTER FIVE

HE'D KNOWN HER eyes weren't that unnaturally intense indigo they'd been at the ball, but the discovery of their true colour had stolen a breath that Damon still hadn't recovered. They were sea green—a myriad of bewitching shades—and he couldn't summon the strength to look away.

She lies.

He reminded himself. Again.

The alluring Princess Eleni Nicolaides had used him and he couldn't possibly be considering kissing her. He'd not been completely certain before but he was now—she was pregnant. To him.

Grimly he shoved himself out of the car and stalked around it to open her door. Impatiently he watched the emotions flicker across her too-expressive face— wariness, curiosity, decision—and beneath those? Desire.

His body tightened. More than anger, this was possessiveness. So off-base. Rigid with self-control, he took her arm, steeling himself not to respond to the electricity that surged between them. It took only a minute to guide her down the steps and along the wooden landing to his yacht. She stopped and stared at it.

'Eleni,' he prompted her curtly. 'We need to talk.'

'You have to take me back soon.' She twisted her hands together. 'They'll be wondering where I am.'

'They can wonder for a while yet,' he muttered.

He hustled her past the cabin and through to the lounge. The windows were tinted so no one on deck could see them, and his sparse crew were under strict instruction to stay out of sight and work quickly. He remained in front of the only exit to the room. He couldn't be careful enough with her.

'Take off the cap.' He could hardly push the words past the burr in his throat, but he needed to see her with no damn disguise.

She lifted the cap. Her hair wasn't long and blue, it was cut to a length just below her chin and was blonde—corn silk soft, all natural and, right now, tousled.

'How did you figure out who I was?' she asked in that damnably raspy voice.

He shook his head.

Once he'd realised who his mystery lover was, he'd been lame enough to look online. But she was more perfect in the flesh. Tall and slender, strong and feminine, with those curves that caused the most base reaction in him. Her complexion was flawless and her sweetheart-shaped face captivating. But her beauty was a façade that apparently masked a shockingly salacious soul. He was determined to get to the truth.

'You knew I was going to be at the hospital,' she said after he didn't reply to her first question. 'How?'

Her fingers trembled as she fidgeted with the cap, but he'd not brought her here to answer *her* questions.

'Were you going to tell him?' he asked.

He glared as she didn't answer. She was so good at avoiding everything important, wasn't she?

He felt the vibration beneath the deck as the engines fired up. About time. Icily satisfied, he silently kept watching. Now she'd be tested. Sure enough, as the yacht moved she strode to the window.

'Where are you taking me?' she asked, her volume rising.

'Somewhere private.' Somewhere isolated. Triumph rushed at the prospect of having her completely alone.

'This *is* private. We don't need to move to make it more so.' Panic filled her voice and turned wide eyes on him. 'This is abduction.'

'Is it?' he asked, uncaring. 'But you agreed to come with me.'

'I didn't realise you meant...' She paled. 'I can't just *leave*.'

He hardened his heart. 'Why not? You've done that before.'

This was the woman who'd had sex with him when she knew she was about to announce her engagement to another man. Who'd then run off without another word. And who was now pregnant and concealing it—apparently from everyone.

The betrayal burned like no other. He hated being *used*. His father had used him as cover for his long-term infidelities. His mother had used his entire existence to promote her political aspirations—hell, she'd even told him she never would have had him if it weren't for the possible benefit to her career. His father had not only agreed, he'd expected Damon to understand and become the same. A parasite—using anyone and anything to enhance success. He'd refused and he'd vowed that he'd never let anyone use him again.

But Eleni had.

Yet that look on her face now was torture—those shimmering eyes, the quiver of her full lips.

Desire tore through his self-control, forcing him closer to her. Furious, he locked it down, viciously clenching his fists and shoving them into his trouser pockets. It was this uncontrolled lust that had got him into this mess in the first place.

It was insane. Once more he reminded himself he knew nothing of importance about her other than her shocking ability to conceal information. But as he watched, she whitened further. Whitened to the point of—

'Eleni?' He rushed forward.

'Oh, hell.' She pressed her hand to her mouth.

Oh, hell was right. He reached for a decorative bowl just in time.

Oh, no. No.

Eleni groaned but the sickness couldn't be stopped. Of all the mortifying things to happen.

'Sit down before you fall down,' he muttered.

'I'm not used to being on the water,' she replied.

'If you're going to lie, at least try to make it believable. It's well known you love sailing, Princess. Your illness is caused by your pregnancy.'

She was too queasy to bother trying to contradict him. What was the point? 'I need fresh air.'

'You need to stay in here until we're away from the island.'

'You can't be serious.' Aghast, she stared up at him. 'You're going to cause an international incident.'

'Do you think so?' He stared at her grimly. 'I think the spectacle is only going to get even more insane when they find out I'm the father of your unborn child.'

She closed her eyes and groaned. 'At least let me use a bathroom.'

'Of course.'

He guided her to a small room. He opened a drawer and handed her a toothbrush, still in its packet. She took it, silently grateful as he left her in privacy.

But he was just outside the door when she opened it again a few minutes later.

She walked back into the lounge just as a uniformed crew member was leaving. The man didn't say a word, didn't meet her eyes. He simply melted from the room.

'Who was that?' she asked.

'Someone extremely discreet and very well paid.'

He'd left fresh water in a tall glass and a few crackers on a plate. She turned away; there was no way she could eat anything right now.

'You're naive if you think he won't sell your secrets.' The man had recognised her. It was only a matter of time before people came to her rescue.

'I've been betrayed before, Eleni. I know how to make my business safe.'

Eleni looked at the hard edge of Damon's jaw and wondered who had betrayed him. 'Your business?'

'My baby.'

Her blood chilled. 'So you planned this.'

There'd been a crew ready and waiting on this boat and no doubt he paid them ridiculously well. He'd gone to huge trouble to get her away from the palace. Maybe she ought to feel scared, she barely knew him after all, but she didn't believe she was in danger. Rather, in that second, the craziest feeling bloomed in her chest.

Relief.

His eyes narrowed. 'You know this isn't about rescuing you.'

His words hit like bullets. She shrank, horrified that he'd seen her *selfishness*. Guilt brought defensiveness with it. 'I don't need rescuing.'

His smile mocked. 'No?'

Damon was more dangerous than she'd realised. She couldn't cope with her reaction to him. It was as if everything else in the world, everything that mattered, simply evaporated in his presence. His pull was too strong.

But then she remembered he wasn't certain she was pregnant to *him*. Perhaps her way out was to convince him he *wasn't* the father. Then he'd return her to Palisades. She'd go to Giorgos. She should have gone to Giorgos already.

'I *can't* stay here,' she pleaded.

'Give in, Eleni,' he replied indifferently. 'You already are. The question is, can you be honest?'

Not with him. Not now.

But she burned to prove that she didn't need 'rescuing'—not from her situation, or from herself. He strolled towards her but she wasn't fooled by the ease of his movement. He was furious. Well, that made two of them.

'How many other possibilities are there?' he asked too softly, his gaze penetrating.

'Excuse me?' She tensed as he came within touching distance.

'Who are the other men who might be the father of your child?' He watched her so intently she feared he could see every hidden thought, every contrary emotion.

'Can you even remember them all?' he challenged.

She flushed at his tone, lost for words.

'You have sex with me at a ball within five minutes of meeting me,' he murmured, continuing his hateful judgment. 'You didn't even know my name.'

'And you didn't know mine,' she flared. 'And we used protection. So there you go.'

'But *I* wasn't engaged to anyone else at the time.'

That one hurt because it was truth. 'Nor was I,' she mumbled weakly.

'Not "officially".' His eyes were so full of scorn that she winced. 'But you *knew*. You knew the announcement was about to be made. You owed him your loyalty and you cheated.'

Damon was right, but he didn't know the reality of the marriage she faced. He'd never understand the scrutiny and crazy constraints she endured in her privileged world.

At her silence now, pure danger flashed in his eyes. She backed away until the wall brought her to a stop. Her heart raced as he followed until he leaned right into her personal space.

'So, how many others?' he asked again, too softly.

She'd brazen it out. Disgust him so he'd take her back to Palisades in repulsion. 'At least four.'

'Liar.' Slowly he lifted his hand and brushed the backs of his fingers over the blush burning down her cheekbones. 'Why won't you just tell me the truth, Eleni?'

His whisper was so tempting.

She lifted her chin, refusing to let him seduce her

again. And at the same time, refusing to run. 'I don't have to tell you anything.'

'What are you afraid of?' he taunted huskily. 'The world finding out your secret? That Princess Eleni The Pure likes dressing up in disguise and doing it fast and dirty with a succession of strangers? That she can't get enough?'

Anger ignited, but something else was lit within as well. That treacherous response. She *had* liked it fast and dirty. With him. She closed her eyes but he tilted her chin back up, holding it until she opened them again and looked right into the banked heat of his.

'Are you ashamed of what happened, Eleni?'

Tears stung but she blinked them back. Of *course* she was ashamed. She couldn't understand how it had happened. How she could have lost all control and all reason like that. And how could her body be so traitorous now—aching for him to take that half step nearer and touch her again?

The intensity deepened in his eyes. A matching colour mounted in his cheekbones.

Hormones. Chemicals. That crazy reaction that she still couldn't believe had happened was happening again.

'You like it,' he muttered. 'And you want it.'

'And I get it,' she spat, reckless and furious and desperate to push him away. 'From whomever, whenever I please.'

'Is that right?'

'Yes,' she slammed her answer in defiance.

He smiled. A wickedly seductive smile of utter disbelief.

'You'll never know.' She was pushed to scorn.

'You don't think?' He actually laughed.

'Maybe I'm pregnant with my fiancé's baby,' she snapped. Reminding him of her engagement might make him back off. She *needed* him to back off.

His smile vanished. 'I don't think so, Princess.'

She stilled at his expression.

'You haven't slept with him,' Damon said roughly. 'I was your first, Eleni. That night with me, you were a virgin.'

She gaped, floundering in total mortification as he threw the truth in her face.

How had he known? How? She pressed against the cool wall, hoping to stop shaking.

'Why lie so constantly?' he demanded, leaning closer, the heat of his body blasting. 'You still have nothing to say?'

How could she possibly explain? She couldn't answer even her own conscience.

'There is nothing wrong with liking sex,' he said roughly. 'But there is something wrong with lying and cheating to get it.'

She trembled again, appalled by how aroused she was. She could no longer look him in the eye; he saw too much. She wanted to hide from him. From herself. Since when was she this wanton animal who'd forgo all her scruples simply to get a physical fix?

'Eleni.'

She refused to look at him.

But she couldn't escape the sensations that the slightest of touches summoned. He brushed her cheek with a single finger, and then tucked a strand of her hair back behind her ear. She stood rigid, desperate not to reveal any reaction.

'Let's try this again, shall we?' He leaned so close.

She bit the inside of her cheek, hoping the pain would help keep her sane, but she could feel his heat radiating through her.

'No lying. No cheating,' he murmured. 'Just truth.'

The tip of his finger marauded back and forth over her lips; the small caress sent shock waves of sensuality to her most private depths.

Her pulse quickened, but his finger didn't. Slowly he teased. Such pleasure and such promise came from a touch so small, building until she could no longer hold still. He teased until she parted her lips with a shaky breath.

He swooped, pressing his mouth to hers, taking advantage to slide his tongue deep and taste until he tore a soft moan from her. So easily. He wound his arm around her waist and drew her close, holding her so he could kiss her. Again. Then again.

After all these sleepless nights he was with her—with all his heat and hardness. She quivered, then melted against him. Immediately he swept his hand down her side, urging her closer and she went—her body softening to accommodate the steel of his.

With his hands and with his lips, he marauded everywhere now. Kissing her mouth, her jaw, her neck, he slid his hand across her aching breasts, down her quivering stomach, until he hit the hem of her skirt. He pushed under and up. High, then higher still up her thigh. Demanding—and getting—acceptance, intimacy, willingness. So quickly. So intensely. She curled into his embrace, then arched taut as a bowstring as he teased her.

'Eleni…' he whispered between kisses and caresses. 'How many lovers have you had?'

Unable to contain her need, she thrust against that tormenting finger that was so close, that was stirring her in a way that she could no longer resist. On a desperate sigh she finally surrendered her not so secret truth. 'One.'

He rewarded her with more of that rubbing designed to drive her insane. She couldn't breathe. Closer, *so* close.

'And how many times have you had sex?'

She shook with aching desire. With the need for him to touch her again. Just once. One more touch was all she needed. 'One,' she muttered breathlessly.

Her answer seemed to anger him again. He held her fast and kissed her hard. Passionate and ruthless, his tongue plundered the cavern of her mouth. He was dominant and claiming and all she could do was yield to his passion.

But the fires within him stoked her own. She kissed him back furiously, hating him knowing how aroused she was. But there was no controlling her reaction. No stopping what she wanted. And she *wanted. Now.*

It was at that moment, of her total surrender, that he tore his mouth from hers.

'How many men have kissed you like that?' he rasped.

She panted, her nipples tight and straining against her suddenly too tight bra. *'One,'* she answered, pushed beyond her limits.

'And how many men have kissed you liked that, but *here*?' His fingers pushed past the silk scrap of material covering her, probing into her damp, hot sex.

She gasped at the delicious intrusion. Her limbs trembled as release hovered only a stroke or two away.

She gazed into his gorgeously fiery eyes, quivering at the extreme intimacy connecting them.

'Answer me, Eleni.' He ground out a brutal whisper.

'None.' Her answer barely sounded.

She registered his sharp exhalation but then he kissed her again. Somehow she was in his embrace, his body between hers. Heaven help her, she went with him to that sofa. She let him. Wanted him. But as he pushed her skirt higher and slid lower so he was kneeling between her legs she realised where this was going. A lucid moment—she gasped and shifted.

'Don't try to hide. I'm going to kiss you. There won't be even an inch of you that I haven't tasted. Every intimacy is *mine*.'

His blunt, savage words stunned her. Blindly she realised that his control was as splintered as her own. That he too was pushed beyond reason. Pleasure surged and she couldn't resist or deny—not him. Not herself.

She groaned at his first kiss, shocked at how exposed she felt and embarrassed by just how much she ached for his touch. It was like being taken over by a part of herself she didn't know was there. That lustful, brazen part. She flung her arm over her face, hiding from him. From herself. But there was no hiding from the sensations he aroused and the delight and skill of his mouth on her. His tongue. There. Right there.

She moaned in unspeakable pleasure.

'Look at that,' he muttered arrogantly in the echo of her need. 'You like it.' His laugh was exultant. 'You like it a lot.'

His attention was relentless. She arched again, pressing her hands against her eyes but unable to hold back her scream as a torrent of ecstasy tore through her. She shuddered, sweet torture wracking her body.

Then she was silent, suspended in that moment where she waited for his next move. For him to rise above her, to press against her, to take her. She ached anew to feel him. She wanted him to push inside and take her completely.

But he didn't. He didn't move at all.

She lay frozen, her face still buried in her arm as the last vestiges of that bliss ebbed. And then shame flooded in. Bitter, galling shame.

She twisted, suddenly desperate to escape. But he grasped her hips hard, prevented her moving even an inch.

'Stop hiding,' he growled savagely. 'There are things we must discuss.'

'Discuss? You think you discuss anything?' She threw her arms wide and snarled at him. 'You dictate.' He *bulldozed*. 'And you…you…'

'Take action.' He finished her sentence for her, as breathless and angry as she. 'And I'll continue to do so. And first up, you're not going to marry Prince Xander of Santa Chiara. You're going to marry me.'

CHAPTER SIX

'I'M NOT MARRYING YOU,' Eleni snapped, furiously shoving him. 'I'm not marrying anyone.'

'Right.' He lazily leaned back on his heels and sent her a sardonic look. 'That's why the world is currently planning party snacks for the live stream of the royal wedding of the century.'

She was sick of his smug arrogance. Awkwardly she curled up her legs to get past him and angrily pulled her skirt down, too mortified to hunt for her knickers. 'I wasn't going to go through with it.'

'Really?' He stood in a single, smooth movement, mocking her with his athletic grace. 'What was the plan?'

She loathed how inept he made her feel. How easily he could make her lose all control. How much her appallingly stupid body still wanted his attention. 'You have no idea how impossible it is for me to get away.'

'As it happens, I do have some insight into the technical difficulties.' His gaze narrowed. Hardened. 'So you were going to go through with it.'

She'd never wanted to but she'd known it was what was expected. Since she'd suspected her pregnancy her desperation had grown. She glared at him from the centre of the room. 'I didn't know what to do.'

'Why not try talking to him?'

She rolled her eyes. He made it sound so easy.

'Giorgos wouldn't listen.'

'Giorgos?' Damon's eyebrows shot up. 'What about the man you were supposed to marry?'

Who? Oh. He meant Xander. As if she could talk to him—she barely knew him.

'I'm guessing you don't love him. Prince Xander, that is,' Damon added sarcastically.

She turned away from Damon. Her heart beat heavy and fast and she perched on the edge of a small chair—far, far away from that sofa. 'Obviously not or I wouldn't have…done what I did with you.'

'Then why marry him?'

'Because it is what has been expected for a long time.'

'So it's duty.'

'It would benefit our countries…'

'Because a royal wedding is somehow going to magically smooth away any serious issues your respective countries may be facing?' He laughed derisively. 'And you'll throw in some rainbows and unicorns to make it all prettier and perfect?'

'You don't understand the subtleties.'

'Clearly not,' he muttered dryly. 'And was my child meant to be the fruit of this fairy-tale unity?' he demanded. 'When in reality she or he will grow up lonely in a house devoid of warmth and love with parents absent in every sense.'

Eleni stared, taken aback by his vehemence. And his insight.

'I'll never let my child be used that way.' His eyes were hard. 'I know the unseen impact of a purely political union and I'll do whatever it takes to ensure my kid doesn't endure that kind of bleak upbringing.'

'I'm not going to marry him,' she said in a low voice. 'I know I can't.'

'But if you don't marry someone, your child will be labelled a bastard. We might live in modern times, but you're a *princess* and there are certain expectations. What kind of life will your child have without legitimacy? Will she be kept cloistered in the shadows, even more stifled than you were? Look how well that turned out for you.'

She flinched. He saw too much and he judged harshly. But the horrible thing was, he was right. She had to think of a better way. She leapt to her feet and paced away from him, twisting her cold hands together. She didn't want to involve *him*—he twisted everything up too much.

'I need to call Giorgos,' she said. It must be almost two hours since she'd left Palisades and her brother would be irate already.

'I agree.'

She spun on the spot. 'You do?'

'Of course. It'll be better if you're completely honest with him. Do you think you can be—or are you going to need help with that again?'

She flushed, remembering just how Damon had dragged the intimate truth from her only minutes ago. Now his biting sarcasm hurt and she felt sick enough at the thought of confessing all to her brother.

'What, you expect me to cheerily tell him I'm here of my own free will?' She flared. 'That you didn't bundle me into a boat and set sail for the high seas before I could blink?'

'The choice was yours.'

'What choice did you give me?' she scoffed.

'To speak the truth, or give you time. I think it was a reasonable choice.'

'It was blackmail. Because you're a bully.'

'You've already admitted you didn't know what to do. You couldn't figure a way out. Here it is and you're happy about it. Don't dramatise me into your villain.'

Eleni rubbed her forehead. Damon's words struck a deep chord. She'd been refusing to admit to herself how glad she was he'd stolen her away. She'd been unable to think up an escape and he'd offered one. She wasn't as much mad with him, but mad with herself for needing it—and for layering on complications with her wretched desire for him. Her emotional overreactions had to end.

She'd been too scared to admit to Giorgos how badly she'd screwed up. But if she wanted her brother to treat her as an adult, she had to act like one.

'Okay.' She blew out a breath and turned to look Damon in the eye. 'I'm not sorry you took me away. You're right. I needed this time to think things through. Thank you.'

'How very gracious, Princess,' Damon drawled. 'But don't be mistaken. Like I said, this isn't a rescue. I'm not doing you a favour. I'm claiming what's mine. And I'm protecting it.' He picked up a handset from a small side table and held it out to her. 'Phone your brother.'

Eleni's hands were slick with sweat as she tapped the private number onto the screen.

'Giorgos, it's me.' She turned away from Damon as her brother answered his private line immediately.

'Eleni. Where are you?' Giorgos demanded instant

answers. 'Come back to the palace now. Do you have any idea of the trouble you've caused?'

'I'm not coming back yet, Giorgos. I need time to think.'

'Think? About what?' Her brother dismissed her claim. 'Your fiancé is already here. Or had you forgotten that you're about to go on tour with him?'

'I can't do it, Giorgos.'

'Can't do what?' Giorgos asked impatiently.

Eleni closed her eyes and summoned all her courage. 'I'm pregnant,' she said flatly. 'Prince Xander isn't the father.'

Silence.

Seven long seconds of appalled silence.

'Who?' Giorgos finally asked in a deadly whisper. *'Who?'*

'It doesn't matter—'

'I'll kill him. I'll bloody— Tell me his name.'

'No.'

'Tell me his name, Eleni. I'll have him—'

'Call off the hounds, Giorgos.' She interrupted her brother for the first time in her life. 'Or I swear I'll never return.' Her heart broke as she threatened him. 'I will disappear.'

Her guilt mounted. Her horror at doing this to the brother she loved. But she pushed forward.

'It doesn't matter who it was. He didn't seduce me. I was a fully willing participant.' She screwed her eyes tight shut, mortified at revealing this intimacy to her brother, but knowing the way he'd assume she'd been taken advantage of because he still thought of her as an innocent, helpless kid. She needed to *own* this. 'I made the mistake, Giorgos. And I need to fix it. Tell

Xander I'm sick. Tell him I ran away. Tell him anything you like. But I'm not coming back. Not yet. Not 'til I've sorted it out.'

'Are you with the bastard now?' Giorgos asked impatiently.

'I'm not marrying him either,' Eleni said.

She didn't catch Giorgos's muttered imprecation.

'This child is mine. Pure Nicolaides.' She finally felt a segment of peace settle in place inside.

This was what she should have done at the beginning. She had to make amends now—to all the people she'd involved. 'And please don't blame Tony for losing track of me. It wasn't his fault.'

'Your protection officer has no idea where you've gone. He's clearly incompetent. He has been dismissed.'

'But it's not his fault.' Eleni's voice rose. Tony had been with Eleni for years. He had a wife and two children. He needed the work. 'I told him—'

'Lies,' Giorgos snapped. 'But it *is* his fault that he lost track of you. His employment is not your concern.'

'But—'

'You should have thought through the consequences of your actions, Eleni. There are ramifications for *all* the people of Palisades. And Santa Chiara.'

Twin tears slid out from her closed eyes. She would make it up to Tony somehow. Another atonement to be made.

'How do I stop a scandal here, Eleni?' Giorgos asked.

She cringed. Was that what mattered most—the reputation of the royal family? But she knew that was unfair to Giorgos. He was trying to protect *her*. It was what he'd always done. Too much.

'I'm so sorry,' she said dully. 'I take full responsibility. I will be in touch when I can.'

She ended the call before her brother could berate her any more. She turned and saw Damon casually leaning against the back of the sofa as if he were watching a mildly entertaining movie.

'Did you have to listen in?' Angered, she wiped the tears away. 'You know they'll have traced the call.'

'And they'll find it leads to some isolated shack in Estonia.' He shrugged. 'I work in the tech industry, Eleni. They won't find us in the next few days, I promise you that. We're hidden and we're safe.'

'What, this is some superhero space boat that can engage stealth mode?' She shook her head. 'They'll be checking the coastline.'

'And we're already miles away from it and your brother knows you're not under duress. You've shocked him, Eleni. I'm sure he'll wait to hear from you. The last thing he'll want now is the publicity from mounting a full-scale search and rescue operation.'

She'd shocked Giorgos. Once he'd got past that, the disappointment would zoom in. She was glad she wasn't there to see it.

'There's one option we haven't talked about,' Damon said expressionlessly. 'It is early enough in the pregnancy for termination to be—'

'No,' she interrupted him vehemently.

She had such privilege. She had money. This child could be well cared for.

And it was *hers*.

That was the thing. For the first time in her life she had something that was truly, utterly her own. Her responsibility. Her concern. Hers to love and protect.

No one was taking it away from her. There was a way out of this if she was strong enough to stand up to her brother's—and her nation's—disappointment. And she was determined to be.

'I'm not marrying Prince Xander,' she said fiercely. 'I'm not marrying you. I'm not marrying anyone. But I *am* having this baby.' She pulled herself together— *finally* feeling strong. 'I have the means and the where-withal to provide for my baby on my own. And that is what I will do.'

'Do you?' Damon looked sceptical. 'What if Gior-gos cuts you off completely? How will you fend for yourself then?'

'He wouldn't do that.' Her brother would be beyond disappointed, but he wouldn't abandon her. She should have trusted him more, sooner.

'Even so, what price will you pay for one moment of recklessness?' Damon badgered. 'The rest of your life in disgrace.'

'I could step away from the spotlight and live in one of the remote villages.' She would ask for nothing from the public purse.

It was the personal price that pained her. She'd let her brother down in both public and private senses. But she would not let this baby down. She'd made her first stand, and now she had to follow through and not let Damon block her way either.

'So that's your escape neatly done,' he noted softly. 'But what price will my *child* pay if you do that?'

She flushed, unsettled by his cool sarcasm. He made it sound as if she was thinking only of herself, not her baby. But she wasn't. She'd understood what he'd said about a child growing up with all that expectation and wasn't this a way of removing that?

But he clearly considered that she'd been stifled and cloistered and, yes, spoilt. He thought her behaviour with him at the ball a direct consequence of that. Maybe he was right. That flush deepened. She loathed this man.

'I'm not marrying you,' she repeated. She *couldn't*.

The absolute last thing Damon Gale wanted to do was marry—her or anyone—but damn if her rejection didn't just irritate the hell out of him. What, was his billionaire bank balance not good enough for her spoilt royal self?

He'd sworn never to engage in even a 'serious' relationship. But the worst of all possible options was a 'politically expedient' wedding. Yet now he was insulted because, while she'd agreed to a political marriage once already, she was adamantly refusing his offer. Why? Because he wasn't a *prince*?

'I'll never let you use my baby for your political machinations.' He glared at her.

All she did was stick her chin in the air and glare back.

His body burned and he paced away from her. That damned sexual ache refused to ease. Heaven only knew why he wanted this woman. But it had been like this since the moment he'd first seen her at that ball. To his immense satisfaction, he'd had her—there and then. He'd immediately wanted more, but then she'd fled.

Now he'd finally found her again, yet within moments of getting her alone on his boat he'd totally lost control and done exactly what he'd promised himself he wouldn't. He'd touched her. Instead of verbally tearing her to shreds, he'd pressed his mouth to her until she'd warmed like wax in his hands. Pliable and willing and ultimately so wanton and gorgeous. It had taken every speck of self-control to not claim her completely there on the sofa.

He knew he could use this mutual lust to get the acquiescence to his proposal he needed, but he wanted more than her gasping surrender. He wanted her to accept that he was *right*. Poor little princess was going to have to marry a mere man. A man she wanted in spite of herself, apparently.

'What were you thinking at that ball?' He couldn't understand why she'd taken such a massive risk. Was it just lust for her too or had there been more to it? Had she been trying to sabotage that engagement? But to throw away her virginity?

'Clearly I wasn't. What were *you* thinking?'

He leaned back against the wall. He'd been thinking how beautiful she was. How something vulnerable in her had pulled him to her.

'I tried to find you because I realised the condom had torn, but you'd vanished from the ball like a—' He broke off. 'I was on a flight the next day. I came back several times, but couldn't find any information about you. I asked—'

'You asked?'

'Everyone I knew. No one had seen you there. You never went back into the ballroom.' He shook his head and asked again. 'Why did you do it?'

Her shoulders lifted in a helpless shrug.

He hesitated but in the end was unable to stop the words coming out. 'Did you even think of trying to get in touch with me?'

Her beautiful face paled. 'I didn't know your name. I wasn't about to run a search on all the guys who'd been at that ball. I couldn't risk anyone suspecting me. How could I tell anyone?'

'How hard would it have been to go through that guest list?' he asked irritably. 'To identify men between a certain age? To look at security footage? You could easily have found out who I was, Eleni. You just didn't want to.' And that annoyed him so much more than it should.

'If I'd tried to do that, people would have asked *why*.'

'And you didn't want them to do that, because you'd already made a promise to another man.' He ran his hand through his hair in frustration. 'I've seen those "official" photos. They weren't taken the day after you slept with me. They were taken before, weren't they?'

She couldn't look him in the eye. 'Yes.'

Damon's blood pressure roared. 'Yet you never slept with him.'

'You're going there again?'

'But you kissed him?' He pressed on, relentless in his need to make his point.

'You can watch it on the news footage.'

He had already. Chaste, passionless kisses. She'd looked nothing like the siren who had writhed in *his* arms and pulled him closer, begging him with her body. The Princess that Damon had kissed was hot and wanton.

'The only time you kiss him is when there are cameras rolling?' He moved forward, unable to resist going nearer to her. 'You don't kiss him the way you kiss me.'

She flung her head up at that. 'Are you jealous?'

So jealous his guts burned right now. 'He doesn't want you,' he said bluntly.

Something raw flashed across her face. 'What makes you say that?'

He stopped his progress across the room and shoved his fists into his trouser pockets. 'If he wanted you the way he ought to, then he'd have moved heaven and earth to find you already. But he hasn't found you. He hasn't fought at all.'

That engagement was a political farce, so he had no reason to feel bad about cutting in and claiming what was already his. They'd sacrifice a year of their lives in sticking it out in a sham of a marriage until the baby was born. That was the only solution. Lust faded and there sure as hell was no such thing as for ever. Princess Eleni here was just going to get over her snobbishness and accept her marriage, and her divorce. And that he was no prince of a man.

Eleni inwardly flinched at that kicker. Because there it was—the cold, unvarnished truth.

Her fiancé didn't want her. Her brother found her an irritant. She had no worthwhile job. And now that her 'purity' was sullied, she'd no longer be desired as a prince's wife anyway. 'I guess my value's plummeted now I'm no longer a virgin,' she quipped sarcastically.

'Your value?' Damon's eyes blazed. 'He shouldn't give a damn about your virginity.'

His anger surprised her. 'In the way you don't?'

A different expression cut across his face. 'Oh, I care about that,' he argued in a slow, lethal whisper.

'It was none of your business,' she said haughtily.

'You don't think?' He laughed bitterly. 'That's where you're so wrong. And who you sleep with is now my business too.'

'I'm. Not. Marrying. You.' She utterly refused.

'It won't be for ever, Eleni,' he assured her dispassionately. 'We can divorce easily enough in time, without destroying the union of two entire nations,' he added pointedly. 'I will retain custody of our child. You will go back to being a princess.'

'Pardon?' The air was sucked from her lungs.

'I'll raise our child alone, without the pressure of public life.'

What? She stared at him, horrified to read the utterly cool seriousness on his face. 'But I'm this child's mother. A child needs her mother.' If anyone knew that, she did.

There was a thick silence.

His expression shuttered. 'A child needs parents who want her. Who love her. And if they're together, they need to be in love with each other.' His words dropped like heavy stones into a still pond. 'While we want each other, we don't—and won't—love each other. This isn't some fairy-tale romance, Eleni. This is real. And we have a real problem to deal with. As adults.'

Not a fairy tale.

She knew theirs was a connection forged by nothing but lust and hormones. But now? What he'd just said came as a greater shock than any the day had brought so far.

He wanted to take her baby from her.

'You've had a long day. You must need something to eat.' He changed the subject easily, as if he hadn't just shaken her whole foundation.

'I couldn't...' She was too shocked to contemplate something so banal as food.

'Suit yourself.' He shrugged carelessly. 'You obviously need sleep to get your head together. But starting tomorrow we'll look at ensuring your diet is appropriate.'

Appropriate? What, he thought he was going to dictate every aspect of her life now?

'How lovely of you to care,' she said acidly.

'I care about my child.' He turned his back on her. 'I'll show you to your quarters.'

Silently she followed him along the gleaming corridor of the large yacht that was still steaming full-speed away from Palisades.

He stopped almost at the end. 'You're in here,' he said briefly, gesturing through the doorway. 'I'm in the cabin next door, if you decide you do need something.'

She didn't move into the room immediately; she was too busy trying to read him. Beyond the too-handsome features, there was intense determination.

A fatalistic feeling sank into her bones. There was no escaping, no getting away from what he wanted. And he didn't actually want *her*—only her baby.

But earlier she'd felt his hardness, his heat, she'd heard his breathlessness as he'd kissed her into ecstasy. Surely he'd wanted her? But he hadn't taken her. And he could have, they both knew that.

All of which merely proved that it had been just sex for him, while she'd thought it had been somehow special…

Strain tightened his features. 'I'm not going to kiss you goodnight,' he muttered. 'I'm too tired to be able to stop it from escalating.'

As if she'd been waiting for him to kiss her? Outraged, she snarled. 'You don't think I could stop it?'

'Maybe you could,' he said doubtfully. 'But I'm not willing to take the risk.'

She stepped into the cabin and slammed the door right in his face.

Not a fairy tale.

No. This was nothing less than a nightmare. She glanced angrily at the large, smooth bed. As if she were ever going to sleep.

CHAPTER SEVEN

'ELENI.'

The whisper slipped over her skin like a warm, gentle breeze. Smiling, she snuggled deeper into the cosy cocoon.

'Eleni.'

She snapped her eyes open. Damon was leaning over her, his face only a breath from hers.

'Oh…hey… What are you doing in here?' she asked softly.

'Making sure you're okay,' he answered, equally softly.

'Why wouldn't I be?' She'd been buried deep in the best sleep she'd had in weeks.

His smile appeared—the magnetic one that had melted all her defences that night at the ball. The one she hadn't seen since. 'Well, I was wondering if you were *ever* going to wake up.'

Why would he think she wouldn't? Had he been trying to rouse her for hours already? His smile diverted her sleepy thoughts onto a different track—had he been about to try waking her with a *kiss*?

Blood quickening, she clutched the sheet to her chest and tried to sit up.

'Easy.' He held her down with a hand on her shoulder. 'Not so fast.' He sat on the edge of her bed and pointed to the bedside table. 'I brought food and water. You must be hungry now.'

The dry crackers on the plate brought her fully awake with a sharp bump. This was no fairy tale. Damon had no thought of romance, only practicality—preventing her morning sickness from surfacing.

'Thank you.' She pulled herself together, determined to be polite and battle him with calm rationality. No more emotional outbursts that only he drew from her. All she needed now was for him to leave.

But clearly he didn't hear her unspoken plea, because he watched her expectantly. With an expressive sigh she lifted the glass of water.

'You normally sleep this late?' Damon asked.

'What time is it?'

'Almost eleven.'

She nearly spat out the mouthful of water she'd just sipped.

That amused grin flashed across his face again. 'I take it you don't usually sleep in.'

Of course not. Never in all her life.

'Has anyone been in contact?' she asked, trying to distract herself from how infuriatingly gorgeous he looked in that old tee and jeans combo.

'You're asking if they've tracked you down?' He shook his head. 'Radio silence.'

She didn't quite know how to feel about that. 'Perhaps they're planning a rescue raid and are about to break in and arrest you,' she muttered acidly. 'Any second now.'

'You came willingly.' That evil amusement lit his eyes. 'More than once.'

Uncontrollable heat washed through her, threatening an emotional outburst. Eleni levered up onto her elbow and glanced about for her robe. It wasn't there. Of course. None of her wardrobe was. The clothes she'd worn yesterday were on the floor where she'd left them. She blushed, imagining the reprimand.

Lazy, spoilt princess.

Awareness prickled. She snuck a look at him from beneath her lashes.

'Got a problem, Princess?' The slightest of jeers, low and a little rough and enough to fling her over the edge.

'Yes,' she said provocatively. 'I don't have anything fresh to wear.'

His eyes widened and for the briefest of seconds his raw reaction to her was exposed. He wanted her still. She was too thrilled by the realisation to stop.

'Hadn't thought of that in all your evil planning, had you?' she purred.

But his expression blanked. 'Maybe I felt clothes weren't going to be necessary.'

'Oh, please.'

But he'd turned that desire back on her, teasing her when she'd wanted to test him.

'You love the idea.' He leaned closer, his whispered words having that warm, magnetic effect on her most private parts. 'And as we're going to be married, there's no need to be shy.'

Her reaction to his proximity was appalling but all she wanted now was to know he was as shattered as she.

'We're *not* going to be married.' She summoned all

her courage and threw back the sheet, meeting his bluff with a fierce one of her own. 'But you want me to spend the day naked?'

As he stared, she fought every instinct to curl her legs up and throw her arms around her knees. Instead she stayed still, utterly naked on the soft white linen.

His gaze travelled the length of her body—lingering on those places too private to mention. She gritted her teeth so she wouldn't squirm. But as his focus trained on her breasts, she felt the reaction—the full, tight feeling as her nipples budded and that warmth surged low within. He looked for a long, long time—and then looked lower, rendering Eleni immobile in the burning ferocity of his attention. Her skin reddened as if she'd been whipped and the slightest of goosebumps lifted. It took everything she had not to curl her toes and die of frustration.

Finally, just when she'd felt she was about to explode, he moved. Wordlessly he pulled his tee shirt over his head and held it out to her.

Desire flooded impossibly hotter still as she stared at his bared chest. Her senses ravenously appreciated his warm tan, the ridged muscles, that light scattering of hair arrowing down to—

'Put it on,' he snapped.

She snatched it from him. But if she'd doubted whether he wanted her as much as she wanted him, she now knew.

Just sex.

She forced herself to remember that this was just sex to him. But a trickle of power flowed through her veins.

He didn't move back as she got out of the bed—he just sat there, too close, his head about level with her breasts. So she stood in front of him—refusing to be intimidated.

The tee skimmed midway down her thighs and swamped her with a sense of intimacy as his scent and warmth enveloped her. Stupidly she felt as if she were more exposed than when she'd had nothing on. Her gaze collided with his—locked, and held fast in the hot blue intensity. She wanted him to touch her again. She wanted more of that pleasure he'd pulled so easily from her last night. She was almost mad with the need for it.

'Stop looking at me like that, Princess,' he said shortly.

The rejection stung. 'Don't call me Princess.'

'Why not?' he challenged almost angrily. 'It's who you are.'

'It's not all I am,' she answered defiantly. 'I don't want that to be all I am.'

She just wanted to be Eleni. She didn't want the reminder of who she *ought* to be all the time and of her failure to do her duty.

Hormones. It had to be the hormones. Here she was facing the biggest mess of her life, rupturing the royal connection of two nations, but all she wanted was for Damon to haul her close and kiss her again. She made herself walk to the door.

'Take me back to Palisades,' she said calmly, trying to sound in control.

'So now that you've used me to hide from your brother's wrath, you want to use your brother to protect you from me.'

She turned back and saw the bitterness of Damon's smile. 'That's not—'

'No?' He shook his head in disbelief. 'Sorry, Eleni,

I'm not a servant who you can order around and who'll fulfil your every whim.'

'No?' she echoed at him angrily. His opinion inflamed her. She stalked back to where he still sat braced on the edge of her bed, his fists curled into the linen. 'But that's what you said I could do. You said I could take what I wanted from you.'

'That's what you really want, isn't it?' he asked roughly, reaching out to grab her waist and hold her in front of him. 'You want me to make you feel good again.'

She wanted it so much—because she wanted it *gone*. But she knew what he wanted too. He might not like her much, but he still wanted her.

'Actually,' Eleni corrected him coolly, 'now I'm offering that to you. Take what you want from me.'

If he did that, she was sure she'd be rid of this wretched, all-encompassing desire. It was too intense— she couldn't *think* for wanting him.

His mouth tightened as he stared up at her, insolence in his expression. 'Look at Princess Sophisticated,' he jeered through gritted teeth. 'What do you think you're doing? Trying to soften me up with sex?'

She froze at the anger now darkening his eyes. 'I just don't think this needs to be that complicated.'

'This couldn't be *more* complicated. And sex only makes things worse.' He laughed unkindly. 'I'll have you again, don't you worry about that. But only once we've reached an agreement.'

He'd laughed that night too. When she'd had the most intense experience of her life, he'd *chuckled*. Her bold pretence fell, leaving angry vulnerability in its wake.

'You can seduce me until I scream,' she said furiously. 'But you can't make me say yes to *marrying* you.'

He stood, slamming her body against his as he did.

She gasped at the intense wave of longing that flooded her. But it roused her rage with it.

'You'll never get my total surrender.' She glared up at him, even as tremors racked her traitorous body as he pressed her against his rock-hard heat.

'And I don't want it,' he growled back, rolling his hips against hers in a demonstration of pure, sensual power. 'Lust passes.'

She hoped to heaven he was right. But his smug superiority galled her. 'You just have to know it all, don't you?'

But she didn't need another overprotective male trying to control every aspect of her life.

His gaze narrowed. 'I only want what's best for my baby.' He released her and stalked to the door, turning to hit her with his parting shot. 'We will marry. The baby will be born legitimately. And ultimately my child will live a safe, free life. With me.'

He slammed the door, leaving her recoiling at his cold-hearted plan. Shame slithered at her lame attempt to seduce him, suffocating the remnants of the heat he'd stirred too easily. He was too strong, too clinical when she'd been confused with desire. She was such a fool.

But that he truly planned to take her child horrified her. She had to fight him on that. She had to win.

Eleni snatched up her skirt. She marched out to the lounge to confront Damon again, only to catch sight of the large screen revealed on the wall. The sound was muted, but she recognised the image. Stunned, she stepped forward to look more closely.

Bunches and bunches of flowers and cards from well-wishers were placed at the gates of Palisades palace. The camera zoomed in on one of the bunches and she read the 'get well soon' message written—to *her*. Giorgos had taken her idea literally and told the world she was too unwell to embark on her tour with Prince Xander.

'There are so many.' She sank onto the nearest sofa.

'Why are you so surprised?' Damon walked forward and sat in the chair at an angle to her sofa, his voice cool. 'You're their perfect Princess.'

She rubbed her forehead. She was an absolute fraud and all those people were being kind when she didn't deserve it.

'It's not a total lie. You *don't* feel well,' he added gruffly.

'I've made a mess of everything.'

'So marry me. We'll live together away from Palisades until the baby is born.'

And then he was going to take her child from her.

Suddenly she broke; tears stung her eyes even as she laughed hopelessly. 'The stupid thing is, I don't even know for sure that I am pregnant.'

'Pardon?'

Of course she was pregnant. She knew it. She was late and there were all those other signs—morning sickness, tender breasts…

'Eleni?' Damon prompted sharply.

She sighed. 'I haven't done a test.'

He gazed at her, astounded. 'How can you not have done a test?'

'How could I?' She exploded, leaping back to her feet because she couldn't contain her frustration a second longer. 'How would I get a test without everyone finding out?' She paced, railing at the confines of the luxurious room and of the life she was bound by. 'I don't even do my own personal shopping—how can I when I don't even carry my own damn *money*?' She'd never shopped alone in all her life. She registered the dumbfounded amazement on Damon's face.

'I don't have any income,' she explained furiously. 'If I want anything I just ask someone and it arrives. Is that someone now you?' She gestured wildly at him. 'I don't have a money card, Damon. Or any cash. I've never needed it. I know that makes me spoilt. But it also makes me helpless.' It was beyond humiliating to be so dependent. 'It makes me useless.'

She flopped back down on the sofa and buried her face in her hands, mortified at the sting of fresh tears. So much for controlling her emotional outbursts.

'All this effort you've gone to, to steal me away might be based on one massive mistake.' She laughed bitterly at the irony. Wouldn't that just serve him right?

Damon hunched down in front of her, his hands on her knees. 'Eleni.'

His voice was too soft. Too calm.

'What?' She peered at him.

He studied her, his expression uncharacteristically solemn. 'Even if you're not pregnant, could you really marry him now?'

'Because I've spent the night on board a boat with another man and no chaperone?' She glared at him, hating that old-school reasoning and the expectation that she'd stay 'pure'—when no prince, no man, ever had to.

But Damon shook his head. 'Because you don't love him. You don't even want him.' He cocked his head, a vestige of that charming smile tweaking his lips. 'At least you want me.'

She closed her eyes. She *hated* him. And she hated how much she wanted him.

There was nothing but silence from Damon. She realised he'd left the room but a moment later he returned, a small rectangular box in his hand.

'You always have pregnancy tests on board?' Humiliation washed over her at her ineptitude.

'No. But as I suspected you were pregnant, I thought it might be useful.' So easily he'd done what she was unable to.

She snatched the box from his outstretched hand. 'I'll be back in a minute.'

CHAPTER EIGHT

DAMON GAZED DOWN at the distressed woman who'd wordlessly waved a small plastic stick at him as she returned to his sofa. The positive proof hit him—she truly had no clue. Her one escape plan had simply been to *hide* and now she was lost. Her lies yesterday had been those of an inexperienced, overly sheltered girl trying to brazen her way out of a dire situation.

He grimaced—was he actually feeling sorry for her now? Fool.

She could be confident when she wanted and had strength when she needed it. She was *spoilt*, that was her problem. Utterly used to getting her own way and never having to wait. He gritted his teeth as he remembered the way she'd flung back her bed coverings and taunted him. So brazen. So innocent. So damned gorgeous he was still struggling to catch his breath.

But she was going to have to wait for that now. And so was he.

Never had he understood how his father could have completely betrayed his mother. Why he'd risked everything he'd worked so hard to achieve. But now Damon understood all too well what could cloud a man's reason and make him forget his responsibilities and priorities.

Shameless lust. The age-old tale of desire.

He was not making the mistakes of his father. He was not abandoning his child to illegitimacy. But nor would he remain in a loveless marriage for years on end.

'You need to marry me, to protect the baby.' He tried to stay calm, but her repeated refusals were galling.

He'd never allow his child to be used for political manoeuvring. His baby would be raised in a safe environment with him. Their divorce would be better than being trapped in a home where the parents tolerated each other only for 'the look of it'.

Eleni paled.

'You know that, away from the palace, my child can have a normal life.' He tried to speak reasonably. 'Not hounded by press or burdened by duty.'

He saw her mouth tremble. He'd known this was how he'd get to her. She'd told him earlier—she didn't want to be *only* a princess.

'*I* can give this child everything,' she argued.

'Really? Can you give her complete freedom? With me, she can be free to do whatever she wants. Study whatever, live wherever. No pressure to perform.'

'And your life isn't in the public eye?' she queried sharply. 'Don't you billionaires get picked for "most eligible" lists in magazines?'

'When you're not a prince and therefore not public property, privacy can be paid for.'

'But this child will be a prince—or princess,' she pointed out, her voice roughening. 'And you can't deny this child his or her birthright.'

'The child can decide whether to take on a royal role when it's old enough.'

Eleni laughed at him. 'You think it's something you can just *choose*?'

'Why not?' Damon challenged her.

She shook her head. 'Giorgos would never allow it.'

'I don't give a damn what Giorgos wants.'

'But I do. Since our father died, he's been brother, father and mother to me and all the while he has that huge job. The hours he works—you have no idea...' She trailed off, pain shadowing her eyes.

Damon remembered when the King had died just over a decade ago. His father had returned to Palisades for the funeral and taken an extra week to visit his long-term lover—Kassie's mother. Grimly Damon shoved that bitter memory aside. But he couldn't recall much about the Queen at all. He frowned at Eleni. 'Where's your mother?'

Eleni looked shocked. Then she drew in a deep breath. 'She died twenty minutes after giving birth to me.' Despite that steadying breath, her voice shook. 'So I know what it's like not to have a mother. And I know what it's like to have your parent too busy to be around to listen... I want to be there for my child. And I will be. In all the ways she or he needs. *Always.*'

Damon stared at her fixedly, ignoring her passion and focusing on the salient information. Her mother had died in childbirth.

He pulled out his phone. 'You need to see a doctor.'

Eleni gaped at him, then visibly collected herself. 'I'm not sure if you know how this works, Damon, but the baby isn't due for *months*.'

So what? She needed the best care possible from this moment on.

'Just because my mother died in childbirth, doesn't mean that I might have trouble,' she added stiffly.

'You need a basic check-up at the very least.'

'Because you don't trust me to take care of myself?'

Blood pounding in his ears, he ignored her petulance. Quickly he scrolled through his contacts to find his physician and tapped out a text asking him to find the best obstetrician he knew. Sure, women gave birth round the world almost every minute, but not always in full health and Eleni's news had caught him by surprise.

'I don't need cotton-wool treatment.' Her tone sharpened.

'I don't intend to give it to you,' he muttered, feeling better for having started the search. 'But I'm not going to ignore your condition either.'

'It's just pregnancy, not an *illness*,' she rasped. 'And I am sensible enough to ensure I get the best treatment when I get back to shore. Trust me, I don't want to die. But you can't make me see someone I don't want to see, nor stop me from doing the things I like.'

Looking at her was always a mistake—especially when she was passionate and vitality flowed from her glowing skin. Had people stopped her doing the things she'd liked in the past? He couldn't resist a tease. 'And what do you like?'

She glared at him, picking up the heavy innuendo he'd intended. 'Not that.'

He laughed even as a wave of protectiveness surged. 'Did you know some women have a heightened libido when pregnant?'

'I'm not one of those women.'

Her prim reply was undermined by the quickening

of her breath. It spurred him to tease her more. 'No, you have the appetite of a nymphomaniac all the time.'

'I do not.'

'Yeah, you do.' He laughed again at her outraged expression. But that sensual blush had spread over her skin and sparks lit up her green-blue eyes.

There was no denying the chemistry between them. But he'd not realised just how inexperienced she was in all areas of life—not just the bedroom. Not to have access to cash? To have any normal kind of freedom?

Yes, she was spoilt, but she was unspoilt in other ways. She'd been too sheltered for her own good. And finally he could understand why. She was the precious baby who'd lost her mother far too soon. Raised by her bereft, too-busy father, and then a brother too young and too burdened to know how to care for a young girl and let her grow. All they'd wanted to do was protect her.

It was a sentiment Damon was starting to understand too well.

And now guilt crept in. He regretted the horrible scenario he'd painted—threatening to take her child from her. What kind of cold-hearted jerk was he?

But he'd been angered by her constant refusals and he'd lashed out, instinctively striking where it would hurt most. He drew in a calming breath. He'd win her acceptance with care, not cruelty.

'So it was the three of you, until your father died?' he asked, wanting to understand her background more.

'My father was a very busy man,' Eleni answered softly. 'He was the King—he had a lot to occupy his time. So for a long while it was Giorgos and me. He's a bit older, but he was always fun.' Her expression warmed briefly. 'When Father died, Giorgos took over.'

'Giorgos was young for that.'

'He is very highly regarded,' she said loyally.

'You're close.'

Her gaze slid from his. 'He has a big job to do. Back then he knew some of the courtiers didn't think he was old enough to handle the responsibility—'

'So he worked twice as hard to prove them wrong.' Damon smiled at her surprised look. 'It's understandable.'

She gazed out of the window. 'He's not stopped working since.'

And she was left lonely in her little turret in the palace. Damon saw how easily it had happened. She was loyal and sweet but also trapped and stifled.

'I'm supposed to marry a royal,' she said quietly. 'It's tradition. I know you think it's stupid, but it's how it's always been. I wanted to do the right thing for Giorgos.'

'Well, I'm not a prince and I never will be.' Damon took a seat. 'But won't it be easier to divorce me, a commoner, than cause conflict with two countries if you divorce your Prince?'

Her lips tightened. 'I'm not supposed to get divorced,' she said quietly. 'That's not part of the fairy tale.'

'Times change. Even royals live in the real world, Eleni. And they get divorced.'

She looked anywhere but at him. 'I barely know you.'

'Do you know Prince Xander?' Damon asked bluntly.

The shake of her head was almost imperceptible.

'Then what's the difference between marrying him and marrying me?' His muscles pulled tighter and tighter still in the face of her silence. The urge to go to her, to kiss her into acquiescence, made him ache. Despite her denial earlier he knew he could do it. All he'd have to do was kiss her and she'd be breathless and begging and he needed to get away from her before he did exactly that. He wanted to hear her say yes to him without that. 'Am I an ogre?'

'You want to take my child from me.'

'And you tried to deny the child was mine. I figure that makes us even.' He stood, unable to remain in the same room as her without succumbing to reckless action. 'Take your time to think about your options, Eleni. I'm in no rush to go anywhere.'

Why didn't she want to marry Damon? Eleni couldn't answer that honestly—not to him when she could barely admit the truth to herself. She'd never wanted anyone the way she wanted him. Her marriage to Xander would have been a loveless union. But safe compared to the tempestuous gamut of emotions Damon roused in her. She was terrified of what might happen to her heart if she stayed with him for long.

She scoffed at her inner dramatics. She needed to grow up and get a grip on her sexual frustration. Because that was all this was, right? Her first case of raw lust.

She turned off the large computer screen and foraged in the bookcase lining one of the walls, her thoughts circling around and around until her stomach rumbled and she realised how ravenous she was.

Quietly she left the room and found her way to a sleek galley kitchen. No one was in there, thank goodness, because she was starving. She located the pantry, pouncing on an open box of cereal.

'You okay?'

'Oh.' She swallowed hastily as she turned. 'You caught me.'

He had been swimming, probably in the pool on deck. Eleni stared, fascinated by the droplets of water slowly snaking down his bronzed chest until they were finally caught in the towel he'd slung low around his hips.

'Not yet.' He walked forward. 'What are you doing that is so awful?'

Staring at your bare chest.

'I shouldn't have helped myself,' she mumbled. 'Eating straight from the packet.'

'That's not awful. That's survival instinct.' He reached into the box she was holding and helped himself to a couple of the cereal clusters. 'Don't you go into the kitchen at the palace?'

She shook her head, forcing herself to swallow.

'You just ask one of the servants?'

'What do you expect?' She bristled. 'I live in a palace and that comes with privileges.'

'But what if you wanted to just make a sandwich?'

'Then someone makes it for me.'

'You never wanted to make your own sandwich?'

'It's not my place to.' She refused to rise to his baiting. 'I'm not going to take someone's job from them.'

He looked at her as she snaffled another cereal snack. 'What would you have done if being a princess wasn't your place?'

'I studied languages and art history.' She shrugged. 'I'd probably teach.'

'But what would you have done if you could have chosen anything?'

Eleni sighed. 'My brother loves me very much but he is very busy and most of my education was left to an older advisor who had ancient ideas about the role of a princess.'

'You're there to be decorative.'

'And quiet and screne—'

'Serene?' He laughed. 'You're a screamer.'

She sent him a filthy look.

'So?' He teased, but pressed the point. 'What would you have done?'

'I wanted to be a vet.' But she'd known it was impossible. The hours of study too intense when she had public duties to perform as well.

'A vet?' He looked taken aback.

'I like dogs.' She shrugged.

'You have dogs?'

'I had a gorgeous spaniel when I was younger.'

'So why not vet school? Did you not have the grades?'

'Of course I had the grades.' She gritted her teeth and turned away because she knew where he was going with this, so she didn't tell him she'd wanted to do Fine Arts first. Again she'd been denied—too frivolous. She was a princess and she had to remain demure and humble. But was hers really such an awful life to bestow upon a child? Yes, there were restrictions, but there was also such privilege. Couldn't she make it different?

'You know I can offer our child a level of freedom that you can't,' Damon said. 'Isn't that what you want, your child not to have to "perform" the way you've had to all your life?'

'I want the best for my child in every way,' Eleni said calmly. And she knew exactly what she had to do for her child now. Nothing was ever going to be the same. She sucked in one last deep breath. 'They're all going to figure out that I was pregnant when we married.'

He stilled; his gaze glittered. 'Either we lie and say the baby was born prematurely, or we say nothing at all.' He cleared his throat. 'The second option gets my vote. There will always be whispers and Internet conspiracy theories but we rise above it with a dignified silence and carry on.'

She nodded. 'I understand what you're saying about giving our child freedom, but I'm its mother and I won't walk away from it. Ever.' She braced and pushed forward. 'If you're serious about doing what's best for our child, then you won't ask me to.'

He carefully leaned against the bench. 'So you'll marry me.'

'If we work out a plan. For after.' When their marriage ended, it needed to be smooth. 'I think there are precedents in other countries for a child not to take a royal title,' she said bravely. Giorgos would have a fit but she would have to try to make him understand. 'We can keep him or her out of the limelight and work out some kind of shared custody arrangement.'

Her heart tore at the thought, but her child had the right to be loved by both its parents.

'Then we'll work it out.' Damon looked out of the window.

'So now you've got what you wanted,' Eleni said.

He looked back at her. His blue eyes had darkened almost to black. 'And what's that?'

'Me. Saying yes.' She watched, surprised to see his tension was even more visible than before. 'What, you're not satisfied?'

'No.'

'Then what do you want?'

He took the two steps to bring himself smack bang in front of her. 'I want my tee shirt back.'

Desire uncoiled low and strong in her belly. 'But I'm not wearing anything underneath it.'

'Good.' His blunt expression of want felled her.

'Are you wearing anything under the skirt?' he asked roughly, gripping the hem of the tee.

She could barely shake her head. 'I thought you said this would only complicate things.'

'Now we're in agreement on the big issues, we can handle a little complication.'

He tugged the tee shirt up. She lifted her arms and in a second it was gone. She was bared to his gaze, his touch, his tongue.

She gasped as he swooped. There was no denying this. He desired her body. Fine. She desired his. Reason dissolved under sensual persuasion. He pressed the small of her back—holding her still, keeping her close, until he growled something unintelligible and picked her up to sit her on the edge of the bench. He pushed her knees apart so he could stand between them. Elation soared through Eleni.

This was what she wanted.

His kiss was nothing less than ravaging. She moaned as he plundered, his tongue seeking, tasting, taking everything and she did more than let him. She gave—straining closer. She wound her arms around his neck, arching and aching. His hands swept down her body, igniting sensation, sparking that deeper yearning. He slid his warm palm under her skirt. She trembled as he neared where she was wet and ready. His kiss became more rapacious still as he touched her so intimately, and her moan melted in his mouth. He lifted away only to tease her more—kissing the column of her neck, down to her collarbones and then to the aching, full breasts pointing hard for his attention.

But the nagging feeling inside wouldn't ease—resistance to this hedonism. It had been wrong before; it was still wrong now. She closed her eyes, turning her face to the side as heat blistered her from the inside out.

'Don't hide.' He nudged her chin. 'Let me see you.'

'I can't,' she muttered, desperately turning her face away.

He pulled back completely, forcing her to look into his eyes. 'You're not cheating. Your engagement is broken now.'

She was ashamed that he knew her desire for him had overruled her duty and her loyalty. Her engagement to Xander had been a loveless arrangement, but Damon was right. She was an appalling person.

'This is nothing much more than what happened yesterday.' Damon tempted her again.

Wrong. It was so much more. If she let him in again, she wasn't sure she could cope. The passion was all-consuming, addictive and all she could think about at a time when she should be concerned with her family. With her duty. But she couldn't think clearly when she was within five hundred paces of this man.

And she doubted him. He'd wanted to find her after the ball only because he'd known there was a risk of pregnancy, not because he'd wanted more time with her. He was only taking advantage of the situation now—certainly it wasn't that he liked her.

But he'd *wanted* her when he *hadn't* known who she was. He wasn't going for the 'perfect Princess' that night, he'd wanted just *her*. There was something still seductive about that.

Damon was studying her too intently. It was as if he could strip back all her defences and see into her poor, inexperienced soul.

'Why didn't you tell me you were a virgin?' he asked softly.

There was no point holding back the truth now. 'Because you would have stopped.'

He expelled a harsh breath and framed her face with surprisingly gentle hands. 'You could have said you were inexperienced.'

'I was pretending I wasn't,' she muttered, mortified. The mask, the costume had combined to make her feel confident. He'd made her feel sexy and invincible. Unstoppable. 'I had a persona that night...now I don't.'

'Are you sure it was a persona?' Damon challenged. 'Or was it the true you?' He skimmed the tips of his fingers down her neck until she shivered.

Was she that person? That woman who took such risks—and found such pleasure?

You want more than what you think you should have.

'There is nothing wrong with liking this, Eleni.' He tempted her to the point of madness.

'But I like it too much.' She confessed that last secret on the merest thread of a breath. 'It's not *me*. It scares me.'

That was why she'd resisted his proposal initially. The intensity of her desire for him terrified her.

His expression tightened. 'I scare you?'

'Not you. Me,' she muttered. 'I never behave like this. Like *that*.' She was appalled at how she'd behaved that night and since. All those outbursts? The waves of emotion? 'You were right. I lied. I cheated. I'm every bit that awful, spoilt person you said I was.'

Damon shifted away from her.

Eleni watched, suddenly chilled at the loss of contact. Her body yearned for the closeness of his again. But he'd switched it off. How could he do that so easily?

Hurt and alarm hit. She shouldn't have spoken so rashly. She shouldn't have stopped him because at least she could've been rid of the frustration that now cut deeper than ever.

'You need to be at peace before this happens again,' Damon said quietly—too damn in control. 'Then you won't need to hide. Then you can truly let go.'

She watched, amazed and horrified as he walked to the doorway. How, exactly, was she supposed to find peace when he was making the decision for her? When he was leaving her this...*needy*.

'I hate you,' she called. One last emotional outburst.

'I'm sure.' Damon glanced back with a smile. 'I'd never dream that you could love me.'

CHAPTER NINE

'I'M NOT WAITING for Giorgos to hunt me down like some fugitive. I want to go to him.' Eleni braced for Damon's response as she sat opposite him at the table the next morning.

She wasn't letting him make all the decisions any more. After the most desultory dinner, she'd spent the night mentally practising her confrontations with both Damon and Giorgos and it was time to put both plans into reality.

Damon arched a sardonic eyebrow. 'Good morning, fire-breathing warrior woman, who are you and what have you done with my meek fiancée?'

'I need to see him,' she insisted.

Damon's answering smile was uncomfortably wicked. 'The yacht turned around last night. We'll be back at Palisades in less than an hour. I've just let him know I have you.'

Eleni stared as his words knocked the wind from her sails.

'Well.' It was going to happen so much sooner than she'd expected. She puffed out a deep breath but it didn't settle her speeding heart. 'We might want to let him know I'm safe on board, otherwise he might try to blow up your boat.'

Damon chuckled. 'I thought Palisades was a peace-loving nation.'

It was, but when Damon's yacht entered the marina, Eleni's nerves tightened unbearably. Never before had she defied Giorgos's wishes and now the weight of his inevitable disappointment was crushing.

'I should handle him by myself,' she said to Damon as she counted the number of soldiers waiting on the pier ready to escort her. It was a heavy-handed display of her brother's authority. 'I should have done that in the first place.'

Damon turned his back on the waiting men with an arrogant lift to his chin. Apparently he was unfazed by the latent aggression waiting for them. 'I'll stay silent if that's what you wish, but I will be beside you.'

Because he didn't trust her?

Except there was something in Damon's eyes. Something more than protectiveness and more than possessiveness. She turned away, not trusting her own vision. Because the last thing she deserved was tenderness.

The military men wordlessly ushered them into a car and drove them straight to the palace. The gleaming building felt silent, as if everyone were collectively holding their breath—waiting for Giorgos's explosion. For the first time in her life Eleni felt like a stranger in her own home. The only person not tiptoeing on eggshells was Damon. He casually strolled the endless corridors as if he hadn't a care in the world.

They weren't taken to either her private suite or to Giorgos's. Instead her brother's assistant led them to a formal room usually reserved for meetings with visiting Heads of State. Chilled, Eleni paused in the doorway. Giorgos grimly waited in full King mode—white dress uniform, jacket laden with medals and insignia, boots polished to mirror-like sheen. All that was missing was his crown.

'I've cancelled an engagement at the last minute. Again.' Giorgos fixed a steely stare on Damon.

But her brother's barely disguised loathing apparently bounced off as Damon blandly stared right back.

'You took advantage of an innocent,' Giorgos accused shortly. 'You seduced her.'

Was she invisible? Straightening her shoulders, Eleni stepped forward.

'Maybe I seduced him.' She clenched her fists to hide how badly her hands were shaking, but she was determined to take control of this conversation. *She* was having the input here, not Damon.

Her brother finally bothered to look at her, but as he faced her he became like a marble sculpture. Expressionless and unreadable.

'Damon and I will be married as soon as possible,' she said, determined to state her case before he tore her to shreds.

Giorgos continued to look unmoved. 'Last time we spoke you insisted you were not marrying either Prince Xander or Mr Gale.'

'I was upset,' she conceded coolly. 'But this is the best course of action, Giorgos.'

'He is not a prince. He has no title whatsoever.'

Of course her brother knew Damon's background already—he'd have had his investigators on it from the moment he'd gotten the message this morning. From Giorgos's frown, Damon's success mattered little to him. 'You know the expectations—'

'Change the law, create a new custom.' For the second time in her life Eleni dared to interrupt her brother. 'You're King. You have the power.'

'And should I abuse power trusted to me, for personal gain?'

'Is it personal gain, or would you simply be granting the same right that any other citizen in Palisades already has?' Why couldn't she have the right to choose for herself?

Giorgos's eyes narrowed. 'So I simply ignore centuries of custom and duty? I abandon all levels of diplomacy and the expectations of our important neighbours and alliances?'

'My personal life shouldn't be used for political manoeuvring.'

'So you got yourself pregnant instead of simply making that argument?'

She recoiled in shock and her anger unleashed. 'Of course I didn't. But would you be listening to me if I *wasn't* pregnant?'

Giorgos sent Damon the iciest look she'd ever seen. 'You know about our mother?'

'Yes. I will ensure Eleni receives care from the best specialists.'

Giorgos shook his head. 'Our doctor is ready to give her a check-up now.'

Eleni gaped. Did her brother think she was somehow incapacitated?

Damon answered before she could. 'I don't think that's necessary—'

'It is entirely necessary. She must be—'

'Stop trying to overrule each other.' Eleni interrupted Giorgos again, her heart and head pounding. 'My medical decisions will be made by *me*.'

'Dr Vecolli is already here,' Giorgos insisted.

'I'm not seeing Dr Vecolli.'

'He's been our family physician for twenty years.'

'Which is exactly *why* I'm not seeing him. He's like a grandfather to me. I would like to see a female doctor.' She glared as Giorgos frowned at her. 'What, do you think no woman can be a doctor, or is it just me you thought so incapable I couldn't even be trusted with animals?'

'I once wanted to be an airplane pilot.' Giorgos dripped cold sarcasm. 'But you *know* we cannot hold down a full-time job while fulfilling royal duty. It is impossible.'

'Why?' she challenged. 'Couldn't I be useful other than cutting ribbons and awarding prizes?'

'You're going to have your hands full with your baby, or had you forgotten that?'

Eleni flared anew at Giorgos's patronising tone. 'So while plenty of other mothers work, I can only be a brood mare? Do you think I'm that incompetent?' She was outraged—and *hurt*.

'I don't think you're—' Her brother broke off and ran a hand through his hair.

'Why are we so enslaved by the past?' she asked him emotionally. 'Just because things have always been done a certain way, doesn't mean they always have to continue in that same way.' And she was more capable than he believed her to be—wasn't she?

Giorgos was silent for a long moment. Then he sighed softly. 'Then how do you plan to manage this?'

'By marrying Damon. I'll have the baby and then...' She drew in a steadying breath. 'Beyond that, I don't really know. But I don't want all those limitations on me any more. They're untenable.'

She braced for his response. She couldn't yet tell him her marriage had an end date already. One let-down at a time was enough.

Giorgos's expression revealed more now. But he didn't need to worry; this wedding wouldn't end the world.

'It could be leaked that Eleni was corralled into the wedding with Prince Xander.' Damon broke the tense silence. 'She was too afraid to stand up to you and the Prince. Public sympathy will be on her side if it is cast as a forbidden love story.'

She didn't deserve public sympathy.

'She fell in love with me during her secret hospital visits.' Damon embroidered the possible story. 'But you refused your consent for her to have a relationship with a commoner. She was so distraught she really did get sick. Only then did you realise how serious she was.'

Eleni winced at the scenario he'd painted. Did everyone need to know she'd been unable to stand up for herself? More importantly, it didn't do her brother justice.

'Do we need to make Giorgos sound such a bully?' She frowned.

Giorgos's eyes widened with an arrested expression.

'Prince Xander is still the injured party,' Damon continued after a beat. 'But it can be spun that they'd not spent much time together. Therefore her defection won't make him appear any less attractive.'

Eleni smothered her startled laugh. Damon was light years more attractive than Xander.

For a long moment Giorgos studied the painting hanging on the wall opposite him. With every passing second Eleni's heart sank—recriminations and rejection were inevitable.

'You might have met your match, Eleni.' Giorgos slowly turned to her, the wryest of smiles in his eyes. 'He won't curl round your little finger.'

'The way you do?' Eleni dared to breathe back.

'You will be married in the private chapel today.' Giorgos's steely seriousness returned. 'I will release a public proclamation together with a few photographs. You will not make a public appearance. Rather you will go away for at least a month.'

'Away?' Eleni was stunned at the speed of his agreement.

'You need to get your personal situation stable while this fluff is spread in the press.' Giorgos's sarcasm edged back. 'You'll go to France. I have a safe house there.'

'But the safest house of all is this one,' Eleni argued. She was not letting her brother banish her. Not when she had to get to grips with a husband she barely knew and to whom she could hardly control her reaction. Staying home would give her the space and privacy to deal with Damon.

'Remaining in Palisades would give Damon a chance to learn palace protocol and understand the expectations for our...*future*.' She glanced at Damon, fudging just how short their future together was going to be.

Damon shrugged but his eyes were sharp. 'I'm happy to hang here for a while if that's what you wish, Eleni.'

'I am scheduled to spend a few weeks at the Summer House,' Giorgos said stiffly. 'So that would work.' He turned icily to Damon. 'But understand that I will be watching you, even from there. I don't trust you.'

'Fair enough,' Damon answered equally coolly. 'If I were you, I wouldn't either.' He smiled as if he hadn't a care in the world. 'I'll not take a title, by the way. I'll remain Damon Gale.'

'While I'll remain Princess Eleni Nicolaides,' Eleni answered instantly.

'And the child will be Prince or Princess Nicolaides-Gale—we get it,' Giorgos snapped. 'Let's just get everything formalised and documented before it leaks. I expect you at the chapel in an hour. Both of you looking the part.'

Her brother stalked towards the door, his posture emanating *uptight King*.

'I'll send someone to the yacht to fetch a suit,' Damon drawled once Giorgos had left. 'I guess you'd better go magic up a wedding dress.'

She stared at her fiancé and clapped a hand over her mouth in horror.

'Don't worry.' Damon's satisfied smile turned distinctly wicked. 'You can wear as little as you like—I will not say no. That busty blue number you wore at the ball would be nice—'

Flushing hotly, Eleni swiftly walked out on him, desperately needing a moment alone to process everything. But her maid hovered at the door to her suite, the woman's expression alert with unmistakable excitement.

'Oh, Bettina. I'm sorry I've been away.' Eleni quickly pasted on a smile. 'And I'm not back for long.'

Bettina nodded eagerly. 'I have done the best I can in the last half hour. I've hung the samples so you can choose. There are nine altogether—from New York, Paris, and one from Milan.'

'Samples?' Eleni repeated, confused.

'The wedding dresses.'

Nine wedding dresses? Eleni gaped. If that wasn't being spoilt, she didn't know what was.

'Would you like to try them on?'

Eleni saw the sparkle in her maid's eyes and realised the fiction that Eleni was marrying her long-secret love had already spread. She drew in a deep breath and made her smile bigger. 'Absolutely.'

But her smile became a wide 'oh' as Bettina wheeled out the garment rack she'd hung the gowns on. And then Eleni surrendered to vain delight—at the very least she could look good on her wedding day.

The sixth option was the winner; she knew as soon as she stepped into it. It was exactly what she'd choose for *herself*—not as something befitting 'Princess Eleni'. The sleek dress with its svelte lines and delicate embroidery was subtle but sexy and she loved it.

As Eleni walked away from her maid, her suite and her life as she knew it, butterflies skittered around her stomach, but she determinedly kept her smile on her face.

She couldn't let the fairy-tale image fall apart just yet.

Giorgos stood waiting for her at the entrance to the private chapel. Her smile—and her footsteps—faltered as she saw his frown deepening. But this might be her only chance to speak to him privately.

'I'm sorry I let you down,' she said when she was close enough for only him to hear.

'You haven't.' Her brother held out a small posy of roses for her.

Tears sprang to her eyes as she took the pretty bouquet from him. 'Thank you,' she whispered.

He nodded, stiffly. 'Do you love him?' Giorgos suddenly asked.

The direct question stole her breath. For the first time that she could recall, her brother looked awkward—almost unsure—as he gazed hard at a spot on the floor just ahead of them.

She couldn't be anything but honest. 'I don't know.'

That frown furrowed his brow again. 'Make it work, Eleni.'

Then he held out his arm, that glimpse of uncertainty gone. She nodded, unable to speak given the lump in her throat, and placed her hand in the crook of his elbow.

As Giorgos escorted her into the chapel, Eleni caught sight of Damon standing at the altar. He was dressed in a stunningly tailored suit. He seemed taller, broader; his eyes were very blue. He claimed the attention of every one of her senses. Every thought. Her pulse raced, her limbs trembled. She tried to remember to breathe. She couldn't possibly be *excited*, could she? This was only part of the plan to secure her child's legitimacy and freedom. This was only for her baby.

But those butterflies danced a complicated reel.

It's just a contract. It's only for the next year. It doesn't mean anything...

But reciting her vows to Damon in the family chapel heightened her sense of reverence. Here—in front of her brother, in front of him, in this sanctuary and symbol of all things past and future—she had to promise to love him.

He's the father of my child.

She could love him only for that, couldn't she? It wasn't a lie.

But a whisper of foreboding swept down her spine

and she shivered just as Damon turned towards her. She met his gaze, almost frozen by the enormity of their actions.

But Damon wasn't frozen. He had that slightly wicked expression in his eyes as he reached to pull her close.

The kiss sealing their wedding contract should have been businesslike, but he lingered a fraction too long. That heat coursed through her veins. She closed her eyes and in that instant was lost. Her bones ached and the instinct to lean into him overwhelmed her. Only at the exact moment of her surrender, he suddenly pulled away. She caught a glimpse of wildness in his eyes but then her lifetime of training took over. She turned and walked with him out of the chapel and into the formal throne room. There she dutifully posed for endless photos with Giorgos on one side of her, Damon on the other. She smiled and smiled and smiled. Perfectly Princess Eleni.

Her brother took her hand and bowed. 'You make a beautiful bride, Eleni.'

Because all that mattered was how she looked and how this arrangement looked to the world? But Giorgos's expression softened and he suddenly gave her a quick hug.

'Take care of yourself.' With the briefest of glances at Damon, her brother left.

A little dazed, Eleni gazed after him. It had been years since he'd hugged her. Her nerves lightened. The worst was over, right? Now she could move forward.

'Eleni.'

She turned.

Damon stood too close, too handsome, his expression

too knowing. That little respite from inner tension was over as she realised the first night of her marriage lay ahead. The beginning of the end of the thing neither of them had wanted in the first place.

'We should take a couple of photos somewhere less formal,' Damon suggested.

Eleni shook her head as his glance around the ornate room revealed his less than impressed opinion.

'There's nowhere "less formal" anywhere in this palace,' she informed him with perverse pleasure.

'What about outside?' Damon eyed up the French doors that no one had opened in Eleni's life.

'That's locked,' she said.

Damon turned the handle and the door opened silently and easily on the hinge.

Of course it did.

He sent her a triumphant smile that did even more annoying things to her insides.

'You're the most irritating creature alive,' she grumbled.

'I know,' he commiserated drolly. 'But you still want me.'

'What are you doing?' she whispered, stalking outside to get away from him as much as anything.

'This is your palace, Eleni. You're allowed to run around in it, right?' He was still too close.

'You're…'

'What?' he challenged, arrogance in his eyes as he wrapped his arm around her waist, stopping her flight and drawing her close. 'What am I?'

Not good for her health.

Eleni half laughed, half groaned as she gave into

temptation and leaned against him. But she refused to answer.

Damon retaliated physically. Magically. Reigniting those embers settled so slightly beneath her skin. The kiss banished the last butterflies and a bonfire burned, engulfing her body in a delicious torture of desire. This time he held nothing back, pulling her close enough for her to feel just how she affected him. Desire flared, compounded by the awareness that, this time, there was nothing to stop them.

Click. Click, click, click.

She put her hands on his broad chest and pushed, remembering too late there was a freaking photographer following them.

'I'm the Princess,' she muttered, mainly to remind herself.

But Damon kept her close with one arm around her waist and a light grip on her jaw. 'I didn't marry "the Princess".'

'Yes, you did.' There was no separating who she was from what she was. She had to accept that and now he did too.

The photographer looked disappointed when Damon sent him away. As he left, thudding blades whirred overhead and she glanced up to see her brother's helicopter swiftly heading north.

'So now we're alone,' Damon said softly. 'And not a second too soon.'

She suppressed the shiver at the determination in his tone and gazed at the rings on her finger to avoid looking at him. He'd surprised her in the chapel, sliding an engagement ring on her finger as well as a wedding band.

'You don't like them?' he asked, inexorably escorting her towards that open French door.

On the contrary, she loved them, but she was wary of showing it. She couldn't quite make out his mood. Was he angry as well as aroused? 'How did you pick them so quickly?'

A grim smile briefly curved his mouth. 'I had just a little longer to prepare for our wedding than you did.'

Even so, his organisational skills were impressive. 'It's a sapphire?'

He shook his head. 'A blue diamond for my blue bride.'

Her heart knocked. The stone's colour was the exact shade of the dress she'd worn that fateful night.

'You still look blue.' He cocked his head curiously. 'Why? You have the support of your brother. Everything that mattered has been resolved. So why so sad?'

Because this wasn't going to last. Because for all the foolishness in the garden, this was as much of a charade as her wedding to Xander would have been. Because she was a romantic fool. Part of her had wanted real love on her wedding day.

You can't be a child any more, Eleni. You're having a child.

Unable to answer his demanding tone, she walked through the palace towards her private apartment. There wasn't a servant or soldier to be seen, as if by some silent decree they knew to stay out of sight. And it was a good thing too. She'd seen the banked heat in Damon's eyes. She knew he wasn't about to show her any mercy.

Her pulse skittered, speeding up the nearer she got to her rooms. At the foot of the staircase he reached out and took her hand.

She tried to hide the quickening of her breath but she knew he could feel the slamming pulse at her wrist and she could see the tension tightening his features too.

He wanted and he would have. Because she wanted too. And maybe this 'want' would have to do. Maybe they could make this work. With the reluctant acceptance of her brother, with the physical attraction binding them, with the baby…maybe this could work *indefinitely*.

She paused at the top of the staircase, drawing in a deeper breath to try to steady her anticipation. Damon released her hand, only to swing her into his arms.

'What are you doing?' she whisper-shrieked, clutching his shoulders as he suddenly strode down the last corridor to her apartment. 'You're not carrying me over my own threshold?'

'Indulge me.'

Excitement rippled down her spine, feathering goosebumps across her skin at his intensity. 'I didn't think you'd be one for wedding traditions.' Her throat felt raspy as she tried to tease.

His grip on her tightened for a nanosecond, and then eased again.

'I was never getting married,' he said carelessly as he kicked the door shut behind them. 'But seeing as that vow has been torn up, I might as well make the most of it.'

She looked into his face as he set her down, wishing she could read his mind. 'Why didn't you want to marry?'

He hesitated for a split second. 'It's not in our nature to be with one person all our lives.'

Our nature, or just *his*? His warning stabbed deep, bursting the warm bubble of desire.

'You don't believe in monogamy?' she clarified, his harsh reality cooling her completely.

'No. I don't.'

So he would cheat on her.

He caught her shoulders, preventing her from walking away from him. 'I think it traps people into a perceived perfection that can't be maintained,' he said quietly, forcing her to meet his gaze. 'No one is infallible, Eleni. Certainly not me. Definitely not you.'

'I can control myself.' Rebellious anger scorched her skin. 'And I intend to keep the vows we just made.'

He smiled. 'Of course you do. And so do I. Until the time when we dissolve the deal. It is just a contract, Eleni. Nothing more.'

Her deeply ingrained sense of tradition and honour railed against that declaration. She'd stood in that chapel and she'd meant those vows. But for Damon, this was nothing more than a business proposition. So why had he carried her only a minute ago?

'But it is a contract with particular benefits,' he added.

'And you intend to make the most of those benefits?' She wasn't buying it.

'As much as you do. Or are you going to try to deny yourself because I've annoyed you?' His smile was all disbelief.

'I'm going to deny *you*.' This might be her wedding night but it made no difference. She wasn't sleeping with him now.

'I've made you angry.' His eyebrows lifted. 'You're very young, sweetheart.'

'No. You're very cynical.' She shoved his chest, but he only took two paces back from her. 'And I'm *not* a child. Just because I haven't slept with half the world, doesn't mean I'm more stupid than you. Sex doesn't make you smarter. If anything it makes you more dense.'

'Come here, Eleni.'

What, he was going to ignore her argument and simply demand her submission just because he knew she found him sexy?

'Get over yourself.'

'You're saying no?' he asked, his early anger giving way to arrogant amusement. 'Because you're the one used to giving orders?'

'No, that's my brother,' she answered in annoyance. 'I'm the one used to standing in the corner doing what she's told.'

'Then why aren't you doing as you're told now?' He stood with his legs wide like some implacable pirate captain. 'Come here.'

The entrance vestibule of her apartment wasn't huge but it might as well have been the Grand Canyon between them.

'You come over here,' she dared, ignoring the pull of his attraction. 'I'm tired of being told what to do. I'm doing the telling this time.'

His eyes widened fractionally. For a long moment he regarded her silently. She could see the storm brewing in him and braced. Him walking closer was what she wanted. And what she didn't want.

'I'm not yours to boss around or *control*,' she said, touching her tongue to her suddenly dry lips but determinedly maintaining her bravado regardless. 'I'm going to do what's necessary. And *only* what is necessary.'

He took those two paces to invade her personal space again and swept his hand from her waist to her hip. 'This is necessary, Eleni.'

She turned her head away, her heart pounding. 'Not any more.'

'Because you're mad with me.' His lips brushed her cheek. 'Because I've ruined your belief in fairy tales? There's only the real world, Eleni. With real complications and real mess.'

'And temporary desires,' she ended the lecture for him.

'That's right.'

'And you're feeling a temporary desire now?' she asked.

'Definitely.'

'Too bad.' She clamped her mouth shut.

He laughed again. 'You say you don't play games.' He gifted her the lightest of kisses. 'Say yes to me again, Eleni,' he coaxed, teasing too-gentle hands up and down her spine. 'Say yes.'

She glared at him for as long as she could but she already knew she'd lost. 'You're not fair.'

'Life isn't fair. I thought you knew that already.' He moved closer still, forcing her to step backwards until she was pressed hard between him and the wall. 'Say yes.'

She could hold out but it would only be for a little while. She wanted him too much. She had from the second she'd seen him that night. And it was just sex, right? Nothing to take too seriously. She might as well get something she wanted from this 'contract'.

'Yes.' It was always going to be yes.

His smile was triumphant but she swore she saw tenderness there too. Except it couldn't be that—he'd just told her this was only temporary. He brushed a loose tendril of hair back from her face.

'Don't pet me like I'm a good dog,' she snapped.

He laughed. 'Definitely not a dog. But very good. And very worth petting.' He put hands on her shoulders and applied firm pressure. 'Turn around.'

She met his gaze and sucked in a breath at the fire in his eyes. Wordlessly she let him turn her, surrendering this once.

'This dress is beautiful,' he said softly. 'But not as beautiful as the woman inside it.'

Eleni bowed her head, resting her forehead on the cool wall. He undid the first button and pressed his lips to the tiny patch of bared skin. His fingers traced, then teased down to the next button. In only a heartbeat Eleni was lost in the eroticism—of not seeing him, but of feeling him expose her to his gaze, to his touch, to his tongue again, inch by slow inch.

Desire unfurled from low in her belly. Her body cared not for the complications and confusion of her heart and mind. Her body cared only for his touch, only for the completion he could bring her.

He teased too much. Too slow. Until she was trembling and breathless.

When her dress slithered to the floor in a rush he put firm hands on her waist and spun her to face him again. She'd worn no bra beneath the gown, so she was left with lacy panties, stockings, kitten heels and nothing else. His gaze was hot and suddenly she was galvanised, reaching out to push him to recklessness again. She wanted him as breathless, as naked—she needed to feel his skin against hers.

But she couldn't undo his buttons. She was too desperate for release from the tension that soared with every second she spent with him. His choked laugh was strained and he took over, swiftly discarding the remainder of his clothes until they lay in a tumble at their feet. For a second she just stared at him. And he at her.

Before she could think, let alone speak, he pulled her close again, as if he couldn't stand to be parted from her for a second longer. He devoured her—with his gaze, then his fingers, then his mouth. He kissed every exposed inch. Somehow they were on the floor and he was braced above her—heavy and strong and dominant. She gasped breathlessly, aching for him. But just at that moment, he lifted slightly away and she almost screamed in protest.

'What?' she snapped at him. Why was he stopping *now*?

His smile was both smug and twisted. 'I've had numerous lovers, Eleni, but you're the first one to run away afterwards.'

'Did I hurt your ego?' She half hoped so; that'd be payback for what he was doing to her now.

'You frustrated me. You still do.' A seriousness stole into his features. 'You know I don't want to hurt you.'

She understood frustration now. 'I'm not afraid.'

And he wasn't going to hurt her—he'd made it very clear that this was only this. Only lust. Only temporary.

'No?' He held fast above her. *So close.* 'You're not going to run away again?'

'Not while I'm this naked.' She sighed, surrendering to his seriousness. 'I can handle you.'

'Then no more hiding either,' he ordered, cupping her cheek. 'In this, hold nothing back.'

She was lost in the blue of his intense eyes. He wanted it all his way—acceptance that this was only sex. But at the same time he wanted everything from her. It wasn't fair. But it was life. And it was just them again.

'Okay.' She breathed. A wave of pleasure rolled over her as she accepted his terms. This total intimacy was finally okay.

Less than a second later he drove deep into her body. She cried out as he claimed her with that one powerful thrust. Trembling, she wrapped her arms around his muscular body. Maybe she couldn't handle him. She couldn't cope with how completely he took her, or how exquisitely he now tortured her by just holding still— his invasion total.

'Easy…' he muttered.

There was no easy. 'Please,' she begged, trying to rock her hips beneath him to rouse him into action. 'Please.'

She needed him to move—to take her hard and fast and break the terrible tension gripping her. Because this was too, too good and she was going insane with the desire for release.

'Damn it, Eleni.' He growled and rose on his hands, grinding impossibly deeper.

Passion washed over her. It felt so good she all but lost her mind in the fire that burned out of control so quickly. She was like dry tinder. With one spark the inferno licked to the bone. But suddenly, blessedly, he flared too. Ferociously he rode her. She moaned with every panting short breath until they bucked in unison. Waves of ecstasy radiated through each cell in her body with every one of his forceful thrusts. Fierce and fast she arched, taut and tight around him.

'Eleni.'

She loved the way he ground her name through

his clenched teeth. Over and over he stroked her. She clenched her fists as the shuddering rush of pleasure started. Gasping for breath, she revelled in the floods of release as he shouted and thrust hard that one last time, pressing her flat against the wooden floor.

Her emotions surged as the waves of her orgasm ebbed. It was shocking how good he made her feel. How *shattered*. She didn't think she could possibly find the energy to stand, let alone smile. And she wanted to smile. More than that, she wanted him again. Already. She struggled to catch her breath before it quickened, but there was no reining in the rapacious desire that he'd unleashed within her. Only then she felt him moving—away.

Damon winced. Every muscle felt feeble. He'd meant to go more gently and ensure she was with him every step of the way. Hell, he'd meant to make her come first and more than once. But she'd provoked him, and he'd wanted her too much, until he'd taken her like this on the floor—unstoppable and unrestrained and so damn quick all over again.

He rolled onto his side to see more of her lithe, passion-slick, sated body. And this time she turned her head to look back at him. Letting him see her. Her green-blue eyes were luminous. His mouth dried as he read the craving within them. For all his teasing, he understood how much she wanted this. As much as he did. Something shifted inside—a warning that this was far too intense. But it was too late.

If he was any kind of a good guy he'd have wed her and then left her right alone, because, as he'd told her, sleeping together again would lead to complication and she was so inexperienced he didn't want to mess with her emotions. But he wasn't a good guy.

Not a prince, remember?

Fortunately he'd recovered from the whim to carry her into the apartment. That action had turned her soft skin pink, so he'd had to remind her of the reality of their situation. His words had snuffed the starry-eyed look from her face. Now all that remained was the flush of raw desire. Because that was all this was. Romance wasn't real. Love didn't last.

So, better him to be doing this with her than some other jerk, right? At least he was the one she wanted.

He was determined to please her. The sound of her sighs and the fierce heat of her hold were his ultimate reward. The intensity of their chemistry both angered and enthralled him. Now his exhausted body roared with renewed energy. He scooped her into his arms and stood. He'd ached to have her this close. To have her unable to say no to him, wanting and welcoming him—and only him.

He walked through the ornate lounge room, going on instinct to find her bedroom—a surprisingly simply decorated room. He was just so glad to see the bed. He placed her in the centre of it, gritting back the primal growl of victory. His skin tightened as his muscles bunched. Now they'd solved the problem of their immediate future, they could thrash this attraction that burned between them. An understanding of pleasure was the one thing he could give her. The enjoyment of what their bodies were built for, with no shame, no reticence and no regret. Just passion and play.

Satisfaction oozed as he started to tease that wild response from her again. He loved finally having her on the bed with all the time in the world to explore her properly. Her cheeks flushed, her eyes gleamed—dazed, passionate, willing.

He'd had her. He'd have her again. But something ached—something that was missing despite the almost intolerable ecstasy of the last orgasm they'd shared.

'Eleni.' He uttered a plea he hadn't meant to let free.

He'd coerced her into this marriage, but while she'd finally agreed—and accepted that it was only a contract—somehow he wasn't appeased. Not yet. Not even when he made her writhe uncontrollably. Not when she moaned again or when her hands sought to hurry him. Because he refused to be hurried. Not this time. He was slow and deliberate and determined to touch and taste and tease every last inch of her. But even when he'd done that, the nagging gap still irked.

Finally he allowed himself to invade her body with his own again. Helplessly groaning at the unbearable bliss, he locked into place. The driving need to get closer consumed him. He craved her heated softness and tight strength.

'Eleni.' He strained to stay in control.

'Yes.' Her sweet answer rasped over his desire-whipped skin and he drove deeper into her fire. Every muscle tensed as he fought the urge to give in already.

Too soon. It was too soon.

'Damon.' She tracked teasing fingers down his chest until he caught her hand and held it close and she whispered again. Sheer lust vocalised. 'Damon.'

His heart pounded. That was what he wanted. His name on her lips. Her eyes on his. Her body drinking his in. Her whole focus only on him. She arched, willing and sultry, and suddenly her enchanting smile was broken by her release.

'*Damon!*'

His name. *Screamed.*

A torrent of triumphant energy sluiced through every cell as the last vestige of his self-control snapped. He could no longer hold back, growling his passion as he furiously pounded his way closer. To her. To bliss. His world blackened as rapture hit and satisfaction thundered.

He had won.

CHAPTER TEN

DAMON QUIETLY PACED about the lounge in Eleni's apartment within the palace. His bags had been delivered before the ceremony yesterday and he drew out his tablet now.

The number of emails in his inbox was insane even for him and it wasn't yet eight in the morning. He clicked the first few open and grimaced at the capital letters screaming *CONGRATULATIONS!* at him.

Rattled, he flicked on the television, muting the volume so he couldn't hear the over-excited, high-pitched squeals of the presenters as they gushed about the surprise nuptials of Princess Eleni. A ticker ran along the bottom of the screen repeating the amazing news that she'd married a commoner—one Mr Damon Gale.

The piece they then played was about him. His business interests got a brief mention while his personal ones were explored in depth and all but invented. They focused on his upbringing, his family, his illegitimate half-sister...

He winced when he saw the media crews camped outside Kassie's small apartment in the village. But the horror show worsened in a heartbeat as his father flashed on the screen. Damon automatically iced his emotions—the response had taken him years to perfect. But the sensation of impending doom increased and he flicked on the audio to hear his father in action. Apparently John Gale was 'thrilled' that Eleni and his son Damon's relationship was finally public. His father didn't use her title as he talked, implying intimacy— as if he'd ever met her? But he wasn't afraid of using anyone to push himself further up the slippery pole of success; Damon knew that all too well.

He could hear his father's avaricious glee at the coup his son had scored.

'You must be very proud of Damon,' one reporter yelled.

His father visibly puffed up. 'Damon is brilliant. He inherited his mother's brains.'

Damon gritted his teeth. His father's false praise poked a wound that should have long healed. His parents were anything but normal. Narcissistic and concerned only with image, neither had hearts. Truth be told, nor did he. That was his genetic inheritance. No capacity for love. No capacity for shame. All his parents had was ambition. He had that too.

But he'd learned to define his own success. To make it alone, be the one in control, be the boss. His parents had been uninterested and absent at best, and abusive at worst, and they'd taught him well. Yeah, now he had the burning ambition not to need them or *anyone*.

'What about your daughter, Kasiani?' Another reporter jostled to the front. 'Is she also a friend of Princess Eleni's?'

His father didn't bat an eyelid at the mention of the daughter he hadn't seen in years and the reference to the women that he'd abandoned entirely—not just emotionally, but financially as well. Damon had actually been jealous of Kassie until he'd learned his father was truly fickle and incapable of any kind of decent emotion.

'I really can't comment further on Eleni's personal relationships.' He didn't need to comment further when the smug satisfaction was written all over his face.

Damon watched as his father walked past the reporter. But as the cameraman swung the camera to keep filming, Damon realised just where the interview had taken place—outside the terminal at Palisades airport.

Which meant his father was here. Now.

Damon muted the sound on the screen and strode from Eleni's private apartment. He needed to speak to the palace secretary immediately.

'Mr Gale.'

Damon stopped mid-stride down the hallway as Giorgos's private secretary called to him.

'It's your father,' the secretary added.

'Please take me to him,' Damon said quietly.

John Gale had been shown to one of the smaller meeting rooms very near the entrance of the palace. Damon's appreciation of Giorgos's secretary increased and he nodded at the man as he stood back respectfully.

Drawing in a breath, Damon closed the door and faced the father he hadn't seen in five years. Not much had changed. Perhaps he had a little more grey in his hair, a few lines around his eyes, but he still wore that surface-only smile, neat suit and non-stick demeanour.

Damon didn't take a seat, didn't offer one to his father. 'Why are you here?'

'I wanted to congratulate you in person.'

The bare nerve of the man was galling.

'You're very quick off the mark. I haven't been married twenty-four hours yet.'

His father's smile stayed crocodile wide. 'I never thought you had it in you.'

'Had what in me?'

'To marry so…happily.'

'Happily?' Damon queried. 'You mean like you and Mother?'

'Your mother and I have a very successful arrangement.'

Yeah. An arrangement that was bloodless and only about making the most of their assets. 'And that's what you think this is?'

'Are you saying you're in love with her?' His father laughed. 'I'm sure you love the power and opportunity that come with her beautiful body.'

Revulsion triggered rage but Damon breathed deeply, settling his pulse. He wasn't going to bite. His father wasn't worth it. But he couldn't help declaring the obvious. 'I'm not like you.'

His father frowned. 'Meaning?'

'You have at least one other child that you have done nothing for. You abuse people, then abandon them.'

His father's expression narrowed.

'How many others are there?' Damon asked bluntly.

'That was one mistake.'

Mistake?

'I saw you with her,' Damon said softly, knowing he'd regret the revelation but unable to resist asking.

'Who?'

'Kassie's mother.' Damon had followed him once, here in Palisades—the opulent island of personal betrayal had taken Damon on a swift bleak journey to adulthood and understanding. He'd seen his father kiss that woman with such passion. Damon had actually thought his father was truly in love. That he was truly capable of it and it was just that he didn't feel it for either Damon or his mother. 'Why didn't you leave us and stay with her?' He'd never understood it.

An appalled expression carved deeper lines in his father's face. 'I would never leave your mother.'

'Not because you love her,' Damon said. 'But because her connections were too important to your career. It was your arrangement.'

Because he was that calculating. That ruthlessly ambitious. That incapable of real love.

'Your mother and I make a good team. We understand each other.'

By turning blind eyes to infidelities and focusing on their careers. They'd used his funds and her family name. Connections and money made for progress in political circles. They'd had Damon only to cement the image of the 'perfect career couple'. Not because he'd actually been wanted, as his mother had told him every time he'd disappointed her. And that had been often.

'So you abandoned your lover and your daughter and refused to help when they were struggling because of the risk to your stupid career and supposedly perfect marriage.' Damon was disgusted.

'I offered her money but she was too proud to accept it. That was her choice.'

'You knew she suffered and you didn't go back.'

'What more could I have done, Damon?' his father asked. 'Was it my fault she chose to remain in that squalid little cottage?'

Damon understood it now—he'd realised the horrific truth when he'd learned how that woman had suffered for so long, so alone. His father had never loved Kassie's mother. He'd wanted her, used her and walked away when he'd had enough. When she'd refused his money his conscience was cleared and he'd considered himself absolved.

No guilt. No shame. No heart.

'It'll look strange if you don't invite us both here soon,' his father said, his callousness towards Kassie and her mother apparently forgotten already. 'Your mother would like to stay as a guest.'

'I'm never inviting either of you here,' Damon said shortly. 'How can you act as if we're close when we haven't seen each other in years?' Bitterness burned up his throat. He wanted the taint of the man nowhere near Eleni.

'We've all been busy.'

His father hadn't realised he'd been avoiding him? 'No. We have no relationship. You're not using this. You're not using me.'

'You can't get away from your blood, Damon.' John Gale laughed. 'You're my son. Just because we're more alike than you want to admit, doesn't mean it isn't so. You can't get away from who you are.'

He'd never wanted to be like either of his parents. They were why he'd never wanted a serious relationship, let alone to marry. Why he'd wanted to build his company—his success—on his own terms. In isolation and not dependent on manipulated relationships.

'I might not be able to deny my blood, but I can deny you access to my wife and to our home,' Damon said coldly. 'You're not welcome here. You'll never be welcome here. I suggest you leave right now, before I have the soldiers throw you out.'

'Your wife's soldiers.'

'Yes.' Damon refused to let his father get a rise out of him. 'Don't come back. Don't contact me again. And don't dare try to contact Eleni directly.'

'Or?'

'Or I'll let the world know just *what* you are.' He'd strike where his father cared the most—his reputation, his image.

John's eyes narrowed.

'It will be much better for you to return to New York and whatever project it is you're about to launch,' Damon said lazily. 'And no more gleeful interviews mentioning Eleni and me. You're showing your lack of class.'

That blow landed and Damon watched as his father's complexion turned ruddy. After that, John didn't stick around and Damon slowly wound his way back up to Eleni's apartment. He'd done the right thing getting him out of the palace as quickly as possible. But his father's slimy insincerity stuck.

He didn't want it getting to Eleni. As soon as the baby was born he'd begin the separation process because she'd be so much better off without him. But he'd still be the Princess's ex-husband, the father of her child. Another prince or princess.

Too late he realised her life was now intrinsically tied to his. His gut tightened as he mulled the possible configurations of their futures and the fact that she would always be part of his world. In the cold light of day he realised he'd not 'won' anything at all.

Nor had she.

But he'd meant what he'd told her. Relationships never lasted. Not for anyone. And certainly not him. Never him. He refused.

He paused for a moment outside her apartment door to draw in a breath. Then he let himself in. It was too much to hope she was still in bed. She was dressed in a simple tee shirt and skirt and his wayward body tightened at the sight of her lithe legs.

'Where have you been?' she asked, sending him a sleepy smile, but her sea-green eyes were too searching for him to cope with.

'I have a company to run,' Damon said sharply, picking up his tablet and staring at it. Hard. 'I've neglected it long enough while tracking you down.'

Silence filled the room, tightening the invisible string connecting his eyes to her body and in the end he could no longer resist the tug.

A limpid look was trained on him. 'Perhaps you should have slept a little longer.'

He couldn't help but smile at that most princess-polite sass.

She wandered over to the window, affording him an even better view of her legs and the curve of her body. She had no idea of her sensuality.

'So what have you been working on that's caused your mood to…deteriorate?'

'It's not important.'

'It wouldn't have anything to do with your father, would it?'

He froze. 'Your palace spies have reported in already?'

'No spies. I saw a replay of the interview with him at the airport.' She turned to face him. 'Is he here?'

'He's already left.'

'You didn't want me to meet him?'

'No.' He didn't want to explain why. But he saw the wounded flash in her eyes. 'He's not a nice man.'

Her lips twisted. 'You don't need to protect me.'

'Yes, I do.' He huffed out a breath and glared at his tablet again, gripping it as if it were his life-support system.

His marriage to Eleni could be nothing like his parents' one. For one thing, it wasn't about to last. It wasn't about his career and never would be. It was about protecting his child. It was about protecting Eleni.

'Are you sure it's me you're protecting?' she asked quietly.

He glanced across at her. 'Meaning?'

'Your father…and you.' She looked uncomfortable. 'You're not close…'

'No.' Damon couldn't help but smile faintly. Definitely not close. 'I haven't had contact with him in almost five years.'

'None at all?'

He shook his head.

'He cheated on your mother.' She still looked super awkward. 'Kassie at the hospital…'

'Is my unacknowledged half-sister. Yes.'

'But you're in touch with her.'

'Yes.' He sighed and put the tablet down on the low table. 'My father isn't. My mother pretends she doesn't exist. Kassie is too proud to push for what she's owed.' He leaned back on the edge of the sofa, folding his arms across his chest. He'd had to find out what had happened. 'I once saw him with her mother,' Damon said. 'Years ago when we lived here in Palisades.'

'That must have been hard to see.'

Damon frowned at the floor. 'I couldn't understand why he didn't leave us for them when it was so obvious...'

'Did you ever ask him?'

About five minutes ago and his father had confirmed what Damon had learned in later years. 'His career was too important. It was always too important to both my parents. The only reason they had me was to tick that box on their CV—happily married with one son...'

'But they must be proud of you.'

He laughed bitterly. 'Proud of a teenager who wasted his time making lame computer games?' He shook his head.

'But now you have a hugely successful company. More than one. How can they not be—?' She broke off and her expression softened. 'You shouldn't have had to "achieve" to get the support any child deserves.'

'I got more than my half-sister did,' he muttered shortly. 'He wouldn't even support them financially. Her mother died a long, slow, painful death. Kassie has been struggling since.'

'Is that why you got in touch with her?'

He nodded. 'But she wouldn't let me help her.' He rolled his shoulders. It still knotted him that Kassie had refused almost everything he'd offered. 'I can understand it.'

Sadness lent a sheen to Eleni's eyes. 'And your parents are still together.'

'Still achieving. Still silently seething with bitterness and unhappiness. Still a successful marriage. Sure thing.'

'He cheated more than once?'

'I expect so,' he sighed.

'So.' Eleni brushed her hair back from her face. 'That's why you made it clear our marriage is only to provide legitimacy for our baby. Why you think no relationship lasts.'

'As I said, a child shouldn't be raised in the household with unhappily married parents.' Unloving parents. 'We married for the birth certificate, then we do what's right. I didn't want this baby to be a tool for some political purpose. Not paraded as the future Prince or Princess or whatever. And I won't abandon it either.'

'I understand,' she said softly. 'I don't want that either.' She bit her lip and looked down at the table between them. 'I'm sorry your parents...'

He held up a hand. 'It's okay. We all have our burdens, right?' She'd lost both her parents. She had expectations on her that were far beyond the normal person's. He shouldn't have judged her as harshly as he had.

'Damon?'

He glanced up at that roughened note in her voice.

Storms had gathered in her sea-green eyes. 'This baby was unexpected, unplanned...' she pressed a hand to her flat belly as she gazed across at him '...but I promise you I'll love it. I already do. I'll do whatever it takes to protect and care for it.'

'I know.' He believed her because she already was. He'd seen her stand up to her brother—knew that had been a first for her. And she was trying here, now, with him.

But somehow it made that discomfort within him worse. He wasn't like her. He didn't understand how she could love the child already. The truth was he didn't know how to love. He had no idea how to be a husband. He sure as hell had no idea how to be a father. When

he'd first suspected she might be pregnant his initial
instinct had been not to abandon his child. He was not
doing what his father had done to Kassie.

But he had no idea how even these next few months
were going to work. The tightness in his chest didn't
ease. Disappointment flowed and then ebbed. Leaving
him with that *void*. He ached for a real escape.

'Is that the photo Giorgos approved for release?'
Eleni's voice rose in surprise.

He glanced at the muted screen still showing the
number one news item of the world.

'Yes.' He cleared his throat. 'There's another with
him in it as well, but this is the one the media have run
with.'

'I can't believe he chose that one. It's…'

'What?'

'Informal.'

Damon knew why the King had chosen that particular picture. Eleni looked stunning with her skin
glowing, her hair and dress beautiful…but it was that
luminosity in her expression that was striking. While
Damon was looking at her with undeniable desire, she
was laughing up at him—sparkling, warm, delighted.
This image, snapped in that moment in the garden,
would sell the 'truth' of this fairy tale.

This image stole his breath.

But now another picture of him flashed on the
screen—him at an event with another woman. Then
another. Inwardly he winced. It seemed anyone who'd
dated him in the past wanted their five minutes of fame
now and had opened their photo albums to show off
their one or two snaps.

'Wow, lots of models, huh?' Eleni muttered, her rasp

more apparent. 'That's very billionaire tech entrepreneur of you.'

'It wasn't a deliberate strategy.' He stepped nearer to her, needing to touch her skin. 'They just happened to be at the parties.'

She subjected him to a long, silent scrutiny. 'You know my history. I don't know yours at all.'

'You mean lovers?' He grinned in an effort to shake off the prickling sensation her piercing greenish gaze caused. 'I've had a few. No real girlfriends. There's nothing and no one to trouble you.'

She didn't look convinced.

He shrugged. 'I'm busy with my work and I like to be good at it.'

The ugly fact was he was a hollow man—as success obsessed as his shallow parents. Just less visible about it. He liked to think he had a smidge more integrity than they did—by refusing to use other people to get to where he wanted to be. Utter independence was what he craved.

'Do you know I've got at least twenty new work offers today purely because of my involvement with you?' he said a little roughly.

She lifted her eyebrows. 'And that isn't good?'

'*I* haven't earned these opportunities, Eleni.'

'Perhaps you could take advantage of them to enable other people to progress as well. To create jobs and other contracts—'

Her naive positivity hit a raw nerve. '*I* built my company from scratch.'

'And you don't want your association with me compromising your success story?' Her cheeks pinked. 'At least you had the choice to forge your own path. I'm one of the most privileged people on the planet and, while I am grateful for that, I'm also bound by the rules that come with it. I couldn't do what I want.'

And it seemed she still couldn't. He grabbed his tablet again and showed her the endless list of invitations and formal appearances the palace official had sent him. 'Is this amount normal?' he asked. 'Which would you usually decline?'

Her eyebrows shot up. 'None.'

None? He paused. 'There are too many requests here.'

Were they were trying to schedule her every waking moment? Damon wasn't having it.

'You don't say no.' The shock on her face said it all.

She really was a total pawn in the palace machine. Well, he wasn't letting them take advantage of Eleni, or her child, or him. Not any more.

'I'm okay with saying no,' he said.

'Well, I don't like to be perceived as lazy.' Her lips tightened. 'Or spoilt.'

And that was why Princess Eleni had always done as she was told —wore what was expected, said what was polite, did what was her duty. She'd obediently played her princess role perfectly for years.

Except when it had come to him. That night with him she'd done what she *wanted*. She'd taken. And since then? She'd argued. She'd stood up for herself. She'd been everything but obedient when it came to him…

He didn't want that changing because she felt some misguided sense of obligation now she was married to him. Hell, she was likely to want to play the part of the 'perfect wife' but he wasn't letting it happen. For the first time in her life, he wanted Eleni Nicolaides to experience some true freedom.

'Why did you want to stay in Palisades rather than go to Giorgos's safe house in France?' he asked roughly.

She looked down. 'This probably sounds crazy, but it's actually more private here.'

'You're *happy* to be trapped inside the palace walls?'

She shrugged her shoulders. 'It's what I'm used to. I can show you how it works.'

He didn't need to know how it worked. He had a headache from all the gilded decorations already. 'I know somewhere even more private.' He rubbed his shoulder. 'I think we should go there.'

'You don't understand—'

'Yeah, I do. I know about the paparazzi and the press and the cell phones in every member of the public's hands. But my island is safe. It's secure. It's private.'

She stilled. 'Your island?'

She really hadn't done any research on him, had she? That both tickled him, and put him out.

'You have your island, I have mine.' He sent her a sideways grin. 'I'll admit mine isn't as big, but good things come in small packages.'

The look in her eyes was decidedly not limpid now. 'Are you trying to convince me that size doesn't matter?' she teased in that gorgeously raspy voice. 'Of course, I have no basis for comparison, for all I know I might be missing out —'

'You're concerned you're missing out?' He rose to her bait, happy to slip back into this tease and turn away from the too serious.

'You tell me.' She batted her eyelashes at him.

This was the woman from that night at the ball—that playful, slightly shy, deliciously fun woman.

'Hell, yeah, you're missing out.'

Her mouth fell open.

'Come with me and I'll show you.'

Her lips twisted as colour flowed into her cheeks.

'It's in the Caribbean,' he purred.

She closed her mouth. 'That is also very tech billionaire of you.'

'Yeah. It is. So let's go there. Today.' He stood, energy firing. For the first time since seeing that damn screen this morning he felt good.

'But Giorgos—'

'But Giorgos what? We can let him know where we've gone.' He paused, waiting to see if she'd defy her brother's orders.

A gleam lit in her eye. Damon suppressed his smug smirk—seemed his Princess had unleashed her latent rebellious streak. He liked it.

'How long does it take to get there?'

CHAPTER ELEVEN

ELENI SAT ACROSS from Damon in one of the large leather recliners in his private jet and tried not to stare at him. Her face heated as she recalled what he'd done to her, what he'd encouraged her to do to him. Last night had been the first time she'd ever shared a bed. The first time she'd slept in a man's arms. She couldn't even *remember* falling asleep, only a feeling of supreme relaxation as she'd lain entwined with him.

'It's a long flight. You should rest while you can.' That wicked glint ignited his smile as if he knew exactly what she was thinking about.

'I need rest?'

'For the days ahead, yes.'

'Empty promises…threats…' she muttered softly.

He leaned forward and placed his finger over her lips. 'Don't worry. I'll make good on every one. When we're alone.'

'I see no cabin crew.' She blinked at him.

'You want them to hear you?' His eyebrows arched. 'Because you're not going to be quiet.'

'I can be quiet.'

'Can you?' He studied her intently, not bothering to add anything more.

Heat deepened and spread, heating her from the inside out. Every, single cell. Realisation burned. She was never going to be quiet with him.

'You're...' She couldn't think of her own name, let alone a suitable adjective this second.

'Good.' Looking smug, he leaned back in his seat and pulled his tablet out. 'I'm very good.'

'Full of yourself,' she corrected.

She couldn't sit for hours with nothing to occupy her except sinful thoughts. She burrowed in her bag and fetched out the paper and small pencil tin that she always had stashed. Sketching soothed, like meditation. And she'd spent so many hours with a pencil in hand, it was calming.

He didn't seem to notice her occupation. She became so engrossed in her work she lost track of time. When she glanced up she discovered he'd closed his eyes. She wasn't surprised; he'd had as little sleep as she. And he'd been worryingly pale when he'd returned to her apartment this morning after that meeting with his father.

With that downwards tilt to his sensual lips now, she understood that he was vulnerable too and much more complex than she'd realised. He'd been hurt. His parents' infidelities, their lack of support and interest. Their falseness.

Yet he'd grown strong. Now she understood his fierce independence and the fury he'd felt when he'd thought she'd somehow betrayed him. He didn't trust and she didn't blame him. He only wanted his child to avoid the hurt he'd experienced.

She looked down at the sketch she'd done of him and cringed. She'd never want him to see this—too amateur. Too embarrassing. She folded the paper over and put it in the small bin just as the pilot announced they weren't far from landing. Damon opened his eyes and flashed her a smile.

'It's just a short hop by helicopter from here,' he said as the plane landed.

'That's what you say to everyone you bring here?'

He met her gaze. 'You already know I never brought any of my women here. This is my home.'

'Heaven forbid you'd let any of them get that close.'

'Wouldn't want them getting the wrong idea.'

'I'm glad I "trapped" you into marriage, then, now I get to kick about on your little island.'

Damon grinned at her. Yeah, he couldn't wait for her to kick about. But he held back as Eleni gathered her small bag and stepped ahead of him to exit the plane. He'd seen her discard the drawing she'd been working on and he was too curious to let it go. On his way out he swiftly scooped up the paper and pocketed it. Given she'd been secretive and clearly hadn't wanted him to see it, he was going to have to pick the moment to ask her about it.

The helicopter ride was smooth but wasn't quick enough. He ached to get there—to his home. His own private palace. His peace.

He breathed out as they finally landed and he strode to the open-topped Jeep that he'd ordered to be left waiting for their arrival.

'Let me take you on a tour.' He winked at her. 'You can see exactly what kind of prize husband you've claimed for yourself.'

'You're not the prize. I am,' Eleni answered sassily as she shook her hair loose in the warm sunshine. 'It really is your island?'

'It's the company compound,' he drawled. 'We futuristic tech companies must have amazing work placcs for our staff. It's part of the image.'

'I didn't think you were a slave to any society's required "image". You're the man who doesn't care what anyone thinks of him, right?'

Right. *Almost.*

Reluctant amusement rippled through him. He liked it when she sparked up.

She stared as the pristine coastline came into clear view. He heard her sharp intake of breath. Now as he drove they could see a few roofs of other dwellings amongst the verdant foliage. He knew it was beautiful, but he was glad she could see it too.

'They live here all year round?'

'No.' He laughed that she'd taken him so seriously. 'It really is just my island. It was a resort, now it's not. My people stay for stints if they need to complete a big project, or to recharge their batteries. Every employee has at least six weeks a year here. Families can come too, of course.' He parked up by the main beach. 'Energy-wise it's self-sufficient, thanks to all the solar-power generation, and we grow as many supplies as we can.'

'So it's paradise.'

'Yeah.' Pure, simple luxury. 'There's no paparazzi. No media. No nosey parkers watching your every move. It is completely private.'

She glanced up into the blindingly blue—clear—sky. 'No drones? No spy cams everywhere?'

'No helicopters. No long-range lenses. No nothing. Just peace and security,' he confirmed, but grimaced wryly. 'And half my staff…but they'll be busy and you can do whatever you want, whenever you want.'

'With whomever I want?' she asked. There was an extra huskiness to her tone that made him so hard.

'No.' He reached across and turned her chin so she faced him. 'Only with me.'

She mock-pouted, teasing in that playful way he adored—demanding retribution of the most erotic kind. But after only a kiss he reluctantly pulled away. He couldn't bring her here and hurry her into bed. He could be more civilised than that.

'Come on,' he said briskly, getting out of the Jeep and pointing to the meandering path through the lush trees. 'I'll show you around the complex.'

Then he'd take her to his house and have her all to himself at last.

Eleni didn't want to blink and miss a moment. His island was like a warm jewel, gleaming with the promise of heat and holiday and indefinable riches. And with that total privacy, it was the ultimate treasure. A feeling of relaxation slowly unfurled through her body, spreading warmth and joy and such anticipation she could hardly contain it.

'This is the "den"—our main office here.'

She followed him into the large building. It was a large open space filled with desks, computers and space for tinkering and was currently occupied by five guys all standing round a giant screen.

'Going from left to right, we have Olly, Harry, Blair, Jerome and Faisal,' Damon said to her in a low voice. 'You have that memorised already, right?'

She smiled because, yes, she had.

'Guys,' Damon called to them. 'I'd like you to meet Eleni.'

Not *Princess*. Not *my wife*. Just Eleni. That different kind of warmth flowed through her veins again.

The men turned and shouts erupted. But not for her. It was pleasure that their boss had returned. One of the guys stepped to the side of the swarm around Damon to greet her.

'Nice to meet you, Eleni.' Olly's accent placed him as Australian.

The other men nodded, smiled and positively pounced on Damon again.

'Look, D—I know you're not here for work, but can I just run a couple things past you?' Faisal asked.

Damon was already halfway across the room, his gaze narrowing at the gobbledegook on the screen. 'Of course.'

All the men perked up but Eleni saw Olly and Jerome exchange a look and a jerk of the head towards her. The next second Jerome walked over.

'Eleni…' Jerome cleared his throat. 'Welcome. You must…ah…'

'I'm really happy to be here.' She smiled to put him at ease. Eleni could make conversation with anyone. 'What is it you guys are working on?'

He led her to the nearest table that was covered in an assortment of electronics components and plastic figurines. 'We're designing a new visuals prototype and we need his thoughts on the latest version.'

'Visuals prototype?'

To his credit, Jerome spent a good five minutes explaining the tech to her and answering her questions. But it was obvious he was eager to talk to Damon too and in the end she put him out of his misery. 'Go ask him whatever it is you need to. I'm fine,' she laughed.

'Are you sure?' Jerome looked anxiously between her and Damon.

'Of course.'

He hurried away to join the conference around the screen. Damon stood in the centre, listening intently then quietly offering his opinion. The Australian was making notes on a piece of paper while Harry asked another question prompting another concise answer. It was evident they valued his every word and had missed his input. Everyone in the vicinity was paying total attention—to him. Eleni gradually became aware she was staring at him too. And for once no one was staring at *her*.

Blushing, she turned away and stepped outside to take in some fresh air. Her muscles ached slightly and a gentle feeling of fatigue made her sleepy. She leaned against the tall tree just outside the building and looked across at the beautifully clear water.

Ten minutes later Damon walked back to where she waited in the shade.

'Sorry,' he muttered as he reached to take her hand. 'That took longer than I realised.'

'It's fine. I enjoyed looking around.'

Damon sent her a speculative look that turned increasingly wicked the longer he studied her. 'What have you been thinking about?' he asked. 'You've gone very pink.'

The heat in her cheeks burned. 'Don't tease.'

'Oh, I'll tease.' He tugged on her hand and pulled her closer to him. 'But first let me show you the rest.'

'I think rest is a good idea.' She wanted to be alone with his undivided attention on *her* again. And right now she didn't care if that made her spoiled.

'There's a restaurant room,' he said.

Of course there was. Right on the beach, with a bar and a woman who waved and smiled at Damon the second she saw him. Eleni's spine prickled.

'Rosa will cook anything you want, as long as you want fresh and delicious.' Damon waved at the relaxed, gorgeously tanned woman and kept walking past.

'This place is just beautiful.' Eleni glanced back at the restaurant.

'Rosa is married to Olly, the guy with—'

'The beard.' Eleni sighed, stupidly relieved. 'The Australian.'

Damon grinned as if he'd sensed her irrational jealous flare. 'They live here most of the year round.'

'Lucky them.' She walked across the sand with him. 'Do you live here most of the year too?'

'Meetings take me away, but I'm here when I can be.'

Eleni could understand why; if it were her choice she'd never leave. But his marriage to her was going to make that problematic for a while. She had duties in Palisades that she had to perform.

'Where next?' she asked. 'Your house?'

'Not yet. You haven't seen the playroom.'

'Playroom?' she asked, startled.

He laughed and gave her a playful swipe. 'Not *that* kind of playroom.' He cocked his head. 'But now I know you're curious...'

'Shut it and show me the room.' She marched across the sand, cheeks burning.

It was a boat shed and it was filled with every watersport toy imaginable—from surfboards, to kayaks to inflatables and jet skis. 'Okay, this is seriously cool.' She stepped forward to get a closer look.

'I knew you liked the water,' Damon said smugly. 'You swim, right?'

'Indoors at the palace,' she answered, checking out the kayaks stacked in racks up the wall. 'Giorgos had a resistance current feature installed so I can train each morning in privacy.'

'You don't swim in the sea?'

'With everyone watching?' She stared at him as if he were crazy. 'Rating my swimsuits every morning?' She shook her head. 'And he'd never let me on a jet ski.'

'No?' Damon's eyes widened.

'Safety issues.' She shrugged and straightened. 'And again, too many photographers.'

'You like to avoid those.'

'Do you blame me?'

'No.' He leaned against the door frame and sent her a smouldering look. 'I'm really good on a jet ski,' he said arrogantly. 'You can come with me.'

She crossed her arms and sent what she hoped was a smouldering look right back at him. 'Can I drive?'

'Sure. I have no problem with that.'

'But what if I want to go fast?' She blinked at him innocently.

'I think I can keep up.' He lifted away from the door frame and strolled towards her.

'You think?' Her voice rose as he stepped close enough to pull her against him.

'I think it's time you saw my house,' he growled.

'It's beyond time,' she whispered.

He guided her across the sand and up a beautifully maintained path through the well-established trees to the gorgeous building at the end.

An infinity pool—the perfect length for laps—was

the feature at the front. Comfortable, beautiful furniture was strategically placed to create space for relaxation, conversation and privacy. The house itself was wooden, with two storeys, and not monstrously huge but nor was it small. Damon didn't speak as he led her inside—he simply let her look around. It was luxurious, yes, but also cosy with a sense of true intimacy. She didn't know why that surprised her, but it did.

He still said nothing, but smiled as if he sensed her appreciation. She took his outstretched hand and he led her up the curling wooden staircase. She assumed it led to his bedroom. Her heart hammered. A delicious languorous anticipation seeped into her bones.

But while there were doors to other rooms on one side, the room he drew her to wasn't for sleeping. It stretched the length of the building. Unsurprisingly it was dominated by symmetrical windows overlooking the sand, sea and sky. A long table took up half the space. It was clearly his desk, given the neatly stacked piles of papers and the writing utensils gathered in a chipped mug. A long seat took up much of the remaining window space. A single armchair stood in front of the large fireplace that broke up the floor-to-ceiling bookshelves that covered the wall opposite the windows. Books were stacked on every shelf. Books that had clearly been read and weren't just there for the look of it. This was more than his workspace. It was his think space—his escape.

'I can see why you love it.' She stood in the middle of the room and gazed from the intriguing space inside to the natural beauty outside.

'Best view on the island.'

'The beauty is more than the view.' She noted the shades for the windows, the pale warmth of the walls, the art that he'd chosen to complement the space. 'The light is lovely,' she said softly. 'The colour. It must help you focus.'

'It's not a palace,' he said with a keen look.

'It's better than any palace.'

A small smile flitted about his mouth. 'So you like it?'

Intrigued that her opinion genuinely seemed to matter, she turned her back on the view to face him directly. 'Did you honestly think I wouldn't?' She wasn't that spoilt, was she?

'There's not a lot of gold leaf and crystal chandeliers.'

'Did you think I wasn't going to like it because there's no ballroom?' She felt slightly hurt. 'You don't need a ballroom—you have a beach.' She looked out across the water again. 'You're lucky to have a home, not a museum in which you live.'

She and Giorgos didn't own the palace, they were the guardians for the future of it, and for the people of Palisades. This small island was utterly Damon's and she had to admit she was a little jealous.

'You can stay here any time,' he said.

She sent him a crooked smile, rueful that he'd so clearly read her mind. She didn't want to think about the future yet. She just wanted to enjoy this freedom, in this moment. Enjoy him, while she had him.

'Thank you.' She faced him, determined to take the initiative, despite the mounting burn in her cheeks. 'So may I sit in the driver's seat?'

His focus on her sharpened. 'Meaning?'

Silently she just looked at him. He knew exactly what she meant already.

'Tell me,' he said softly—a combination of demand and dare. 'You can tell me anything.'

His easy invitation summoned that streak of boldness within her, just as it had that very first night. Something in him gave her the courage to claim what she wanted. The courage she got only with him. Only for him.

'I want to kiss you,' she muttered huskily and swallowed before continuing. 'The way you've kissed me.'

He stared at her so intently she wondered if he'd turned to stone.

'I dare you to let me,' she whispered.

'Is this what you've been thinking about?'

'All day,' she admitted with a slow nod.

His smile was as rueful—and as honest—as hers had been only moments earlier. He lifted his hands in a small gesture of surrender. 'That's why you drew this?' He held up a piece of paper.

She winced as she saw what he was holding. 'I put that in the rubbish.'

'Which was a shame.'

That he'd seen that drawing was the most embarrassing thing. Because it was him. Half nude. Heat flooded her. Mortifying, blistering heat.

'Why didn't you study Fine Arts?' he asked.

'It would have been arrogant to assume I had talent.' She hadn't been allowed.

'You do have talent.'

His words lit a different glow in her chest but she laughed it off. 'You're just flattered because I gave you abs.'

'I do have abs.'

'I don't usually draw…' She couldn't even admit it.

'Erotic pictures?' He laughed. 'What do you usually draw?'

'Dogs,' she said tartly.

'The pictures in Kassie's ward at the hospital are yours, right? You draw them for the children.'

He'd seen those? 'They're just doodles.' She shrugged it off.

'You're talented, Eleni.'

'You're very kind.' She bent her head.

He gripped her arms and made her look at him again. 'Don't go "polite princess" on me. Accept the compliment for what it is—honest.'

That fiery heat bloomed in her face again.

'Do you paint as well?'

'Sometimes, but mostly pen and ink drawings.'

'You're good, Eleni.'

'You promised me you were good,' she whispered.

A smile sparked in his eyes but he shook his head. 'You're trying to distract me.'

'Is it working?'

'You know it is. But why can't you take the compliment?'

Because it was too intimate. Too real. It meant too much. His opinion of her shouldn't matter as much as it did. But she didn't say any of that. She just shrugged.

'You have a lot to offer the world,' he said softly.

For a moment it was there again—that flicker of intensity that was different from the pure desire that pulled them together in the first place. This was something deeper. Something impossibly stronger. And she backed away from it.

'Stop with the flattery or I'll never leave,' she joked.

There was a moment of silence and she couldn't look at him.

'Where will you have me?' With those husky words

he let her lead them back into that purely sensual tease. The easier, safer option.

'Here. Now.'

She walked, nudging him backwards. All the way to that comfortable armchair. She pushed his chest and he sat. She remained standing, looking down at him. He'd not had the chance to shave since their flight and the light stubble on his jaw lent him a roguish look. That curl to his lips was both arrogant and charming.

She leaned forward. 'Damon,' she breathed as she kissed him.

'Yes.' He held very still beneath her ministrations.

'You're irresistible.' She sent him a laughing look.

He chuckled. 'I'm glad you think so.' He tensed as she slowly undid his buttons. 'What a relief.'

'You don't seem very relieved.'

'I'm trying to stay in control.'

'Why would you want to do that?'

'I don't want to scare you.'

She laughed. 'You're no ogre.'

'I don't want you to stop,' he whispered.

'Why would I? I want you to lose control. You make me lose control all the time.'

'Eleni…'

'It's only fair,' she muttered. Not teasing.

'Fair? You know that's not how it works.'

A frisson of awareness reverberated through her body. Delight. Desire. Danger. That intensity flickered again. But she moved closer. Took him deeper. Stroked him harder. Doing everything she'd secretly dreamed of doing. She'd show him *not fair*.

He groaned. 'Don't stop.'

Pleased, she kissed him again and then again. His

hands swept down her sides, stirring her to the point where she couldn't concentrate any more. She drew back.

'Stop touching,' she growled at him. 'It's my turn.'

He half laughed. She squeezed. Hard.

'Mine,' she said seriously—and for more than just this 'turn'.

He met her gaze. The blue of his eyes deepened as that something passed between them. No matter that she tried to dance past it, it kept curling back—entwining around them.

He lifted a hand, threading his fingers through her hair to cup the nape of her neck. 'Mine.'

His echo was an affirmation, not an argument. He was hers to hold. Hers to have. And yes, she was his too.

For now. Only for now.

She closed her eyes and let herself go—taking exactly what she wanted, touching in the way she'd only dreamed and never before dared. She liked feeling his power beneath her. Liked his vulnerability like this—letting her pleasure him.

'Eleni.'

She felt his power and restraint and fought to topple it. He curled his hands around the armrests and she heard his breathing roughen. His muscles flexed and she tasted salt as sweat slicked his skin.

'Eleni.'

She tightened her grip, swirling her tongue, and simply willed for him to feel it the same way she did—that unspeakable bliss. 'Let me make you feel good.'

That was what he did for her.

Spent and satisfied physically, a different need surged fiercely through Damon. He didn't want her doing this out of gratitude or pity. He lifted her onto his lap and cupping her chin, stared hard into her eyes—heavy-lidded, sea-green storms of desire gazed back at him. Dazed, yet seemingly seeing right into his soul.

Pure instinct drove him. He kissed her, slipping his hand under her skirt, skating his fingers all the way to her secret treasure. His heart seized as he discovered how hot and wet she was and satisfaction drummed in his heart. She'd not gone down on him from a sense of obligation; she'd almost got off on it. The least he could do was help her get the rest of the way. This thing between them had them equally caught. Her need—her ache—was his. Just as his was hers. She moaned as he flicked his fingers and pushed her harder, faster. He kissed her again and again, almost angry in the pleasure and relief of discovering her extreme arousal. It took only a moment and then she was there, pleasure shuddering through her body.

She was inexperienced, yet lustful. Her shy but unashamed sensuality felled him—he wanted to make it better and better for her. But there was no bettering what was already sublime. No beating the chemistry that flared so brightly whenever they came into contact.

He held her in his arms and stood, carrying her down the stairs to the comfort of his bed. In this one thing, at least, he could meet every one of her needs.

Again, again, and again.

CHAPTER TWELVE

'I THINK YOU can go a little faster than that.' Damon double-checked her life vest and then dared her.

'It's even more fun than I imagined.' Eleni smiled at him from astride the jet ski.

He grinned at the double-meaning glint in her eye. With wild hair and without a speck of make-up his Princess was more luminous than ever. With each moment he spent with her, he grew more intrigued. But he forced a laugh past the lump in his throat. 'Because you like fast.'

'I must admit I do.'

'Then why not see if you can beat me.'

Her eyes flashed again and he relished the way she rose to his challenge. He liked seeing her this happy. The one thing he could do was give her more moments of freedom before she returned to full-time royal life and that damn goldfish bowl she lived in.

He got on the other jet ski. 'Come on, we'll go to the cove.'

Her laughter rang out as she took off before he was ready. Grinning, he revved his engine and set out to hunt her down.

Two hours later Eleni sat on the beach suffused with

a deep sense of contentment. The place was paradise—
and Damon in paradise? Heartbreaking. He talked,
teased, laughed. But she liked him like this too—just
sitting quietly alongside her, relaxed and simply enjoying the feel of the sun.

Now she understood why he'd been unable to trust
her initially. Why he didn't want his child caught between parents knotted together unhappily. But now that
she knew, things had changed. Her feelings for him
were deepening, growing, causing confusion.

She sat forward as a shiver ran down her spine. She
didn't like the cold streak of uncertainty; she'd bring
forward warmth instead. She sent him a coy look. 'I
think I should go back to the house and have an afternoon nap.'

'Ride with me this time. One of the guys will come
get the other jet ski later.'

He sped back to the main beach while she unashamedly clung, loving the feel of the wind on her face and
the spray of the sea, taking the chance to rest before
what was to come. But when they walked up to the
house, he diverted to the staircase, turning to her with
a smile on his face.

Eleni stood on the threshold and stared at the new
desk that had replaced the window seat in Damon's office. It was angled, an artist's desk. A cabinet stood
beside it, together with a folded easel. Boxes of art supplies were neatly stacked on the top of the cabinet and
instinctively she knew that were she to open the drawers, she would most likely find more. Paper, paint, pens,
pencils, pastels, ink, brushes, canvas—so many art supplies and a desk and chair that were not for Damon to
use. But for her.

Her heart raced. 'When did you arrange this?'

Why had he arranged this? She stared at the beautifully set out equipment and then looked at him.

That gorgeous smile curved his mouth but he just shrugged. 'I unleashed one of the graphic designers in an art store in the States. He got in last night and set it up while we were out just now.' His gaze narrowed on her. 'Would it have been better for you to choose the supplies yourself?'

'No. No, this is…amazing. It's so much better than what I use at home.'

He nodded slowly. 'You don't spend money on it because— '

'It's just a hobby,' she answered quickly.

'But it's more than a hobby to you.'

She was unbearably touched that he understood how much she loved it. 'It's not going to bother you that I'm working here?'

Damon's smile faded, leaving him looking sombre, and suddenly that intensity flared between them. That silent pull of something that tried to bind them closer. 'I'm not going to tease you with the obvious answer because this is actually too important.' He reached out and cupped her face. 'I don't want you to sit in the corner and be decorative and silent. I like your company. And not just…'

He let the sentence hang and his smile said it all.

Eleni stared up at him, her own smile tremulous. He'd put her in his space—placed her desk next to his and drawn her close to his side. He wanted her near him. Eleni had never had such a gift.

'Thank you,' she said softly. 'I like your company too.'

* * *

When she woke the next morning Damon had already risen. She showered and put on a loose summer dress. She took some toast and fruit from the breakfast tray and climbed the stairs to see him. He glanced up from the book he was reading. In his white tee, beige trousers and bare feet, he was too gorgeous.

Even more so when that roguish smile lit up his eyes. 'I thought you might sleep in.'

Heat burned in her cheeks as she remembered the little sleep they'd stolen through the night. But she was determined to tease him every bit as much as he teased her, so she adopted her most princessy tone.

'I might take a nap later. You may care to join me then.' She gestured at her desk. 'I thought I'd take a look at my new toys, if that's okay.'

He shut his book with a snap and sent her a stern look. 'You ruined it with that last bit. You don't need my permission. You're free to do whatever you want.' He reached for another book on his desk. 'I'm not your King, Eleni. Not your master.'

She knew that. 'I was just trying to be polite.'

'You don't need to try to be anything with me, Eleni. You can just be yourself.'

She was self-conscious to start with, too aware of how near he was and nervous of making too much noise as she removed plastic wrap and opened packets. She'd never really shared space like this with anyone.

'I'm messy,' she said, glancing at the bottles of ink she'd opened to test out. 'Sorry.'

'That's okay. I'm messy too.'

That was a lie; his desk was immaculate. But as the morning progressed, the piles beside him began to grow.

He read more than she'd have thought possible. He sent emails in batches, took video calls over the Internet. His focus didn't surprise her, nor his ability to recall facts or tiny facets of design and interface.

Rosa appeared with another tray of food—fresh, beautifully prepared and presented. Eleni was used to immaculate service but this was different. This was more intimate, more relaxed, more friendly. Just like the island itself. He had such privacy and freedom here. It was the perfect holiday escape for her.

But it was his reality. His life. The space he'd secured for himself to think and create and build.

He connected or disconnected from the rest of the world as he pleased. No wonder he'd looked so uncomfortable at the thought of spending serious time in the palace. It wasn't that he couldn't handle it, it was just that he didn't want to. He had other things to think about—fascinating things, much more meaningful to him than gallery openings and charity visits.

And he had history back in Palisades—bitter family history that hurt. She understood that, for him, attendance at glittering events was only to promote the fallacy of his parents' marriage. He thought everything about those evenings was false. But he was wrong.

They did important work. They had value too. She just had to help him understand it.

Lost in thought, she opened the drawers of the cabinet and selected a sheet of paper. She needed this time out to figure out their future. To accept it.

As she settled into her exploration of pen nibs and ink and the tin of beautiful pencils, time snuck away. When light glinted on the glass of water beside her desk, she looked up from the picture she'd fallen into drawing. To her surprise, the sun was almost at its zenith and she knew both the sand and the water would be warm. Her whole body melted at the thought.

'I just need to get this message sent and I'll go with you.'

Startled, she glanced over and met Damon's knowing gaze. He smiled at her and then looked down to his tablet, his fingers skipping over the keyboard.

She sat back, relaxing as she appreciated how hard he worked. People counted on him and he delivered. No wonder he'd become as successful as he had. An outlier—fiercely intelligent, gifted, and hard-working. But he liked to do things his way—in his place, in his time.

'It's looking good.' Damon rose and studied her page.

She chuckled and shook her head.

He pointed at the faint lines she'd drawn in. 'You've had training.'

'Well, drawing classes were quite an acceptable occupation for a young princess.'

'Until you wanted to get serious about it?' Damon was too astute.

Even she'd understood that it was impossible—as had her art professor. She still saw him sometimes. 'I used my interest to become knowledgeable about the art and antique treasures in the palace.' She stood and stretched, keen to get out to the warm sunshine. 'I like to take the tours sometimes.'

'As the guide?' Damon's eyes widened.

She nodded, laughing at his expression.

'No wonder they're always booked out so far in advance—they're all hoping to get on one of your days.'

'I don't commit to an exact timetable,' she admitted.

'Because you don't want to become an exhibit your-self.'

No. Trust him to understand that. And she hadn't wanted to disappoint people. She turned to get past him and head out to the beach.

'I don't see why it has to be only a hobby,' he said, still studying the incomplete drawing. 'You could sell them. People would buy them.'

Eleni laughed again. 'They'd sell only for the sig-nature. There'd be no honest appraisal from anyone. Some fawning critics couldn't be objective for fear of offending the royal family while others would damn me to mediocrity for daring to think I could do some-thing with skill.'

'You're afraid of what they think.' He sent her that stern look again. 'You don't need to give a damn, Eleni. You could sell them for charity. Imagine what you could raise.'

'But I do give a damn and so I raise money anyway. But I don't want this tied to that. This is my escape.' Just as this island was his.

'Then do it anonymously. We could find a dealer.'

'Or I could just do them for myself.' She sent him the stern look back. 'For my own enjoyment.'

'They'd bring joy to other people too,' he said charm-ingly.

'Flatterer.' She mock slapped him as she walked away.

'I have no need to flatter you when I already own your panties,' he called after her.

She stopped and swivelled to send him a *death* stare that time. 'Oh, that is—'

He threw back his head and laughed. 'True. It's true.'

* * *

Playing in the sea with Eleni was too much fun. She was so beautiful, lithe and, as he'd suspected that very first moment he'd seen her, strong. Now, as he sat on the sand beside her and let the sun dry his skin, satisfaction pooled within him. The same feeling that had crept up on him while she'd been seated beside him upstairs all morning.

But it was the quiet moments like these that unsettled him the most—when he felt too content.

Moments like these became too precious. And moments didn't last. Nor did marriages.

He stood, needing some space for a second to get them back to that light teasing. He turned and tugged her to her feet. He only had to whisper a dare and they raced back to the house. Play came so easy with her now she was free.

'How do you ever force yourself off this island?' she asked, breathless as he caught her.

'Actually we're leaving in the morning,' Damon muttered.

'What?' Her shocked query made him turn her in his arms so he could see her eyes.

'It's only twenty minutes by helicopter to the next island,' Damon quickly explained. 'There aren't many shops but…' He strode to a small cabinet in the lounge and retrieved a small purse that he tossed to her. 'Here. You can go wild, practise counting out the right currency before you hit the big cities.'

She caught the bag neatly with one hand but wrinkled her pretty nose. 'I don't want your money.'

'Well, until you earn your own I think you're stuck with mine, because I'm your husband and apparently that makes me responsible.' He sent her a deliberately patronising smile. 'I can give you an allowance if you'd like.'

The nose-wrinkle morphed into a full-face frown.

Chuckling, he backed her up against the wall. 'If our positions were reversed, you'd do the same for me,' he whispered.

'Don't be so sure.'

'Oh, I'm sure.' Laughing, he kissed her.

But her lips parted and she didn't just let him in, she pulled him closer, hooking her leg around his waist, her towel dropping in the process.

'If you keep this up I'll get you a credit card, so you don't even have to count.' He rolled his hips against her heat, giving into the irresistible desire she roused in him.

'Payment for services rendered?' she asked tartly. 'Finally you've figured out I married you for your money.'

'I knew it.' He failed to claw back some semblance of sanity from the ultimate temptation she personified.

'It certainly wasn't for your charm.' She glared at him.

'Then spend every cent.' He smiled, loving the sparks in her eyes. Those few shops mainly stocked bikinis. The thought made his mouth dry. 'Meanwhile...' he stepped back and unfastened his shorts '...I was thinking you might want me to model for you.'

'You're...' Her gaze dropped and her words faded.

'You're not concerned about people taking photos?'

He shook his head as their helicopter descended. 'The people here appreciate the privacy of their visitors.'

To be frank, the island was barely larger than Damon's. There were only a few shops along the waterfront and, when Eleni saw this, her expressive features were a picture of mock outrage. He laughed, enjoying his little joke.

'They sell bikinis.' He held up his hands in surrender. 'I thought you'd love it.'

'You're the biggest tease ever.' She growled at him with a glint in her eye. 'You're the one who wants me to get the bikinis.'

'Have you ever bought a bikini before? All by yourself?'

'Actually I have. Online.'

'In the privacy of the palace.'

'Of course.'

'Well, you can cruise the whole mall here.'

She rolled her eyes.

'If you don't want to shop for skimpy little swimsuits, why don't you spend some coin and buy me an ice cream?' He dared her.

'Because you don't deserve it.'

She flounced off to the bikini store and he lazily loitered outside, watching her through the wide open doors as she browsed the racks. In less than five seconds she lost that faux indignance and relaxed. As she chatted to the woman serving behind the counter she relaxed even more and that gorgeous vitality oozed from her skin. His gaze narrowed as it finally clicked—*interaction* with others was what gave her that luminescence. The ability she had to be able to talk to anyone, and to put them at ease, wasn't just learned skill from being 'the Princess', it was a core part of *who* she was. Warm, compassionate. Interested. Caring.

So much more than him.

Now she'd stopped to talk to another couple of customers and she was positively glowing. One of the women was balancing a wriggling toddler in her arms. Damon watched as Eleni turned to talk to the child, who immediately stopped wriggling and smiled, entranced— as if Eleni was some damn baby whisperer. Of course she was—she had that effect on everyone, big and small. They stopped what they were doing and smiled when she came near. Because she was like a beautiful, sparkling light.

She was going to be such a great mother, given her truly genuine, generous nature. He narrowed his gaze as his imagination caught him unawares—slipping him a vision of how she was going to look when cradling their child in her arms. Primitive possessiveness clenched in his gut, sending a totally foreign kind of heat throughout his veins.

His woman. His baby. His world.

He blinked, breathing hard, bringing himself back to here, now, on the beach. Her body had yet to reveal its fertile secret—while her breasts were slightly fuller, her belly had barely a curve. But their baby was safe within her womb.

Despite the summer sun, a chill swept across his skin and he cocked his head to study her closer. The baby was safe, wasn't it? And Eleni. She was slim but strong, right? But icy uncertainty dripped down his spine—slow at first, then in a rush as he suddenly realised what he'd been too full of lust and selfish haste to remember.

Eleni's mother had lost her life in childbirth.

Damon felt as if some invisible giant had wrapped

a fist around his chest and was squeezing it, making his blood pound and his lungs too tight to draw breath.

How could he have forgotten that? How could he have dragged her here to this remote island without seeing that damn doctor back in Palisades? He'd promised her brother that she'd get the best care, yet he'd been in too much of a hurry to escape his own demons to put her first. To put his child first.

He'd been thinking only of himself. His wants. His needs. His father had done that to Kassie and her mother. Now Damon was as guilty regarding Eleni and their unborn child.

How could he have neglected to tend to something so fundamental? He'd been so smug when he'd texted his assistant to find an obstetrician that day on the boat. As if he'd thought of everything—all in control and capable.

But he wasn't either of those things. Turned out he was less than useless—to not even have a routine check done before flying for hours out to somewhere this isolated? What the hell kind of father did he think he was going to make anyway?

He'd failed before he'd even begun. Both his wife and child deserved better. He huffed out a strained breath. At least seeing the truth now cemented the perfection of his plan. They'd be better off apart from him. He'd always known that, hadn't he? Wasn't that why he'd insisted on his and Eleni's separation in the first place?

This whole marriage and kids and happy-ever-after was never going to be for him.

Except, just for this little while on his island, he'd let himself pretend.

That he could have it all with her. Be it all for her.

But he couldn't.

Bitterness welled, a surging ball of disappointment within himself. For himself.

'Are you okay?' Eleni gave him a searching look as she joined him to stroll along the beach.

'Fine.' He flashed a smile through a gritted jaw and kept strolling along the beach, staring down at the sand.

But he wasn't and wasn't it typical that she'd already sensed that? She was too compassionate. Too empathetic.

'Did you spend up large?' He made himself make that small talk.

'Every cent.' She held up a carrier bag and shook it, a twinkle in her eye that he couldn't bear to see right now.

'Then let's go back,' he said briskly.

He sensed her quick frown but she simply turned and quietly walked alongside him.

Of course she did; that was Eleni all over—doing what was asked of her, knowing her place, unquestioning when she sensed tension.

It was how she handled Giorgos, how she handled the public and palace demands on her. And, apparently, it was now how she handled him.

It was the last damn thing that he wanted. He wanted impetuous, spontaneous, emotional Eleni who liked nothing more than to challenge him. But what he wanted no longer mattered. Because she was vulnerable and he didn't have the skills that she was going to need long term. He'd just proven that to himself. The lust they shared wasn't ever going to be enough and the sooner they separated, the better.

He was such a damn disappointment to himself—let alone to anyone else.

'I'm going to the workshop for a while,' he said the second their helicopter landed.

'Sure.'

He turned his back on that hint of coolness in her voice. The tiniest thread of uncertainty. Of hurt. He had to walk away to stop hurting her more. That was the point.

The guys were heads down, but he waved them away when he walked into the room. He'd rebalance in here. Get stuck in another of the projects. But while he could take in the info his team had sent him, he couldn't make it stick. The future kept calling—her pregnancy, the baby. What he was never going to be able to do for them both.

'Which do you want to go with?' Olly ventured over to Damon, showing him three designs for a new logo.

'I need to think about it.' Damon lifted the sheet displaying the three options, his gaze narrowing as he registered the colours. He wanted to do more than think about it. He wanted to ask Eleni. She had a better eye than any of them.

'I had a call from one of those futurist foundations,' Olly said as Damon headed to the door. 'They'd like you to speak at next year's gala.'

More like they wanted him to bring his beautiful Princess wife. He did *not* want her used that way.

'Next year?' Damon asked idly, still staring down at the sheet.

'They're planning well ahead of time. Futurists,' Olly joked.

Time. Damon walked out of the den. In time, according to Damon's plan, he and Eleni would be sharing custody but living separately. They'd be on their way to divorce already. She wouldn't be curled next to him in bed, or sitting at a desk at his side any more. And their child would be a few months old. Their tiny baby with its tiny heart would still be so vulnerable. His chest tightened. He had no idea how to provide the required protection. How did he protect Eleni? How did he give either of them what they needed when he hardly knew what that was? When he'd never had it himself?

Eleni had changed so much in the few days she'd had of freedom. He realised now how much more she needed. How much more she deserved. She was loving and generous and kind. She deserved someone who could give all that back to her tenfold.

She was going to be a far better mother to their child than his mother had been to him. She was open; she was generous. She was loving.

What did *he* have to offer her? She had a workaholic brother and no one else close in her life. She needed a husband who could offer her a warm, loving family. All he could offer were sycophantic grandparents who'd leech everything they could from the connection—and offer nothing. No warmth. No love.

Damon had money, sure. But King Giorgos would never let his little sister suffer financial hardship. There was nothing else he really had to offer her—other than orgasms and the occasional cheesy line that made her laugh. He didn't know how to be a good father, or a good husband. She deserved more than that. She deserved the best.

And he had to help her find that somehow. He owed her that much at least, didn't he?

He walked to the house, missing her already, wanting her advice on the decision he couldn't quite make, just wanting to be near her again. He found her at her desk—her new favourite place—clad in a vibrant orange bikini that was bold and cheerful and sexy as hell. She wore a sheer white shirt over it that hung loose and revealed a gently tanned shoulder. Her hair wasn't brushed into smooth perfection but looked tousled and soft and there wasn't a scrap of make-up on her glowing skin.

She looked beautiful and relaxed; he'd never seen her look happier. She was thriving, from so little. She should have so much more. More than he could ever give her.

Her welcoming smile pained him in a way he'd never been pained before.

'You're busy.' He hesitated, staying at a distance, trying to resist that fierce, fierce pull.

She deserves better.

'It's okay.' She put down her pen and turned her full focus on him. 'What did you want?'

He'd forgotten already. But her gaze grazed the paper he was holding.

'I just...' he glanced down at the images he held '...wanted your opinion on this.'

'My opinion?' she echoed softly.

'You have an artist's eye.' He gruffly pushed the words past the block in his throat. 'I wanted to know which you think is better.'

Eleni blinked, pulling her scattered wits together. He walked in here looking all stormy and broody and sexy as hell and then wanted her opinion on something he was clinging to as if it were worth his very soul?

'Are you going to let me see it?' She smiled but he didn't smile back.

He put the page on her desk. She studied the three

designs that had been printed on it. That he valued her input touched her and it took her a moment to focus on what he'd asked her to do. 'I think this one is cleaner. It stays in the mind more.' She pointed to the one on the left. 'Don't you think?'

'Yes,' he said, nodding brusquely. 'Thank you.'

A defiant, determined look crossed his face as he stepped back from her. She stilled, trying to read all the contrary emotions flickering in his expression. He always tried to contain such depth of feeling, but right now it was pouring from him and she could only stare, aching to understand what on earth was churning in his head.

'What?' His lips twisted in a wry, self-mocking smile. 'I don't know why you're staring at me when you're the one with ink on her nose.'

'Oh.' Embarrassed, she rubbed the side of her nose with her finger.

He half snorted, half groaned. 'Come here,' he ordered gruffly, tugging a clean tissue from the box on his desk.

She loved being this close to him. Loved the way he teased her as he cared for her. She held ultra-still so he could wipe the smear from her face. He was so close, so tender and she ached for that usual teasing. But his eyes were even more intensely blue and his expression grave. He focused on her in a way that no one else ever had. He saw beyond the superficial layers through to her needs beneath. Not just her needs. Her gifts. He saw *value* in her and he appreciated it. That mattered to her more than she could have ever imagined. Suddenly, thoughtlessly, she swayed, her need to be closer to him driving her body.

'Eleni?' He gripped her arms to steady her, concern deepening the blue of his eyes even more. 'You okay?'

All the feelings bloomed in the face of the irresistible temptation he embodied—the capricious risk he dared from her with a mere look. But beneath it was the steadfast core of certainty. He'd caught her. Just as he'd caught her and held her close that very first night. Somehow she knew he'd always catch her. He was there for her in a way no one had ever been before. That spontaneous tide of emotion only he stirred now swept from her heart, carrying with it those secret words until they slipped right out of her in a shaky whisper of truth that she breathed between them.

'I love you.'

CHAPTER THIRTEEN

'I'M NOT SORRY I said that,' she said shakily, determined to believe her own words.

Impulsive. Impetuous. Spontaneous. *Stupid.*

Because he stood rigid as rock, his fingers digging hard into her upper arms and his eyes wide. But his obvious shock somehow made her bold. She could have no regrets. Not about this. Not now. So she said it again—louder this time.

'I've fallen in love with you, Damon.'

It felt good to admit it. Terrifying, but good.

His expression still didn't change. Just as it hadn't in the last ten seconds. But then he released her so quickly she had to take a step back to maintain her balance.

'You only think you're in love with me because I was your first.' He finally spoke—harsh and blunt. And then he turned his back on her.

That was so out of left-field that she gaped as he walked away towards his desk. 'Give me some credit.' She was so stunned she stormed after him and yanked on his arm to make him face her again. 'Even just a little.'

But he shrugged her hand off.

'Eleni, look…' He paused and drew breath. 'You've

never felt lust before. You haven't had the opportunity until now. I'm just the first guy you've met who got your rocks off. But lust doesn't equal love. It never does.'

'Actually I do know that.' She wasn't stupid. And she didn't understand why he was lashing out at her. She was utterly shocked.

'Do you, Eleni?' He looked icier than ever. 'You've got freedom here that you've never had in all your life. I think you're confused.'

'Because I've been able to hang out at the beach without worrying about any photographers in the bushes? You think that's made me think I'm in love with you?' She couldn't believe he was saying this. 'I might not have had a million lovers, but I know how to care. I do know how to love.'

'No, you know how to acquiesce,' he said scathingly. 'How to do as you're told while suffering underneath that beautiful, serene exterior. While not standing up for yourself.'

'I'm standing up for myself now.'

He shook his head 'You're confused.'

'And you're treating me like the child my brother sees me as. You don't think I'm capable of thinking for myself?' Was he truly belittling her feelings for him? He didn't believe her and that hurt. 'This is real.'

'No, it isn't.'

'Don't deny my truth.'

'Eleni.' He closed his eyes for a second but then he seemed to strengthen, broadening his stance. He opened his eyes and his stark expression made her step back.

'I have used you. I have treated you terribly. You can't and don't love me.' He drew in a harsh breath. 'And I'm sorry, but I don't love you.' He seemed to brace his feet a bit further apart. 'We are only together now because you're pregnant.'

His words wounded where she was most vulnerable. Because underneath she'd known this had never been about *her*. He never would have sought her out again if he hadn't been worried about the contraception mistake that night. He'd never wanted to see her again—not just for her.

'This has only ever been for the baby,' she said softly.

'Yes. For its legitimacy and protection.'

'Yet you were happy to sleep with me again.'

His gaze shifted. Lowered.

He'd been happy to string her along. 'And Princess Eleni was an easy conquest because she was so inexperienced and frustrated it took nothing to turn her on… is that how this has been?' She couldn't bear to look at him now, yet she couldn't look away either.

'Eleni—'

'Maybe I was inexperienced and maybe I was starving for attention—' She broke off as a horrible thought occurred to her. 'Have you been laughing at me this whole time?'

Suddenly her skin burned crimson at the recollection of her unbridled behaviour with him. So many times.

'Never laughing.' His skin was also burnished. 'And I'm not now. But you *are* mistaking lust for deeper affection.'

She didn't believe him. She couldn't.

'So you don't feel anything for me but lust?' When he sat with her on the beach and they talked of everything and nothing? When they laughed about stupid little things?

There was a thin plea in her voice that she wanted

to swallow back but it was too late. Maybe he'd been trying to keep his distance and now she'd forced him into letting her down completely. 'You don't think we could have it all?'

'No one has it all, Eleni. That's a promise that doesn't exist.'

'No. That's your excuse not to even try. It works out for plenty of people. Maybe not your parents—' She broke off. 'Is this what you learnt from them? Not to even try?'

'Yes.' He was like stone. 'I'm not capable of this, Eleni. Not marriage. Not for ever. Certainly not love.'

'You don't mean that.'

'Don't I?' He laughed bitterly. 'How can you possibly think you're in love with me?' He stalked towards her. 'I seduced you—an innocent. I knew you were shy that night. I knew you weren't that experienced. Did I let that stop me from taking you in a ten-minute display of dominant sex? No. It made it even hotter. But I got you pregnant. Then I kidnapped you. I forced you into marrying me. Tell me, how is that any kind of basis for a long-term relationship?' His short bark of laughter was mirthless. 'It will *never* work.'

'It wasn't like that.'

'It was exactly like that.'

No, it hadn't been. He was painting himself as a villain like in one of the games he'd once designed.

'You don't care about me at all?' She couldn't stop herself from asking it.

'Enough to know you deserve better.'

'Better than what—you?' She stared at him. 'You're more sensitive than you like to admit. More caring. You're kind to your employees, you've been kind to *me*.' She tried to smile but couldn't because this was too important and because she could already see he wasn't listening. And he certainly wasn't believing her. 'You're thoughtful, creative. And you think I don't mean it.'

'You only think you mean it.'

Could he get any more insulting? She'd prove him wrong. She glared at him. 'I know you don't want any part of royal life. You don't value what I am. So I will relinquish my title.'

'What?' He looked stunned—and appalled.

'I'll tell Giorgos that I want to live as a commoner. We could live anywhere then. Here, even. Maybe I could get a normal job, not just cut ribbons and talk to people. I could do something useful.'

He laughed.

Eleni chilled and then burned hot. He'd thrown it back at her—her love. Her proof. He was treating her as everyone else in her life had—as if she were a decorative but ultimately pointless ornament with no depth, no real meaning. No real value. When for a while there, he'd made her think he felt otherwise. That he saw her differently—that he thought she had more to offer. He'd shown her such caring and consideration. Hadn't he meant that at all?

'Why won't you believe me?' she asked him, so hurt she couldn't hide. 'Are you too scared to believe me?'

He just stayed frozen. 'You don't mean it, Eleni.'

'Why is it so impossible to believe that I could love you?' She demanded his answer. Because she was certain this rejection came from fear. 'Or that I could want to give up everything to be with you?'

'So now you think there has to be something wrong with me because I don't want your love?' he asked cruelly. 'Maybe you suddenly want to give up your title because *you* don't like being a princess.'

'Poor me, right?' she said bitterly. 'I have to live in a castle and wear designer clothes and have all these things—'

'You're not materialistic,' he interrupted harshly. '*Things* aren't what you want. What you *want* is out.'

'No. What I want is *you*.'

He stared at her.

'I want you with me,' she carried on recklessly. 'At the palace. Not at the palace. I don't care. I just want you there wherever I am. I want to know I have you by my side.' She totally lost it. 'I don't care what companies you own or what tech you help create. I just want the man who makes me smile. Who laughs at the same things I do. The man who's passionate and who, usually, can think like no one else I've met.' She drew in a short breath. 'What I'm trying to do is put you first. Put you ahead of my brother. My family. My duties and obligations. Don't you get it? I want *you*.'

'I don't want that,' he said harshly. 'I don't want you like that.' His eyes blazed. 'I'm not in love with you, Eleni. Don't you understand that I'll *never* be in love with you? And you'll soon realise you're not in love with me.'

She sucked in a shocked breath as his total rejection hit like a physical blow.

Hadn't the first rejection been humiliation enough? No. She'd had to go on and argue. But the fact was he didn't want to love her. He never had.

All their time together had been nothing but a physical bonus while he put up with their marriage to make the baby legitimate. Eleni was simply a temporary side issue.

She'd mistaken his affection and amusement for a growing genuine attachment, but the support he offered her was probably the kind he'd give any of his cool employees.

'I have to leave,' Eleni said dully. There was no way she could stay here with him now.

'You're going to run away?' he asked coldly. 'Because that's always worked so well for you in the past.'

No. She wasn't going to run away. In that one thing he was right. Running away never worked.

'This child is a *Nicolaides*.' She drew herself up tall. 'She or he will be royalty. And until Giorgos finally has a family of his own, she or he will be next in line to the throne after me. It seems there's no getting away from that. So I'm going to return to Palisades.' She was suddenly certain. And determined. 'That is where I belong.'

He stood very still. 'You won't see out these few months?'

If she hadn't believed that he didn't love her before, she did now. He had no emotion at all—no understanding of just how cruel that question was.

'I've just laid myself bare for you, Damon,' she choked. 'And you don't accept it. You don't accept me. You don't believe in me.' Her heart tore as she accepted *his* truth. 'You want me, but you don't love me. That's okay, you don't have to.' But bitterness choked her. 'One day, though, you are going to feel about someone the way I feel about you. And then you'll know. Because no one is immune, Damon. You're human and we're all *built* to feel.'

She stared hard at him as she realised what she'd failed to see before—and she hit him with it now. 'But what you feel most of is fear. That's why you hide away on your island paradise. Controlling every one of your interactions, having those brief affairs when you go to some city every so often. Keeping yourself safe because you're a coward. I get that your parents were less than average. I get that they hurt you. But don't use them as your excuse to back out of anything remotely complicated emotionally.'

She drew in a desperately needed breath. 'You don't think what I do has value—that I deserve more? Well, you're right, but not in the way you think. I help people. It may not be much, it may appear superficial, but in my role as Princess of Palisades I can make people smile. And I do deserve more. As a *person*. How can you possibly think I could stay here with you like this but not get all I need from you?' It would destroy her slowly and utterly.

The irony was *he* was the one to have shown her what she could have. What she'd hoped to have with him.

'You can't give me what I need, but I can't settle for less,' she said. 'So no, I won't "see out these few months". I can't stay a second longer than I have to.' Even though it was just about going to kill her to leave.

Eleni might never be loved personally. But as a princess she was. And that would have to do.

CHAPTER FOURTEEN

DAMON PACED ALONG the beach, waiting for her to finish packing. She couldn't leave soon enough. He'd spoken the truth. She didn't 'love' him. She was in 'lust'—with him a little, but mostly with the freedom he'd provided for her. It wasn't *him personally*. It was the situation. Any other man and she'd feel the same about him. It was only fate that had made Damon the one.

He clenched his fists, because she offered such temptation. She made him want to believe in that impossible dream. In her.

But it was better to end it now. The pain in her eyes had been so unbearable he'd almost had to turn away. He hadn't meant to hurt her. But she was inexperienced and naive and he realised now their divorce might hurt her more if they didn't part now. He didn't want to lead her confused emotions on.

She didn't look at him as she climbed into the helicopter that would take her back to his jet, and then to Palisades.

'I'll have rooms set aside for you,' she said regally. 'You may visit at the weekends, so we maintain the illusion of a happy marriage until after the baby is born.'

He *'may'*? His brewing anger prickled at her tone. 'And after?'

'You may visit whenever you want. I won't stop you from seeing the baby.'

Even now she was generous. His anger mounted more, but he contained it. She would care for their child better than he ever could. He understood that now. Because his father had been right—they were alike. Damaged. Incapable and frankly undeserving of love.

He couldn't damage Eleni or his child any more than he already had.

The sun and the sand mocked him. His team were abnormally quiet and left him alone. He stood it for only two days before summoning the jet. He needed to get further away. San Francisco. London. Berlin. Paris.

He wanted her. He missed her. But he did not love her. He did not know how to love. It was easy to stay busy in cities—to arrange endless, pointless meetings that filled his head with fluff. But people asked about the Princess and he had to smile and pretend.

She was better off without him.

His head hurt. His body hurt. His chest—where his heart should be if he had one—that hurt too. But he didn't have a heart, right?

Yet all he could think about was Eleni. He spent every moment wondering what she was doing. Whether she was okay. If she was smiling that beautiful smile at all.

She'd given, not taken. She'd offered him the one thing that was truly her own—her heart. He knew she'd never done that before. She'd been at her most vulnerable. And he'd rejected her.

But he'd had to, for her. Because he didn't deserve her love. He had no idea how to become the man who did. If she was freed from the marriage to him, she might find some other man to treat her the way she deserved. That would be the right thing to do.

Hot, vicious, selfish anger consumed him at the thought of someone else holding her. Of someone else touching her. Of someone else making her smile.

He didn't want that. He *never* wanted that.

He clenched his fist, emotions boiling into a frenzy. He had no freaking idea how to manage this. And that was when he realised—so painfully—how much he didn't want to let her go. He *never* wanted to let her go.

He logged into his computer, searching for somewhere to go and sort himself out for good. Far from Palisades. Far from his own island that was now too tainted with the memories of her presence. He had to escape everything and pull himself together. But as he scrolled through varying destinations, his emails landed in his inbox.

There was one from the palace secretary.

Damon paused. It would probably be another schedule of engagements that they wanted him to approve or something. Unable to resist, he clicked to the email and opened it. But it wasn't a list. It was a concise couple of sentences informing him that Princess Eleni had seen the obstetric specialist of her choosing who'd written a brief report, the contents of which had been inserted into the email. In one paragraph it explained that the baby was growing at a normal rate. That the condition that had taken Eleni's mother was not hereditary. That the pregnancy posed no abnormal risk to her. That everything was progressing as it ought for both mother and baby.

His breath and blood froze. There was an image file attached to the email. Dazed, Damon opened it on auto. A mass of grey appeared. He looked at the arrow and markers pointing out a particular blob set in a darker patch in the middle of the picture. It was an ultrasound scan. It was his baby.

He tried to breathe but he just stared at that tiny, little treasure in the centre of his screen. It was there. It was real. It was happening. Heat swept through him in a burning drive to claim what was—

Mine.

Both hands clenched into fists.

Eleni.

The thought of her consumed him—her strength, her decisions, her role in all this. She was well. She was strong. She was safe. He ached to reach for her, ached to see her smile as she saw this picture—he just knew she'd smile at this picture. And the realisation rocked him.

Ours.

They had made this beautiful child *together*. That night she'd come with him and he'd claimed her and somehow in that insanely wonderful moment they'd created this miracle. It never should have happened— but it had. And Eleni was taking it on. She was doing her bit and she was doing it so damn well. And if he wanted to be part of that, *he* was the one who had to shape up. Seeing this now, reading Eleni's results, he realised just how much he wanted in and he burned with acidic shame. He'd missed so much already. He wished like hell he'd been there with her when she'd seen this doctor and when she'd had this scan. He should have been holding her hand for every damn second.

* * *

He bent his head, squeezing his eyes shut so he could no longer see the image on that screen. But the truth snuck in and stabbed him anyway. The fact was he had a heart. He really, truly had a heart and it hurt like hell. Because it was no longer his.

Eleni had it. It was all hers. He had to tell her. He had to apologise. He had to get her back. Groaning, he closed the picture file and read the doctor's report again. And again. Sucking in the reassurance that Eleni was healthy. Strong. Safe.

She'd asked if he was scared of love and at the time he'd refused to answer. He'd been utterly unable to. But now he faced the stark facts. He was terrified. Like a freaking deer in the headlights he'd simply frozen.

Frozen her out.

Where she'd been brave, proudly standing up to him, he'd been unable to admit, even to himself, how much he wanted her in his life. And when she'd unconditionally offered him everything she had, he couldn't believe her. No one had ever offered him that before.

Eleni had been right. He was a coward. He hid because it was easier. But in truth he was no better than his parents—putting all emotion aside for work. But she'd got under his skin and he'd been unable to resist—he'd taken everything she'd offered. He'd even convinced himself he was doing her a favour. He'd encouraged her to blossom and let all that sweet enthusiasm and hot passion out. He'd thought she'd needed freedom away from the palace. Freedom to take what she wanted—to ask for what she wanted.

And she had.

Eleni had offered him her love. And she'd asked for his in return.

But he'd rejected her. The worst thing he could have done was not take her seriously. Only he'd done even worse. He'd scoffed at her.

That hot streak of possessiveness surged through his veins as he clicked open that ultrasound image again. But he sucked in a steadying breath. He didn't get to be possessive, not without earning her forgiveness first. Not without begging to make everything better. And how did he get to her now she was back in that damn prison of a palace?

CHAPTER FIFTEEN

'ARE YOU SURE you're feeling up to this, ma'am?' Bettina asked Eleni carefully.

'That's what blusher is for, right?' Eleni answered wryly. 'And I still have quite the tan on my arms.' She forced a smile for her maid. 'I'm fine to go. It'll be fun. But thank you.'

She needed to fill in her day. She needed to feel *something*.

She'd been buried in the palace for almost a fortnight, hoping she'd hear from him. But she hadn't. She couldn't face drawing, couldn't face the pool. She'd tried reading. But her mind still wandered to him. She hated how much she ached for him.

He doesn't deserve me.

She tried to remind herself, but it didn't lessen the hurt. Hopefully this gallery visit would take her mind off him even for a few minutes. The fact that it was a children's tour was even better because children asked questions fearlessly—with no thought to privacy or palace protocol. It would be a good test. She'd have to hold herself together when they mentioned his name. And they would ask. They'd want to see her engagement and wedding rings. They'd want to see her smiling.

They expected a blushing, beyond happy bride.

Giorgos had sounded harried when he'd phoned, which was unlike him. And for whatever reason that he hadn't had time to explain, he was still residing at the Summer House and he'd asked if she'd attend the small gallery opening on his behalf. Of course she'd agreed. She'd been going insane staying inside. She needed to build a busy and fulfilling life. Then she could and would cope with the break in her heart.

But she'd appreciated the concern in Giorgos's voice. Just as she appreciated Bettina's quiet care. And her bodyguard's constant, silent presence.

She smiled as Tony opened the car door for her. 'It's nice to have you back.'

'Thank you, ma'am.'

'I promise not to disappear on you today,' she teased lightly, determined not to hide from the past.

'I understand, ma'am.' Tony's impassive expression cracked and he smiled at her. 'You won't be out of my sight for a second.'

'I understand and I do appreciate it.'

It was a beautiful late summer morning but she'd added a light jacket to complement the floaty-style floral dress she'd worn to hide her figure and deflect any conjecture and commentary. That suspicion would be raised soon enough. But preferably not today.

Twenty minutes later she stepped out of the car at the discreet side entrance of the new art space. She took a moment to accept a posy of flowers from a sweet young girl. But as she turned to enter the gallery she froze, her heart seizing. She blinked and moved as Tony guided her forward. But she glanced back as something caught her eye. For a second she'd thought she'd seen a masculine figure standing on the far side of the road—tall, broad, more handsome than Adonis...

Wishful, impossible thinking.

Because there was no man there now.

Releasing a measured breath, she walked with the small group of children through the new wing of the gallery, focusing her mind to discuss the paintings with them. But despite the easing of her morning sickness over the past few days, maintaining her spark during the visit drained her more than she'd thought it would. She was relieved when she saw Tony give her the usual signal before turning slightly to mutter into his mobile phone.

Damon had half expected soldiers to swoop on him and frogmarch him straight to the city dungeons, but the coast was clear and the path to the car easy. It was unlocked and he took the driver's seat, waiting for the signal. Anticipation surged as his phone rang. He could hardly remain still.

Finally the passenger door opened. He heard her polite thanks.

He started the engine. As soon as she'd got into the car and the door closed behind her, he pulled away from the kerb.

'Tony?' Eleni leaned forward in her seat.

'Damon,' he corrected, a vicious pleasure shooting through his body at just hearing her voice again.

He glanced up and looked in the rear-view mirror and almost lost control of the car in the process. She was so beautiful. But that soft colour slowly leeched from her skin as she met his gaze in the mirror and realised it truly was him. If he'd suffered before, he really felt it then. He'd killed her joy. The make-up stood out starkly against her whitened face. She'd had to paint on her customary vitality—her luminescence stolen. By him.

Her eyes were suddenly swimming in tears but she blinked them back. The effort she was expending to stay in control was immense. He hated seeing her this wretched. But at the same time, her distress gave him hope. His presence moved her. She hadn't forgotten him. Hadn't got over him.

He didn't deserve her.

'Why are you here?' She demanded his answer in the frostiest tones he'd ever heard from her.

All he wanted was to enfold her in his arms but he couldn't. She was furious with him and she had every right to be. He had to talk to her. Ask for forgiveness. Then ask for everything.

When he'd already rejected her.

He gripped the steering wheel more tightly as anxiety sharpened his muscles and he tried to remember where the hell he was going. Because this was going to be even harder than he'd imagined. And he'd imagined the worst.

'I'm kidnapping you.' He ground the words out, holding back all the others scrambling in his throat. He needed to get them somewhere that they could talk in private.

He glanced back at the rear-view mirror. Her emotion had morphed into cold, hard rage.

'I'm not doing this to Tony again,' she snapped, turning to look out of the window behind her to see if any cars were behind them. 'He'll be following. He doesn't deserve—'

'Tony knows you're with me,' he said quickly. 'So does Giorgos.'

She flicked her head back, her eyes flashing. 'So you planned this with everyone but me?'

He didn't want to answer more. He was only making it worse. Damn, it turned out he was good at that.

'This is *not* okay, Damon,' she said coldly.

'None of this is okay,' he growled, swerving around the nearest corner. 'And I can't wait—' He broke off and parked on one of the narrow cobbled streets.

'Can't wait for what?' she asked haughtily.

Eleni waited for his answer, trying to remain in control, but underneath her calm demeanour her heart was pounding and it was almost impossible to stop distress overtaking her sensibility. Damon was here. Not only that, he'd colluded with her brother and her bodyguard and she couldn't bear to think about *why*.

It mattered too much. *He* mattered too much.

But it was too late. He'd made his choice. He'd let her go. He'd let her *down*.

She refused to believe in the hope fluttering pathetically in her heart. This was too soon. She hadn't grown a strong enough scab over her wounds to meet him yet.

'Eleni.'

She closed her eyes. He couldn't *do* this to her.

One look. One word. That was all it took for her to want to fall into his arms again. She refused to be that weak. She couldn't let him have that power over her.

'Take me back to the palace,' she ordered.

He killed the engine. She watched, frozen, as he got out of the car and swiftly opened the rear passenger door. But before she could move he'd slid into the back seat with her and locked the doors again.

'Give me ten minutes,' he said, removing his aviator sunglasses and gazing intently at her. 'If you wish to return to the palace afterwards, then I'll take you there. I just want ten minutes. Can you give me that?'

She wanted to give him so much more already. But she couldn't. She'd been a fool for him already; she wasn't making that mistake again. 'What more is there to say, Damon? We want different things.'

'There's plenty more to say,' he argued shortly.

'Too late. You had your chance.' She glanced behind her, hoping Tony was less than a block away. But there was no car. No people.

'Ten minutes,' he pushed. 'I'm not letting you go until you listen to me.' He was silent for a moment. *'Please.'*

At that urgent whisper she turned back to face him. Starved of his company for days, she couldn't help drinking in his appearance now. He was studying her with that old intensity. Always he'd made her feel as if she were the only thing in the world that mattered.

Not fair. Not true. Not for him.

'Five minutes,' she answered flatly.

Only five. Because tendrils of hope were unfurling, reaching out, beginning to bind her back to him. That weak part of her wanted him to take her in his arms and kiss her. Then she might believe he was actually here. That he'd come back for her. But at the same time she knew that if he touched her, she'd be lost.

His smile was small and fleeting and disappeared the second he opened his mouth again. 'I'm so sorry, Eleni.'

Her heart stopped. Her breath died. She didn't know

if she could take this. Not if he wasn't here to give her everything.

'Words said too easily,' she whispered.

'That night at the ball—'

'No,' she interrupted him furiously. 'We're not going back there. You're not doing this.'

'Yes, we are. It's where it all began, Eleni. We can't forget what's happened. We can't ignore—'

'You already have,' she argued. 'You already denied—'

'I lied,' he snapped back. 'Listen to me now. Please. That night was the most extreme case of lust I've ever felt,' he confessed angrily. 'And for you too. You know how powerful it was. How it *is*. You never would have let just any man touch you that way, Eleni. You never would have let just any man *inside*.'

She sucked in a shocked breath.

'I know I didn't want to admit it,' he said. 'But what's between us is something *much* more than that.' He gazed at her so intently, the blue of his eyes so brilliant it almost blinded her.

But she shook her head. Not for him, it wasn't.

'For me too,' he declared, rejecting her doubts. 'It was and is, Eleni. I've denied it for too long.' He bent closer, forcing her to look him right in those intense eyes. 'You were flirtatious, you were shy...so hot and so sweet.'

She winced. She couldn't bear for him to revisit her inexperience. Her naiveté. He'd thought she had nothing more than a teenage *crush* on him. He'd felt sorry for her.

'I belittled you when you told me your feelings,' he said. 'I didn't believe you. I couldn't...and I'm so sorry I did that to you.' Somehow he was sitting closer, his voice lower. His gently spoken words hit her roughly. 'I never should have let you go.'

'Why shouldn't you have?' She succumbed to the hurt of these last intolerably lonely days. 'You miss having my adoration? My body? My naive protestations of love?' She was so mortified. The imbalance was so severe. It was so unfair.

'Not naive.' He shook his head. 'Not you. *I'm* the ignorant one. I didn't know what love was, Eleni. I've never had someone give me what you've given me. And like the idiot I am, I didn't know how to handle it.' His gaze dropped. 'I don't know how to handle you or how I feel about you. It is so…' He trailed off and dragged in a breath. 'It's huge.' He pressed his fist to his chest. 'I was overwhelmed and I threw it away like it was a bomb you'd tossed at me.' His voice dropped to a whisper again. 'But the fact is, you'd already detonated my world. You took everything I thought I knew and turned it on its head. I thought I had it all together. The career. The occasional woman. The easy stroll through life. No complications. Every success was mine…but you made me *feel*.'

'Feel what?' she asked coldly, twisting her fingers together in her lap, stopping herself from edging anywhere nearer to him. She needed to hear him say so much more. She still couldn't let herself *trust*—

'Need,' he said rawly. 'Need to be with someone— to have you to talk to, to laugh with, to show everything, to hold, to just keep me company…to love…' He trailed off.

'So this is about *your* need?' She sent him a sharp look.

A harsh breath whistled out between his clenched

teeth. 'I don't know how to be the kind of father that this baby deserves,' he gritted. 'I don't know how to be the kind of husband that you deserve. I have had awful examples of both and for a long time I believed...' Words failed him again.

Eleni didn't speak. She couldn't believe and it was becoming too hard to listen.

'I never imagined this would happen to me. And for it to be *you*?' He visibly paled. 'You deserve so much more than what I can give you.'

She shook her head, her rage surging. 'That's a cop-out, Damon.'

'You're a princess—'

'That's *irrelevant*,' she snapped.

'I don't mean your lineage. I mean in here.' He pressed his fist to his heart again but gazed at her. 'You're generous, loyal, loving, true...that's what I mean. You're not like other people—'

'I'm just like other people,' she argued fiercely. 'I'm human. *Most* people are loving and loyal, Damon. Most people are generous and honest.'

That was what he needed to learn and it crushed her that he hadn't learned it as he should have, that his life had been so devoid of normal family love.

'I'm nothing special,' she added.

'You're special to *me*!' he bellowed back at her. 'You're more generous, more loyal, more loving than anyone I've ever met and *all* I want is to be near you. You don't value yourself the way that you should.'

But she did now. She did, because of him. That was what he'd taught her. That was why she'd walked away from him. Because she knew what it was to truly love. And that she deserved more than he'd wanted to give her.

'Yes, I do,' she flung back at him brokenly. 'That's why I'm back in Palisades.' That was why she'd left him when it had almost killed her to do so. Because staying would have been an even more painful experience. She wasn't going to settle for less. Not now. Not from him. She couldn't exist settling for less from him. 'That's why I couldn't stay with you. Because I do need…'

The words stuck in her throat as the pain seeped out. She knew he'd been hurt, but that he couldn't push past it for her? That hurt *her*.

He was staring into her eyes but his face blurred as her tears spilled—hot, fast, unstoppable, stupid tears.

'I'm so sorry, darling, so sorry I did this to you.' He reached out as she tried to turn away from him. His fingers were gentle as he captured her close and wiped the tears from her face. 'Please don't say I'm too late. It can't be too late. Because I love you, Eleni. Do you understand? I love you, I do.' He leaned closer as she remained silent. 'Eleni, please don't cry. Please listen to me.'

Her breath shuddered as she tried to still, needing to hear him.

His hands framed her face and he kept talking in those desperate hushed tones. 'Until you, I had no idea what love was—what it means, how to show it. And I want to love you, so much, but I don't know where to start. I don't know how to make this right. I'm begging you here, Eleni. How do I become the man you need?'

'You're *already* what I need,' she whispered hoarsely, so annoyed that he still didn't get it. 'You're everything I need. Just you. You're enough exactly as you are.' That was what he needed to learn too. 'And you have started.'

She pushed past the ache in her throat. 'By showing up. By being here.'

By coming back for her.

He stared at her for a moment and then with the gentlest of fingertips he traced down her cheekbone. She struggled to quell her tremors at his tenderness.

'See? So generous,' he murmured, almost to himself. But then he cleared his throat and leaned that bit closer, his gaze fierce and unwavering. 'I love you, Eleni.'

Once again he said it. What she'd been too afraid to believe she'd really heard. And the words weren't whispered, they were strong, almost defiant.

He shook her gently. 'Did you hear me?'

Two more tears slowly rolled down her cheeks.

'I am so, so sorry it has taken me so long to figure it out. I miss you like—' He closed his eyes briefly but she'd already seen the stark pain. He opened them to stare hard at her. To try again. 'These past couple of weeks have been—'

That weak scab across her heart tore as he choked up in front of her. He couldn't find the words. She understood why—it was indescribable for her too.

'I know,' she whispered.

A small sigh escaped him. 'I don't deserve it, but please be patient with me. Talk to me. Talk like you did that hideous day you left me. I need your honesty... I just need you.'

She drew in a shaky breath, because she wanted to believe him so much. But she needed to understand. 'What changed? What brought you back?'

'Misery,' he said simply. 'I was so lonely and it hurt so much and I tried to escape it—you—but I couldn't.

And finally I got thinking again.' He shook his head as if he were clearing the fog. 'I haven't been able to think clearly since that first second I saw you…it's just been blind instinct and gut reaction—equal parts lust and terror. I'd got *so* defensive and then, when I could finally think, I realised you were right. About everything. But I'd pushed you away. You're worth listening to, Eleni,' he whispered roughly, edging closer to her again. 'When you told me you loved me, I couldn't believe you… I was scared.'

'You don't think I was scared when I said it to you?'

The corner of his mouth lifted ruefully. 'You know my family doesn't do emotions. They do business connections. I want to do more than that, to be more…'

'You're more than that already. You just need to believe it.'

'I know that now. Because somehow, in all this, you *did* fall in love with me.' A hint of that old arrogance glinted in his eyes and his fingers tightened on her waist. 'You do love me.' His chin lifted as he all but dared her to deny it.

But she saw it in his eyes— the open vulnerability that he'd refused to let show before.

'Of course,' she said softly. 'I stood no chance.'

'Just as I stood no chance with you.' His hands swept, seeking as if he couldn't hold back from caressing her a second longer. 'And I'm afraid I can't let you go, Eleni. I can't live through you leaving me again.' He gripped her hips tightly. 'I'm taking you with me. I'm kidnapping you and I'm not going to say sorry for that.' Determination—desperation—streaked across his face.

At that raw emotion the last of her defences shattered.

'You're not kidnapping me.' She sobbed, leaning into

his embrace. 'I choose to come with you.' Just as she'd chosen to be with him that first night. 'I choose to stay with you always.' She drew in a breath and framed his gorgeous face with her hands. 'I chose to marry you. I meant my marriage vows.'

'Thank God.' He hauled her into his lap with barely leashed passion. 'I love you. And I promise to honour you. Care for you…always.' He drew back to look solemnly into her eyes. 'It's not just a contract for me, Eleni.'

Her heart bursting, she flung her arms around his neck, kissing him with a hunger that almost overwhelmed her. 'I missed you so much,' she cried.

'*Eleni.*'

She heard the joy, the pure love in his voice. She felt it in his tender, fierce embrace and in the heat of his increasingly frantic kisses.

'I love you,' he muttered, kissing her desperately. 'I love you, I love you, I love you.'

It was as if he'd released the valve holding back his heart and now the most intense wave of emotion swamped her. Finally the veracity of *her* feelings could flow again. She had complete freedom to say what she wanted. To be who she was—who she'd wanted to be.

His lover. His beloved.

He held her so close, wiping away yet more tears that she didn't realise were tumbling down her cheeks. Opening her eyes, she saw a softness in his strong features that she'd not seen before. She trembled as she registered just how good this felt—how close she'd been to losing him. He'd been gone from her life too long. She needed his touch, his kiss, his hold—*now*.

'It's okay, sweetheart,' he soothed, kissing her again and again as she shuddered in his arms. 'It's okay.'

It was better than okay. It was heaven. And now she clung—unashamedly clung, needing to be so much nearer to him. 'Don't let me go.'

'Never again. I promise.'

But he'd hardly kissed her for long enough when he lifted his lips from hers and rested his forehead on hers, his breathing ragged. 'People are going to see us if we stay here too much longer…a palace car, illegally parked on the side of the road…'

'It doesn't matter.' Her voice rasped past the emotion aching in her throat. 'They know we're passionately in love.'

For real. Not just a fairy tale for the press. She ached to have him again completely.

He read her expression and groaned with a shake to his head. 'We can't be that reckless. And I'm crushing your pretty dress.' He lifted her from his lap, puffing out a strained breath. 'You're Princess Eleni, and this isn't right for you.'

She stilled, a thread of worry piercing her warmth. 'You don't like the palace.'

'I can learn to like it.' He brushed back her hair. 'I can learn a lot, Eleni. I can become the man you need. We can make it work.'

'You're already the man I need. You just need to stay—'

'Right by your side.' He met her gaze with utter surety in his. 'I know.'

Her eyes filled again. 'Where were you planning to drive me to?'

'Back to the boat.' A wry grin flitted across his lips.

'There aren't that many ways to kidnap a princess from Palisades. Damn palace is a fortress.'

She chuckled.

'But the treasure that was locked in there…' His old smug smile resurfaced. 'That's my treasure now.'

'And you're going to keep it?'

'Oh, I am. For always.'

'Then what are you waiting for? Let's get to the marina.'

His face lit up and then tightened in the merest split of a second. 'You can't imagine how much I need you—'

'Actually I think I can,' she argued breathlessly.

His laugh was ragged. 'You're hot and sweet, Eleni.' He swiftly climbed over to the driver's seat and started the engine.

'So, Giorgos and Tony were in on this?'

'I'm afraid so.' He drove quickly, confidently. 'You didn't stand a chance.'

'No?' she asked archly as he pulled into the park by the yacht.

'Believe it or not…' Damon got out of the car and opened her door '…they want you to be happy.'

'And they think being with you means happiness for me?'

'Does it?'

She stepped out of the car and reached up to stroke his face, seeing that hint of vulnerability flicker in his eyes once more. 'It does now, yes.'

He swiftly turned. 'We need to get on board. Now.'

'Are we going to sail off into the sunset?' She was so tempted to skip.

'Not for ever.' He winked at her. 'Palisades needs its Princess but I'll admit I'm going to push for part-time status.' He suddenly turned and swept her into his arms. With that gorgeous effortlessness he carried her across the boardwalk, onto the boat and straight into the bedroom. 'Because she'll be busy with her baby. And meeting the needs of her husband. And she'll be busy drawing and being creative with all the other things she's not let herself take the time for until now.' He paused, holding her just above the bed. 'Does that sound like a good plan to you?'

'It sounds like a brilliant plan.'

It was only moments until they were locked together. He was so close and she stared into his beautiful eyes.

'Take what you want from me, my beautiful,' he muttered. 'Anything and everything I have is yours.'

'I have your body,' she murmured. 'I want your heart.'

'It only beats because of you.' He laced his fingers through hers. 'I wasn't alive until I met you. You're everything to me. I love you, Eleni.'

'And I love you.' She wrapped around him, letting him carry them both into that bliss.

'Too quick,' he groaned, and gripped her hips tightly, slowing her.

Amused and beyond aroused, she tried to tease him. 'But what does it matter? We can go again, now we have all the time in the world.'

'Yes.' Those gorgeously intense eyes focused on her with that lethal desire and her heart soared as he answered. 'We have for ever.'

* * * * *

If you enjoyed
PRINCESS'S PREGNANCY SECRET
why not explore these other
ONE NIGHT WITH CONSEQUENCES *stories?*

CONSEQUENCE OF HIS REVENGE
by Dani Collins
CONTRACTED FOR THE PETRAKIS HEIR
by Annie West
CLAIMING HIS NINE-MONTH CONSEQUENCE
by Jennie Lucas
A BABY TO BIND HIS BRIDE
by Caitlin Crews

Available now!

#3629 BLACKMAILED BY THE GREEK'S VOWS
Conveniently Wed!
by Tara Pammi
Discovering her passionate marriage was a business deal devastated Valentina. Yet before granting a divorce, Kairos demands she play his wife again. And soon their intense fire is reignited...

#3630 A DIAMOND DEAL WITH HER BOSS
by Cathy Williams
While pretending to be her sexy boss Gabriel's fiancée, Abby can't resist the temptation of a burning-hot affair. But soon Abby must decide: Can she share her body—*and* soul—with Gabriel?

#3631 THE SHEIKH'S SHOCK CHILD
One Night With Consequences
by Susan Stephens
When innocent laundress Millie succumbs to Sheikh Khalid's touch, she's overwhelmed by the intensity of their encounter. But becoming Khalid's mistress isn't the only consequence of their reckless desire...and Millie's scandalous news will bind them permanently!

#3632 CLAIMING HIS PREGNANT INNOCENT
by Maggie Cox
Lily doesn't expect her landlord to be gorgeous billionaire Bastian. Antagonism leads to a sensual encounter, and shocking consequences! They'll meet at the altar, but will a ring truly make Lily his?

HPCNM0518RB

Get 2 Free Books,
Plus 2 Free Gifts—
just for trying the *Reader Service!*

HP17R3

*When desert prince Dal's convenient bride is stolen,
he must find a replacement—immediately. Suddenly,
his shy secretary, Poppy, has been whisked away to
Dal's kingdom, Jolie...where she'll find herself tempted
by his expert seduction!*

Read on for a sneak preview of
Jane Porter's next story
KIDNAPPED FOR HIS ROYAL DUTY,
part of the **STOLEN BRIDES** miniseries.

Before they came to Jolie, Dal would have described
Poppy as pretty, in a fresh, wholesome, no-nonsense sort
of way with her thick, shoulder-length brown hair, large
brown eyes and serious little chin.

But as Poppy entered the dining room, with its glossy
white ceiling and dark purple walls, she looked anything
but wholesome and no-nonsense.

She was wearing a silk gown the color of cherries,
delicately embroidered with silver threads, and instead
of her usual ponytail or chignon, her dark hair was down,
and long, elegant chandelier earrings dangled from her
ears. As she walked, the semisheer kaftan molded to her
curves.

"It seems I've been keeping you waiting," she said,
her voice pitched lower than usual and slightly breathless.
"Izba insisted on all this," she added, gesturing up toward
her face.

At first Dal thought she was referring to the ornate silver earrings that were catching and reflecting the light, but once she was seated across from him, he realized her eyes had been rimmed with kohl and her lips had been outlined and filled in with a soft plum-pink gloss. "You're wearing makeup."

"Quite a lot of it, too." She grimaced. "I tried to explain to Izba that this wasn't me, but she's very determined once she makes her mind up about something and apparently, dinner with you requires me to look like a tart."

Dal checked his smile. "You don't look like a tart. Unless it's the kind of tart one wants to eat."

Color flooded Poppy's cheeks and she glanced away, suddenly shy, and he didn't know if it was her shyness or the shimmering dress that clung to her, but he didn't think any woman could be more beautiful or desirable than Poppy right now. "You look lovely," he said quietly. "But I don't want you uncomfortable all through dinner. If you'd rather go remove the makeup, I'm happy to wait."

She looked at him closely, as if doubting his sincerity. "It's fun to dress up, but I'm worried Izba has the wrong idea about me."

"And what is that?"

"She seems to think you're going to…marry…me."

Don't miss
KIDNAPPED FOR HIS ROYAL DUTY
available June 2018.

Coming next month—the first installment
in Michelle Smart's
RINGS OF VENGEANCE miniseries!

Benjamin Guillem was once Luis and Javier Casilla's
closest friend. Until the day the brothers stole from
him. Now they are enemies, and nothing will stand
in the way of their revenge!

Billionaire Benjamin has the ultimate plan for vengeance
on those who betrayed him: steal his enemy's fiancée,
Freya, and marry her himself. It's meant to be a convenient
arrangement, yet the cool, collected prima ballerina
ignites a passion in his blood! There's nothing remotely
convenient about the red-hot pleasures of their wedding
night—and Benjamin is tempted to make Freya his for
more than revenge…

Find out more in Benjamin and Freya's story
Billionaire's Bride for Revenge

And look out for Luis's and Javier's stories

Coming soon!